FROM the OTHER SIDE of the TRACKS

Volume 1

ALEXIS SOLEIL

PAGE PUBLISHING, INC.
New York, NY

First originally published by Page Publishing, Inc. 2016

ISBN 978-1-68139-707-8 (pbk)
ISBN 978-1-68139-708-5 (digital)

Printed in the United States of America

For my family, Irene Dolores Johnson,
Anthony Eduardo Rivera-Arroyo and Savannah Arroyo.
RIP

Introduction

've been a screenwriter for over twenty years and have written stories from drama to horror. Writing is my passion, and I haven't stopped. The Romeo and Juliet idea hit me years ago while I was on the train going to school. I asked myself, what is a bad boy? Is it the African-American or Latino male between the ages of fourteen to twenty-five or older who resides in underprivileged communities, who wears baggy urban gear, who has tattoos and earrings, who speaks slang intertwined with profanity, who is high school dropout? Is it the one who has babies with multiple women, abuses them only to make their lives a living hell? And then these bad boys (deadbeat dads) finally leave?

In a lot of cases, these things are true. But you never know about someone. Just because a college-educated man who makes eighty thousand a year or more lives in the suburbs and has two or three cars and a wife and no more than two kids doesn't mean he's always wholesome. Unfortunately, in this society, the bad boy—or the other word that is frequently used, *thug*—is the one followed around the store, feared by their persona, profiled by police, and even murdered at the hands of anyone. The whole bad boy (thug) issue has become a so-called black issue. No, this is a universal issue. African-American men who have made it complained why African-American females are dating thugs. No other race talks about this, but us. The bad boy (thug) issue occurs with people from every walk of life. There are impoverished communities in United States, Canada, Japan, Mexico, South Africa, etc. Where there is poverty, there's crime, and there'll be bad boys.

Are these so-called bad boys *monsters*, or simply misguided? What is the difference between a monster and a bad boy? The bad boy walks the walk, talks the talk, and gets into his fights, if he can or just put up a front. Basically, he wants a brighter future, so he resorts to making mistakes in the process. He gets involved in with the wrong crowd and winds up serving prisons terms or even death. Now, the monster, a malevolent-minded individual, brutally murders innocent victims. The victims have done nothing wrong to him or never knew their killer.

As far as my main character, Seven, he's no monster. He's judged by others in the story along with people who are even reading his story. A lot of my peers loved the story and loved Seven. They clearly understood him, but people who weren't of my peer didn't. They simply judged my main character on the subplot of the story and not the main plot. Surprisingly, I shouldn't have been surprised. I guess because it was in screenplay form, and the limit was one hundred twenty pages or less. Or it was just their bias against this type of young African-American male.

I had many different versions of the story and couldn't fit everything into a one-hundred-twenty-page script. So I decided to write a novel. For years, people have been telling me to write *From the Other Side of the Tracks* into a book. But I was stuck in the screenplay zone for years until finally I came to my senses. Anyway, the story gives more depth of how my main character, Seven, became the street-racing ruffian who was feared by many and loved by one affluent girl who knew him inside out.

Shakespeare's Romeo and Juliet is another theme I love so much. And yes, this street-racing ruffian has a heart. He's in love, and there's nothing wrong with it. Seven's not a wimp, a pussy, a sucker, a herb, or a mangina. Seven's a man—mind, body, and soul. He's a fighter. A real fighter. If challenged, Seven will bring everything he's got, verbally and physically. Seven will bring his true feelings, profanity, fists, knives, and guns to set fools straight. He's not one dimensional. Seven's a lover and fighter. Some people would say he can't be both. I say, yes, he can. It's because, they don't have the guts to show love toward a female. They're afraid of what their peers would say. Seven's human.

There are a lot of women who are attracted to so-called bad boys. Yes, I can see where they're coming from with the swagger. This thug displays strength, daring, and sex appeal. All women want their man to be strong, not weak. That's what they want from these guys: protection and love. Instead, the women will get dogged out. From my own experience, I've been dogged by the conservative type of guys, so an eye should be kept on them as well.

I would like for the reader to experience this read with an open mind and see how this twenty-something-year-old man went from his humble years to his fierce years. Check out how Seven is as an individual—when he fights, he fights; when he loves, he loves; and he is true to everything that a man is supposed to be. In other words, Seven's not a bad boy. He's a *bad man*.

Chapter 1

July 27 was the hottest day of the summer, with its breaking temperatures of 101 degrees. In this modest community of Long Island, New York, the average income for a family was forty thousand or less annually. These days, it's either rich or poor. Whoever isn't living the high life is considered poor. There's no more middle class. The residents of this particular community knew how to cope with this extreme heat wave.

On this blazing afternoon, the neighborhood kids clamored in the sprinklers, squirted one another with water guns, and threw water balloons. The elderly remained indoors to avoid the harmful rays of the sun that could become fatal. Some neighbors had to do what they had to do by keeping their lawns and hedges trimmed regardless of the weather. The blaring of a diesel train chugged along the tracks rapidly. It always drowned out the sound of the birds, the wind blowing, or neighborly communication. The railroad gate was closed, with its red signal. Before it was a line of cars sat waiting for the locomotive to pass by. Then the screeching wheels of a green Audi cut the corner and halted behind the line of cars. Eighteen-year-old Darren Thomas, an African-American male, sported a camouflaged t-shirt and jeans as he occupied the driver's seat of his green Audi.

"Damn!" he yelled as he pounded his fist against the steering wheel. There was nowhere to go. He turned to the backseat, where his sister, Ingrid Miles, an African-American female, light complexioned, pretty, in her late twenties, panted as she held her round belly. Ingrid sported a blue maternity jumper with sneakers. A hospital band was strapped around her wrist due to her having contractions a few days earlier. Sweat poured down her face as her mother, Madeline Thomas, a sweet-faced, pudgy woman in her late sixties, wiped away every drop and held her hand.

"Breathe, baby! Breathe!" Madeline encouraged with her stern tone. Madeline held Ingrid's hand as this child was ready to be brought into the world right now. The contractions became stronger and stronger.

"It's coming! It's coming!" Ingrid hollered in agony. Ingrid prayed to God she would have an easy childbirth. She carried this baby for nine months too long. Ingrid had to endure the pains of a natural childbirth like every woman. Ingrid felt the baby coming from between her legs. "Oh my God!" Ingrid shouted as she quickly took off her jumper from the shoulders down to her feet.

Madeline rushed to get the garment off Ingrid. Then Ingrid opened her legs as Madeline could see the little head peering out of Ingrid's vaginal area. Madeline had no time to smile about this little precious angel that was about to arrive. She had to act fast. "Push, Ingrid!" Madeline encouraged.

Ingrid made up her mind this was going to be the last and final push. She wanted this over with. She inhaled and gave an enormous one. Ingrid caught her breath. Not there yet. The rest of the child's head emerged out of Ingrid's birth canal.

Darren smiled and became teary eyed because of the miracle being presented before his eyes. This new life was ready to say "Hello" to the world. A Volvo was in front of the green Audi. The fifty-two-year-old driver heard Ingrid's screams despite the train's chugging along the tracks. He could see all the action through his rearview mirror. "What the hell!" he mumbled to himself.

The locomotive passed. The railroad crossing signaled green. The wailing of a baby erupted like a fire alarm. In the rear of the green Audi, Ingrid gave birth to a bouncing baby boy. Madeline wrapped her newborn grandson in her blue jumper.

Ingrid held her bundle of joy in her arms as she shed tears of joy. "Hey, baby boy! How are you?" Ingrid greeted her son in a loving tone.

The fifty-two-year-old gentleman got out of his car and strutted over to the Audi. "Are you guys—oh, wow! Do you guys need any assistance to the hospital?" asked the middle-aged driver as he peered into the backseat and saw Ingrid with her bundle of joy.

"We're cool!" said Darren, nonchalant.

"Are you sure?"

The railroad gate then opened. As soon as Ingrid and her baby boy arrived at the hospital they were assisted by nurses. Once the newborn was in the maturity ward, the doctor immediately checked the time on his watch. He jotted down the time for the newborn's birth 2:37 p.m., which was hospital time. The baby was checked from head to toe by the doctor to make sure the baby was in good health. They measured, weighted, checked his heartbeat, and then took the child's first photo.

Two days later, Madeline, Darren, and the rest of Ingrid's kin entered the hospital room. They brought balloons, clothes, and other gifts for the baby. Excitement was in the air as relatives sighed at the sight of the newborn.

Ingrid cradled her son in her arms. She was thankful to God for a successful birth. Ingrid glared at her fidgety, cooing baby as she felt the healthy weight of her son. She knew her son was strong because he was a Leo. Family members offered their gifts. Ingrid opened a large blue box and pulled out a blue blanket with a baby race car driver on it. "This is so adorable." Ingrid cried. Ingrid unwrapped the next gift. It was a pair blue pajamas. Then she went to the next gift. "This is so cute," Ingrid said. She dangled a pair of baby sneakers by the laces. "He's going to be something else!" Ingrid said as she smiled.

Someone was missing. Where was the father of this child that Ingrid carried for almost a year? No call. No show. Ingrid had worries of raising her child alone. She wanted her marriage to work. Her husband, William Miles, always came home late nights, stayed away for days or weeks at a time. This made Ingrid definitely suspicious.

Then the new father made his entrance. William was a tall African-American male in his early thirties, brown skinned, bald, and medium build. He took baby steps over to see his child with blue balloons, flowers, and a teddy bear.

"It's about time!" Ingrid shouted without giving William a chance to explain himself. She sneered at him.

Madeline and Darren gave William sour expressions. Madeline never really cared for William. She always knew William was no good. A bum. A loser. He always took odd jobs or either gambled to get some cash. On the other hand, Darren wanted to beat William to a pulp for being a total asshole. Darren could not comprehend what Ingrid saw in this bum. He couldn't intervene until shit hits the fan. For now, he had to mind his own business.

William bashfully, with tears in his eyes, "May I hold my son?" Without hesitation, Ingrid handed her son to his father. William kissed his son on the forehead as he paced back and forth. Ingrid's other relatives smiled due to the father-and-son bond. But Ingrid, Madeline, and Darren weren't. Ingrid wanted to let him have it, but no. Ingrid allowed William to bond with his son. Ingrid's relatives left the room as they gave Ingrid, William, and child a chance to bond.

William attempted to give Ingrid a kiss on the lips, but she turned the other cheek. "I'm sorry. I got caught in traffic," William explained.

Ingrid wasn't buying the lame story. She knew there was someone else. Ingrid should have listened to her family about this piece of shit. "Lies! Lies!" Ingrid said as she shook her head. "What are you going name him?"

"I don't know," William said as he shrugged his shoulders like a dumb little kid.

"Name him after you." Ingrid snapped.

"I'll come up with something," William said as he kissed his pride and joy.

The next morning, Ingrid and her bundle of joy were wheeled out in a wheelchair by William. Madeline and a nurse were also by her side. They halted at the front desk. The birth certificate was typed up by a pretty receptionist with short bob haircut, who smacked on some chewing gum. She frowned at the blank space where there was no first name. Everything else was filled out on it, the last name, address, hospital information, birth date, weight in ounces, etc.

The receptionist scrambled from her swivel chair and marched toward William and Ingrid. "Ma'am, what's the baby's name?" the receptionist asked as she proceeded to smack on her gum.

Ingrid held her head down in shame. She stared at William and then punched him on the arm. "You were supposed to name him!" Ingrid shouted.

"You had him. Isn't that your job?" William shouted in response.

"You're the father! The father names the son! You know what, I'll name him." Ingrid agreed. Ingrid eyed the birth certificate as William glared at it from over her shoulder. Ingrid could sense William "so-called" taking an interest in his child when confronted. Ingrid looked back at William. "Did you think of anything?" Ingrid asked.

"No," William said abruptly.

"These nurses don't have all day! This is the simplest thing to do." Madeline sighed. Madeline took a seat as she exhaled with Ingrid's duffel bag in her hand. She shook her head in disappointment.

The new parents continued to glare at the birth certificate as they mumbled to themselves. William noticed the repetitive 7s on the birth certificate. "Ingrid, check out the sevens here." William indicated. "July, the sixth month of the year."

"July is the seventh month," Ingrid corrected him.

"July is the sixth month, Ingrid!" William argued.

"You really need to go back to elementary school, William. July is the seventh month of the year."

William turned his back as he counted on his fingers like a child learning his numbers. "You're right. July is the seventh month," William mumbled as he held his head in shame.

"And look at his time of birth, 2:37 p.m.," Ingrid said. Ingrid wanted to give her child a nice, unique name. But what? Something that would make her son stand out from the crowd. Then the idea hit her like a bolt of lightning. "Seven!" Ingrid said proudly as an enormous smile surfaced on her face. She knew in her heart that was the perfect name.

William sneered at Ingrid and then shook his head in disagreement. "That's a street name!" William shouted.

"No! It's a unique one! You couldn't think of anything!"

William gawked at his son. He knew the number 7 was lucky. This little boy would have lots of luck. From Ingrid's point of view, it was a blessing. Not only did Seven sounded unique, it was also hip and cool. He would be cool. William nodded in agreement with the name.

The receptionist continued to smack on her gum as she rolled her eyes, waiting for the child's name. "What's it going to be?" the receptionist asked.

"Seven. That's going to be his name," William said with pride.

Ingrid smiled due to William coming around. The nurse typed in the baby's first name on the computer in the space of the first name on the birth certificate: S-e-v-e-n. A copy of Seven's birth certificate was printed from the computer.

Chapter 2

Cartoons played on television as a black toy Mustang remote control car zoomed through the living room, where nine-year old Seven Miles imagined himself in. He hoped to be behind the wheel of a muscle car someday. The toy car zoomed under the kitchen table, where it hit Ingrid's feet as she read the Sunday morning paper. A clock of the Last Supper hung above the sink. A Jesus figurine wobbled due to the remote control toy bumping the legs of the table. Ingrid sipped her coffee and nibbled on a doughnut. Seven then grabbed a powdered doughnut from the box.

"Don't eat too many, Seven. You'll get a stomachache like the last time," said Ingrid as she gave him the look of "mother knows best."

Seven paid his mother no mind and bit into the pastry. He then guided the remote control toy out of the kitchen.

Creflo Dollar, a televangelist, could be heard from Madeline's bedroom. Seven guided the remote control toy car down the hallway. Madeline sat in her lounge chair as she listened to the minister on her twenty-four-inch television. Madeline, her husband, Moses Thomas, along with Ingrid fled from an unpleasant, crime-ridden community to the American dream, which was a home in the quiet suburbs. Moses promised he'd buy his family a home on Long Island where there were friendly neighbors, fear of being mugged or the "Ick" of stepping in dog feces. Moses purchased their dream home after working thirty-five years as a school custodian. Unfortunately, he only experienced his American dream for a year and a half. Moses suffered a severe stroke due to the years of his dedication and hard work.

Seven navigated the remote control toy into his grandmother's bedroom. It bumped into the bottom of her dresser. "Sorry, Grandma," Seven said innocently.

"That's all right, baby." Madeline sighed in her loving tone.

"What are you watching?" Seven asked.

"Creflo Dollar," Madeline answered. Madeline clutched Seven and kissed him on the cheek.

Seven always saw his grandmother as an angel. He believed she came from heaven to take care of the family. Madeline was very understanding and warm when it came to him. Even when Seven acted up, Madeline knew how to humble Seven. Seven knew his grandmother watched a lot of religious television programs. The house felt like heaven.

"What kind of name is Creflo Dollar?" Seven asked as he frowned.

"And what kind of name is Seven?" Madeline answered the question with a question. She glared directly into Seven's eyes.

"That's because of my birthday, you know that, Grandma!" said Seven as he stomped his foot on the floor.

Madeline gave Seven the look. Seven toned down his attitude. He held his head down shamefully. He then picked his head up and gave his grandmother a smile. Then Madeline returned the smile.

"Creflo Dollar teaches about God, right?" Seven asked bashfully.

"Right! Seven, I want you to say this with me. The Lord is with me. I am a successful person. Say it," Madeline demanded in a gentle voice.

"The Lord is with me. I am a successful person," Seven repeated as he seemed somewhat puzzled. Then he smiled with confidence. Seven knew what his grandmother was talking about.

"Now you always remember that, you hear?" said Madeline.

"Yes, Grandma," Seven replied in a submissive tone. He gave Madeline a peck on the cheek. "See you, Grandma." Seven steered his remote control car out of his grandmother's bedroom as he departed behind his toy.

In a dimmed bedroom, clothes were thrown around as deep snoring filled the atmosphere and could be heard miles away. The remote control Mustang toy car made its way into Seven's parents' bedroom. It bumped into the bottom of the dresser. Seven claimed his toy car, but the snoring of his father grabbed his attention. He tiptoed over to his father's bedside. William slept on his stomach as he wore a white undershirt.

"Dad?" Seven called. The snores continued as William was in another world. "Are we going out today, Dad?" Seven asked in a shy voice. The snores became deeper and more intensified. Seven nudged his father. Nothing could have brought this man out of his sleep. "Dad!" Seven shouted.

William abruptly raised his head from his pillow. His eyes were halfway opened. William scanned his surroundings as he noticed Seven at his bedside. "What's up, son?" William yawned. William blinked his eyes to clear his blurry vision. Then Seven's presence was crystal clear before him.

"Are we going to the car show today?" Seven questioned.

William glared at his son and nodded his head. "Give me about an hour. It's father-and-son time today." William yawned.

Seven rejoiced. The child jumped for joy as the deep tone of the doorbell rang. "I'll get it!" Seven shouted as he scrambled out of the bedroom with the remote control in his hand, leaving his toy car behind. Seven dashed to the front door.

"Seven, ask who it is!" Ingrid hollered from the kitchen.

Seven swung the door open as a skinny brown-skinned African-American female in her midthirties stood before him, holding an adorable two-year old baby girl with pigtails in her arms. The stranger was Maureen. A pink diaper bag hung on Maureen's shoulder. She had the nastiest expression on her face. It's the kind that made any-one head for the hills.

"Is William here?"

"Yes," Seven replied.

"Are you, Seven?" Maureen asked again with her disgusting attitude.

Seven sneered at this strange woman as if she were conjured up from hell. He didn't like her disposition at all. Maureen peered over Seven's shoulder to see who's in the house. She could only see the living room with the television on. "Who are you?" Seven questioned the evil woman.

"Maureen," Maureen exhaled. Her eyes wandered around. "Here, take your sister. I'm late for work," said Maureen as she placed the two-year-old baby girl in Seven's arms. Maureen handed the pink diaper bag to him as well.

Seven held the baby girl with her soaked diaper, which made her heavy. Maureen stormed away as the baby reached out to her mother. The baby girl screamed and cried. Tears streamed down the child's face. Seven comforted the baby as he headed back inside. Seven approached Ingrid with the baby in the kitchen. "Mom, when did you have another baby?"

Ingrid threw down her newspaper on the table as she rose from her seat. Her jaw dropped. "Where did that baby come from?" Ingrid bellowed.

"Mommy," the baby girl continuously cried.

William dragged his feet into the kitchen. He squinted his eyes, and then they bulged.

"Daddy," the baby girl cried as she opened her arms to him.

William's going to feel Ingrid's wrath. This was the other life that he kept from her. William snatched the baby girl from Seven's arms. Seven wondered what he did wrong. He wondered if he could play with the baby.

"Daddy?" Ingrid asked as her face alternated to a hellish red.

William stormed out of the kitchen with the baby in his arms. Ingrid followed with heavy pounding footsteps that could have brought down the house. William sat the child in the middle of the king-sized bed. William kissed the baby on the cheek. "Hey, Athena. How's daddy's girl?" William asked.

"How's daddy's girl?" Ingrid mocked William.

He took off his undershirt and put on a fresh one. Seven stood in the doorway as he gazed at the beautiful baby girl. Baby Athena sucked her thumb. Seven hopped on the king-sized to play with the baby.

"You've got another child? How many other kids?" Ingrid questioned. William grabbed a pair of pants. "Answer me, William!"

"Shit! Please don't make Athena nervous!"

Baby Athena began to wail as Seven took the baby in his arms. Seven heard the baby's name. Athena. What a beautiful name. Seven always wondered if names had meanings, just like his.

"What happened? Maureen's got your tongue!" Ingrid questioned as she tried to snatch William's pants out of his hand. The couple wound up playing tug-of-war with the garment.

"Get off my pants!" William yelled. The pants tore from Ingrid's grip. William made a sour face at Ingrid as she gave a sour expression in return. William then put on another pair of pants as Ingrid nagged him.

Seven observed the negative interaction between his parents. How did this happen? Why all the fighting over something Seven couldn't understand. He's too young to understand the situation. Seven was concerned about the baby girl, who arrived on their doorstep. It was like the stork delivering the babies to their new mothers. In this case, it was an evil old crow.

"Her diaper needs to be changed, Dad?" Seven interrupted his parents' argument.

"Seven, stay out of grown folks' conversation!" Ingrid said with a stern tone.

"What's the commotion?" Madeline hobbled in, out of breath.

Ingrid pointed at the baby that sat in Seven's arms. "That's the commotion!"

Madeline saw the beautiful baby girl in Seven's arms. Her heart melted just looking at the living doll. Seven rolled his eyes at his mother for taking her frustrations out on him. Seven never dared to challenge his mother's authority. Things were about to change.

"Athena's diaper needs changing!" Seven insisted as he glared at Ingrid.

Ingrid gave Seven the evil eye. "You are really trying me, boy!"

"Get off his case! Take your wrath out on me, Ingrid!" William bawled. William attended to Athena. He took off the urine-soaked diaper from Athena's bottom.

Ingrid stormed out of the bedroom in tears. Madeline scoffed at William and stormed out as well. William put a fresh diaper on Athena and dressed her. "Are you ready for the car show?" William asked Seven as he smiled at his son.

Later, William, Seven, and Baby Athena exited the home toward William's car. Ingrid dashed out of the house in tears.

"Seven, get in the back with the baby," William insisted.

Seven got in the backseat as he held Athena in his arms. He fastened his seat belt on both of them. He could see the tension in his father's face. Seven hoped this friction would not ruin their time together.

William hurried into the driver's seat. He slammed the door and started up the engine. Ingrid pounded on the driver's side window. "I'm filing for divorce! You hear me, William!" Ingrid hollered. Seven never saw his mother in such pain. He wanted to stay home with his mother, but Seven had faith. She'd be all right. William sped off in his Toyota Camry. The engine roared. Seven stretched his neck as he witnessed his mother fall to her knees from the rear windshield.

Ingrid sobbed. Her heart ached due to William's infidelities, a love child arriving on their doorstep, and an evil mistress. Madeline consoled Ingrid as she wrapped her arms around her. Seven couldn't bear to watch this sight anymore. He turned around in the seat and clutched Baby Athena.

A few hours later, a showroom of luxury and sports cars sparkled like jewels in a jewelry store. Techno music blasted through the atmosphere. Car corporations were in full attendance to present their new products. Glowing neon lights brought an abundance of excitement. The latest Dodge Viper in silver sat on a revolving stage as red velvet ropes surrounded it.

Seven maneuvered his way through the crowd. William took big steps to catch up to Seven as he held Athena snoozing in his arms. William stood behind Seven as a Dodge representative introduced the latest Dodge Ram. Seven glanced over his shoulder at his father. William smiled at Seven. Seven was thrilled to see all the beautiful cars. He was like a kid in a candy store.

Moments later, Seven raced toward the latest Ferrari displayed behind some red velvet ropes. Seven looked behind him. He didn't see his father around. Then he spotted him. "Dad, hurry up!" Seven said, filled with enthusiasm.

"Whoa! Check out that, baby." William admired.

"Isn't she a beauty? I'm gonna have car like that someday," Seven said with confidence.

"I'm sure you will, son," said William as he patted Seven on the head.

Later, a BMW executive in a three-piece suit stood before the latest BMW model. The enormous crowd watched the video of the NASCAR champ Todd MacKenzie testing out the vehicle. In the demonstration video, the NASCAR champ raced the car around the auto track. The BMW bellowed with its turbo-charged engine. Seven's eyes were glued to the screen as they sparkled. William crept up behind Seven, tapping him on the shoulder. "Having a good time?" William asked.

Seven nodded, with a smile from ear to ear. Seven then focused his attention back to the screen. Todd MacKenzie proceeded to demonstrate the BMW's performance. William whispered in Sevens' ear. Seven's eyes bulged as he nodded in agreement to whatever it was.

Moments later, there was a Go-kart track outside of the convention center. Drivers both young and old raced the little motorized vehicles around the track. Seven drove one of the go-carts as he waved to his father holding Athena in his arms, who was wide awake. The baby smiled. "You see your big brother?" William said to Athena as he pointed to Seven.

Then Seven, William, and Baby Athena ate at a themed restaurant. It was busy of course; waitresses served customers with parties of two or more. The placed was dimmed nicely, with cherry-colored booths, tables, and chairs. Paintings and wall decor hung on the walls. Pop music played at a medium volume. Seven, William, and Baby Athena resided at a booth. Seven poked the ziti on his plate with his fork. He stuffed pasta in his mouth. William fed Athena some baby food as he ate a steak and shrimp. William chewed with his mouth opened as if he raised on a barn.

"You did real good with your driving," William praised Seven as he nudged him. "Where did you learn that?" William wondered.

"My remote control car," Seven responded. He continued to eat and gulp his drink.

"That's my boy!"

Seven took another bite of his food. He chewed slowly and constantly looked at his father. William caught Seven's eyes and his body language. Seven swallowed his food and wiped his mouth with his napkin. "Is Athena my sister?" Seven questioned as he cocked his head and glared directly into his father's eyes.

"Yes. She is," William answered. Baby Athena touched Seven on the shoulder. Seven kissed her hand. "She's definitely your sister. You two are bonding already," William said. "No matter what happens, I will always be here for you. All right, Seven?"

"Yes," Seven replied.

That night, the Toyota Camry stopped at the curb in front of the Thomas/Miles' residence. Crickets chirped. A neighbor's dog barks echoed through the community. Seven and William exited the vehicle. William held Baby Athena as she slept in his arms again. Seven saw his father's clothes and other items on the front steps. Seven turned around to see William's reaction. William slowed down his stride as he sighed at the sight of his belongings. Ingrid thrust the front door open. Seven hurried inside without greeting his mother. He knew she was still in an extremely bad mood. William stomped up the steps as Ingrid gave him a look that would kill.

"Are you serious, Ingrid! Are you serious!" William said excitedly as he had the baby in his arms.

Throughout the house, Ingrid's and William's voices could be heard from miles away. Seven sat with Baby Athena on the living room couch. Athena began to whine. She reached out to Seven. Seven took her in his arms. Lots of racket came from the master bedroom. It became more and more intensified. Athena cried.

Madeline resided in a lounge chair with her Bible in hand. She did the sign of the cross. "Heavenly Father, help my family!" Madeline prayed.

"Don't disrespect my property!" William argued.

"You disrespect me! Your son! And a child shows up on my doorstep! How does that make me feel!" Ingrid cried. She began to sob.

The doorbell rang. "Lord, I hope that's you at the door," Madeline said as she kissed the good book.

Seven carried Baby Athena in his arms as he opened the door. Again, Maureen stood before Seven as she smirked.

"How's my baby?" Maureen said as she reached out to grab her child. Maureen gave Baby Athena an abundance of kisses.

Madeline noticed Maureen and her sarcastic disposition. Madeline rose from the recliner, not pleased at all. "Are you this child's mother?" Madeline asked.

"Yes, I am! And who are you?"

Seven turned red in the face due to this crazy woman being disrespectful to his grandmother. Seven wanted to punch her in the face.

"I don't appreciate you popping on my doorstep with a child," Madeline lectured.

Loud arguing between Ingrid and William came from inside of the home. Seven hated this woman but loved Athena. Seven gave Maureen the baby's diaper bag.

"Say good-bye to your big brother," Maureen said sarcastically. Baby Athena sucked her thumb as she rested her head on her mother's shoulder.

Seven frowned as Maureen strutted away with the baby. Seven wondered if he'd ever see the baby again. He loved the idea of being a big brother. He would be someone that Athena could look up to. Maybe not. Seven became disgusted with everything that was going on. He slammed the door. Seven balled up his fist, ready for the biggest dare of his life. He was going to do it because he was a Leo. A lion could take on everyone and everything. Seven stormed in the master bedroom. "Shut up! Shut the fuck up!" Seven cursed. Then there was dead silence.

Chapter 3

Seventy-six degrees was the temperature on this gorgeous spring morning in late April. The birds sang with their uplifting melodies as the sun beamed through an opened shutter into the kitchen of the Thomas/Miles' residence. A radio played with reports of news and weather. Seven sat at the table eating a bowl of fruity pebbles. He was dressed in black jeans, shirt, and sneakers. Seven glared at the information about the Todd MacKenzie challenge on the back of the cereal box. The challenge was where you could win a trip to Houston, Texas, to watch Todd MacKenzie at a NASCAR race, meet him, and other fabulous prizes. Seven knew he had no time to daydream as he usually did whenever he got the opportunity. But he knew he had to get to school. He pushed the cereal box away. Seven switched the radio station to hip-hop station. There was no harm in a little music before hitting the books. The rap music blasted through the air. Seven bopped his head to the rhythms as he increased the volume.

"Seven, turn that down!" Ingrid yelled. Seven turned the volume down. Then he focused his attention back on the cereal box. He noticed the picture had little white boys smiling with Todd MacKenzie. There was not one boy that looked like him. Seven finished his cereal and wondered if it were possible for him to get into that white affluent sport. He was determined that it was going to be his goal. All of a sudden, Ingrid roared. "Seven!"

In Seven's unkempt bedroom, Ingrid stirred about, gathering up Seven's toys, throwing his dirty laundry in the hamper, and folding his clothes. Besides the mess Seven left behind, it was like any other boy's room. For Seven, there were Todd MacKenzie posters, along with other race car posters, and a NASCAR model car that sat on his desk with an old computer. Ingrid proceeded to fold Seven's fresh garments. Seven swaggered to the doorway of his bedroom. He could see that his mother wasn't pleased with the pigsty.

"Seven make your bed, please," Ingrid asked with displeasure in her voice.

As Seven did what his mother demanded, he could see her browsing around his desk. Seven straightened out the sheets and fluffed his pillows. Ingrid held an x-rated magazine in her hand. Seven's heart raced as he saw his mother glaring at the front cover of it. It was a girl with her finger in her vagina, pleasuring herself. Ingrid then flipped through the periodical. There's a photo of a man and woman engaged in anal sex, then a man with his penis on a woman's breasts. Ingrid waved the x-rated garbage in the air. "Seven, what are you doing with this?" Ingrid bawled with a displeased expression on her face. "This is not you!"

Seven didn't understand why his mother was so upset. Sex is what two people do when they love each other. Right? Or wrong? These were natural feelings he had going into manhood—pretty soon. Seven couldn't help but to be honest with his mother. "It's no big deal!"

"It is a big deal!" Ingrid argued in return.

"How do you think I got here!" Seven raised his voice at Ingrid. Seven gave his mother a dirty look. Ingrid gave Seven one right back.

"Who do you think you are, young man?" Ingrid asked as she placed her hands on her hips and frowned.

"Seven Miles. That's who I am," Seven answered sarcastically. Seven grabbed his book bag and stormed out of the room.

"Get over here! Where do you think you're going?" Ingrid yelled.

"School!" Seven shouted.

Madeline waddled into Seven's bedroom, dressed in her nightgown and pink robe. "What's going on, Ingrid?" asked Madeline as she squinted her eyes.

"This!" Ingrid handed the porno magazine to her mother.

Madeline's jaw dropped as she saw the smut. Madeline shook her head and then shrugged her shoulders. "Don't jump on the boy. It's too early for that."

"It's never too early. Or it'll be too late," said Ingrid. Madeline gave the magazine back to Ingrid. Ingrid ripped it up and threw it in the garbage.

Moments later, Seven swaggered alone down the street on his way to school. He was in no hurry to get there. He took his time as he looked at everything in sight while taking nonchalant steps. Seven wasn't angry with his mother due to her finding the dirty magazine. It was because of her new job. Seven hardly saw his mother. Ingrid was a nanny. She took care of a little girl of an affluent international realtor. What was so special about this kid that Seven had to lose his mother? Was this the little girl that Ingrid might have wanted? Instead of him? Was it because she came from a very wealthy background? No. It's because Ingrid had to take care of Seven and the family. The only time Seven got to see his mother was once or twice a week. But in the morning, that's when she took out all her frustrations out on him. Ingrid was pissed off about Seven not keeping his bedroom neat or taking the garbage out or keeping his grades up in school. All Seven knew was he missed his mother.

A cute small school building sat with beautiful surroundings of manicured lawns, trimmed hedges, and full trees. School buses dropped off students as well as parents who escorted their kids by car. Seven bumped into his friend Chad, an African-American male, dark skinned with hazel eyes, nine years of age, clad in blue denim and black shirt, wore his baseball cap backwards. Chad was similar to Seven. He was a hip kid who loved rap music and wanted to drive fast cars. Chad wasn't thinking about any NASCAR like Seven. But fast cars was their thing.

The late bell rang as Seven and Chad took their time heading up the steps. They gave each other high fives. During class, a nerdy, glasses-clad female student, Allison, eight-years old, read her essay in front of the class. She smiled because she had the class's full attention. Seven's teacher, Mr. Kincaid, was a slacks-wearing, shirt-and-tie gentleman in his midforties, who was thin and had curly hair. He leaned against the desk as he listened to the young girl's career goals. Seven and Chad were seated in the back of the classroom. Chad doodled a picture of a guy and girl engaged in penile-vaginal intercourse. Seven just sat at his desk, bored out of his mind. He wanted so badly to go home. Seven then tried to pay attention to his fellow classmate who dreamed of becoming an ornithologist. That's the study of birds. As Seven kept listening, it sounded corny. Who the hell wanted to study some birds? That's nothing compared to what Seven wanted to do. Then there was a loud sound that came from outside. It grabbed Seven's attention like a child waking up Christmas morning. Seven dashed to the window. It was a Porsche Carrera GT in mango color that stopped at a red light. Chad was right behind Seven.

"That's the latest Porsche GT!" Chad said with enthusiasm.

"That's a cool car. Check out the color," said Mr. Kincaid as he smiled at the two young boys. Then the other students peered out of the window as well. They admired the Porsche that still sat at the red light.

Allison noticed that everyone's attention shifted from her to outside. "Hello! It's me, Allison, the ornithologist. The study of birds," said Allison.

"You are a bird!" Chad responded.

The students guffawed as Allison marched back to her desk. Seven and his classmates were excited by the car's roaring sound as if they're at the drag strip. Then the traffic light turned green. The Porsche blasted off. The engine's sound penetrated through the air like a knife cutting meat. Seven and his classmates went crazy. The Porsche weaved between other motorists. They honked their horns. There were cheers and applause from Seven and his classmates.

Moments later, Allison stood before her class again to proceed with her essay about her goals. It was the same reaction that the class had before when Allison spoke. Boredom. Especially Seven's attitude. Seven just glared at Allison. He tried to give his attention to her, but

Seven was only thinking of himself. Seven could see himself driving that Porsche. He didn't write his essay. He'll probably get an F.

It was now Seven's turn to tell his classmates about his dream. Seven stood up in front of everyone as he spoke from his heart. Mr. Kincaid noticed Seven had no paper in his hand. Seven's teacher didn't say a word. Seven took the class on a ride of their lives. He told about the different sports cars, from muscle cars to foreign cars. He told about Todd MacKenzie, the greatest NASCAR racer in the world, who won multiple races consistently. Seven wanted to be just like him someday. As Seven continued to tell his goals, his eyes scanned the class to see if anyone was smirking or laughing at his ambition. If there were, that person would have to pay the consequences with Seven's fist in their face. The class smiled with pleasure and saw that Seven's dream was unique.

After school, Seven and Chad scrambled into the candy store, along with other kids from school. The establishment was small, colorful, and where the latest and old-fashioned candies were sold. The goodies caused every child's eyes to become bigger than their stomachs. Seven and Chad bought everything in sight. Seven grabbed two bags of M&M's, a Snickers bar, Jolly Ranchers, and bubble gum. Chad snatched up three bags of chips, Three Musketeers, and a few lollipops. The two boys were exactly that "kids in a candy store."

The leaves of the trees ruffled as the warm breeze blew through them. Seven and Chad swaggered down the street as they ate their goodies. The air felt so good that it would have made any kid not want to do their homework. The two young men approached Chad's residence, where he lived half of his life with his mother.

"Are you gonna come back outside?" Seven asked Chad.

Chad shook his head as he took a bite of his candy bar. "Give me about an hour. I'll holler at you," Chad replied. He gave Seven a high five and dashed into the house. Chad's mother, Mrs. Richardson, a thin, fragile woman in her late thirties, greeted him at the door with a smile. She waved to Seven.

Seven waved back as he watched Chad's mother shut the front door. He took a deep breath as he proceeded home. He lollygagged through the park, where some kids clamored. An old man fed some birds. The ducks and their ducklings swam in the pond. Some squirrels scurried around for food as a chocolate Labrador pursued it. The dog owner restrained her four-legged friend. Seven chuckled as he witnessed the two creatures in conflict. Then he proceeded on home.

The aroma of Sunday cooking filled the air from the Thomas/Miles' residence. In the warm, cozy kitchen Madeline cooked roast beef, mashed potatoes, vegetables, and corn bread. She did all this work even on a school day. The food was the only thing filling the atmosphere. The joyful sounds of Gospel music did the same. Good for your spirit. Keys rattled at the door as Seven stepped inside. He dropped his book bag on the couch.

"How are you, Grandma?" Seven greeted his grandmother.

"How are you, baby? How was school today?" Madeline asked, startled. She wiped his hand with the dish towel.

"Everything smells good," Seven said as he greeted the cook with a kiss. Seven grabbed a soda from the refrigerator and cracked open the can. Seven gulped down the soft drink and released an enormous belch. Madeline was displeased with Seven's ill manners. "Sorry," Seven apologized. Seven sat down at the table and grabbed a doughnut. Madeline hummed to the gospel tunes. She loved that music. That's what made her so angelic. Seven wanted to listen to some rap music, but it was his grandmother's time. And even when Seven did listen to his rap music, he would turn the volume down or listen to it through headphones.

The beautiful breeze blew through the cracked kitchen window. It was as if the spring air was calling Seven to go out and play. But Seven didn't want to leave his grandmother alone in the house. He didn't like the idea of her being alone. "Grandma!" Seven cried. "Is it all right if I go out and play for a while?" Seven asked in a submissive tone.

"Yes, you may," Madeline replied as she turned away from the sink. Madeline washed pots and pans. She placed a long metal pan in the dish rack.

Seven sprung from the kitchen table. He took the last bite of his doughnut and tossed the soda can in the garbage. "I promise. I won't stay out long, Grandma," Seven said as she kissed her on the cheek.

Moments later, Seven swaggered toward Chad's house. There was no one in sight. Seven was about to ring the doorbell as Chad thrust the door open. The two young men gave each other high fives.

"How did you know it was me?" Seven asked.

"I saw you coming down the street. Duh!" Chad replied. Then there was the clamoring of a black Volkswagen Jetta that blasted past them. Seven's and Chad's eyes widened with excitement. "That's my man, Polo," said Chad.

"What are we waiting for? Let's go," Seven insisted. The two young boys fled on foot as they pursued the sound. The Volkswagen Jetta pulled into an opened car garage. Seven and Chad dashed in as twenty-two-year-old Polo—an African-American male, dark skinned, good-looking, thugged out—emerged from the driver's seat of the vehicle. He puffed on a Philly blunt that he held in his hand. He noticed Seven and Chad approaching him. Chad gave Polo a high five. Chad then introduced Seven to Polo. Polo greeted Seven with a high five. Seven noticed Polo had a love for fast cars. They all had something in common. Polo popped the hood of his Volkswagen Jetta. Seven and Chad saw the clamoring turbo engine. It was shiny silver, with all kinds of technical parts, wiring, nuts, and bolts, and it had a blower, which gave the vehicle boost that increased its speed. Seven was fascinated with the motor. He wanted to learn everything about engines and cars that were compatible with them. Polo revved the engine. Seven got startled a bit as he stepped back. But he still kept his attention on that magnificent machinery. Polo smiled at Seven as he then sat behind the wheel, revving the Jetta even more.

Chad resided in the passenger's seat. Chad grinned at Seven. "Cool, right?"

"Yeah." Seven nodded in agreement. Seven just remembered he promised his grandmother that he wouldn't stay out long.

Later, Seven swaggered toward his home. He knocked on the rear glass door. There was no answer. It was quiet. Seven could see the food on the stove. "Grandma!" Seven called. Still there was no answer. Seven ran to the front door and rapped at it. No answer. "Grandma, it's me!" Seven cried. Seven scrambled to the side of the house. He tried to open up the basement window. No luck. Then he tried to pry open a second window with a stick. Success. The window opened slowly as Seven forced it all the way. He slid his body halfway in. Seven landed on a bed. Then he closed the basement window, but he was unable to lock it. Seven stomped upstairs. Seven marched into the kitchen, where the aroma of his grandmother's cooking was still fresh. He lifted the lid of the mashed potatoes in the pot, vegetables, and the well-seasoned roast beef in the Crock-Pot.

"Grandma! Can I eat now!" Seven crept into his grandmother's bedroom. The preachings of Creflo Dollar emerged from the television. Madeline slept in bed as she clutched her Bible in her arms. Seven stepped closer and closer to her bedside. He smirked at his grandmother. Madeline rested due to all the cooking she put such effort into.

Seven swaggered back into the kitchen, where he fixed himself a plate. He devoured down the roast beef and veggies then sipped his soda from a glass. Then the phone rang, and it startled Seven as he choked a bit. Seven answered the telephone.

"Hello," Seven answered.

"Seven, hey baby. How are you?" Ingrid said, delighted to hear her son's voice.

"Mom, when are you coming home?" Seven sighed.

"I'll be home in a few days," Ingrid replied as Seven heard the sweet little feminine voice of a child as he spoke to his mother. Seven so badly wanted to curse at the little girl that was taking his mother from him. But he held his tongue and composure. "Where's Grandma?" Ingrid asked as she hushed Angelika in the background.

"She's asleep." Seven replied.

"All right. Did you do your homework?" Ingrid said, concerned.

"I'll get to it." Seven said.

"Ask Grandma if you need help, okay?" Ingrid advised. Angelika could be heard over the phone.

"Hi, Seven!" Angelika shouted through the receiver.

Seven immediately snatched the receiver from his ear due to Angelika trying to deafen him. He took a deep breath as he decided to be polite. "Hello," Seven greeted Angelika with a low tone.

"When are we going to meet?" Angelika asked.

"I have no idea," Seven answered as he was getting annoyed.

"How old are you?" Angelika questioned as she pestered him.

Seven took another deep breath. "Could you please put my mother back on the phone!" Seven said in an aggressive tone.

"Seven, don't be so rude!" said Ingrid.

"When are you coming home?" Seven said in his quivering voice.

"Don't worry. I'll be home before you know it," Ingrid promised.

"Where's my father?" Seven asked.

"You're father's out there somewhere. Everything will be all right, Seven."

Tears trickled down Seven's face as he began to sob. Seven tried to hold back his tears, but he couldn't help himself. He's never been away from his mother.

"Grandma will be up in a little while. I promise."

Seven trusted his mother's words and held back his tears. Ingrid told Seven that she loved him and threw him a kiss over the phone. Seven then hung up. He wiped his tears. Seven knew he had to be strong. As a matter of fact, boys don't cry. That's a girl thing. Seven sat back down and proceeded with his dinner.

That night, crickets could be heard chirping from outside of Seven's cracked bedroom window. A light, warm breeze blew in, gently touching Seven's face. Cartoons played on television as he did his homework before bedtime. The house was too quiet for him. Seven sprung from his bed. He tiptoed down the hallway to his grandmother's bedroom. Now, the preachings of Charles Stanley played on the television as it gleamed throughout the dark bedroom. Seven's eyes bulged as he began to panic. He turned the lights on. Madeline still lay in bed, clutching her Bible.

"Grandma!" Seven shouted. There was no response. "Grandma!" Seven shouted even louder. Still no response. "Grandma, wake up! Wake the hell up!" Seven swore. Unfortunately, there's no response. Seven touched his grandmother's hand. She was cold as ice. Then he felt Madeline's face. It was also ice-cold. Seven backed away in tears. His grandmother had left him.

Red and blue siren lights flashed as police and an ambulance surrounded the premises. Chad and his mother and Polo were by Seven's side. Seven cried in Chad's mother's arms. Earlier, Seven felt like a tough kid, and now he's a wimpy one. A taxi pulled up to the house as Ingrid hopped out.

"Mom!" Ingrid shouted as she dashed to the paramedics carrying Madeline out on the stretcher. She lifted the sheet from her mother's face. She released an enormous cry like never before, plummeting to her knees with tears streaming down her face. The neighbors comforted her. The paramedics carried Madeline into the ambulance. Seven dashed from Chad's mother's arms to his own mother's arm. Seven and Ingrid held each other as they cried.

A week later, it was a dismal morning where the rain was about to pour down on an old cemetery. Seven, his family, and his friends came to lay Madeline Thomas to rest. Seven and Ingrid clutched each other. Ingrid couldn't keep a dry eye. Seven laid his head on his mother's arms. Madeline was an angel that was sent from God to take care of her family, and now Madeline has returned home to be with God. Roses blanketed Madeline's chestnut coffin. A minister preached about Madeline's life, how she loved her daughter and her proud grandson, Seven, and everyone that she came in contact with. Madeline had a kind heart.

Hours later at the Miles' residence, Seven's family and friends comforted one another in this time of mourning. Seven laid in his bed, dazed. He stared up at the ceiling and wondered what was going to happen next. Seven closed his eyes, trying to think of something more pleasant. But he couldn't; his grandmother kept popping up in his head. Seven began to cry.

William entered Seven's bedroom. William comforted Seven in his arms. "It's all right. Your grandmother's in a better place now. She'll still be with you," William said.

"She'll be watching me from heaven?" Seven asked.

"Yes," William answered.

Just by the thought of Madeline being with God and all his wonders gave Seven comfort. Seven wiped his tears and stuck his chest as a posture of bravery. But, Seven thought about who would take care of him. His mother has to take care of someone else. Seven doubted his father would be around, because he was out there doing God only knows what. Did he have to stay by himself? Seven hoped not. He's not ready for that yet. Especially after experiencing his grandmother's passing.

Chapter 4

A couple of weeks after Seven's grandmother's untimely death, Seven and Ingrid rode in a taxi. It was early May. Of course, the weather was gorgeous. Eighty-one degrees was the low, and the high was going to be a summer temperature. There were no words exchanged between him and Ingrid. Just the engine of the taxi gently ran. Ingrid swiped her powder foundation on her face as she gazed into the mirror. Then she applied lipstick and blotted her lips. Ingrid smiled at Seven.

Then there was a bawling sound of a car engine. Seven glanced over both of his shoulders to see what kind of car it was. A blue Mustang with black stripes on the hood breezed past the taxi and then switched lanes. Seven loved the highway. It was like the car show. Seven saw Mom and Pop vehicles, sports, American, and foreign cars. Seven wasn't looking forward to meeting Angelika. Seven hoped she wouldn't take his ear off like she did over the phone. Chances were, Angelika was going to be a pain in the butt. She'd brag about her family, how much money they had, and the places she traveled to, such as California, London, Paris, Tokyo, and Milan. Today was going to be torture for Seven due to a little girl's riches being thrown in his face. Seven knew all he had to do was act like he was rich too—point-blank.

The cab drove down a well-paved cemented road. Then it made its way around a curvy lane. As Seven gazed out of the window, he saw a street sign that read, Old Westbury Road. The taxi halted at an enormous black fence with brass on the top. A security guard emerged from a booth with a gun in his holster. Seven cocked his head as he squinted his eyes. He heard aggressive voices. Seven saw two more security guards who carried firearms as they stood guard in front of the estate. Their walkie-talkies were loud with lots of static. The guard checked the identification of the cab driver, Ingrid, and Seven. Seven shied away as the guard stared him down. Then the guard gave the thumbs-up to the other guards. The large gates opened slowly as the taxi sped down a straight pavement. Tall hedges and well-cut grass enhanced the entrance.

Was Angelika a princess? Seven thought to himself. Were they royalty? As the cab drove farther on to the property, it zoomed up a winding pavement to a beautiful three-story brick mansion. It stopped. Seven was in wonder.

"Is this were you work, Mom?" Seven asked as his jaw dropped. Ingrid nodded and smiled. "This place is beautiful!" said Seven with excitement.

Ingrid's smile turned to a frown as she took a deep breath. "Seven, don't think you're going to come here and play. You're gonna study, and I've got some chores for you to do. You got that?" said Ingrid. Ingrid just had to rain on Seven's parade. Just to think Seven was going feel like he was rich.

By him visiting this mansion was the best feeling in the world even if he had chores to do. The taxi driver opened the door for Seven as he stepped out as if he were getting the red-carpet treatment. Ingrid followed behind. They headed toward the front door as the housekeeper, Olga, held it opened. Olga, a heavy accent Hungarian immigrant, hunchback, late-fifties, greeted Ingrid with a kiss. Then Seven was introduced to Olga by his mother. Seven extended his hand to Olga. It was a firm and friendly grip.

"How are you, Seven?" Olga asked as she greeted Seven with a kiss.

As Seven headed into the foyer of the home, he was taken by the huge crystal chandeliers in the ceiling. The marble table held a large bouquet of flowers. Seven saw the beautiful staircase that led to a second and third level. Ingrid and Seven marched up to third floor. They headed down the hallway as Angelika ran from room to room, playing with her dolls.

"Angelika?" Ingrid called. Ingrid dropped her bag as she opened her arms to the little girl. Angelika raced into Ingrid's arms. They clutched each other like mother and child.

"Ingrid, you're here," Angelika cheered. "I'm so happy."

Seven eyed Angelika and Ingrid; it was as if they were mother and daughter. Seven could automatically feel their bond. Ingrid introduced Seven and Angelika. Seven shook the hand of the beautiful, fair-skinned, brunette, angelic, five- year old child. Angelika was warm and very friendly. She then gave Seven a welcome hug. Seven didn't reciprocate the greeting. Seven made a sour expression. Angelika was a little too friendly.

Not long after Angelika's hug, Seven, Angelika, and Ingrid headed into a dim marble study where there was a fireplace that crackled. Books were the main decor of the atmosphere—books on real estate, how to start your business, and a lot of fiction novels. Jazz trumpeter Dizzy Gillepsie bellowed from the Bose radio. Seven frowned at the sound of this annoying art form. Angelika couldn't stand Jazz. Angelika sat in the lounge chair as she covered her ears. Seven checked out Mr. Westland's CD collection against the wall. It was mostly Jazz and classical, but Seven was familiar with R&B singer Luther Vandross. An enormous globe sat next to a dark cherry wood desk with an executive's chair right behind it. There were Thomas Kinkade paintings on the walls with some angelic art. It was as if Seven were on a field trip with his class at the museum.

A slender elderly gentleman, Ben, poured coffee into a cup. Seven sniffed the Colombian coffee–beaned air. Even though Seven was too young to be a coffee drinker, it smelled good. Ben turned and gave Ingrid a kiss on the cheek. Ingrid introduced Seven to Ben. Ben gave Seven a firm handshake. Seven noticed Ben spoke funny, because he was from England. Ben seemed to be a very boring guy who drank tea all day. Ben reminded Seven of the old television show *Mr. Beveledere*. By the strong handshake he gave Seven, he seemed cool.

And then the boss, Mr. Westland, strutted in. He was an African-American male of mixed heritage, creole, but had a mocha complexion, slender, mid-thirties. His presence made him stand out in a crowd. Mr. Westland didn't acknowledge that Seven and Ingrid were present in the room. Ben served Mr. Westland his coffee. Mr. Westland took a couple of sips as he sat in his executive's chair. He maneuvered it close to his desk and turned on his computer. Seven felt the arrogance from this man. Mr. Westland invested in real estate internationally, in places like France, England, Spain, and other parts of Europe, Canada, the Virgin Islands, and the United States. That's how he made his millions. He was very passionate about his business.

"Daddy!" Angelika shouted excitedly as she sprung from the lounge chair. Angelika rushed into her father's arms.

"Good Morning, Angelika? How are you?" Mr. Westland greeted his daughter with a kiss.

"Good morning, Mr. Westland?" said Ingrid nervously.

Mr. Westland heard Ingrid greet him but chose to ignore her. He focused his attention on Angelika.

"I'm starving. I'm gonna go get some breakfast. See you later, Dad," Angelika said as she waltzed out of the study.

"Good morning," Mr. Westland greeted Ingrid with a high and-mighty attitude.

Seven couldn't figure out why Mr. Westland was acting so cold towards his mother. What did she do wrong? Was she not doing her job? Then it hit Seven that Mr. Westland thought he was better than them. Mr. Westland felt that because he was wealthy, he could look down upon everyone else. Seven didn't like him. Seven gave Mr. Westland a dirty expression. He wanted so badly to punch Mr. Westland in the face. If Seven were older, he would do more than that. He would've given Mr. Westland the worst beat-down ever. As Seven continued to give Mr. Westland a dirty look, both Seven and Mr. Westland eyed each other with the most hateful expressions.

"This is my son, Seven," Ingrid introduced.

Then Mr. Westland snapped out of the trance. He focused his attention on Ingrid. Mr. Westland gave a slight smile, but he didn't give his condolence for his grandmother's death. Instead, Mr. Westland glared at Seven again. Mr. Westland felt intimidated by Seven being so little and tough as a lion. Mr. Westland didn't like this child, this strange boy, around Angelika. God only knows what he would do. Then Mr. Westland erased the negative thoughts from his mind and gave Seven a phony smile.

Seven gave a grin in return. Seven felt tough. He felt good. He scared an adult with the evil eye.

That afternoon, a navy Jaguar was parked in the front of the mansion. The luxury vehicle was being washed by Rocco. He was an overweight gentleman who wore the chauffeur attire. He scrubbed the hood of the car with soapy water. There were lots of studs. Mr. Westland and Seven exited the mansion. There were no words exchanged between him and this child. Seven knew that Mr. Westland didn't like him. Mr. Westland escorted Seven toward Rocco. Seven was introduced to Rocco by Mr. Westland.

Seven smiled as he saw the Jaguar. Seven was going to do something he loved: cars. Rocco gave Seven a firm handshake. This was another strong handshake from someone that was cool. Rocco and Seven gave mutual smiles. Mr. Westland strutted away and felt he was punishing Seven. But he was doing Seven a favor.

"I'll finish washing the car for you?" Seven volunteered. He grabbed the cloth from Rocco's hand. Rocco didn't resist. He backed off and allowed this tough kid that he just met to give the car a wash. And moments later, Seven waxed the jaguar with an electronic buffer. He started on the hood.

"You're real good at this, Seven. Where did you learn to do this?" Rocco asked.

Seven shrugged his shoulders. "I have a love for cars," Seven responded proudly.

"Can I watch?" Angelika asked in her sweet voice. Angelika stood there dressed in her girly attire. She wore a pink T-shirt, fuchsia jeans, and pink sneakers as she held her Barbie doll in her hand.

"Yeah. Just stay out of my way," Seven said with a stern tone. Seven proceeded to clean the Jaguar.

Angelika sat down on the stone-made steps. She placed her Barbie doll down next to her. Seven concentrated on getting this luxury ride to shine. He didn't pay Angelika any attention. Mr. Westland peeked from behind some fancy curtains of the window on the first floor of the mansion. He kept an eye on Angelika as she sat on the steps. Then he saw Seven washing his Jaguar as Rocco supervised. Mr. Westland gave a slight smile. "You did a real good job, Seven," praised Rocco.

"You washed the car fast," said Angelika as she applauded.

As a reward, Rocco gave Seven a couple of books about cars. Seven flipped through them with enthusiasm. There were pictures of sports cars, their compatible engines, parts, what type of gas they ran on. Then a silent engine could be slightly heard as a cream-colored Bentley parked in front of the mansion.

"Mommy!" Angelika cried. The Bentley was grill to grill with the Jaguar. Another chauffeur, Tomas, a Latin male in his midforties, exited the driver's side as he opened the door for lovely, blond, early-thirties Raquel Westland. She wore a black-and-white dress with black pumps. Mrs. Westland wore her hair in a bun. She exited the Bentley with some shopping bags in her hands. Tomas took the bags of luxuries from Mrs. Westland. Mrs. Westland helped Mr. Westland with the success of his real estate empire. She did this for the love for her husband and running a successful business. But Mrs. Westland's parents turned their backs on her when they found that she was in love with an African-American man. Mrs. Westland came from old money and usually didn't associate with people of color or poor people. But Mrs. Westland found love with her husband and followed her heart.

Angelika dashed into her mother's arms. "How's my darling?" asked Mrs. Westland as she clutched Angelika in her arms. Mrs. Westland gave Angelika constant smooches. Seven saw how beautiful Mrs. Westland was, and he could see where Angelika got her looks from. Mr. Westland headed out of the mansion as he greeted his wife with a kiss. Seven continued buffing the car. He noticed the

Westlands embracing each other. They must have been the happiest family in the world, especially with all this. The family marched into the mansion.

Later on, Mrs. Westland showed the new dresses she brought for Angelika to Ingrid. Angelika played with her Barbies in her magnificent dollhouse. Along with Angelika's dollhouse were collectible dolls, figurines, stuffed animals, and a music box. Angels adorned the ceilings, paintings of angels, pictures of Angelika from birth until the present day. She had a full-sized bed with a fancy pink bedspread. Angelika's entire bedroom was in shades of pink—baby pink, pink, and hot pink.

Seven swaggered into Angelika's bedroom. "Mom!" Seven called. Seven saw Mrs. Westland and his mother chatting. Angelika ran to Seven as she dropped her Barbie on the floor. She gave Seven another hug. Not again, not another hug from Angelika. Seven had enough but had to deal with it. He made a sour expression. "Mom, this is Ingrid's son," said Angelika. Mrs. Westland and Ingrid laughed as they saw Angelika being overfriendly with Seven. Mrs. Westland stepped toward Seven as she extended her hand to him. Mrs. Westland didn't give a firm handshake. It was light. It was an "I don't want to touch you, I'm not too crazy about meeting you" handshake. Mrs. Westland chuckled as she eyed Seven from head to toe. Seven felt Mrs. Westland was uneasy about him. *Is it because I'm here at the house with her little darling daughter? I know that's it,* Seven thought to himself. Seven knew these rich people like he knew the back of his hand.

Mr. Westland tiptoed into Angelika's bedroom and snatched Angelika into his arms. "How's my baby?" Mr. Westland shouted.

Seven observed the Westlands' happy interactions once again. "Could they really be this happy?" he thought. It was an unfortunate situation for his parents. They're always at each other's throats. Yelling and screaming. Two women fighting over a man. "Wasn't it supposed to be the other way around? The man fighting for the woman. That's manly," Seven recalled. That's what he always saw on television. Whether it be cartoons or some movie. It was better being with the Westlands than at home, where there was nothing but chaos. Seven kind of liked watching Angelika interact with her parents. It was like he was watching television. Angelika was funny. She was always giggling and cracking corny jokes. Angelika was so corny. It was funny. Seven's visit was an eye-opener to a whole new world.

That night, Seven got dressed into his pajamas in the bathroom. Seven noticed the enormous mirror where he stood. His reflection stared back at him. There was marble everywhere. Seven approached the shower and opened the heavy glass door. It was marble. The shower had five showerheads that would release water from every angle. Seven saw the two toilet bowls. One of them was a normal-looking toilet, but fancy. The other was a funny-looking toilet, but still fancy. Seven wondered why there were two toilets. Then Seven got it. One was for number 1. And the other was for number 2. "*But, it all goes down to the sewage.* Do they have one for the rich and the other for everyone else?" Seven thought.

As Seven exited the private bathroom, he heard Angelika praying. "Now I lay me down to sleep, I pray the Lord my soul to keep." Angelika proceeded to pray. Ingrid taught Angelika about God. Angelika loved to hear about this mysterious man in the sky. It was like her imaginary friend. Mr. and Mrs. Westland were nonbelievers. Angelika's parents didn't like the idea of her being taught about God, because it wasn't Ingrid's place. Ingrid may have been the nanny, but she was more of a mother than Mrs. Westland was. Seven headed out into the hallway and stood by Angelika's bedroom door and eavesdropped. He shook his head. Ingrid stopped giving Seven that type of attention when he was eight. The bedtime stories and kisses were gone. Seven didn't want any more of that baby shit, especially since Seven was a Leo.

Seven headed back to his guest bedroom. He swaggered in and checked out his surroundings. The guestroom was nice but not so fancy. Seven leaped upon the full-sized bed. Seven got under the covers and laid down. As he looked around the room, the walls were bare. Seven wanted so badly to pin up some posters that he liked. This was so Seven would feel like he was in his own bedroom at home. The guest bedroom wasn't his, and he couldn't touch anything that didn't belong to him. Seven got into a comfortable position and closed his eyes. Even the help got a taste of the good life.

The next morning, it was a dismal day. The birds still chirped. The sun tried its best to peek out from behind the clouds, but Mother Nature wouldn't let it. Seventy-nine degrees was the low for this morning. The high was in the mid-eighties. The flowers were in full blossom, trees sat gracefully on the Westland estate, and the birds danced in the gardens. There were two separate vehicles in front of the villa—the Jaguar and a taxi. Angelika and Seven were escorted out by Angelika's parents and Ingrid. Angelika held Ingrid's hand rather than her mother's. Seven noticed that Mrs. Westland stole a kiss from Angelika. Then Angelika kissed her father. "Have a good day," Mrs. Westland cried.

"I will," Angelika responded. Angelika then gave Ingrid the last kiss. Seven observed it all. Then Ingrid gave Seven her last kiss.

This is a fuckin' confusing! Whose mother is who? Seven thought. Seven got in the taxi as Ingrid shut the door. She waved to him. Angelika made her way toward the Jaguar and hopped in. Rocco resided in the driver's seat. Of course, the Jaguar headed out first with the taxi behind. Both vehicles made their way out of the large iron gates. The cars drove in opposite directions. Seven thought he'd be driven to school in the Jaguar since he washed it. He got put in the cab.

On Seven's drive to school, he lay back in his seat and didn't move a muscle. Seven even brought one of the auto books that Rocco gave to him. You would think he would've at least flipped through that. No, Seven wondered what kind of school Angelika went to. He knew it was school for the rich. *What kind of things do they learn? Are the subjects different? How do the classrooms look? Are they fancy?* All these questions Seven asked himself. He already saw how Angelika lived, so he wanted to know about her education.

Later that morning, Seven's teacher Mr. Kincaid lectured about the solar system. Most of the students listened as one student slept. A girl read a pop magazine. Chad was busy with his nasty ways. He drew x-rated pictures. Seven had his science book in front of him as he listened to Mr. Kincaid. Seven was so eager to read one of his car books. He eased the car book from under his desk. He placed it in between his science textbook. Seven had it halfway exposed while under his science book. He read along with the class and then was able to read his book on cars.

"Seven, do you wanna read?" Mr. Kincaid asked.

Seven nodded his head as he concealed his car book. He read the paragraph about the solar system to the class.

That afternoon, school was out. Seven and Chad swaggered out of the building. Chad wanted to go to the park, but Seven had to get to his aunt's house, which was a lie. He wasn't going to tell Chad where he was really staying. Chad noticed Seven taking the taxi. That was unusual. He never did that before. Chad shrugged his shoulders as he and Seven gave each other high fives and went on their ways. Seven hopped in the taxi as it took off. As soon as Seven got back to the mansion, he made his way through the gardens of the estate with his books. Seven promised his mother he was going to do his homework. He tried to find himself somewhere quiet where he could so-called study. But Seven wound up giving himself a tour of the estate. He strolled across the lawn as he looked down at the beautiful swimming pool that had a plastic cover on it. It wasn't hot enough yet to take a dive. In a couple of months, it'll be ready to go. Seven proceeded through the gardens. There was a rose garden that released its fragrance through the air. Then he strolled past a garden of color-ful tulips. The surroundings were very colorful with lots of greenery. Seven swaggered across a bridge over a lake, where the swans and ducks graced the body of water. Then he made his way down some stone-like steps, where he came to a stone altar. It seemed like a quiet place where he could have some peace. This altar was adjacent to another lake with ducks and geese as the mansion was right behind the lake.

As Seven looked at his surroundings, he thought of his grand-mother. *Is heaven like this? Is this where she's spending the rest of her life with God? An enormous garden with flowers, trees, and birds? If so, I'm happy that she's in his hands,* Seven thought to himself. Seven walked into the altar. He gazed up at the glass on top. It was gorgeous. Seven felt as if he had died and gone to heaven. Seven sat down and read his car books instead of doing his homework. He indulged in his world of fast cars, engines, nuts, and bolts.

"Hi!" a sweet little unknown voice greeted. Seven looked around and saw no one. As soon as he turned around, Angelika stood right before him in the altar. Seven was startled by Angelika. Not only was Angelika too friendly, she was a bit creepy. "What's your problem, Angelika?" Seven yelled. Seven sucked the air through his teeth and stared at Angelika.

Angelika smiled in return, and then her smile dropped. "What's wrong?" Angelika asked in a submissive tone.

"Why are you sneaking up on me?"

"I just wanted to see what you were doing'". Angelika responded as she sat beside Seven. Angelika flipped through the car book. "What are reading?" Angelika asked.

Seven snatched the book out of Angelika's hand. "Don't worry about it. Would you stay out of my way!" Seven yelled again.

Angelika became teary eyed, and she headed out of the altar. Seven felt guilty. He knew his grandmother was watching him down from heaven and shook her head in disappointment at her grandson's bad behavior. "Angelika!" Seven exhaled as she marched away. Seven ran behind her. He blocked Angelika's path. "Don't cry, Angelika. I'm sorry," Seven apologized.

Angelika walked in the other direction. She didn't want to hear it. Seven tried blocking Angelika's path again. "Do you want to learn about cars?" Seven asked. Angelika held back her tears. She didn't say a word. "Girls like boys with cars," said Seven. "Would you like to see my favorite muscle car?" Seven asked jokingly.

Angelika frowned. "What's a muscle car?"

"A Dodge Charger, Challenger, Mustang, or Camaro," Seven answered. "I know you would love to see me in one of those cars. Right?" Seven smiled. He tried to get Angelika to smile. Success. Angelika laughed.

Moments later, Angelika and Seven got along just fine like two best friends. This was an opportunity for him to tell all his dreams to her. Angelika shook her head and loved what she heard. Angelika then told Seven about her goals. She wanted to be a ballerina. Angelika took lessons every Saturday and hoped to audition for the role of Clara in *The Nutcracker* on Broadway. To Seven, that wasn't very interesting, but he tolerated it. Then she told Seven she wanted to be a photographer as well. Or maybe go into real estate like her father. Angelika had so many goals; she wasn't really sure what she wanted to do. But, she loved taking pictures.

The two children enjoyed each other's company as they spent many days together until the end of the school year.

Chapter 5

Eighty-nine degrees was the temperature on July 3—time for T-shirts, shorts, beaches, swimming pools, and barbecues. One of the biggest holidays was the next day, July 4. It was noon at the Westland mansion, where Angelika plummeted into the enormous swimming pool. Angelika wore a one-piece bathing suit in pink with a fuchsia child lifesaver around her waist. She kicked her feet and swam toward Ingrid. Ingrid waited in the shallow end of the pool where she sported a one-piece pink swimsuit. Ingrid was delighted to see Angelika swimming. Seven swaggered out in his blue trunks. Angelika swam towards Ingrid in the shallow water of the pool. She then sat on the shallow pool steps.

"Hello, Seven. Get in! It's fun," Angelika shouted. Seven did an Olympic-styled dive from the deeper end of the pool. Seven learned to swim in the local neighborhood YMCA. Seven would go with his father, where he gave him swimming lessons like diving, holding your breathing, backstroke, etc. Surprisingly, Seven knew how to hold his breath for quite a while. He loved swimming under water in pools that is. He hated the beach because of the salt water burning his eyes and God only knows if you'll encounter a sting from a jellyfish or some unknown predator of the sea. The sun's rays beamed through the blue water making it a lighter shade. Seven loved that type of mood lighting it felt heavenly. The water was like a safe haven for Seven. He couldn't hear or see anything or anyone that vexed him until he got to the surface. As Seven proceeded to swim underwater, Angelika and Ingrid's eyes bulged. It was shocking how long Seven could hold his breath. Was Seven meant to be in the Summer Olympics or something related to swimming? Ingrid thought to herself. Angelika didn't know what to think, but just that it was pure magic. Seven made his way towards the shallow water where Angelika and Ingrid were. Finally, Seven made it to the surface. He inhaled the fresh air into his lungs. Ingrid and Angelika applauded. "Very impressive, Seven.," said Ingrid. Seven took sharp breathes as he sat on the steps of the pool in the shallow water.

Later, Angelika and Seven ate burgers and fries on the West porch, which was on the west wing of the mansion. It was like eating at a fancy restaurant, with ceiling fans keeping the air cool from every angle. Angelika and Seven joked and laughed as they ate. Ingrid sat at the table, watching the children. He wondered if he was gonna stay there forever. After eating a huge lunch, Angelika and Seven marched toward a group of party planners. They were setting up for the Westland's huge Fourth of July bash. There were gonna be fireworks, of course, a huge barbecue, music, and fun for the kids. A group of men assembled a Ferris wheel.

"A Ferris wheel!" Angelika shouted. Angelika scrambled toward it.

Seven was right behind her. "This is nice," Seven admired. *Is this what rich people do? They can build an amusement park in their own backyard,* Seven thought.

Mrs. Westland instructed the party planners and others where to set up and what to do. Mrs. Westland noticed Angelika and Seven at the Ferris wheel. Mrs. Westland strutted over. "Hello, Angelika," she greeted as she gave Angelika a kiss. Mrs. Westland was just like her husband. She'll stare at you for a moment without uttering a word if you're not one of them.

"When will the Ferris wheel be ready?" Angelika asked.

"Tomorrow," said Mrs. Westland as she stroked Angelika's brunette hair.

"I want to take a ride today." Angelika sighed.

Mrs. Westland noticed that Angelika was unsupervised. Mrs. Westland looked around. Seven noticed whom Mrs. Westland was looking for.

"Angelika and Seven!" Ingrid cried.

Mrs. Westland heard Ingrid's cries. She saw Ingrid scurrying across the lawn. "Angelika here, Ingrid." Mrs. Westland cried. "Angelika, don't run away from Ingrid. Don't worry her," Mrs. Westland insisted.

Seven could see that Mrs. Westland didn't even acknowledge him and his whereabouts. It was all about Angelika. Well, it's was understandable. Angelika was a little girl.

It was Independence Day. The Westland mansion was ready for the most enormous Fourth of July celebration ever. The party planners made their last preparations for the event. They draped fancy tablecloths on the tables, set up chairs, and made other seating arrangements. The chefs set up the barbecue grills as steaks, chicken, ribs, vegetables, fruits, alcoholic and soft drinks, and goodies for the kids were hauled in by food vendors. Red, white, and blue aluminum and latex balloons were hauled in.

Seven and Angelika watched the whole thing unfold from his guest bedroom window. Cartoons played on television. The kids were excited about the most important holiday for America. "I can't wait to go on the Ferris wheel!" said Angelika.

"This is gonna be the best of Fourth ever! We could hang together." Seven suggested.

"Yeah, we will," Angelika agreed.

As Angelika and Seven continued chatting about the big night, Mrs. Westland heard voices coming from the guest bedroom. Mrs. Westland heard Angelika and Seven hanging out. Mrs. Westland picked an outfit for Angelika to wear at the party. She was in the walk-in closet in Angelika's bedroom. It was adjacent to the guest bedroom that Seven occupied. Mrs. Westland shook her head as she eavesdropped on the kids' plans. Mrs. Westland picked out a red, white, and blue dress, with black patent leather shoes. Mrs. Westland wasn't too crazy about Angelika associating with the underprivileged.

Mrs. Westland came from a family of wealth that went back four generations. Mr. and Mrs. Westland's love wasn't approved of by her parents. They strongly denounced it. It wasn't over the fact that Mrs. Westland was given some money from her father as a birthday present. It was that Mrs. Westland had fallen head over heels for an African-American man. Mrs. Westland's father wanted so badly to sue his daughter in order to get the money back, but it was a gift, so there was no case. Her father held bitterness for his daughter's disloyalty. Mrs. Westland was headstrong and didn't believe in arranged marriages. Her father did. Her family wasn't some affluent family from another country. They were American. But she knew of some affluent American families who actually practiced arranged marriages. Anyway, Mrs. Westland had to get the word to her husband about Angelika's associations.

That evening, dozens of luxury vehicles pulled up in front of the mansion. Valets thrust open the doors of expensive automobiles as guests strutted into the biggest Fourth of July bash ever. The party guests wore fancy casual summer outfits. They were Mr. and Mrs. Westland's business associates, neighbors, and closest friends. They all had one thing in common: money.

A band played jazz music. Everyone sipped on wine or whatever else they preferred and nibbled on hors d'oeuvres. The Westlands mingled with their guests. Angelika, Seven, and the other rich kids played. Angelika and Seven rode on the Ferris wheel. Ingrid was right there watching the two as they enjoyed themselves. Angelika waved to Ingrid. "Hey, Ingrid!" Angelika shouted.

Ingrid waved back as she saw how much fun the kids were having. Angelika and Seven ate hot dogs and other goodies. The kids waved and threw sparklers into the air. Mr. and Mrs. Westland observed as Angelika and Seven were having a blast. Then it happened again— the staring battle between Mr. Westland and Seven. Mr. Westland glared at Seven as he played with Angelika and the other kids. Seven then caught Mr. Westland's eyes. Seven challenged him at the staring game. Seven knew this wasn't any game. This was serious. He knew it was because Angelika and he were acquainted. Then the drum solo of the jazz music played. Seven and Mr. Westland continued to glare;

it was like they were two cowboys at a showdown. They were right ready to brandish their guns, releasing bullets into their foe. Seven wished he could fire a bullet in Mr. Westland's ass. He'll survive that.

"Charles!" Mrs. Westland cried. Mr. Westland snapped out of the challenge as she kissed and embraced Mr. Westland. "What are you glaring at?" Mrs. Westland wondered.

Mr. And Mrs. Westland strolled away. Seven won this battle again. He was proud of himself. Seven wanted Mr. Westland to stop giving him the dirty stares.

Then it was the moment they've all been waiting for. The enormous fireworks show were colors of red, white, and blue that burst into the night sky. Seven and Angelika gasped at the sparkling, fiery display of patriotic symbols representing our great nation. Like the American flag, the bald eagle, a flute, drum, etc. Ingrid stood directly behind the kids as she smiled and saw how happy the kids were. But Mr. and Mrs. Westland weren't. The couple had to keep a smile on their faces in order to play it off. But, their smiles dropped every time they laid eyes on Seven.

The extravaganza was over, and the last few guests exited the mansion. Mrs. Westland thanked them for coming. Valets pulled up to the front door with the guests' luxury vehicles. The party guests hopped in their cars and sped away from the mansion. Meanwhile, Mr. Westland lounged in his office. He kicked his feet up as Ben lit his cigar for him. Mr. Westland inhaled as he puffed smoke into the air. The scent of cigar overwhelmed the room. Three ceiling fans cleared out the disgusting smell to some degree, bringing about fresh air. Mr. Westland flipped through the channels on the television. He watched the news. Ben tidied up the office before calling it a night.

There was a knock on the door, and Ben answered it as Ingrid headed inside. "Hello, Mr. Westland. You wanted to see me?" Ingrid asked in curiosity. Mr. Westland rocked back and forth in his chair. Mr. Westland cut right to the chase. He wanted Ingrid to find a babysitter for Seven. Mr. Westland claimed he understood that Angelika and Seven were kids, but things do happen. "Things like what?" Ingrid asked.

Mr. Westland didn't answer her and gave her pay for the week. It wasn't much for her family. And she definitely couldn't hire a babysitter. Ingrid was paid as if she worked at McDonald's; that's how cheap Mr. Westland was. Ingrid had to figure out something fast.

The next morning, Ingrid and Seven exited the mansion. The taxi driver grabbed their bags and placed them in the trunk of the taxi. He shut the trunk. Mr. and Mrs. Westland just glared at them as if they were happy to see them leave, especially when it came to Seven.

Angelika rushed to hug Ingrid. "When are you coming back, Ingrid?" Angelika asked as her voice cracked. Tears streamed down her rosy cheeks. She sobbed.

Ingrid comforted Angelika as if she were her own. "I'll be back in a couple of weeks." They were closer than Angelika and Mrs. Westland were.

"What about my birthday?" Angelika asked.

What about my birthday? Seven asked himself. But he erased the selfishness from his mind. He knew that Angelika's birthday was three days after his. He couldn't stand to see Angelika in tears. It reminded him of his baby sister, Athena. Seven knew his mother would be back for Angelika's birthday. Angelika and Ingrid gave each other a long hug as if a child were being taken away from her mother. Mrs.

Westland then pulled Angelika away from Ingrid. Ingrid waved to Angelika. Seven then waved to Angelika from the taxi. Ingrid got into the taxi as the door slammed. Then it drove away from the mansion and through the iron gates.

Chapter 6

"Happy Birthday, Seven!: read a humongous banner with royal-blue background with silver lettering. July 27 was the date Seven and his family and friends celebrated ten years of his life. On this hot afternoon, the sun beamed as a sizzling barbecue released more hot air into the atmosphere. Hot dogs and hamburgers were flipped on the grill and served to party guests. Rap music blasted from a deejay's stereo. Seven, Chad, and his other neighborhood friends goofed around while the adults engaged in the latest gossip. Then ten candles were lit on a Carvel ice cream cake as Ingrid held it in her hand. She marched toward the picnic table. The cake was placed down before Seven. Everyone sang "Happy Birthday" to Seven. Seven smiled as he was happy to see everyone coming together. But someone was missing—his grandmother. Seven felt some sadness because she wasn't around. He wanted to cry but couldn't. He closed his eyes for a second in order to hold back the tears.

"Make a wish!" Ingrid commanded. Seven closed his eyes. He wanted his grandmother back, but that wasn't going to happen. So he wished for his father. Seven hadn't seen his father in a great while. Seven hoped his father didn't forget his birthday. Then he blew out the candles. Everyone applauded. Moments later, Seven's guests were enjoying their Carvel ice cream cake. It was everyone's favorite. It was layered with vanilla ice cream on top, chocolate chips crunchies in the middle, and chocolate ice cream on the bottom. Seven, Chad, and a couple of other boys had their boys talk. Of course, the topic was cars. They spoke about different vehicles, street racing versus professional, to the Fast and the Furious films. Seven wanted his father so badly. He needed his father. Seven loved that male bond that he had with his Pops.

Is Athena gonna get all my father's attention? Seven thought to himself. Seven didn't want to take anything out on Athena because she was just a baby. Seven knew whom to direct his anger toward. *Why couldn't things work out between him and my mother?* Seven asked himself. Seven then snapped out of it. He continued to chat with his friends about their dreams of driving fast cars.

That evening, Ingrid and Chad's mother threw out trash in large garbage bags. They picked up paper cups, paper plates, and plastic utensils. Seven and Chad were in the living room, watching late cartoons. Then the doorbell rang. Seven leaped from in front of the television. He swung the front door open as William, his father, stood there in the doorway. Seven was overjoyed to see his father. But he was late. Better late than never. Seven gave his father an enormous hug.

"Happy birthday, Seven!" William shouted. "I'm sorry I'm late," William said in an apologetic tone.

Seven overlooked his father's tardiness. He's just happy to see him. Then William rolled in a brand-new NASCAR Todd MacKenzie dirt bike. It was black with green designs just like the signature designs that were on Todd MacKenzie's NASCAR race car. Chad dashed to Seven and William. Chad saw the dirt bike and was a little excited about the dirt bike. But he wasn't really into professional car racing. Seven wheeled his brand-new bike from the front door through the living room to the kitchen to the double slide-in door that led to the backyard.

"Mom, look at my bike!" Seven shouted, excited. Ingrid smiled as she saw her Seven with his shiny new bike. Seven rolled it toward his mother. Seven hopped on his bike and rode it around the yard a bit. Seven was so excited; he couldn't help but hear his parents' argument.

"The party is over, William!" Ingrid shouted as she continued to throw more party favors in the trash bag. Mrs. Richardson kept collecting trash as she could hear the frustrations of Seven's mother. Seven stopped riding his bike as Chad approached him.

"That's cool," Chad said as he eyed the bike's every detail.

"You like it?" Seven asked. "It kind of looks like Todd MacKenzie's race car, right?" Seven said.

As the two boys were excited about the new bike, they made plans to race each other the next day and pretend that they were drag racing on the block. As the boys continued to plan their expedition for the next day, they ended their conversation and heard the intense words between Ingrid and William. Ingrid needed William to watch Seven for a few days. William made up nothing but excuses. Seven became a little nervous for Mrs. Richardson. Plus it was embarrassing for him. Thank goodness his guests left. Then it happened again.

"Shut the fuck up, please!" Seven bellowed.

"Watch your mouth, young man," Ingrid suggested.

"Get off his case! You can see he's upset," William said.

Ingrid's jaw dropped as she pointed a plastic fork in William's face. "This is your doing!" yelled Ingrid. From this point on, Ingrid and William's heated exchange of words started again. Seven was off the hook for his sinful words. Seven exhaled as he looked as Chad. Seven could see the look of embarrassment, especially on a special day like his birthday. Seven couldn't wait to ride his bike to get away from it all.

The next morning, Seven pedaled his bike at a fast pace on the side of the road. A few cars passed him on the opposite side. Already sweat poured down Seven's face on this hot and humid day. He wiped the perspiration from his face as his heart raced. Seven was getting as far away from his parents as possible. Just for the day. The verbal fighting between his parents bothered him. So he ran toward his imagination of racing with the use of his bike.

He approached Chad's house. Seven marched up to the door and rang the doorbell. Chad opened the door. "Are you ready?" Seven asked. A few moments later, Seven and Chad were on their dirt bikes, riding through a dirt-like field. They made their laps around the track, jumping small hills as dirt emerged from the rear of their tires. Seven no longer saw his brand-new Todd MacKenzie dirt bike. Instead, he visualized himself in the driver's seat of a navy-blue Mustang Cobra, and Chad occupied the driver's seat of a silver Camaro. Clouds of smoke emerged from the rear tires of the muscle cars. The monstrous engines bellowed as they swerved on to Sunrise highway with screeching wheels. The Mustang and Camaro weaved in and out between vehicles. The motorists cursed as the kids showed off. Seven put his pedal to the metal as the Mustang went faster. He was right on the Camaro's tail. Then the Camaro sped into the distance. The engine roared through the air. Seven sped up in this Mustang to catch up with Chad.

"Seven!" Chad called. Chad gawked at Seven. He could see Seven was in a daze.

Seven then snapped out of it as he noticed Chad was on the side of the track with his bike. Seven pulled to the side. "How did you get there?" Seven asked shockingly.

"You were daydreaming." Chad laughed as he clapped his hands.

"What's so funny, asshole!" Seven cursed.

"I was trying to get your attention several times," Chad answered.

Seven then shook his head as he felt a bit embarrassed.

Later, at Chad's house Mrs. Richardson fed Chad and Seven burgers and fries as they sat in the small so-called dining area. The boys devoured the food as NASCAR played on television in the living room which was adjacent to the dining area. Multi engines bellowed from the box with the Dolby surround sound. Chad hopped from his seat to hear what the sound would be like on high. He grabbed the remote and pressed the volume button. Then the engines overwhelmed the entire house with those NASCAR engines. The house vibrated due to the powerful sound.

"Chad, turn that down! You're gonna wake up the dead!" Mrs. Richardson shouted.

Chad lowered the volume on the remote. "It's so much fun," Chad suggested.

"Do you want the police called on us?" Mrs. Richardson asked as she placed her hands on her hips.

Seven and Chad had the same conversion all the time: cars. Seven and Chad proceeded to share their goals. Seven then thought of what happened to his grandmother. He promised that he wouldn't stay out too long. And he felt guilty when she died. Seven left the house earlier that morning without telling his mother where he was going. Seven took the last bite of his hamburger. He leaped from the table. Seven thrust the front door open. Seven hoped that Chad and his mother understood him leaving so suddenly.

"I'll see you later, man," Seven said as he and Chad exchanged high fives. Chad gave a slight smile. Seven could tell that he understood his dilemma. Seven hopped on his bike and rode off down the road.

Meanwhile, Ingrid wiped her eyes as she placed a bowl of chicken soup on the table. She washed the dishes in the sink. In the rear glass door, Seven arrived on his bike. He knocked on the door.

"Mom!" Seven called to his mother. Ingrid turned abruptly from the sink and unlocked the door. She slid the glass door open as she clutched Seven in her arms. Ingrid began to sob. Seven knew about his mother's episodes. And he really couldn't understand it. But he knew she was very depressed due to his grandmother passing away and the fighting with his father. What could he do to make things right? Seven was just a kid. "I can't depend on your father to do anything," Ingrid explained as she glared into Seven's eyes. "You understand. Don't you?" Ingrid asked. She rubbed Seven's cheek.

Seven shook his head. "Yes." Seven really didn't understand.

Chapter 7

Seven and Ingrid were off to the Westland estate again. It was July 29, another sizzling summer morning. A taxi picked Seven and Ingrid up from their home. Seven had something to look forward to. That was riding his new Todd MacKenzie bike and hanging out with Angelika. But there was something Seven wasn't looking forward to: enduring more staring competitions with Mr. Westland. Seven dreaded the thought. The man hated him with a passion. Why? The question ran through Seven's brain.

The taxi zoomed through the enormous iron fence along a long stretch of pavement that lead to the mansion. It parked in front of the house. Rocco was waxing the hood of the jaguar as he smoked a cigar. Olga opened the red door of the mansion as she smiled and waved to Ingrid and Seven. The cab driver hopped out of the vehicle and grabbed Seven's bike from the trunk. Ingrid and Seven escorted themselves out of the cab. When you're poor, you have to do things on your own, like escorting yourself in and out of a taxi, making your own food, and doing things independently. Seven would've loved the red carpet treatment, but no.

"Hello, Ingrid. Angelika's tooth is loose," Olga told Ingrid.

Angelika was Ingrid's first priority. She made it her business to attend to the child. In Angelika's private bathroom, Mrs. Westland had a string tied around Angelika's tooth. Angelika stomped her feet on the floor due to the pain. And even more pain was about to come. "Mommy, why is it taking so long to come out?" Angelika cried.

Ingrid rushed through Angelika's bedroom and into the private bathroom. Ingrid clutched Angelika as Mrs. Westland scurried away. "I've got to run. I'll see you later, Angelika. Everything will be fine," Mrs. Westland said as she stormed out of the bathroom. Mrs. Westland breezed past Seven without even acknowledging his presence. Seven stepped into the doorway of the bathroom, it matched Angelika's angelic bedroom. It was pretty and pink, with angelic wall decor and some cartoon characters. Fancy fuchsia towels and washcloths hung on the racks, and some water toys sat in the corner. After Seven gave himself a tour of the bathroom with his own eyes, he couldn't help but see Angelika in the pain and frustrations of trying to get her tooth out. Seven's mother was a pro when it came to getting things wrapped up.

"Sweetheart, stop crying. On three," Ingrid said. Angelika nodded her head in fear. Seven saw Angelika had to trust Ingrid. "Ready? One. Two. Three." Ingrid counted. Then there was a small snap and trickling to the floor. Seven picked up the bloody baby tooth and glared at it. He then passed it to his mother. "You see. That wasn't so bad, was it?" Ingrid asked with her loving tone.

"No." Angelika sniffled with her baby tone of voice.

"You're very brave. I'm proud of you, Angelika," Ingrid praised the child.

Angelika looked at Seven and grinned with her missing front tooth. Seven scoffed as he saw the funny-looking kid with no front tooth.

Angelika looked as if she had been in a boxing match. Ding-Ding! It was a silly thought that just across Seven's mind.

Through a beautiful park full of bloomed trees, trimmed grass, and people enjoying the summer afternoon with their families, friends, pets, or just strolling alone. Seven pedaled fast on his Todd MacKenzie bike, leaving Angelika and Ingrid behind.

Angelika pedaled as fast as she could on her pink-and-white Huffy bike. She wore a pink helmet. "Seven, wait up!" Angelika shouted.

Ingrid rode on a mountain bike as she and Angelika tried catching up to Seven. Seven looked behind him and saw his mother and Angelika way behind him. Seven cackled at the thought.

Again, a black Dodge Challenger spun out of control on a highway as the brakes screeched. The muscle car switched lanes as it left every car in the dust. Seven, a young adult, glanced in his rearview mirror and saw other racers behind him. He guffawed. Then Seven snapped out of his fantasy as he slammed on the brakes of his bike. Seven's bike skidded across the pavement and stopped before a woman and her Yorkie pooch. A middle-aged woman snatched her dog as she gawked at Seven.

"Are you okay, sweetie?" the forty-something-year-old woman asked. Seven lay on the concrete with his bike and an enormous black skid mark on the ground. The people in the park came over and saw the tire markings. Ingrid and Angelika rode towards Seven and saw him in distress.

"Seven, are you alright, baby!" Ingrid hollered as she sped towards him on her mountain bike. She hopped off and comforted Seven.

"I'm cool. Look what I did!" Seven said proudly.

Angelika stopped her bike and approached Seven. "Are you okay?" Angelika asked. Even more people passing by noticed the large skid marks surrounding Seven and his bike. Seven jumped to his feet and saw it. Seven grinned because he knew from that skid mark he was bound for street racing or some kind of professional car racing.

On the way back to the Westlands', Ingrid had a taxi make a stop at her home. Seven and Angelika resided in the backseat. The two kids glanced at each other and grimaced. The taxi halted at a red signal at a railroad crossing. As Seven glared out of the window, he knew this was the way home.

"I'm gonna pick up some fresh clothes for you," Ingrid responded. Moments later, the taxi parked in the driveway of Ingrid's home.

Angelika glared at the small house as she looked over both of her shoulders. "Is this where you live, Ingrid?" Angelika asked.

"Yes," Ingrid answered. Seven as well as Ingrid got themselves out of the taxi. Seven dashed around to the other side and opened the door for Angelika. She exited the vehicle with a smile on her face.

"Thank you," Angelika said. Seven smiled in return. He knew they weren't at the mansion, but Angelika was used to being waited on hand and foot. He knew it was the right thing to do. Ingrid watched Seven's every move when it came to Angelika, just like Mr. Westland. Ingrid witnessed Seven's gentlemanly act. She nodded to Seven with her proudest smile ever.

While, Ingrid packed some fresh under clothes, shirts, socks, and other garments into a duffel bag, Angelika browsed around noticing Seven's NASCAR items and love for the sport. Seven eyed Angelika carefully to make sure she didn't break anything.

"I like your house, Ingrid," said Angelika as she continued to browse Seven's room.

"Thank you, Angelika. It's small," Ingrid said.

"It's not small. It's beautiful," Angelika complimented. Angelika didn't turn her nose up at anything they had. She smiled at everything she saw, especially Seven's remote control car. "What's this?" Angelika asked as she grabbed the remote control for the car. Seven grabbed it from her hand.

"Don't touch that please. I don't touch your stuff," Seven said.

"Seven, be nice," Ingrid suggested.

"That's okay," said Angelika as she backed off and respected his wishes.

"You kids go out and play for a minute," Ingrid insisted as she continued to pack Seven's things in a duffel bag.

Moments later, Seven and Angelika played in the backyard, where there was a pond with some ducks and lots of geese. The children watched the birds as they tossed rocks into the water. Seven's rocks skipped the body of water until they finally went under. Angelika threw hers. Seven noticed Angelika wasn't good at doing what he was doing. *Because she's a girl. And girls don't have a clue about anything.* Seven proceeded to toss the rocks as they skipped the waters. Angelika watched Seven as he did it. Angelika held the stone in her hand and allowed her wrist to release it from her hand. The stone skipped the water. "I did it," Angelika said with a proud smile on her face.

"Did what?" Seven asked in return.

"You know. I tossed the rock like you did," Angelika said.

"You don't know anything," Seven said.

"Yes, I do. I know a lot," Angelika informed Seven.

"What do you know?" Seven asked as he sucked his teeth. He continued to toss rocks into the lake.

"I know ballet, tap, and jazz dancing. Do you know how to dance?"

"I don't know about any ballet jazz shit. All right?" From the corner of Seven's eye, he saw Angelika was looking at him. Seven gave direct eye contact with Angelika. Seven raised an eyebrow. "What's the problem, Angelika?"

"What does *shit* mean?"

"Shit means . . ." Seven took a deep breath. "How the fuck can I explain this? Don't you know anything?"

Angelika shrugged her shoulders. "It's a curse word. It sounds bad."

"It is bad."

"So why do you do it?" Angelika asked.

"Because I'm not rich. Rich people don't curse."

"Yes, they do. My dad does."

"What does he say?"

"Darn!"

"That's not a curse word," Seven cackled.

"Shit is a curse word?" Angelika questioned Seven with her squinting eyes and curious expression.

"Yes," said Seven as he continued to hurl stones into the pond.

"Come on, kids! It's time to go!" Ingrid alarmed them.

Angelika and Seven dashed to the taxi. Seven allowed Angelika to get a head start. Their feet trampled on the concrete as the taxi driver heard them. He waited in the cab for a while with the meter running. The fair was getting expensive. Angelika hopped in the backseat first, with Seven directly behind her. The door shut. Then Ingrid hurried out of the house with a duffel bag and hopped in the taxi.

Back at the Westland mansion, Angelika and Seven hung out around the lake where there were swans. Seven did the same thing he always did: tossed rocks into the lake. Angelika was right by his side. "Do you like it here?" Angelika asked shyly.

Seven shook his head and stared into the distance. He could see Angelika looking directly at him. Seven had a feeling Angelika must have a crush on him. He kind of liked her too. But she's just a baby, like his half sister, Athena. But Athena was much younger. Seven abruptly turned to Angelika. "Why are you looking at me like that?" Seven asked with a straight face. He shook some rocks in the palm of his hands.

"I don't know. I'm just looking," Angelika replied. She looked away bashfully.

"Angelika!" called a mysterious girly voice in the distance.

Angelika saw her friend Cassandra. Seven noticed the beautiful brunette Caucasian female, Angelika's age. Cassandra wore yellow overalls with a white T-shirt and white tennis shoes. Angelika and Cassandra were so beautiful; they looked like sisters, except Angelika was biracial and Cassandra was white. For a moment, Angelika was doing the same thing Mrs. Westland did to Seven earlier. She ignored him. Seven was invisible. Then Angelika came to her senses. Angelika introduced Cassandra to Seven. Seven was going to be nice. He smiled at Cassandra. Instead, Cassandra turned her nose up at Seven. Cassandra whispered in Angelika's ear. Seven knew it was rude.

"He's my friend. I can't do that," Angelika shouted at Cassandra.

Cassandra made eye contact with Angelika. Cassandra then pulled Angelika to the side. "Why are you playing with the help?" Cassandra whispered to Angelika.

Seven glared at Angelika to see if she was going to take her friend's advice.

"If you're going act like that, then you can't come to my birthday party," Angelika said in a stern voice. Seven knew Angelika would come around for him. Cassandra then stormed away from Angelika. Angelika strutted back to Seven's side. She then grasped Seven's hand as they smiled at each other.

Chapter 8

I t was July 31, Angelika's birthday. Party planners were at the Westland estate, making preparations for her special extravaganza. Hundreds of balloons of latex and aluminum in every color were blown up. There were some men assembling a beautiful carousel, tablecloths were draped over the table and chairs. There were lots of party favors, food, and candy. Seven gazed from his guest bedroom window at Angelika's birthday celebration being set up before his eyes. Angelika wasn't by his side to watch the whole thing take place. At this point, Seven felt alone. Ingrid had no other choice than to bring Seven with her to work. She refused to leave Seven home alone. Mr. and Mrs. Westland let it go, but Mr. Westland had his eye on Seven. Ingrid was in Angelika's bedroom, attending to her. Seven plopped down in the lounge chair and watched television. His cars books were by his side on the table. Seven hoped he could attend Angelika's party. A bunch of rich kids were going to be there. They probably wouldn't associate with him. Because he would be considered "poor" in their eyes. Then voices were heard coming from Angelika's bedroom. Seven sprung from his seat and opened the door. He peered into the hallway and tiptoed toward Angelika's bedroom door.

In Angelika's vanity mirror, Ingrid brushed Angelika's long ebony hair. Seven watched as his mother helped Angelika get ready for her big day. Angelika was like a movie star. Everything was handed to her on a silver platter. But Angelika was still down-to-earth and seemed to do the right thing due to her heart, not what her parents tried to instill in her. Angelika began to pick up Ingrid's religious ways. She had a big influence on Angelika when it came to God. Angelika would ask her own mother about God, but she told Angelika he didn't exist. Still Angelika looked to the sky and believed this invisible man lived there was responsible for creating heaven and earth.

"Do you want your hair curly or straight, Angelika?" Ingrid asked as she tried to figure out a beautiful style for the child. "I want curls," Angelika responded in her soft tone.

"Okay, sweetheart," Ingrid answered.

"Ingrid?"

"Yes, baby."

"Do you think of me as your little girl?"

"Yes."

"I can be your little girl. Just like you have a boy. You can have both," Angelika said.

"Angelika, close your eyes." Angelika closed her eyes as Ingrid placed a beautiful crucifix necklace with a ruby birthstone around her neck. "Surprise!" Ingrid whispered. Angelika opened her and saw the beautiful necklace. The child gave Ingrid a hug. Then the double doors swung open as Mrs. Westland waltzed in. She wiped her eyes with a tissue.

Seven saw the pain in Mrs. Westland's eyes just through the cracked of the door he peered in. Maybe, she was experiencing the same thing that his mother was. Seven thought, maybe someone died. Did she and Mr. Westland have a fight? The crude thought ran through Seven's mind. He then stopped trying to figure out these people lives and focused on Angelika.

Mrs. Westland stroked Angelika's hair. "Ingrid, could you get Angelika's Burberry shoes?" Mrs. Westland asked Ingrid.

"Yes, Mrs. Westland," replied Ingrid as she went to fetch Angelika's apparel for the party. Mrs. Westland brushed Angelika's hair. "I want curls, Mommy," Angelika suggested.

"Okay," Mrs. Westland answered.

"Look at what Ingrid gave me, Mommy," Angelika said.

Mrs. Westland saw the crucifix with Angelika's birthstone . Mrs. Westland wept, concerned with her own problems. She didn't ignore Angelika's birthday. And of course, Mrs. Westland saw the crucifix and knew it represented Christ, but overlooked it for now.

"What's the matter?" Angelika questioned. She immediately embraced her mother.

"Nothing." Mrs. Westland answered as she fought back further tears.

"I'm just so happy you're growing up. It's your birthday."

"You should be happy, not sad," said Angelika.

Mrs. Westland clutched Angelika in her arms. Mrs. Westland kissed her daughter on the forehead. "Go get ready," Mrs. Westland advised.

Angelika left her mother's side to get dressed into her outfit for her big event. Mrs. Westland couldn't help but face herself in the mirror. She then broke down into tears. Seven's eyes widened. He thought all rich people were supposed to be happy. Seven headed back to his room.

Later that afternoon, Angelika's birthday party was in full swing. All her guests were kids from school and the neighborhood. They were from families of generations of wealth, just like Angelika. The kids ran and clamored around the estate with balloons and party favors. There were clowns and some sideshow performers. Loud music chimed from the beautiful merry-go-round as the kids laughed and waved to their parents. Angelika rode on a white stallion as she was decked out in her red chiffon dress with her white Burberry shoes. Next to Angelika, Cassandra was on a black stallion dressed in a yellow dress. The girls giggled and waved to everyone watching them.

"Where's Timothy?" Angelika cried. She glanced behind as she saw her friend Timothy. Timothy Zoeller was a rich neighborhood kid and who went to school with Angelika. Of course, Timothy came from a family of old money. His father was a stock broker over in London and New York while his mother stayed at home. Timothy, a blond, ten years of age, and good looking, wore stylish glasses for a kid his age.

"I'm right behind you!" Timothy shouted as he rode a beautifully crafted lion.

"Hey, Ingrid!" Angelika shouted as she waved to her.

"Having fun, sweetie?" Ingrid asked as she was so delighted.

"Yes," Angelika said.

Seven gazed out of the window at the kids. The entire estate had been transformed into a small carnival—a carousel, a sideshow, clowns, games, and other sorts of entertainment on your birthday. Seven wanted to go, but who would he hang out with? Angelika's busy with her friends. He just decided to stay indoors. Seven plopped down in the lounge chair again. Seven flipped through the television channels. Nothing was on. The cartoons were boring. There were some old movies on from the olden days as any young kid would call it. Then there was a knock at the door. Olga entered the guest bedroom as she held a tray of food from the party. There were two hot dogs with mustard, potato chips, pretzels, candy, and soda.

"Seven, come and get your goodies from the party," Olga said in her heavy accent.

Seven smiled as she placed the tray on the nightstand. Seven devoured some of the goodies.

"Why don't you come to party?" Olga asked Seven.

Seven shrugged his shoulders and bit into the hot dog. "There's no one for me to hang out with," Seven said with his mouth full.

Olga grabbed Seven by the hand and kissed it. "You are a handsome young man. You should be at the party. All the young girls would love to see handsome boy like you."

Seven shook his head in disagreement. He chugged down his soda and released an enormous belch. "Excuse me," Seven said. Olga turned her nose up at Seven. "That's no good," Olga exhaled and threw her hands up. "Maybe, later you'll come to Angelika party."

"Maybe."

"Bye-bye," Olga said as she left the guest bedroom, shutting the door behind her.

Later, Seven's tray of birthday refreshments was half gone. He took the last sip of his soda. Then he grabbed his car books again. He began reading info on the vehicles. Seven read about the latest Dodge Viper. He could hear the roar of the Viper's engine right in his head. Everything else was blocked out. Then he went on to read about the Dodge Charger from the seventies in comparison to the latest Dodge Charger. Seven loved the look of the latest Charger because it had a stockier build than the old one. Then singing was heard in the distance. "Happy birthday to you! Happy birthday to you!" Seven sprung from his lounge chair and rushed to the window. Seven could only see a large crowd of Angelika's friends-hundreds of them, rich and pretty just like Angelika. Just by the looks and the sound of it, it was a delightful scene. Seven then regretted not being there but then headed toward the door and exited the guest bedroom.

"Make a wish, sweetheart," Mrs. Westland said to Angelika.

Angelika closed her eyes and mumbled to herself. Then she blew out six sparkling candles on a four layered red velvet cake. Everyone applauded. As Angelika looked across, she saw Seven standing in the distance. He stared at Angelika with a smirk on his face. Angelika reciprocated the smile. Mr. and Mrs. Westland embraced Angelika and kissed her. Angelika's guests ate cake, drank soda, and danced. Pop music blasted from the speaker where the DJ played the latest songs. Angelika, Cassandra, and Timothy danced to the rhythm. Seven eyed Angelika having a good time with her friends. He was halfway done eating his cake. Mr. Westland eyed Seven from a distance. Seven didn't notice that his mother's boss was right behind him. Seven smiled and laughed as Angelika and her friends danced very silly. Seven then grabbed his soda from the side of him and noticed Mr. Westland right behind. The two made eye contact once more. No words exchanged, just the eyes telling Seven something was wrong. Seven shook his head and then focused back on the fiesta.

Angelika then ran towards Seven. "Seven, come and dance with me!" Angelika shouted. She grabbed Seven by the hand. Seven looked at Mr. Westland, and he gave a smirk. Everyone cheered and saw the handsome young man that caught Angelika's heart. Mrs. Westland noticed as she glanced at her husband. Mr. Westland's smile then dropped to a frown. Ingrid was happy to see Seven and Angelika interacting happily. Ingrid and Olga giggled and clapped their hands to the music. Seven and Angelika danced to the music.

Angelika's birthday celebration was over. It was early evening, and the kids left with party favors and candies. Angelika said good-bye to them. Seven stood by the Jaguar with Rocco as the kids left one by one. Then Timothy made his way out of the mansion, and then he kissed Angelika on the cheek. Seven sneered at the pompous kid with the Richie Rich resemblance. Seven ignored the kiss and acted as if he never saw it. Seven wondered what Timothy got for Angelika for her birthday. *Was it better than the necklace my Mom and I picked out for her?* Seven thought to himself. *And if so, does that make Timothy better than us?* Seven thought again. All these thoughts ran thorough Seven's brain like crazy. Then Seven swaggered upstairs.

That night, Seven lay in his bed and watched television. He heard gift paper being unwrapped as Angelika screamed her head off at every gift she got. Seven smirked. He was happy Angelika got all that she wanted.

"I want to show, Seven!" Angelika cried. Seven heard her voice from her bedroom. Then small footsteps approached the guest bedroom door. Angelika abruptly opened it. Seven didn't mind. But Mrs. Westland told Angelika to knock on the door before entering. Angelika didn't pay her mother any attention. All she wanted to do was show off her birthday gifts. Angelika showed Seven her new digital camera. It was a pink and white striped one. "Seven, smile," Angelika said. She snapped a picture of Seven as he lay in bed. Angelika checked out the results of the photo with viewfinder. "Your picture came out nice," Angelika said proudly. "Look at the pictures I took." Angelika showed Seven the pictures she took of her mother and father and some of Ingrid. Seven nodded his head. The pictures Angelika took were pretty good for a six-year old.

"Let Seven get some rest. Let's all get some rest. We've had a long day. Especially you, Angelika," said Mrs. Westland. Mrs. Westland escorted Angelika out of the guest bedroom. They shut the door behind them. Seven scoffed and continued to watch the box. Then Seven saw a shadow from under the doorway. It was as if someone were spying on him. Seven discreetly sprung to his feet and crept to the door and opened it with caution. It creaked. Seven peered down the hallway and saw Mr. Westland quickly hid. Seven was pissed off with all the spying and staring. Seven began to think the worse of him. *Was he a killer or something?* Seven hurried back in and locked the door.

Chapter 9

I t was a dismal day as the rays of the sun tried to break their way through the clouds, but it was still hot and humid. The scent of rain overwhelmed the atmosphere. Seven added soapy water to the hood of the Bentley in the driveway of the Westland mansion. Rocco lounged in a patio chair watching Seven do the so-called hard work. Olga scurried over with two glasses of soda on a silver platter. Rocco took a sip of the soft drink and nodded to Olga as a sign of "Thank you."

"Seven, soda!" Olga offered.

"No. Later," Seven said. He proceeded to add soap to the windshield and all over the vehicle.

"Do you like those books. I gave you, Seven?" Rocco asked as he enjoyed his drink.

"Yes."

"Tell me about what you're reading?" Rocco asked, curious.

Seven didn't read the books. He only read a few paragraphs and just admired the pictures of the muscle cars. Then Angelika came with her new camera in her hands. She smiled and didn't say a word. Angelika just started snapping shots. She took shots of Seven from every angle as he continued to wash the Bentley. Then a Caucasian

GQ gentleman—brunette, in his midthirties with light facial hair—
stood a few feet behind Angelika.

"Happy belated birthday, Angelika!" said the handsome gentleman. He was Christian Covington, Mrs. Westland's brother.

Angelika scrambled into her uncle's arms with her camera in her
hand. "You missed my party," Angelika shouted as she stomped her
foot on the pavement.

"I had a lot of work to catch up at the office." Christian
explained. He gave Angelika a large brown box with a pink bow on it.

Seven eyed the Dapper Don–looking gentleman. *Was he a snob
too?* Seven thought.

Christian eyed Seven and smiled. "How are you, young man?"
Christian greeted Seven.

"I'm cool," Seven responded.

"Cool." Christian nodded as he grimaced at Seven.

Seven could see large holes in the brown box. He knew it was
some sort of live animal. *Maybe a dog or a cat? Maybe a hamster?*
Seven guessed in his mind.

Angelika aggressively tore off the ribbon and lifted off the top.
Her eyes widened, and she gasped, "A puppy!" Angelika lifted up the
very small Pomeranian pup in her hand. Seven's eyes almost popped
out of his head due to the pup being so tiny. "She's so tiny," Angelika
said.

"She's a Pomeranian," Christian informed Angelika.

Angelika cuddled the pooch in her arms. Everyone took a lik-
ing to the pup. Ingrid made her way out of the mansion. "Angelika,
where were you?" Ingrid asked.

"Look at my puppy, Ingrid!" Angelika said excitedly.

Then Ingrid fell in love with the Pomeranian.

"How are you, Ingrid?" Christian greeted his charming smile.

"How are you, Mr. Covington?" Ingrid greeted in return with
a submissive tone.

"Ingrid, you don't have to call me Mr. Covington. Christian
will do just fine." Christian smiled with the "It's okay" feeling. Rocco
and Olga also fell in love with the pooch. Seven didn't move a muscle. He continued to stand there with the sudsy sponge in his hand.

He observed these adults clamoring like children over a puppy. Seven felt like the more mature one. The Pomeranian was cute, but not that cute. Then Mrs. Westland strutted out of the mansion. She greeted her brother, Christian with open arms. "How are you, Christian?" Mrs. Westland asked.

Christian exhaled and explained how sorry he was for missing Angelika's birthday. But he still made it his business to get Angelika's gift. Seven watched as everyone interacted with one another. He proceeded to wash the Bentley.

September made its way in and it was back to school. The leaves on the trees began to turn orange, yellow, and red. It was Indian summer. Seven put on his new T-shirt with black jeans and sneakers in front of a full-length mirror.

Ingrid thrust the bedroom door open. "Seven, hurry, you don't want to be late on your first day," Ingrid demanded.

Seven grabbed his book bag and headed out the door. The taxi and Jaguar had their engines running, ready to take Angelika and Seven to school. Mr. and Mrs. Westland kissed Angelika good-bye. Angelika couldn't forget to give Ingrid a kiss. Seven noticed how much Angelika loved his mother. Angelika loved Ingrid more than Mrs. Westland. He then kissed his mother, Ingrid, good-bye.

As usual, the kids were escorted to different vehicles. The Jaguar drove off first, then the taxi. The two vehicles approached the main road and headed in different directions. While on Seven's way to school, he didn't ask himself any questions about Angelika's educational background. "It is what it is," Seven said. He got used to it already. Opposites. Seven's mind went blank. Not a thought crossed Seven's mind. He laid his head back as the quiet engine of the taxi was music to his ears.

During recess, the students clamored on the school playground. Seven and Chad hung out on the concrete steps. Chad and Seven discussed what they did on their summer vacations. Seven allowed Chad to talk about his first. Chad went to Atlanta, Georgia, to visit his grandmother and other relatives from his mother's side of the family. They went to the movies, public swimming pool, barbecues, etc. As Chad was going on about his summer, Seven had to think of something quick about his summer vacations, something that would be similar to Chad's. Seven couldn't tell Chad that he was living with rich people. Then the school bell interrupted Chad's vacations adventures. Seven was saved by the bell. Chad was so caught up in himself that he forgot to ask Seven about his. That was all right with Seven.

After school, Seven studied in the stone altar that was on the Westland estate. He watched the swans and ducks as he had his math textbook and notebook in hand. Seven focused on solving math problems. Then Seven heard skipping approaching. Angelika popped up with her camera in her hand. Immediately, she started snapping shots of Seven. Seven felt as if he were a celebrity being harassed by the paparazzi. But he ignored Angelika. Angelika continued to take pictures of him. "Why are you taking so many pictures?" Seven wondered.

"Because you're my friend. That's why," Angelika answered. Angelika stopped and noticed Seven with his schoolbooks. "What are you doing, Seven?"

"I'm doing homework."

"We don't get homework on the first day of school," Angelika said.

"When you get older, you'll get it on the first day and weekends," Seven said. "Where's your puppy?" Seven asked.

"Upstairs," said Angelika.

Seven shook his head and proceeded with his studies. "What did you name it?"

"It's not an it. She's a she.," said Angelika with an attitude.

"What did you name her?" Seven asked, disgusted.

"Emily."

"What kind of name is that for a dog! Angelika, think of something different," Seven advised.

"That's her name," Angelika said.

"Why aren't you upstairs with her? She's just a baby," Seven advised.

Angelika took another picture of Seven and strutted away.

It's early evening, when sunrays peered through the west wing porch. Seven ate steak, potatoes, and veggies at the beautiful round marble table. Angelika approached the table with Emily in her hand. Seven gawked at Angelika. Seven could tell Angelika was being arrogant. "You're not supposed to have the dog at the table," said Seven.

"Yes, I can. Emily's just a baby." Angelika said.

"Angelika, you can't have Emily at the table," Ingrid suggested.

"All right." Angelika left the table with her puppy in her hand. She marched away. Angelika and Mrs. Westland crossed paths as she sashayed on the porch.

"Where are you going, darling," Mrs. Westland asked.

"I'm not supposed to have Emily at the table." Angelika proceeded on.

"Angelika's such a smart child. I taught her very well," Mrs. Westland said.

Seven glared at Mrs. Westland for a moment. He noticed how Mrs. Westland liked to give herself credit for something she didn't do. Ingrid gave Angelika advice on things. Mrs. Westland was hardly ever around. This time, Mrs. Westland was home from work early. She was so busy at the office most of the time, just like her husband Mr. Westland. He worked long hours and came home late every night.

Moments later, before eating dinner, Angelika did the honors of blessing the table. "God is great. God is good. Let us thank him for this food. Amen," Angelika concluded her prayer. Mrs. Westland gawked at Angelika. She was a bit offended that Ingrid taught Angelika about an invisible man in the sky. But she then let it go. Seven, Angelika, Ingrid, and Mrs. Westland ate dinner while the soothing melodies of Enya played from the Bose radio. Mrs. Westland ate her food with tiny bites of her pasta salad and chewed slowly. She also took tiny sips of her water from a glass. Ingrid stuffed her mouth with penne pasta and took large gulps of her water. Angelika chewed with her mouth open. Mrs. Westland didn't say a word.

"Angelika, chew with your mouth closed," Ingrid advised.

Angelika took Ingrid's advice and chewed with her mouth closed. Seven observed Mrs. Westland again. He was waiting to see if she was going to take credit for this one. But Mrs. Westland didn't say a word.

After dinner, Ingrid gave ideas about having a Halloween party for Angelika—the idea of dozens and dozens of Halloween-shaped black, yellow, and orange balloons, Halloween decor, clowns, lots of food, etc. Mrs. Westland never thought of that until Ingrid brought it up. The Westlands rarely threw Halloween parties. And of course, Mrs. Westland took credit for this one.

Seven glared at Ingrid, wondering why she didn't speak up. He could understand his mother's submission to these arrogant fucks. Ingrid was nothing but a nanny. And it was her job to stay there. *This is what rich people do also—take credit for ideas that aren't theirs,* Seven thought. Seven turned red in the face. He wanted so badly to slap Mrs. Westland because she was a self-centered bitch. He could see right through her. Mrs. Westland was just like her husband. Seven hoped that Angelika didn't turn out like them.

Chapter 10

Jack-o'-lanterns of all sizes were everywhere on the grounds of the Westland mansion. It was a hot Halloween, temperature-wise. There were hundreds of orange, yellow, and black balloons, streamers, confetti, party favors, food, and goodies for Angelika and her guests. They danced to the "Monster Mash" song. Angelika wore a ballerina costume, and her guests were dressed from the scariest costume to the most popular culture. Ingrid stood on the side as she watched the kids have a good time. She was dressed as Tina Turner. She wore the sixties dress, high boots, and a wig. Ingrid cheered Angelika on as she danced the night away. Mrs. Westland strutted into the party, dressed as a jazz singer from the 1920s. She wore finger waves in her hair, a tassel dress, old-fashioned shoes, and a long pearl necklace.

Seven watched the whole Halloween party unfold before his eyes from his guest bedroom window. Seven really didn't like Halloween. It was crap to him, people dressing up in scary costumes for one day. Seven looked back into his room, where there was some Halloween decor. There were some goodies on the side table untouched. The movie *Halloween* played on television. Seven sneered at the Michael Myers film and sucked his teeth. Michael Myers couldn't beat a fly as far as Seven was concerned. Then Seven's eyes bulged as he saw shadowy footsteps from under the door. Seven crept towards it. He then opened the door with caution. Seven poked his head into the hallway. There wasn't a sign of anyone. The end of the hallway was dark. He knew it was nothing. Seven slammed the guest bedroom door. Seven lounged in the recliner as he munched on some potato chips and chugged down a soda. Then there's a *thump*. Seven took short breaths as his eyes wandered around the room. Then the "Monster Mash" song ended.

Then the "Bela Lugosi's Dead" song played. The beginning of the song was creepy. Seven then slowly looked at the door of the guest bedroom. He saw shadowy footsteps pass by the door. Seven tiptoed to the door as he balled his hand into a fist. He swung the door opened. No one was in sight. The hallway was murky at the end. How could he get out of the house without being freaked out? Or was it just his imagination? Seven closed his eyes and poked his chest out. He closed the door behind him and crept down the hallway. Seven got closer and closer to the darkened area of the corridor. His pace slowed down even more. He glanced over his shoulder. Then he tiptoed downstairs to the second level. Seven heard another thump. He looked over his shoulder and saw a shadowy figure. Seven raced down the steps. He tripped down about a couple of bottom steps on the second floor. Seven looked up and saw the shadowy figure still approaching. He sprinted down the next flight of stairs that led to the first floor. Seven scrambled into the murky living room. He found himself a good hiding spot, but little did he know he hid next to an eight foot creepy statue. Seven's eyes popped out of his head as his heart raced. Seven released a loud gasp. He immediately covered his mouth with his hands. He heard the creepy individual taking his time down the steps to the first floor. Seven still couldn't make out who it was. All he knew was he had to get out of there. Seven raced out of the living room and hid in the bathroom.

In the murky bathroom, Seven couldn't see a thing. But, he noticed his slight reflection in the mirror on the other side. The bathroom door creaked open as a masked man reflected in the mirror. It was a werewolf rubber mask and a hairy costume. Seven couldn't believe what he was seeing. *Is this how the rich lived, by acting weird?*

Seven thought. *Who was that behind the mask?* Seven thought again. *Was it Mr. Westland? Was it Rocco or maybe Ben?* The masked gentleman kept glaring directly in the mirror. Seven hoped that whoever it was didn't notice him hiding behind the door.

Then the bathroom door closed back slowly. Seven exhaled as he slid his back against the wall to the floor. He sat in almost complete darkness but wasn't scared at that moment. Then there was a roar of cheering from outside. Seven dashed to the bathroom window and saw hundreds of balloons flooding into the air.

"Happy Halloween!" the party guests shouted. Then Michael Jackson's "Thriller" blared from the speakers. Seven knew everyone was having a good time. He felt a bit out of place because of Mr. Westland. *Was Mr. Westland a part of a secret society?* Ever since Seven met Mr. Westland, questions about him have been going nonstop. He never discussed it with his mother. He couldn't; it was her job. Seven didn't want her to be angry with him. Seven kept it to himself. "Should I go to the party and try to fit in? I don't have a costume. Nah. They're a bunch of rich snobs." Seven thought. He cautiously opened the door and headed back upstairs to his room.

Seven swaggered down the hallway as he poked his chest out. He noticed his bedroom door was cracked open. Seven halted in the middle of the murky hallway. His heart raced and hands trembled. Then he crept towards the door. He opened the door with caution. Angelika was watching the movie Halloween as she sat on the floor without a care in the world. "Angelika!" Seven cried out to her.

Angelika screamed. "You scared me, Seven."

"I'm sorry. What are you doing in here?" Seven asked.

"I wanted to watch *Halloween*." Angelika responded.

Seven didn't argue about that. At least, he had company. Seven grabbed some Halloween candy from the silver tray. Of course, he shared with Angelika as they indulged in the horror movie classic.

Chapter 11

November 28 was turkey day. Snow fell to the ground, leaving a couple of inches. It only snowed once in a while around Thanksgiving. It was beautiful, especially on the Westland estate.

Seven slept in his bed. He tossed and turned, only to be awakened by the bright white stuff that lit up the guest bedroom. He sprung from his slumber and saw the winter wonderland from his window. "Wow!" Seven said to himself. He wondered what was in store for the holiday. Seven immediately thought of his father. *Why hasn't he seen me in so long? Does he still love me? Is it my fault that my parents didn't get along?*

Angelika invited herself in unexpectedly. There was no knock. No nothing. Seven knew Angelika didn't care if she was interrupting anything. Angelika did this when it came to Seven. Because she liked him. She joined Seven as both of them gazed out of the window as the snow blanketed everything in sight.

Ingrid rushed into the guest bedroom. She clapped her hands to get the kids' attention. "Good morning, kids. Happy Thanksgiving," said Ingrid as she greeted them with a kiss. Isn't it beautiful outside?" Ingrid asked with a delightful smile on her face. The brightness of the snow reflected on Ingrid's face, which made her look angelic. Seven smirked as his mother was in good spirits, especially on this holiday.

A few hours later, Angelika, Ingrid, and Seven clamored on the snow-covered grounds of the Westland estate. Angelika dragged her sled behind her. She wore her winter coat, scarf, hat, and gloves. Seven swaggered directly behind her. He glared at Angelika as she was so indulged in the wintery scene. Ingrid was right behind the kids, keeping an eye on them. Ingrid helped Angelika drag her sled through the white stuff. Seven still proceeded to lag behind, taking his time in the crunchy icy snow. Seven sensed the feeling that someone was watching him. He knew that, of course, God was. But someone else was too. Seven turned, and there he was, Mr. Westland staring from the master bedroom window. Seven didn't back down. He gave Mr. Westland the glares right back. There was a long distance tension between them. Seven continued walking through the snow. Mr. Westland didn't take his eye off Seven. He watched Seven make his way from the mansion and into the garden.

Four o'clock was turkey time. Ben set the delicious golden-browned bird in the middle of the long cherry table, which sat thirty guests. Mr. Westland's relatives and business colleagues came over for dinner. The only relative that came from Mrs. Westland's side was her brother, Christian. He brought a date, a ginger-haired beauty who wore an orange turtleneck, and anyone could tell she wore no bra. Every time she laughed, her breasts jiggled like crazy. Seven kept peering at them. Ingrid nudged Seven. *Where are Mrs. Westland's parents? Are they prejudiced? They probably are,* Seven wondered.

Mr. Westland sharpened the butcher knife with a knife sharpener. He carved the turkey. There was no saying grace. Mr. Westland didn't believe in God. He believed in himself and his money. So he gave thanks to himself. Ingrid felt uncomfortable without the Lord's blessings. Seven knew it, but as usual, Ingrid's job was to take care of Angelika. Seven looked at the food on the long table. They had mashed potatoes, corn, rolls, and some other types of food that were ritzy. Seven got a couple of white slices of turkey, a spoonful of mashed potatoes, stuffing, corn, and roll. *Is this what rich people eat? Boring foods?* Seven thought. He immediately thought of his grandmother, how every holiday the house was filled with the richness of macaroni and cheese, stuffing, sweet potatoes, sweet potato pie, and of course, a seasoned turkey. The Westlands turkey was dry, and it was hard to chew. The roll was hard as a rock, and stuffing was bland. Seven sneered at his plate. Ingrid played along with the situation. Seven shook his head. *This Thanksgiving fuckin' sucks,* Seven shouted in his mind.

After dinner, Seven and Angelika were in his room watching *March of the Wooden Soldiers.* Ingrid sat in the lounge chair reading her Bible. The kids laughed at the film. Then there was a knock at the door. Olga entered with some sandwiches, drinks, and snacks on a silver tray. Seven knew it would be better than that horrible Thanksgiving dinner. Seven grabbed the sandwich and took a huge bite. It was really good. He had no idea what he was eating, but it was a kind of salty pinkish meat with a little fat.

"Is this corned beef?" Angelika asked. Olga answered Angelika with a smile as she nodded. Angelika then grabbed a sandwich and devoured it. That corned beef sandwich was the best Thanksgiving dinner Seven ever had. Ingrid munched on some potato chips.

Then Mrs. Westland barged into the room with a ballerina Christmas ornament in her hand. "Look at what I found, Angelika," said Mrs. Westland. The crystal ornament dangled from Mrs. Westland's hand.

Angelika raced to her mother and grabbed it with caution. "Where did you find it?" Angelika asked with sparkles in her eyes.

"I found it in the storage room with all the other ornaments," Mrs. Westland replied.

In the living room, Ben and other servants of the Westland estate helped to assemble a ten-foot white flocked Christmas tree. Angelika made her way downstairs with Seven behind her. Seven slowed down his pace as he was mesmerized by the gigantic snowy Christmas tree. Then Ben connected the lights and lit it up. It looked like Rockefeller Center. He continued down the stairs. Johnny Mathis Christmas music bellowed from the Bose radio. Seven stood back and watched Angelika and Mr. and Mrs. Westland gather around the tree. Angelika hung a red bulb on a branch. The Westland family was ready for Christmas already.

Thanksgiving really isn't a holiday on its own, because Christmas intervenes. People are already putting up their trees, decorating, and shopping for gifts.

Ingrid came downstairs and saw the beautiful sight. Her eyes lit up as Angelika ran into her arms.

"Look at the tree, Ingrid," said Angelika. Angelika pulled Ingrid toward the tree. "Help us decorate," Angelika suggested.

Ingrid joined the Westlands trimming the tree. Everyone was into the holiday spirit. Seven swaggered through the house and stumbled upon the ballroom. It had huge red walls and a large floor for dancing. Another Christmas tree was being assembled by Rocco. The tree was another ten-foot snowy Christmas tree. Rocco saw Seven in the background. He cracked a smile with his pudgy face. "Seven, give me a hand here," Rocco demanded.

Seven immediately rushed to Rocco's side. Seven helped fluff the tree by spreading out the branches. Seven saw there were some extra ornaments on the side. They were black, white, and silver. Seven knew those colors would make the tree unique. As Seven and Rocco kept fluffing the tree, Mr. Westland stood right in the doorway as he eyed them.

"Do you like the tree, Seven?" Mr. Westland asked as he sashayed towards him. "Wish you could have a tree like this. Right?" Mr. Westland asked sarcastically.

Seven knew where his mother's boss was coming from. He insulted him about being "poor." Mr. Westland's eyes were fixed on him. Seven sighed and wished he could go home. This place was beautiful, but weird.

Later, Mrs. Westland wore her beautiful red wool coat as she strutted to the Bentley that awaited her and Mr. Westland. Rocco held the rear passenger's side door open. Mrs. Westland hopped inside, with her spouse right behind. Rocco then shut the door. Angelika waved to her parents as the Bentley drove away.

"Mr. and Mrs. Westland were off to do their holiday shopping or off to visit friends. Who cares?" Seven thought. He just couldn't wait to go home.

Chapter 12

I t was Black Friday, the busiest shopping day of the season. Finally, Ingrid and Seven were on their way home. Seven felt relieved. He missed his home and sleeping in his own bed. He didn't have to look over his shoulder. And maybe, he'll get to see his father. Seven swaggered toward the taxi.

Ingrid kissed Angelika good-bye. "I'll see you in a couple of days, Angelika," Ingrid said.

"Okay, I'll see you. Love you, Ingrid." Angelika sighed. Angelika hated for Ingrid to go even if it was just for a couple of days. "Bye, Seven," Angelika said. Seven waved to Angelika.

Mr. Westland witnessed Ingrid and Seven's departure. "Good-bye," Mr. Westland said sarcastically with a fiendish grin. He grabbed Angelika by the hand. Seven could tell by the tone in Mr. Westland's voice that it wasn't nice. Ingrid felt it as well. But she played along. Ingrid gave a slight smile and got in the taxi. Mr. Westland slammed the door behind as he stared into the cab. Seven felt Mr. Westland's presence hovering over the window where Ingrid sat. He was like the devil trying to get their souls. The taxi then sped away. It zoomed through the iron gates. Seven didn't attempt to look back because it would only anger him.

Home sweet home. The taxi pulled to the curb in front of their home. Keys rattled at the front door as Ingrid and Seven stepped in. Seven headed straight to his bedroom. He opened the door as he looked around. Seven smiled. Then he plopped on his bed and put his hands behind his head. Seven gazed up at the ceiling. He missed doing that. Seven bet the ceiling missed him. Seven closed his eyes and was at peace.

Meanwhile, Ingrid searched through her cupboards in the kitchen to fix dinner. She noticed the canned goods were expired. Then she went to open the refrigerator, and it stunk. The foul odor overwhelmed the entire kitchen. She noticed the box of Arm & Hammer baking soda had expired as well. Then the doorbell rang. Ingrid hurried to the door. She thrust the front door open as William stood there with Athena in his arms. Ingrid frowned.

Seven was awakened to voices of Ingrid and a man. Seven opened his eyes and knew it was his father. William stormed into Seven's bedroom with Athena. Seven embraced his father and hugged his baby sister, Athena. Just by them coming to see him, Seven knew he was definitely home. Home is not just a place. It's where the heart is. And it's the people in your heart.

The smell of baby lotion filled Seven's room from the Athena's tiny body. She stood up in Seven's bed and jumped around. Seven held on to her to make sure she didn't fall. William gave Seven a shopping bag. It was an early Christmas present for Seven. He grabbed a package of Todd MacKenzie bedsheets and a Mustang model car. Seven checked out the box and saw that he had to assemble the thing. Seven became a little discouraged about it. Seven sighed.

William saw the discouragement in Seven's face. "What's the matter, Seven?" William asked.

Seven shrugged his shoulders and didn't answer. "This looks hard," Seven said.

"Seven, you can do this. You love cars. Don't you?" William asked. "This can help you in the future. You can do it, Seven," William encouraged. Seven smiled as his father patted him on the back.

Moments later, Seven was right in the middle of assembling his model car. Two bottles of glue, an instruction manual, and a couple of screwdrivers sat on his desk. NASCAR played on the television. The roaring of the race cars bellow throughout Seven's entire bedroom. His mind was solely on his model car. Athena drank her bottle and watched NASCAR on Seven's bed. Of course, Athena was just a baby, but the fast cars captured her attention. Seven saw that the baby was drawn into the sport. Seven smiled. *Am I going to have some competition?* Seven thought to himself. Seven wasn't serious about the thought that went through his mind. It was just so cute to see his baby sister watching an intense sport. For a toddler, it was like a kids' show to her. It was just so cute to see. Seven proceeded on with his model car. He was determined to assemble this car. He's got to learn more about building cars, even fixing them. He wasn't going let anything stop him.

A few hours later, Seven did it. He finished the model black Mustang car. He was very proud of himself. He looked over on his bed as Athena fell asleep. Seven headed over to his bed and placed two pillows on both sides of Athena to prevent her from falling. Milk dripped one by one from Athena's bottle on Seven's bed. It was a small soaked spot. Seven placed the bottle on his nightstand. Seven then held his model car in his hand as if it were a trophy. He carried it into the living room.

Ingrid cooked roast beef, potatoes, and veggies just like his grandmother did. Seven noticed his father was nowhere in sight. Unopened boxes of perfume and jewelry box were on the table. Seven's heart began to race. He was irate. William came in and out of his life. *What kind of father is he?* Seven thought. Ingrid kept herself busy in order not to cry. Whenever she was upset, Ingrid wouldn't make eye contact with anyone. So Seven turned around and headed back into his bedroom.

Then the doorbell rang. Seven halted in his tracks. He answered the door. Maureen stood in the doorway. She was dressed holiday-like. She actually smiled for the first time. *How did she know that Athena is here? Why didn't my father pick Athena up?* Seven questioned to himself. Seven's heart raced again as Ingrid headed toward the door. The women glared at each other as if they were going to go at each other. But peace was made.

"Happy holidays, Ingrid." Maureen greeted as she gave a slight smile.

"Happy holidays, Maureen," Ingrid greeted her in return with a grimace. "Seven, the baby," Ingrid reminded Seven.

Seven scrambled away from the front door. There was dead silence between the two women. Seven hurried to the door with Athena. Maureen grabbed her child into her arms.

"Hey, Athena," Maureen said to her baby. "Thank you so much." Maureen gave her gratitude to Ingrid and Seven. Maureen left.

Seven was grateful his mother and Maureen didn't go to blows. *Was my dad trying to start a fight?* Seven asked himself. The situation didn't sit well with Seven. But thank goodness everything went smoothly. They kept peace on this holiday season.

Chapter 13

December 23, the Westlands held a Christmas party in their enormous ballroom with the tall white tree. Black, white, and silver ornaments adorned every branch on it. Johnny Mathis holiday music blasted from the speakers. The Westlands' guests were decked out in holiday outfits. The women strutted in red, green, gold, and pewter gowns while the men sported tuxedos. Mrs. Westland nibbled on a finger sandwich as she held a champagne glass in the other. She wore a fabulous red high neck crepe opened back gown with a foot long train. Mr. Westland wore a tuxedo from Giorgio Armani with a touch of grey in it. Angelika sported a red satin dress with a big bow in the back from David Charles. Her hair was straightened with curls on the ends. Angelika played with Cassandra who wore a black hearted embossed peplum dress from Armani juniors and Timothy who was tuxedo-clad also from Armani juniors.

Ingrid sat in the corner as she chatted with Ben, along with Seven nearby. Seven observed everyone as he resided in a chair. He ate a piece of red velvet cake. Seven picked small pieces of it with his fork. He wore a shirt, tie, and slacks. Seven was very handsome, better than Timothy and most of the affluent little boys at the party, Seven thought. Seven noticed Angelika whispering in Cassandra's ear across the ballroom. The girls burst into laughter. Timothy engaged in some intellectual conversation with the guys. *Stuck up!* Seven thought to himself. He sucked his teeth and then started to stuff a larger piece of the cake in his mouth.

Angelika took baby steps towards Seven. Puppy love could be seen in Angelika's eyes. Seven sat his cake on his chair and made his way to Angelika from the other side of the ballroom. It was like a kiddie version of *West Side Story*. They came face-to-face. Angelika grimaced. "Merry Christmas," Angelika greeted Seven. "Merry Christmas, Angelika," Seven greeted as his cheeks blushed.

Mr. and Mrs. Westland slow-danced as they gazed into each other's eyes. Seven saw the loving couple in the holiday spirit. It was as if they were the only ones in the room. Seven focused his attention back on Angelika. "What's up?" Seven asked.

"Nothing much," Angelika responded. She smiled at Seven as they both looked away from each other for a moment. "How The Grinch Stole Christmas is coming on television in a little while", Angelika insisted.

"I'm too old for that," Seven answered.

"You never too old. It's Christmas." Seven and Angelika smiled at each other once more. Seven was nervous. He wanted to tell Angelika how beautiful she looked on an occasion like this. But the cat had his tongue.

"You look very handsome, Seven," Angelika complimented. Angelika beat Seven to it. She admired him first. "I know you would look real handsome in a tux," Angelika complimented again. Seven smiled because he loved the compliment, especially coming from her. Seven experienced every aspect of the Westlands' lives—the wealth, the soirees, and the people. Especially the people. Seven glanced over his shoulder at Mr. and Mrs. Westland. They were still indulged in each other. "How does it feel to be rich, Angelika?" Seven asked. Angelika really didn't know how to answer. It was just normal to her. Angelika shrugged her shoulders. Then Angelika asked a question with a question. "How does it feel to be rich, Seven?"

"I'm not rich. You are."

"If I'm rich, then you're rich," said Angelika.

"How do you figure that?" Seven wondered. He frowned due to his disbelief.

"You live here. Right?" Angelika said.

Seven shrugged his shoulders. "Right."

Moments later, Seven stood in front of a full-length mirror as he buttoned up a white dress shirt and wore black slacks in Mr. Westland's walk-in closet of his master bedroom. The closet was full of apparel from top to bottom—expensive suits, ties, shoes, sneakers, etc., all designers' brands like Giorgio Armani, Brooks Brothers, and Rockafella. The white dress shirt fit Seven perfectly, but the pants were a bit too big. "You look just like an executive," Angelika complimented. She then helped Seven try on the matching jacket. "You look so handsome."

"Thanks." Seven smiled with gratification.

Angelika snatched a bottle of men's cologne and gave Seven a couple of spritzes of it. "Try this."

"Pew! That smells like shit!" Seven shouted. He waved the mist away from him.

Angelika snickered. Then she grabbed a second bottle of men's cologne. Angelika sprayed some of it on Seven.

He smiled. "That's what I'm talking about."

"You can have it if you want," Angelika insisted.

"But it's your father's."

"He has so much cologne." Then heavy footsteps approached the walk-in closet.

"Angelika, where are you?" Mrs. Westland cried in the distance. "It's time for Santa's grab bag." Mrs. Westland sashayed into Mr. Westland's walk-in closet. Her jaw dropped as she saw the slack drop to Seven's ankles. Seven covered up his important parts. "What the hell!" Mrs. Westland shouted.

Minutes later, Mr. Westland rocked in his executive's chair of his study. Ingrid stood before Mr. Westland like a peasant begging for mercy to the king. Tears streamed down her face as she wiped them away. Seven sat in the corner, facing judgment. He held his head down in shame as he continuously peeked up at Mr. Westland. Mrs. Westland paced the floor with her high heels. "Ingrid, where were you? You were supposed to be watching them!" Mrs. Westland cried as her voice reverberated through the air.

"I'm sorry, Mrs. Westland. Mr. Westland, you know I've always kept a close eye on Angelika," Ingrid pleaded.

"But this time you didn't," Mr. Westland said.

"Seven's a good child. He didn't mean any harm. Really," Ingrid pleaded.

Mrs. Westland stomped her foot on the floor. "What do you mean? Really?"

Ingrid tried to hold back the tears that were about to make their way down her cheeks but couldn't. "I promise. It won't happen again, Mr. Westland," Ingrid wept.

Mr. Westland smiled devilishly. "You're right. It won't happen again."

Moments later, a taxi driver loaded Seven's Todd MacKenzie bike in the trunk of the cab. Ingrid and Seven made their way to the vehicle with duffel bags of their apparel and personal items. Seven didn't expect to go home on terms like this. Ingrid got fired on his account. Seven knew his mother was going to make him feel guilty about losing her job. They hopped into the taxi.

Angelika dashed to the rear window of the cab, crying hysterically. Ingrid's feelings were mutual. It was as if Ingrid's child were being taken away. Ingrid suffered from more emotional pain. She lost her mother, lost her husband to another woman, and lost her job and the little girl whom she loved dearly. And Christmas was in two days. How could someone be so heartless? It was a misunderstanding. But Mr. Westland didn't care. He wanted to get rid of Ingrid, not because she wasn't doing her good job, but because of Seven being around his precious angel. "I love you guys," Angelika cried. Mr. Westland snatched Angelika away from the cab. It zoomed away from the mansion and exited through the iron gates.

A few moments later, there was utter silence in the taxi. Seven wanted to console his mother but was too afraid. He blamed himself for his mother losing her job. Maybe if he had stayed in that corner like a child on timeout, nothing of this would have happened. Seven peered at his mother, but Ingrid kept her eyes focused right in front of her. She wouldn't say a word to Seven. All you could hear was the sound of the engine. That's usually music to Seven's ear.

The taxi parked in front of Seven's home. The taxi driver helped to unload Seven's bike and their clothing and personal items. Ingrid paid the cab driver. The taxi drove off as Ingrid and Seven grabbed their things and marched toward the house.

Moments later, the house was the way they left it. Ingrid sat at the table as Seven resided across from her. "How am I supposed to keep a roof over our heads and pay the bills? What am I going to do about Christmas? What were you doing in my boss's closet? With Angelika?" Ingrid asked question after question.

"I just wanted to know what it felt like to be rich," Seven answered.

Ingrid shook her head. "Richness comes from within. It doesn't matter how much money you have or if you have the biggest house," Ingrid expressed.

Seven's posture in this chair across from his mother was similar to his posture in the chair at Mr. Westland's study. He was slumped over. Seven felt guilty about the whole thing. What could he do to make it up to her? How could he make things right? There was nothing he could do. And Seven's father was nowhere in sight. No call. No show.

"Go to your room!" Ingrid shouted.

Seven scrambled from the kitchen table and went to his bedroom. In Seven's bedroom, he undressed by removing his sneakers, shirt, undershirt, and pants. Seven left only his boxers on. He hopped in bed as he threw the comforter over himself. He stared at the ceiling. This was going to be the worst Christmas ever. No dad. No presents. No job for Mom. No Angelika. No fun. No Christmas. There weren't any Christmas decorations in the house because Seven and Ingrid were expected to stay with the Westlands until after New Year's. Some holiday. Seven didn't get the chance to say good-bye to Rocco. Seven had the books on cars that Rocco gave to him. They were still packed in his bag. He was too upset to even look at them at the moment. Rocco was like his mentor. But who did Seven have now but God? Seven kept his eyes on the ceiling (God) and closed his eyes.

On Christmas Eve, Ingrid and Seven remained at home. Throughout the day, Seven wanted to apologize to his mother. Seven stayed in his bedroom all day. He got funny feeling in his chest for the first time. He didn't understand what it was. It wasn't physical. It was emotional. Ingrid fixed Seven breakfast, lunch, and dinner. Still, there were no words between them. Seven resided in his room for most of the day like a prisoner. The only freedom he had was when it time to eat. He watched more Christmas specials that came on television and read car magazines. Dr.Seuss "How The Grinch Stole Christmas." cartoon and the motion picture with Jim Carrey ran on television most of the day. Speaking of the Grinch, that was Mr. Westland. He was the Grinch who stole our Christmas, Seven thought to himself. Then there were other shows that came on, like Santa Claus Is Comin' to Town, Rudolph the Red-Nosed Reindeer, etc. The only thing Seven heard was banging of pots and pans in the kitchen from his bedroom. Luther Vandross Christmas music bellowed from the radio. Seven wanted to see if his mother was all right. But he didn't budge. He gazed up at the ceiling (God) as he usually he did. "God, don't allow this Christmas to be a messed up one. It was my fault. I was in Mr. Westland's closet. I ruined everyone's Christmas." Seven then shook his head and tried to fight back tears. No success. Seven opened them as tears flowed down his face. Seven wiped his tears but fought back further tears. He then shut his eyes again and didn't reopen them.

The sun beamed on this beautiful summer day. Seven sped down the road in his black Camaro. The engine bellowed like a lion. He loved to need to speed. Sirens screamed behind him. Seven wasn't stopping. He put his pedal to the metal as the muscle car took the boys in blue for a ride. The black Camaro weaved in and out of traffic. The cops were right in Seven's tail. Seven exited off the highway and entered the expressway. On the expressway, Seven really picked up speed. He cut off other motorists. Seven laughed as he left the police in the dust. Two more police cars made their way on to the expressway. Cops were in pursuit. Seven observed the whole thing in his rearview mirror. He maneuvered his muscle car around an eighteen-wheeler truck. Seven laughed as he left the two patrol cars behind. Seven turned as an elderly woman right before him stood in the middle of the road. It's wasn't his grandmother, but she was similar to her. Angelic that is. Seven swerved the car, as it flipped over multiple times and exploded into a ball of fire.

Seven abruptly woke up from his sleep. His heart raced as he heard sizzling coming from the kitchen. He noticed it was evening. A full moon glistened in the dark sky which could from his bedroom window. His clock read 6:48 p.m. Seven didn't want to think about the bad dream he just had. He just wanted to forget about it. Then the doorbell rang. Seven sprung from his slumber and raced to the front door. He swung it open. And there stood his father, William, with a handful of Christmas gifts in his arms. This was the best Christmas present ever—Seven having his father. Seven leaped into his father's arms. Seven and his father really couldn't embrace each other because of the load of presents in his arms.

"Merry Christmas!" William shouted. Ingrid entered in the living room and saw William playing Santa. William was the man with empty promises. Ingrid wasn't impressed. Seven grabbed his gifts from his father. Seven got Grand Theft Auto, Todd MacKenzie's NASCAR adventures, and other car related video games. That was the only gift Seven could open. He raced to his bedroom with excitement and immediately overcame his emotional pain. While in Seven's bedroom, he indulged himself in the game. He didn't move a muscle from the television and then the mini movie played. William and Ingrid bickered in the kitchen. Seven heard it, but ignored the commotion. Then William waltzed in and sat beside his son. He watched the mini movie along with Seven. The short movie involved street gangs, profanity, and violence in Miami and other large cities in the United States. William lectured Seven about self-defense. Not necessarily, Karate or Kung Fu. But, if someone messes with Seven to let them have it. But, Ingrid disagreed with the whole thing. She felt Seven was being taught to be a hoodlum. If that was the case, then so be it. As long as no one messed with Seven. He always took his father's advice. William raised his fist in the air and told him that this was what made a man out of him.

"No, I don't want Seven learning any of that street nonsense!" Ingrid argued as she marched into Seven's bedroom. She heard William's bad teachings all the way from the kitchen. Ingrid proceeded to bitch about losing her job, putting food on the table, keeping a roof over their heads, and clothes on their backs.

"How the fuck did you lose your job!" William hollered.

"Watch your mouth, William!" Ingrid hollered in return. She took a deep breath and told him what had exactly happened between Seven and Angelika and that it was just a misunderstanding. William continued to curse like a sailor. Seven then told his father Mr. Westland gave him dirty looks. William was ready for war with that rich stuck-up Negro. William promised he was going to provide for Seven. Ingrid didn't believe a word he had to say.

"Let's go get a tree, Seven." William said as he marched out of his son's bedroom. Seven made eye contact with his mother. Seven's guilt overwhelmed him again. He didn't know whether to stay with his mother or go with his father. Seven headed to his closet and grabbed his coat. Ingrid sobbed. Seven kissed his mother's hand and exited his bedroom. The best thing for Seven to do was hope for the best on Christmas day.

Christmas morning, Seven's father brought them a six-foot-high live tree. Seven and William decorated it the way Ingrid wanted. There was an abundance of gifts under the tree and a turkey roasted in the oven. Seven and William spent all day purchasing a tree and lots of food, so they could have a beautiful holiday. Seven unwrapped another gift of his. It was a model car, a 1960's Dodge Charger. Ingrid didn't bother to open up any gifts at all. She just resided at the table staring at how happy her son was. But, it was the reverse for Seven. He noticed how unhappy Ingrid was. Seven grabbed the gift that he picked out for his mother and presented to her. Ingrid slightly smiled. Maybe, that gift would build their bridge. Ingrid embraced Seven.

"Seven, it wasn't your fault. These things just happen," Ingrid said. She looked at him with tears in her eyes.

"Are you sure?" Seven asked.

"Yes. I saw the way Mr. Westland looked at you. I didn't like it."

"Merry Christmas, Mom."

"Merry Christmas, son. As long as we've got each other, we're gonna be fine." Ingrid and Seven engaged in the longest embrace ever. Seven felt like a baby again. He had a slight recollection of his mother holding him as an infant. He recalled getting his diaper changed, and on one occasion, Seven was being fed baby food. He even remembered the taste of two of them. One of the baby food was a mixed vegetable, and the other was a custard dessert. Most people don't have any recollection of them as babies, not even one occasion.

Then the doorbell rang. Seven swung the door open. Seven reached out and grabbed baby Athena from his father's arms. "Athena!" Seven shouted. He held his baby sister in his arm and kissed her on the cheek. Baby Athena smiled, and she knew she was in good hands. Seven was nervous about Ingrid's reactions to the baby. Ingrid was fine. Baby Athena reached out to Ingrid with open arms.

"Merry Christmas, Athena," Ingrid greeted the toddler with open arms and a kiss. Seven, Baby Athena, Ingrid, and William sat around the Christmas tree and exchanged gifts, because of God's blessings on this holiday.

Chapter 14

The New Year rung in, where everyone was looking forward to a fresh start—new outlook on life, goals, changes, and other resolutions people promised to keep. On this frigid Monday morning of January 4th, there were a couple of inches of snow and ice on the ground everywhere. The thermostat was on eighty-five in the Mileses' residence. Seven put on his black sweater with blue jeans and construction boots as he stood in front of his dresser mirror. Seven was in no hurry to get to school because he had to walk in this seventeen-degree weather.

"Your breakfast is on the table," said Ingrid as she stood in the doorway for a second and then scrambled away. Seven swaggered into the kitchen as he saw his mother at the table looking through the want ads of the newspaper. Seven wondered what kind of job his mother was going to find. Another rich little girl to take care of, Seven hoped not. He didn't want to go through staring games with some old rich guy who thinks he's king of the world. He hoped his mother would find something good. Seven poured some Fruity Pebbles in a bowl and then added milk and ate. Ingrid smiled.

An hour later, Seven exited his house. He shut the door behind him as he saw his breath visible through the cold air. Seven took his time walking on the sheet of ice right in front of their door. He slid a couple of times but didn't hit the ground. Seven headed down the street with his backpack on his shoulder. As he was on his way to school, he felt as if he were in another world—winter wonderland, that is. It was beautiful. He loved it. But it was too cold. Seven walked at a faster pace to get his blood flowing in order to keep warm. Plus Seven didn't even have a hat on.

Moments later, Seven arrived at school. He hurried upstairs and dashed into his classroom. Seven hung up his coat in the closet and resided at his desk. He sat across from Chad. They gave each other high fives. Chad kept his eye on something or someone. He then nudged Seven. "Check it out, yo," Chad said. Seven saw the beautiful dark-skinned girl who occupied a desk in the first row, third seat from across the room. She had a rich complexion and wore her hair in a bun. Nicely. She was very feminine—from her pink sweater, blue jeans, and pink winter boots to her notebook, books, pencils, and pens. Her name was Dilbrina. That was an unusual name, but pretty. Dilbrina smiled and seemed happy with her classmates. Seven couldn't keep his eyes off her.

At lunchtime, students packed the cafeteria. There was clamor in the air due to relief from all the stressing schoolwork. Seven and his classmates stood in line to get their lunches. Seven and Chad were right alongside each other. They grabbed a hot tray with a hamburger, french fries, an apple, and milk. Seven and Chad sat at the extremely long lunch table. Seven still couldn't keep his eyes off Dilbrina.

"Do you think she noticed me?" Seven asked nervously.

"What are you scared of? You've got to be fuckin' kidding, yo," said Chad. Chad stuffed french fries in his mouth. "Just talk to her."

Seven gazed down at the other end of the table where Dilbrina mingled with the other girls. Then Seven caught Dilbrina's eye. Seven gave Dilbrina a big smile, and she gave him one in return.

"You see. How hard was that, man?" Chad said.

Meanwhile, there was a heavy-set kid by the name of Monster. He was a dominating force within the school. He sat with some other students that were smaller and who followed him. He stood five eleven, was brown skinned and chunky. Monster dressed similar to Seven by wearing all black, whether it be jeans, shirt, or footwear. Monster threw his weight around. He laughed and picked on other students. Monster rose from his seat and grabbed a couple of students' milks and cookies. "This shit is mine," Monster bellowed as he sat down at the other end of the table.

Seven and Chad observed Monster's boisterous behavior. Seven noticed Monster's followers were smaller than him. "He can't fight. His posse isn't even his equal," Seven said to Chad.

"Someone needs to fuck 'em up," Chad responded.

Then Monster rose from his seat again and wandered around the lunchroom. Seven and Chad eyed his every move. Monster made his way toward his table, but he went to the other end where Dilbrina was. Monster immediately gave Dilbrina the evil eye. "You look like you have a chocolate doughnut on your head. You look stupid," Monster teased.

Dilbrina looked around in embarrassment. Seven still observed the whole thing.

"Go back to your motherfuckin' table, bitch," Seven cursed.

"Who the fuck said that!" Monster shouted. He swaggered around to see who his challenger was. Seven stood up from his seat and approached Monster. When the two boys came face-to-face, Monster was obviously bigger than Seven. But Seven wasn't afraid, because he was a lion. "Who the fuck are you?" Monster yelled.

Seven got up directly in his face. "I'm your worst nightmare."

Monster pushed Seven. Then Seven pushed Monster back to the point where he landed on the floor. Like the saying goes, "The bigger they are, the harder they fall." It was just that when it came to Monster. Seven balled his fist and was ready to take this beast out. Monster then lunged at Seven. The two boys hurled punches at each other. The lunchroom erupted into students clamoring due to the fierce fight. The teachers and the principal separated the boys.

Moments later, Seven and Monster sat in the dean's office. Both sat on a bench on opposite ends. Seven and Monster stared each other down just like the good old Mr. Westland days.

"Yo, you need to mind your business," Monster said.

"Fuck you!" Seven told him.

Mr. Mattina, a good-looking Caucasian male, medium built, in his late forties, was a tough man who's familiar with street lingo and urban music. That's not usually expected for a white man to have knowledge of these things in order to relate to the kids.

"What's up, fool!" Seven shouted he challenged Monster again.

"You won't fuckin' last, bitch!" Monster attempted to lunge at Seven. Mr. Mattina got in between Seven and Monster.

"What's up with the fighting? Especially, you Rene!" Mr. Mattina bellowed in Monster's face.

"Rene?" Seven said, surprised. He snickered.

"What's so funny?" Monster asked with embarrassment in his face.

"That's a girl's name. In other words, a sissy's name," Seven insulted.

Monster lunged at Seven. The two boys wrestled to the floor. Mr. Mattina put Monster in the headlock. He dragged the bully to the other side of the room. Seven jumped to his feet and punched Monster twice in the face. Blood dripped from Monster's nose and mouth.

"Seven, you're suspended for a week."

"I don't give a fuck," Seven cursed.

Later, Ingrid rushed to the dean's office to pick Seven up. Seven and Ingrid exited the building. On their way home, Ingrid didn't get mad or show any signs of anger. She was nonchalant. They went to the supermarket, and Ingrid allowed Seven to get whatever he wanted. Seven headed over to the deli. The deli manager assisted Seven as she smiled. Seven ordered some corned beef, then he picked out Kaiser rolls, a bag of chips, soda, etc. Seven wondered why his mother wasn't irate.

Ingrid headed to the cashier to pay for the food. Seven packed the things in a bag. The cashier looked at Seven and smiled. "Thanks for bagging," said the cashier to Seven.

"You're welcome," Seven said as he swaggered away.

Ingrid was right behind him. She walked at a slow pace. Seven turned around and saw Ingrid lagging behind. Seven rushed back to his mother's side. "Are you all right, Mom?" Seven asked.

"Yes, I'm fine. Just tired," Ingrid replied.

Seven walked at the same pace by his mother's side.

At home, Seven ate his corned beef sandwich and chips while watching television. Seven noticed everything was quiet. Ingrid wasn't in sight. Seven left the table and went to his mother's bedroom. The door was closed. Seven knocked, and there was no answer. He just opened it. Seven saw his mother in bed, asleep. *Is Mom tired or sick?* Seven thought to himself. It was like history repeating itself when his grandmother passed away. "Mom, are you okay?" Seven asked in an aggressive tone.

Ingrid tossed and turned in her slumber. "I'm fine, Seven. I'm just a little tired."

"I got suspended from school."

"I know. Why?" Ingrid said in a whispering tone.

"Because there was some bully motherfucker picking on a girl in my class."

"Watch your mouth, Seven," Ingrid said. "That was a good thing, but you have to be careful that you don't stick your nose in for the wrong girl. You did something most boys and even men won't do. I'm proud of you," Ingrid said as she shut her eyes.

Seven kissed her and left the room. The doorbell rang. He thrust the door open. William stood there with a sour expression on his face. "Why did you get suspended?"

"Like I told Mom, there was a bully motherfucker picking on a girl in my class," Seven explained.

"That's some heroic shit. Don't put yourself in jeopardy for a girl again."

"Am I grounded?" Seven asked.

"No," William answered.

Seven went to his bedroom and did whatever homework he had. Cartoons played on television. He worked on his language arts. Then he read a couple of magazine on cars. Then he ate a sandwich and then his dinner. Seven read some more. He really wasn't paying attention to the television. It played for nothing. That's all Seven did his entire suspension. He ate, slept, read, and watched television. The next day, Seven repeated the same routine. Seven opened the refrigerator door and grabbed the jug of milk. He poured it into a bowl of Fruity Pebbles. Due to Seven being home, he ate everything in the refrigerator. Seven gained some weight. It's not a bad thing for a growing boy. It's a good thing.

Ingrid spent time with Seven at home. Besides Seven eating, sleeping, and watching television, Ingrid and Seven talked about life lessons and reading the Bible. Seven read, "The Lord is my shepherd" from Psalms of the Bible every night. It gave Ingrid comfort. She wanted Seven to read the Bible because she wanted him to do the right thing. Ingrid didn't want Seven to become another statistic. She didn't want Seven to follow in William's footsteps. Seven didn't really know what that meant, because he was still young. But Seven knew God and a fast car would protect him. With God, he would help Seven to get a fast car. Then the doorbell rang. Seven thrust the front door open. There stood beautiful Dilbrina. There was a maroon Volvo car waiting for her with its engine running. Seven smiled from ear to ear. "Dilbrina, hi."

"How are you, Seven?" Dilbrina greeted him.

"What brings you here? How did you know where I live?" Seven asked.

"Chad told me. Here's the homework," said Dilbrina. She had given him the homework assignments.

"Thanks, Dilbrina."

"When are you coming back?"

"On Monday," Seven said.

"And thanks for sticking up for me," said Dilbrina. She kissed Seven on the cheek and went on her way.

Ingrid stood in the background and watched. She smiled. "You're blushing." Ingrid laughed.

A week later, Seven was back in school. Everything was pretty cool. Seven did his schoolwork, studied hard, and caught up with his classes. But in the cafeteria, Seven and Monster still had a deep-seated animosity for each other. They didn't exchange any words but stared each other down. Monster wasn't going around taking any milk from the other students; he just remained in his seat. Mr. Mattina had his eyes on both Monster and Seven.

It was a hot summer day, eighty-nine degrees. The school bell rang as students ran out of the building like a herd of wildebeest. It was the last day. Seven and Monster had this planned for this day. They took it to the streets. An enormous crowd of young people, rooted for Seven as others cheered for Monster. The two young men fought with fists. Seven threw multiple punches to Monster's body as quickly as he could. Monster tried to throw as many as he could but couldn't keep up. Monster was out of breath. He slumped over as Seven hurled an enormous punch to his abdominal area. Monster spat up blood. The kids were screaming for Seven to stop. But Seven showed no mercy. Then Seven gave Monster an uppercut. Seven's punches became more and more fierce and raw. Monster had a bloody nose and mouth. Seven saw the blood and halted. He gazed at Monster. Blood dripped on Monster's his shirt and some on his hand. Monster cried like a baby. It was like a David and Goliath. Seven couldn't believe how much blood he drew. Chad and the other boys praised Seven for taking out the beast. "Thank you so much, Seven," said a gratified glass-clad nerdy student. He shook Seven's hand. Dilbrina witnessed the battle. She and Seven made eye contact. Dilbrina gave Seven a smile and walked away with her friends.

Chapter 15

Mid-July, the heat wave of ninety-two degrees was climbing, and it was just the break of dawn. The sunrays peered through Seven's bedroom blinds. A small fan rotated around, giving relief. Seven tossed and turned as he sniffed the air. He sat up in his bed and smelled coffee and waffles. He sprung from his bed. Seven swaggered in the kitchen to find his mother cooking breakfast. He only wore boxers and no shirt.

"Seven, good morning. Put some clothes on," Ingrid demanded.

"Are we going somewhere?" Seven asked.

"No," Ingrid said.

Seven opened the refrigerator and saw there was no orange juice. He closed it and headed back to his room. Moments later, Seven ate a stack of Eggo waffles on the table. It was drenched in syrup and butter. Seven then chugged down a tall glass of milk. There were red ink marks on the want ads that Ingrid went through. Ingrid still received some back pay from the Westlands. It was good enough to hold Ingrid and Seven for a while. But Ingrid knew this money would run out quick.

"What are you going to do today?" Ingrid asked.

Seven shrugged his shoulders as he chewed his food. Seven told her he was going to go bike riding with Chad. But Chad wasn't around. He was in Atlanta, visiting his aunt. Seven stuffed the last piece of waffle in his mouth and tossed his plate in the sink. He kissed Ingrid on the cheek and swaggered away. Seven slowly pedaled on his Todd MacKenzie bike. He was nervous about going to Dilbrina's house. Seven thought he should turn around and go back home. This kind of felt like being with another rich girl again. Seven didn't really know if Dilbrina was rich. But he knew Dilbrina's family probably had more than his. But the thing that kept Seven pedaling that bike was that Dilbrina was beautiful.

Then Seven arrived at a beautiful white cottage home. The grass was well kept, including the hedges. The birds sang their songs like crazy through the atmosphere. Seven parked his bike at the bottom of the steps. He made his way up to the door and rang the doorbell. It was an unusual ringing. It sounded very sweet, like very high-pitched chimes that he never heard before. Then a ginger-haired Caucasian woman, Caroline Burton, in her early fifties, opened the door and gave a smile as she saw Seven standing on the other side. Then she opened the screen door.

Do I have the wrong house? Seven thought to himself.

"Are you, Seven?" Mrs. Burton asked.

"Yes," Seven answered.

Then Dilbrina ran to the door with a big smile on her face. Dilbrina hugged Seven, and then she introduced Seven to her mother. Of course, not her real mother, her adoptive mother. Seven's jaw dropped when he saw that Dilbrina had a white mother. Dilbrina wasn't mixed. She was full African-American. *I'm surrounded by rich people everywhere I go,* Seven thought to himself. First, Angelika, and now Dilbrina. But Seven wasn't going to let someone's economic background stop him. Seven just wanted to enjoy the day.

Later, Seven and Dilbrina sat in her enormous backyard. It wasn't as big as the Westland estate, but it was bigger than his. Then the kids spoke about their lives. Dilbrina told Seven that she was adopted by the Burtons when she was three months old. She never knew her real family, and she didn't feel like she was missing out on anything. Dilbrina was happy with her parents, Mr. and Mrs. Samuel Burton. Dr. Burton was a surgeon, and Mrs. Burton was a stay-at-home mom. Dilbrina told how Mrs. Burton was an excellent cook because she used to go to culinary school. Also, Dilbrina had an older brother, Douglas. He was away in college and would come home on the weekends. Seven asked Dilbrina a lot of questions. He asked her if she ever felt out of place at times by being with a white family. Dilbrina saw them as her real mom and dad.

As the day went on, Dilbrina bragged about how great her dad was, how Dr. Burton was the greatest surgeon in the world. He operated on several Siamese twins. Seven could tell that Dilbrina was exaggerating about her dad's accomplishments. But Seven knew Dr. Burton was a legit man of society. As Dilbrina went on about her family, Seven got bored. She wasn't as down-to-earth as Angelika was. And Angelika came from a wealthy background.

Moments later, Seven got on his bike and waved good-bye to Dilbrina.

"Come back tomorrow, Seven," Dilbrina said.

Seven began to pedal fast on his bike as he sped away. Seven didn't plan on seeing Dilbrina again. She was full of herself, and all she did was brag about how great her family was. She was definitely a showoff. Dilbrina didn't ask him one question about himself and his life. It was all about Dilbrina. That was a real turnoff.

Minutes later, Seven arrived home. He made his way around the back of the house. He slid the glass door open and entered with his bike. Ingrid cooked lunch in the kitchen. "You've been gone for quite a while," said Ingrid.

"I'm sorry." Seven parked his bike in the corner of the kitchen. He grabbed a soda from the refrigerator, opened the can, and chug it down. Seven exhaled heavily and then released an enormous burp. Ingrid gave Seven the evil eye.

"Excuse me," Seven apologized. Seven took a seat at the table.

"Pig," Ingrid insulted Seven as she glared at him.

Seven sat at the table and thought. Every time he met someone, they were somewhat high class and it turned out to be a disaster. He missed Chad and Polo. Polo probably moved. Seven rang Polo's bell a couple of times, but there was no answer. Seven wanted to be in good company with good friends like Polo and Chad. Seven wondered what kind of summer this would be. Seven headed into his bedroom and plopped on the bed. He flipped through the channels of the television. NASCAR was on.

"Gentlemen, start your engines!" the NASCAR announcer shouted. The engines revved of the stock cars as they made their laps on the track. The racers drove about one hundred miles per hour. It was mesmerizing to Seven. He sat erected in his bed as his eyes were glued to the tube. Then the list of the drivers displayed on the screen. Todd MacKenzie was at the top of the list. Seven made it just in time for NASCAR. If Dilbrina had been nice, he would have missed out on NASCAR. It was a good thing that Dilbrina was full of herself.

"Mom, come quick!" Seven shouted.

"I'm coming!" Ingrid cried from the kitchen. Ingrid raced into Seven's bedroom with an empty soup can in her hand. "What's the excitement?"

"Todd MacKenzie's racing! I'm gonna race a muscle car just like him!"

Ingrid made a sour expression and turned off the television.

"Hey! Why did you do that?" Seven sighed.

"I want you to go to the store and get some milk." Ingrid said.

"Can I have a dollar?" Seven asked as he held out his hand.

"Only spend a dollar and bring my change back." Ingrid demanded as she placed a ten dollar bill in his hand. "I'm running low on money, Seven!"

Seven raced out of the bedroom. Seven grabbed his Todd MacKenzie bike from the corner of the kitchen and exited the rear glass door. Ingrid's right behind him as she closed the door back. Seven glanced back and saw his mother watching him as he rode off.

Seven pedaled fast on the side of the road. Cars passed him by as Seven continued his navigation to the store. Horns of the vehicles honked.

"Get off the road, kid!" a truck driver shouted.

Seven pedaled toward a convenient store up ahead. He noticed four hoodlums acting boisterously. One was tall and fat, the other short and fat, and the other guys were skinny as sticks. They were cursing, wrestling, goofing off, and drinking. Seven approached slowly as he parked his bike in front of the store. Then the hooligans stopped as they eyed Seven. He then entered into the store.

In the store, Seven browsed in the candy aisle as he grasped the container of milk in his hands. Seven eyed sweets on the shelves. Seven's mother told him not to spend all her change. He wanted every candy there was. "Fuck it!" Seven whispered to himself. Seven snatched a Snickers bar, peanut M&M's, a bag of Doritos, and soda. Seven marched up to the cashier. She scanned all the items. "That'll be six, seventy-two," said the cashier. Seven handed the cashier the ten-dollar bill. The sound of the register with its drawer opening and coins trickling around was another sound that was like new music to Seven's ears. He cautiously peeked over the counter to see the money and coins in it. The cashier slammed the drawer shut and gave Seven his change. She then packed the items in the bag. "Have a nice day."

"Thanks," said Seven as he grabbed his bag as he swaggered out of the store. Seven's eyes bulged as she saw the overweight kid riding away with his bike. "Hey!" Seven shouted. The other two skinny guys snatched his bag. Seven turned around and proceeded after the two skinny guys for his items. Several thoughts ran through Seven's mind while this was all going simultaneously. If he didn't get his mother's stuff, he would never hear the end of it. And if he lost his bike, he would never hear the end of it from his father. Seven ran as fast as he could to get his bike that his dad got for his last birthday. His dad would really kick his ass. The overweight thug pedaled slow on the Todd MacKenzie bike. Seven caught up to the thug. As Seven grabbed his shirt, it ripped. Then the fat thug halted.

"That's an eighty-dollar shirt!" the overweight thug roared. A black Lexus with tinted window turned the corner and made its way down the street. In the backseat sat DeShaun Stewart, a very handsome, thirty-something, well-dressed thug decked out in black. He puffed on a cherry-flavored Philly blunt. The smoke was released through the crack of the rear seat window. DeShaun's eyes widened as he saw the overweight thug punching Seven. Seven plummeted to the ground. "Skeeter, stop the car!" DeShaun hollered. The wheels of the black Lexus screeched. DeShaun swaggered out of the vehicle and grabbed the overweight thug by the throat. "Are you fuckin' stupid! Fuckin' bitch!" DeShaun punched the overweight thug in the face. Seven witnessed this stranger hurl multiple punches to the thug's face and abdominal area. The overweight thug coughed up blood. Then as Seven lay on the concrete, Skeeter, an African-American male wearing cornrows, a streetwise hoodlum, reached his hand out to Seven to help him to his feet.

"Are you all right, little man?" Skeeter asked. Seven nodded. DeShaun glared at Seven.

Seven became a little afraid. *What did I do? I'm the one that got knocked the fuck out,* Seven thought to himself.

DeShaun then kicked the overweight thug in the butt. He collapsed to the ground in agony. DeShaun grabbed Seven's bike. "Is this yours?" DeShaun asked in a hostile tone.

"Yes," Seven answered.

Then DeShaun kicked the thug in the stomach as he laid on the ground. He then made it to his feet. He staggered down the street, bleeding. "Don't let me catch your ass around here again!" DeShaun yelled. Then DeShaun hovered over Seven like some kind of powerful being not of this world, but something good. Maybe it was a guardian angel sent by Grandma from heaven, Seven thought.

Later, Seven held a tissue to his bloodied nose as he sat on his bike before DeShaun. DeShaun sat in his parked car with backseat door open. Seven sniffled as he held back tears from the bad experience. Luckily for him, DeShaun came to his rescue in the nick of time. Skeeter exited the store with a container of milk and candy. He handed the bag to Seven. "Here you go, my man," said Skeeter. DeShaun introduced himself and his partner, Skeeter. Then Seven introduced himself. DeShaun and Skeeter were blown away by such a unique, cool name. Seven told how it was given to him due to his date of birth, July 27th at 2:37 p.m. DeShaun continued to ask Seven a lot of questions about himself. He asked Seven about his family and friends. Seven told about how his father brought him that Todd MacKenzie bike and how his father wasn't really around. DeShaun empathized with him due to his father being absent in his life.

As the two got to know each other, Seven noticed DeShaun kept glaring at him funny. Seven became nervous and hoped this wasn't another Mr. Westland experience. It wasn't. DeShaun told how one night he lost his eight-month-old baby boy in a fire. It was caused by his negligent ex-girlfriend, who decided to go to the club with some friends in the middle of night. The baby was left alone in the apartment as the child slept. The blaze started from a flat iron that was left on. Neighbors smelled smoke as flames quickly spread throughout the apartment. One neighbor heard the baby's cries. He burst down the door as flames engulfed his body. It was also too late for the eight-month infant. A tear trickled down DeShaun's face as he told Seven about his baby's terrible death. "My son is in heaven," DeShaun said softly as he continued to fight back tears.

"I'm sorry that happened," Seven said.

"Too bad I didn't get a chance to see him grow up." DeShaun immediately changed the subject and saw noticed the Todd MacKenzie bike that Seven had. "I can see that you're a real Todd MacKenzie fan," DeShaun said.

Seven went on to tell DeShaun how the NASCAR races were on television and so forth. Seven felt as if he were talking to his own father by talking to DeShaun. DeShaun jotted down his phone number on a piece of paper and handed it to Seven. "If you want to talk or need anything, Seven, just holler at me."

Seven took DeShaun's number. He said "Thank you" and rode away on his bike.

Moments later, the bowl of chicken soup sat waiting on the table for Seven. Ingrid sat in a chair across from the empty seat where Seven usually sat. Seven wheeled his bike toward the glass door. Ingrid rushed to the door and slid it open. Ingrid was horrified to see Seven holding a bloodied tissue to his nose. "Lord have mercy! What happened, Seven!" Ingrid shouted. Seven didn't answer as he parked his bike in the corner of the kitchen. He dashed to the bathroom. Ingrid gave chase.

In the bathroom, Ingrid applied a peroxide-soaked cotton ball to Seven's nose. Seven cringed as the medication stung. "Ouch! Ow!" Seven hollered.

"I'm sorry, baby. Look at what the bully did to my baby's face," Ingrid said in a soft tone. She kissed Seven on the forehead. "What happened?"

"He tried to take my bike. And I kicked his fat ass." Seven cursed.

Ingrid gave Seven a dirty look because she didn't like profanity, especially coming from her son's mouth. Then the doorbell rang. Seven rushed out of the bathroom. "Your father's gonna have a fit!"

Seven swung the front door open as his father stepped inside. William noticed Seven's nose. William grabbed Seven's face and noticed the blood from Seven's nose.

"Don't worry. I kicked the shit out of his fat ass," Seven swore.

"Are you sure about that?"

"Yes."

"What did I always tell you?" William asked Seven. William held both of his fists in the air. "This is what makes a man out of you!"

"Don't encourage him into all that street nonsense. You talk out your problems."

"Talking doesn't work, Ingrid."

"And fighting does?" Ingrid asked.

Later, the bowl of chicken soup was half eaten. Seven and William watched the NASCAR races on television in the living room. Ingrid watched the father and son duo from her seat in the kitchen. She didn't want to disturb them, because Ingrid knew how important it was for Seven to have his father. But something was really eating Ingrid. She relaxed and let the boys enjoy their afternoon.

"Todd MacKenzie needs one more lap and he's got it!" Seven said excitedly. "He's gonna get that NASCAR cup!" On the television, Todd MacKenzie drove stock car number 4. The stock car was decorated with advertisements of today's latest products. Also, they're sponsors of Todd MacKenzie. The engines of the stock cars became more and more fierce as the race was about to end. Seven's heart raced as he knew his hero was gonna get that NASCAR cup. Then car number four made across the finish line. Seven and William jumped for joy. They danced around. "He got it!"

"He's the man," William said. Seven and William watched as the crowd of Todd MacKenzie fans roar throughout the race track. Seven then looked at Ingrid as she resided at the table. Ingrid seemed disturbed. Seven knew something was bothering her. He didn't want to tell her that he lost her change due to the fight he had at the convenience store. But he had to. Seven took baby steps into the kitchen. Ingrid glared at her son. "Mom, I lost your change," Seven said. Ingrid shook her head and slammed both hands on the table. "William, do you have any money? I'm dead broke!" Ingrid roared.

"Don't start any shit now!"

"What the hell did you come here for!" Ingrid screamed.

"To spend time with my son. Is that okay with you!" William responded.

"I only have about two hundred dollars," said Ingrid as her voice began to crack. Ingrid rushed into bedroom.

William started to pace the floor. He threw his hands in the air. "Damn! It's always some shit!" William whispered to himself.

Seven plopped in the recliner as he prepared for another episode of "William versus Ingrid." "I lost Mom's change."

"Shit happens." William cursed.

Ingrid ran into the living room. She threw the two hundred dollars in his face. Seven watched as his mother was in tears again. Maybe he should've kept his mouth shut. William reacted with the same type of behavior as Ingrid. He gathered up the money, and as he was about to throw it in Ingrid's face, Seven said, "Don't do that! It was my fault! Mom told me to bring her change back and I lost it!" Tears streamed down his face. William consoled Seven. Ingrid stood alone in tears without anyone comforting her. Seven saw his mother in tears and always alone, hardly ever happy. William put his arms around Ingrid and kissed her. This was what Seven always wanted to see, someone comforting his mother, especially his father. He wanted his mother and father back together.

"I'm gonna fix this," William said as he swaggered to the door. He exited and slammed the door. Seven was pleased that his father was gonna make things right. Seven then embraced his mother.

Night approached as the crickets chirped and fireflies flew through the hot summer air. Seven gazed at the ceiling while in bed. He wore only his boxers and undershirt. Seven wiped sweat from his forehead then tossed and turned. Seven closed his eyes and tried to go to sleep but couldn't. He was too hot. Seven went to open the window wider. But there was still no cool air. Seven hopped back in bed and forced himself to get some sleep. All he could think about was his birthday. Seven wanted a party, but a peaceful one with his parents.

Several hours later, Seven laid on his side with his head on the pillow. The birds sang. Dawn broke as the sunrays peeked into Seven's bedroom window. Then there was a loud scream. The scream then turned into loud crying. "No! It can't be!" Then there was another scream. Seven's eyes opened in surprise. His heart raced as he clutched his pillow hard. Seven sat up slowly and looked around his room. He then crept to his door and opened it with caution. He heard the static of walkie-talkies from the living room. Ingrid's cries became louder and louder. Seven proceeded to make his way to his mother as she sat in the recliner with police officers hovering over her.

"How could this have happened?" Ingrid cried.

"We're sorry for your loss," said an officer.

Seven maneuvered his way between the police officers. Seven reached out to his mother. "Mom," Seven called. Seven and Ingrid embraced. Ingrid sobbed as she held Seven in her arms. She then made direct eye contact with her son. Tears kept streaming down her face like water dripping from a faucet.

"Your father . . . he's in heaven now." Ingrid said as her voice quivered.

"He's in heaven? What?" Seven responded in disbelief.

"Yeees." Ingrid answered her son slowly as she was about shed tears some more.

"Not again. Just like Grandma," said Seven. He stormed away from his mother's side. Seven scrambled into his bedroom. He slammed the bedroom door. Seven looked at everything in it. He thought about his birthday that was coming up on the twenty-seventh. This was too much for a kid to take. Seven tossed over his desk, knocked the books off the shelves, smashed his model car, and then punched his fist into the dresser mirror. A bloody spot was left in the crack of the mirror. Seven screamed in agony as blood streamed down his hand. "Mom!" Seven cried.

Ingrid swung the door open as her eyes widened. She clutched Seven. "My God! I've got to get you to the emergency room!" Ingrid said.

Chapter 16

This was Seven's second funeral that he attended. He resided next to his mother, dressed in his black three-piece suit. It's the same suit he wore to his grandmother's funeral the year before. Seven's bandaged hand ached a bit. Punching his dresser mirror with his fist was a painful thing after hearing the disturbing news. *Who did this to my father? And why?* Seven thought to himself. William's family and friends were definitely asking the same questions themselves. Why? They packed the church to pay their respects. Seven and Ingrid sat in the front row. Ingrid also wore the same black dress to her mother's funeral. Maureen and Baby Athena sat two rows away. Athena's cries echoed throughout the church. Seven glanced over his shoulder and saw his half sister in Maureen's arms. Then Seven faced forward and saw his father lying in his black casket.

William was dressed in a navy-blue suit with a rose clipped on the jacket pocket. His arms were crossed against his chest as he lay very peacefully. To Seven, it seemed as if his father was sleeping just like at home. Nothing really happened to William; it seemed that way to Seven. Seven didn't see any marks, wounds, or bruises on his father's corpse, so he couldn't really cry right now. He was angered that his father was going to be out of his life permanently. *Who's next? My mother?* Seven thought to himself.

The preacher got in the pulpit and gave William's eulogy. There wasn't a dry eye in the congregation. Ingrid wept every few minutes, and then she took a breather. Death came at any time, any day, any moment. Seven thought even deeper, *Why doesn't God stop this death thing that lingers around us? He put us here to live, right? It's a waste of time giving us life when we're sure to die at any time of day.* Seven expunged the malevolent occurrence from his mind.

On their way to the graveyard, Seven focused on every car that passed by the black car they rode in. This was no time for cars. Seven had to think about his father. He couldn't help it. Seven noticed a black Mercedes-Benz that sped along the highway. He thought of his own death. How would he die? Would Seven die of sickness? Murder? Or an accident? Especially a car accident? If he were to die, let it be an automobile accident. It's crazy. Live by speed, die by speed. Unusual thoughts for a child. Seven preferred a car wreck.

At the cemetery, gravediggers shoveled up the soil of the earth and placed William's casket six feet under. Seven, family, and friends head back to their vehicles as they said their final farewell. Seven stood there as he watched gravediggers toss soil into his father's grave. "Please, God, take my father and let him be with Grandma. He wasn't a bad person, please. Take my father into heaven. Amen," Seven prayed. Seven thought of all the disgusting things that are in the ground as your body lay in the coffin—all sorts of insects crawling all over you and eating you. That scared Seven; he cried as he did an about face and marched to the black car.

That afternoon at the Miles' residence, the sun gleamed with its rays hitting every angle of the earth. Seven's family and friends comforted one another in this time of need. Ingrid sobbed at the table like crazy. Everyone tried to console her, but she couldn't stop crying. Seven ran out of his bedroom, dressed in his T-shirt and blue jeans. Seven was tired of his mother in such pain, constant pain—whether it was his father causing Ingrid to become lovesick or now with the loss of his own life. Thank goodness people were around. Seven knew he had to get out of there. He rolled his bike out of the corner of the kitchen. Seven slid the rear glass door open with one hand, he had some difficulty, but was able to leave without anyone noticing. Then Seven slid the rear glass door back and rode away on his bike.

During Seven's bike ride, he pedaled slow and steered with one hand as the other was bandaged up. It was challenging, but Seven had it pretty much under control. Seven remembered the address and phone number DeShaun gave him. Then Seven arrived at a gas station and minimart that were adjacent to one another. A couple of customers pumped their own gas while other people exited the minimart. Seven rode toward the minimart. He looked around cautiously to make sure there weren't any hoodlums around to steal from him again. The atmosphere seemed nice. To be on the safe side, Seven wheeled his bike into the store. The bell chimed. Seven looked around and saw a female cashier at the register. She was busy scanning a customer's items. Seven was a little unsure if this was the correct address. He scanned the supermarket with is eyes. The isles, the abundance of foods, and the registers made the business condensed.

"Excuse me, is DeShaun here?" Seven asked with the look of uncertainty written on his face. The cashier was a fabulous ghetto type of chick. She wore bright-red Bozo the Clown hair with big gold earrings, a red T-shirt, and blue jeans. *Yuck! She is ugly,* Seven thought to himself. Seven continued to stare at her even harder and noticed that she wasn't really ugly. It was just the circus hair. Seven took notice of her name badge Tiana. And she was such a loud mouth. Tiana screamed as if someone were killing her. Then Skeeter hustled from the cereal aisle with a clipboard in his hand.

"What's the problem, Tiana?" Skeeter hollered. Skeeter noticed Seven and, of course, his bandaged hand. Skeeter smiled at Seven but then frowned. Seven could see that he was getting pissed off. "How are you, Seven?" Skeeter asked and eyed him. "What happened to your hand?" Skeeter asked in a stern tone.

Seven's eyes became watery. The tears streamed down his face. "DeShaun, hurry yo!" Skeeter commanded.

DeShaun swaggered from one of the aisles taking his time as if he were a king. Seven then saw DeShaun heading towards him. Seven held back his tears and took a deep breath. Seven respected him and knew DeShaun was strong. He didn't like tears. As DeShaun got closer and closer to Seven, he didn't smile at all because he saw Seven's bandaged hand. DeShaun's heart raced, balled his hands into fists, and grinded his teeth. He glared at Seven directly in the eyes. "Did that kid do this to you, Seven? Tell me. I've got you. Trust me." DeShaun said in a stern tone. Seven turned his back and cried like a baby. He was ashamed. DeShaun turned Seven facing him. "Tell me!" DeShaun shouted. "My dad. He's in heaven now." Seven wept. DeShaun embraced Seven in his arms, and they both now had something in common.

July 27 was another birthday, Seven's twelfth birthday, that is. He celebrated by staying home with his mother and a bandaged hand. Ingrid did the best she could with what little she had. She baked a red velvet cake for him. There was no party for him this year, just he and his mother. They ate cake and talked about the people they lost in their lives—the loss of his grandmother and father and the loss of his friendship with Angelika. Angelika was like a daughter to Ingrid.

Seven and Ingrid shuffled through the old pictures of Seven and Angelika at the Westland mansion. There were photos of Rocco, the chauffeur, as well. Ingrid wondered how Angelika was doing since her birthday was coming up. She wanted to send Angelika a gift. But she couldn't because she was fired, and she didn't have the money. All Ingrid could do was pray that God would allow Angelika to have the most wonderful and blessed birthday ever. Seven wished the best for Angelika as well. But he wondered if Angelika was thinking of them. Probably not. She's now being taken care by another nanny that she considered to be her mother.

Anyway, Seven got some phone calls from relatives to wish him a happy birthday, especially from his uncle Darren, who was in the marines. Seven wondered when he was coming home. Darren didn't have any idea of when that would be. Darren wanted Seven to do good in school and do the right thing. Seven promised to do that and hung up the phone.

Then the doorbell rang. Ingrid scrambled away from the table. She swung the door open. "Oh my God! What's this!" Ingrid bellowed. She grabbed the three wrapped birthday gifts with "Happy birthday" gift wrapping paper on it. Seven raced toward his mother and saw the gifts in her hands. "These are for you," Ingrid said. Ingrid placed the gifts in Seven's arms.

Seven was excited by the presents. He raced to the couch and opened them. He didn't bother to read the card. Seven grabbed a black long-sleeved T-shirt with a marijuana leaf on it. Ingrid's eyes bulged and wondered. Then Seven opened up another gift—a pair of brand-named black construction boots. He got a black Rottweiler T-shirt, another T-shirt in black with a marijuana leaf logo, a pair of black sneakers, and two model cars. Seven then read the card. Ingrid glanced over Seven's shoulder and read along with him. It read, "Happy birthday, Seven. You're twelve years old today. Way to go, my man. Your friends, DeShaun and Skeeter."

"Who is DeShaun?" Ingrid asked. Seven didn't know how to answer his mother. She asked repeatedly. He still didn't answer her. Ingrid then became uneasy about the situation. "Are you taking things from strangers?" Ingrid asked.

"No," Seven answered.

"Who is DeShaun?" Ingrid asked once more.

"My friend."

"What friend gives a twelve-year-old a shirt that encourages drug use?"

"It's not drugs."

"Marijuana is a drug, Seven. You're gonna give those gifts back to DeShaun or whoever he is." Ingrid demanded.

"No."

"Don't fight with me."

"It's my birthday. DeShaun gave them to me. So I'll keep them!"

"Give those gifts back, Seven. And that's final!" Ingrid argued.

A couple of hours later, DeShaun's minimart was busy as usual, with customers doing their more convenient shopping. There was a short line of people at the gas station. Then Seven headed toward the mini mart as he carried all his birthday gifts in a bag. He entered into the establishment. Then a few moments later, DeShaun smiled at Seven due to it being his birthday. He was proud that he befriended this young man and wondered what was going to become of his life.

Whatever Seven chose in life DeShaun would back him one-hundred percent. But, Seven wasn't smiling. He loved the gifts DeShaun gave to him, but he couldn't keep them because of his mother. Ingrid fussed at Seven for taking gifts from strangers. A child wasn't supposed to do that. DeShaun got the picture, and knew exactly what to do.

Later, the black Lexus pulled into the driveway of Seven's home. DeShaun and Seven exited the car, closing the doors on each side. Seven was thrilled that DeShaun wanted to meet his mother. The two of them made their way around to the rear of the home. Seven knocked on the glass sliding door as he held the gifts from DeShaun. The aroma of roasted chicken and sweet potatoes filled the air. Ingrid knew Seven was hungry and prepared this slaving over the stove meal for her baby. Ingrid turned and saw Seven accompanied with a menacing stranger. Ingrid's heart race as she noticed this new friend of Seven's was in fact an adult. The new friend held a dozen roses and a fruit basket in his hands.

"Open the door, Mom," Seven said. Ingrid hesitated to open the door. On the other side of the glass, she saw a good-looking but very intimidating gentleman dressed in black. He gave a devilish grin. "Mom, this is my friend, DeShaun."

Ingrid slid the rear glass door open with caution as Seven and DeShaun entered into the house. DeShaun offered Ingrid the dozens, but she made a sour expression and refused his so-called gentleman- like ways. She didn't know this man who arrogantly swaggered into her home. DeShaun then placed the fruit basket down on the kitchen table beside the Jesus figurine. Seven felt his mother's nervousness about the whole thing. He also noticed how DeShaun gazed into his mother's eyes. "Is he in love with my mom? She is beautiful. Is he going to become my new Dad?" Seven thought. DeShaun offered the roses again to Ingrid with a smile on his face. He didn't utter a word as he spoke with his eyes. Finally, Ingrid gave in and clutched the bouquet of roses in her arms. Seven cracked a smile. Ingrid looked like Miss America by winning the crown and receiving that bouquet of roses for being the most beautiful woman in the world. Seven could certainly see that in his mother. Then DeShaun and his mother engaged in some conversation. He then swaggered to his bedroom with his gifts.

In Seven's bedroom, he hung up his shirt and kept his black construction boots in its box to keep them brand-new looking. He began assembling the model car. He had a bottle of glue and a small screwdriver on his desk. The old model car his biological father gave him used to be on the top shelf. After hearing the bad news about his father, Seven blocked it out of his mind and proceeded on with his project.

"Get out of my house! You hoodlum!" Ingrid shouted from the kitchen. Seven scrambled out of his bedroom. Seven witnessed DeShaun grabbing and kissing his mother. Then Ingrid slapped DeShaun. He didn't retaliate. DeShaun took the smack like a man and smiled devilishly. "Get out of my house!" Ingrid shouted once more. DeShaun glared at Ingrid for a second, then he placed down a bundle of cash on the table. DeShaun headed toward the door as he passed by Seven. He halted in his tracks. DeShaun gave Seven a high five. Seven escorted DeShaun to the door. DeShaun looked back at Seven. "We're still cool. Aren't we, Seven?" DeShaun asked.

"No doubt," Seven responded.

"I'll check you later. I've got some things to discuss with you."

"Cool," Seven answered.

DeShaun jumped in his black Lexus and sped away. The wheels screeched, leaving a small cloud of smoke. Seven wondered if DeShaun drag-raced himself. Probably not. Seven could hear his mother's cries from inside. Seven took a deep breath and closed the front door. He headed in to the kitchen, where his mother sat at the table. Ingrid held the money in her hand and then tossed it in the trash. Seven ran and snatched the bundle of money out of the garbage can. "Seven, leave that dirty money alone!"

"What are we going to do to keep a roof over our heads! We need this!" Seven lectured. Seven slammed the cash back on the table. "We're keeping the cash, and that's it!" Ingrid cried her eyes out as Seven embraced her. Seven was just as nervous about this situation as she was. But they needed help from someone. And that someone was DeShaun.

Chapter 17

A couple of weeks later, Seven held a nine-millimeter handgun in his hand for the first time. It was black, heavy, and menacing. He felt good to have that power right in the palm of his hand. But Seven always remembered what his father taught him. When it came to fighting with fists, that's what made a real man out of you. For now, Seven erased that from his mind and aimed the firearm at the target of a man's silhouette. Seven released several shots into it. DeShaun cheered and applauded at Seven's excellent gun firing. "Yeah, man! Do it, baby!" DeShaun praised. DeShaun, Skeeter, and other members of his posse stood around as they supervised Seven, Chad, and three other boys around twelve or thirteen years old target practicing.

Chad was by Seven's side, also pumping bullets from a .57 magnum gun. Chad's shooting was good, but he wasn't satisfied with the way the gun looked. He turned to DeShaun and wanted a more threatening firearm. DeShaun refused Chad's request and told him to work with what was given to him. Moments later, DeShaun had Seven, Chad, and the other boys gathered around a table before him. Seven felt like he was in school again. But he knew it would be something interesting.

The other three boys were fraternal triplets named BiBi, Bay, and Boo. They were good-looking dark-brown-complexioned young men searching for a world of trouble. DeShaun was looking for young soldiers to make his crew bigger. DeShaun wanted to be king of the streets, and he needed a strong army. He already had his older crew, but he needed young ones to do the dirty work, which was delivering packages to certain people and putting in overtime on the corner. DeShaun wanted everyone to live good because members of his posse have been to jail and needed help with their families and so forth. That was just like in Seven's situation. He lost his grandmother, then his father, and then his mother lost her job, and help came around. Seven was too young to think about the consequences. He was just a kid. DeShaun was a hero to him, someone to look up to, a father figure.

Few minutes later, DeShaun opened a door when everyone was dressed in plastic pants with no shirts, even the women, titties hanging. This was DeShaun's drug room, where the people inside cut the crack and place them in the vial. When Seven saw the women with their breasts exposed, he thought it was a type of sex thing for a second, but then he saw the blocks of crack being cut. Then DeShaun gave them a tour of how the crack was made. The smell was chalky, which made Seven and the boys choke a bit. It also got in Seven's throat, which made him cough even more. DeShaun even coughed a bit. BiBi snickered as they saw one woman's breasts. "Check out her tits. They look deflated." BiBi snickered. DeShaun heard what BiBi said and cracked up himself. But DeShaun made it clear there was a time to play and a time to be serious. And this was the time to be serious.

Later, Chad and Bay hurled punches at each other. This wasn't a real hard-feelings fight, but a practice fight. DeShaun had them do this to see how strong they were with fists, because DeShaun believed in fists as well. Punks fought with bullets while real men fought with fists. The reality was it was all about guns, especially on the streets. Chad and Bay's fight was like a boxing match at Caesar's Palace in Las Vegas. DeShaun and his posse cheered on the fight between the two young boys. Chad and Bay threw punches at each other like crazy as

DeShaun and his posse went crazy, cheering and wildly applauding. As a result of the fight with no hard feelings, Chad and Bay both wound up with bloody noses. DeShaun and his posse pat them on the back for their courage.

Now it was Seven's chance to prove himself. "Seven, my man. I know you can pull this off," DeShaun said. He patted Seven on the back. He swaggered to the center of the floor and then came Boo. Boo was the same size as the kid that Seven fought on the last day of school. Seven kept his cool and did what he had to do. This time, Seven could get his ass whooped, not in front of DeShaun; that would be embarrassing. "Ready! Go!" DeShaun commanded.

Seven and Boo danced around like professional boxers in the ring. Boo threw the first punch. Luckily, Seven ducked, and then he uppercut Boo. Boo staggered and then caught his balance. "Holy shit!" DeShaun hollered. Then Boo charged at Seven like a bull. He hurled multiple punches hitting Seven on every part of his body. Then Seven of course, hurled the same amount of punches at every angle of Boo's abdominal area. Seven knew he had to win this one. The fight became serious and fierce. Blood drew from both young men. Seven and Boo wound up with busted noses and lips. DeShaun and his posse saw how serious it was getting and then broke the fight up. Both boys were exhausted and bloodied as they shook hands and went their separate ways. "You put up a good fight. You're real hood, you know that." DeShaun praised.

In DeShaun's office, the jetscan counted up large sums of money. DeShaun, Skeeter, and his associates eyed the green with passion. DeShaun then snapped out of it and gazed at Seven. Again, Seven held a bloody tissue to his nose as he lounged in a chair. Another bloody nose due to fists flying. Seven didn't think about his future or his mother's feelings. Seven just thought about his physical pain at the moment. Then Seven looked around and saw photos of a baby boy on the wall. This must've been DeShaun's baby, the baby he lost in that terrible fire. Seven felt bad. *How could any mother leave their child alone like that? I was never left alone, even though at times I felt alone. If there was no one to take care of me, my mother took me with her,* Seven thought.

Later, Skeeter shoved bundles of cash in Seven's backpack. DeShaun lectured Seven on how to pedal as fast as he could. Seven had to make a delivery to a Peruvian drug kingpin named Lalo. Seven was nervous about his first job for DeShaun. "I want you to get this to the Peruvian Palace restaurant over on Sunrise Highway. I'm counting on you, Seven. All right?" said DeShaun. Seven nodded his head nervously. Skeeter then placed the backpack over Seven's shoulder. Skeeter shook Seven's hand and patted him on the back.

Moments later, Seven pedaled as fast as he could to get to Peruvian Palace on Sunrise. He rode through different parking lots of different businesses and alongside cars that beeped at him. Seven kept focus on his task and didn't want anything to go wrong. The Peruvian Palace restaurant stood sky-high as if it were one of the Seven Wonders of the World. It was majestic. Seven halted in front of the entrance of the restaurant as he wheeled his bike inside. A gorgeous Latina female in her midtwenties stood at the booth as she escorted customers to their seats. She noticed Seven and knew what the deal was. The hostess nodded to Seven, picked up the phone, and made a quick call.

A few minutes later, the Latina hostess escorted Seven through the kitchen. The cooks were busy preparing various Latin dishes while communicating in Spanish. The place was so hot and steamy. Seven wiped the sweat from his forehead. Spices, cooked chicken, and beef overwhelmed the air. Then Seven and the hostess headed down a dark stairwell into the basement. Seven couldn't see that well. It was pitch-black. Seven began to take baby steps because he didn't want to trip or bump into anything. Then there was light. Several good-looking, robust Latino henchmen guarded the premises as if they were protecting royalty. A red glow shone on Lalo, a handsome fifty-something gentleman with beautiful, well-groomed black hair and was dressed casually. He and his henchmen ate an enormous Latin feast with luxurious glass of wine. Paintings and photos of the country of Peru adorned the walls. Flowers adorned the place. Seven and the hostess approached Lalo with caution. The hostess spoke in a very submissive tone to Lalo in their native language. He stopped in the middle of his dinner and glared at Seven and the hostess. Lalo wiped his mouth with his napkin and washed his food down with a sip of wine. Seven poked his chest out and knew not to back down. He was on a mission. *I have to be a man and face this dude,* Seven thought to himself.

"Are you Seven?" Lalo asked in a stern tone.

"Yes, I am," Seven responded with a stern tone.

"DeShaun sent you?" Lalo questioned.

"Yes," Seven answered. Then Seven handed Lalo the bag. Lalo unzipped it and pulled out the bundles of cash. Lalo addressed his henchman in Spanish. Then later, one of Lalo's henchman stuffed several kilos of cocaine in Seven's bag. This felt like the movie *Scarface.* This was real. Seven knew he had to get this product to DeShaun safely.

Minutes later, Seven rode on his bike as fast as he could. When Seven rode his bike, he visualized it being a muscle car. He had to stay focused. Whenever Seven rode his bike it gave him drive. Determination. Seven arrived at the minimart and wheeled his bike into the store. Seven panted. The cashier saw him and waved. Seven nodded and raced downstairs with the backpack on. The basement was dimmed with advertisements of soft drinks and alcoholic beverages. DeShaun gave Seven a dead-hard stare. *What did I do,* Seven thought to himself. *Did I go to the wrong place?* Seven's heart pumped fast.

DeShaun snatched the backpack off his back. DeShaun unzipped it and pulled out the kilos of coke. He then turned to Seven. Sweat poured down Seven's face as if he were still in that Peruvian kitchen. "Seven, you're a genius!" DeShaun shouted. DeShaun gave Seven a high five. Seven was relieved. He did it—a job well done.

Throughout the summer, Seven ran lots of errands for DeShaun. Seven rode on his bike and weaved in between cars. They honked their horns. Seven paid no attention to their road rage. Seven didn't allow anyone or anything to distract him. Seven made more deliveries from DeShaun to Lalo. Then Seven returned to DeShaun with several kilos of cocaine. Seven was doing pretty good at this task. There was more that DeShaun wanted to teach him. At night, a lamppost burned bright on a street corner. The black Lexus parked at the curb. Skeeter occupied the driver's seat as DeShaun sat in the passenger's seat. Seven rode in the back. A twenty-something-year-old kid, Russell, counted money in his hand as DeShaun stepped out of the car. Russell looked up as he saw DeShaun approaching him. He extended his hand to give DeShaun a high five.

"What's up, DeShaun?" Russell greeted him with a smile from ear to ear. Out of nowhere, DeShaun hurled a punch to Russell's face. Seven witnessed the whole incident before his eyes. "Where the fuck is my cash!" DeShaun demanded. Russell handed over the dough with no hesitation. DeShaun beat Russell to a pulp. Russell tried to put up a fight, but it didn't work. He knew he couldn't win. Russell took his beating like a man. Seven turned his head away because he felt sorry for him. Russell's bloodied face was something out of a horror movie.

"Seven, come here," DeShaun hollered. Seven's heart pumped fast. He opened the car door and closed it back. Seven took baby steps. "Seven, let's go!" DeShaun hollered. Seven picked up his pace as he scrambled to DeShaun's side.

Why is DeShaun yelling at me? Seven thought.

"You see this shit. When a motherfucker doesn't pay up, you fuck his shit up and empty his pockets," DeShaun lectured in a stern voice. When DeShaun wanted his money, he wanted it. He'll beat or even kill you for it. He showed no sympathy and no excuses. DeShaun instilled in his entourage not to have any sympathy for any of these fools. The other drug runners watched in shock. "Don't you motherfuckers owe me some cash! Hand it over!" DeShaun glared at Seven and nodded. Seven automatically knew what to do. Seven took deep breathes and collected the cash from the other drug runners. They were much older than Seven. For a minute, Seven felt the respect that he was getting from these older guys. It felt good. "Hurry the fuck up!" Seven began to shout. The drug runners handed over their money to this little twelve-year-old kid quickly. Seven handled a batch of cash in both hands. "Have a good evening, fools!" DeShaun and Seven hopped into the black Lexus. The wheels screeched as it sped away.

Seven and DeShaun counted up the cash. DeShaun puffed on a Philly blunt while in the passenger's seat. He turned and smiled at Seven. "How much do we have back there?" DeShaun questioned with laughter. Seven proceeded to count the money. "Twenty, forty, sixty, eighty—" Seven was halted in his counting.

"Check it out. The easiest way to count is with twenties. You count by twos to make it easier."

Seven began to count the twenties again. "Two, four, six, eight, ten, twelve . . ." Seven continued to count the bundle of cash. "Three hundred forty," Seven said.

"Let me count that," DeShaun said. Seven gave the stack of cash to DeShaun. He recounted the cash as his Philly blunt hung from his mouth. Gradually, a smile appeared on DeShaun's face. "You're right. Three hundred forty dollars. I'm proud of you," DeShaun praised Seven as he patted him on the head. Then they were on their way to another street corner. On this corner, three guys were busy smoking blunts without a care in the world. The black Lexus stopped short at the corner. DeShaun and Seven stepped out of the vehicle with a job to do. Seven's head was on cloud nine. DeShaun looked at Seven and nodded.

"Hand over the cash, fools!" Seven demanded. The three thugs looked at Seven and erupted into laughter. They didn't even recognize DeShaun standing right behind him. They were high as a kite. Embarrassment overwhelmed Seven as if he were in class being picked on by the other students. Seven looked to DeShaun. "Handle it, Seven. You know what to do," said DeShaun.

Seven turned back to the three thugs laughing their asses off. Seven's heart raced. He had to do something quick and think fast. He had to get the money from these clowns. Seven looked around. DeShaun and Skeeter observed Seven's actions. They both smiled and allowed Seven to handle it his way, by any means. Then a large glass bottle came crashing over one of the thugs' head. Blood dripped profusely down his face. The thought of a bloody scene in a horror movie popped in Seven's head. At this point, Seven didn't give a fuck. The thug screamed and shook like a leaf. He felt the warmth of the blood and placed his hand on his head.

"Where the fuck is the cash? DeShaun's cash, motherfucker!" Seven shouted. The other two thugs' jaw dropped as they saw DeShaun standing right behind him. The cowards trembled.

"DeShaun, holy shit! I didn't notice you were there," One of the thugs said as his voice quivered.

"You heard what the little man said. Hand over my money!" hollered DeShaun. The thug with the bloodied head gave Seven all his money.

Seven snatched it. "Yuck!" Seven said as he tried to avoid touching the bloody cash. The other two drug runners immediately gave Seven their cash. Seven grabbed it and smiled. Seven never felt so much power in his life. Money was nice. But the power felt greater.

Back in the Lexus, Skeeter had his one hand on the steering wheel as he looked in the backseat at Seven counting a bloody stack of cash. "One hundred, two, four, six, eight. One hundred eighty," Seven counted for DeShaun. Then DeShaun recounted the money and agreed.. He gave Seven a high five.

As time went on, Seven graduated junior high school. He was thirteen years of age, handsome, and his body structure became stocky. Seven and his entire graduating class threw up their caps. They cheered and rejoiced. The graduates received hugs and kisses from their families and friends. Seven swaggered out of the auditorium with Chad. Ingrid and Mrs. Richardson waited with gifts and cards.

"My baby, Seven. I'm so proud of you," Ingrid cried. Chad received hugs and kisses from his family. "I'm the proudest mom in the entire world," Ingrid said.

"Seven!" Seven turned and he saw DeShaun. They exchanged high fives and embraced.

"What's up, DeShaun?"

"Congratulations, man," said DeShaun.

Ingrid's smile turned upside down. Seven couldn't wait to hang out with DeShaun. He wanted his mother to come along just for lunch. But Ingrid refused. Seven didn't like the idea of his mother always shying away from an event, especially when it came to her son.

"Are you sure you don't want to go, Mrs. Miles?" DeShaun asked.

"I'll be fine," Ingrid said. She kissed Seven and walked away. "I'll see you at home."

Seven ran behind his mother and blocked her path. "Mom, why don't you come hang out with us?" Seven asked.

"No!"

"This is my day," Seven said.

"This is not only your day. This is your life, Seven. DeShaun's a big drug pusher," Ingrid said.

"If it weren't for him. We'd be out in the streets, Mom."

Tears streamed down Ingrid's face. She sobbed.

Seven comforted his mother and couldn't stand to see his mother in pain. *How much pain is my mother going to endure? I've got to do something to make her happy,* Seven thought. Ingrid pushed Seven and stormed away. Seven looked on as his mother headed into the distance. He wanted to cry so badly but had to hold his feelings in.

DeShaun put his hand on Seven's shoulder. "Is everything all right, man?" DeShaun asked.

"Not really," Seven said in a depressed tone.

"Don't worry. Your mother will be just fine. Cheer up. It's your day, Seven." DeShaun laughed.

That night, Seven and DeShaun went for a drive through the beautiful neighborhood where the rich lived. The mansions stood very majestically behind the iron gates with well-trimmed hedges. This placed looked very familiar to Seven. He looked up at the street signs, but none of them read Old Westbury Road. They were some other streets' names. DeShaun talked about moving up in the world. And his goal was to become the biggest dealer on the street and then get out before he gets caught by the authorities. DeShaun puffed on a Philly blunt as always. He gave it to Seven. Seven took a puff of the blunt without choking. He blew rings into the air.

"That's some good shit, right?" DeShaun guffawed. Seven snickered. "Take the wheel, yo!" DeShaun said. DeShaun put on the brakes of the black Lexus. Seven and DeShaun switched sides. DeShaun took the passenger's seat as Seven occupied the driver's seat.

"Do you really trust me with your ride?" Seven asked.

"Why would you ask a question like that?"

"I'm just a kid."

"Drive this motherfucker, Seven." DeShaun cursed.

Seven took deep breath, and his hands became sweaty. He then thought of his fantasies driving, especially when it came to speed. There's no reason for him to be nervous. Seven could do this. Seven looked at DeShaun. DeShaun relaxed in the passenger's seat, waiting to be driven home. Seven had his foot on the brake as he started up the engine. Then he put the car into drive and hit the gas. The vehicle took off as Seven's driving was a bit awkward. While on the road, Seven picked up his speed. DeShaun constantly watched Seven as he drove his baby. "Seven, don't mess up my car," DeShaun said nervously.

"I won't," Seven replied. Then Seven's driving became smoother, and it was a pleasure.

DeShaun praised Seven. "In about a year or two, I'll get you a car."

"That's cool."

The black Lexus parked in the driveway of DeShaun's home. It was a beautiful house. It wasn't luxurious, but it was comfortable. Later, Seven sipped on a soda as he sat in a recliner in the living room. *The Jeffersons* played on television, an old sitcom. "For you," DeShaun said as he gave Seven three hundred dollars.

"Thanks."

"You've proven yourself. My rules are, when a thug is in training and succeeds, he gets to mingle with the lions and the wolves," said DeShaun with a dead-hard expression. Seven knew this was like stepping into a forest of wolves or the African plans with a pride of lions.

An hour later, Seven sat at the dining room table with these wolves that have been in and out of prison or have spent several years there. DeShaun introduced Seven to his crew. None of them were crazy about dealing with a little kid. Because they felt Seven may fuck things up. Chief, Ronell, Tool, Nugget, Pop, Napoleon, TaTu, Raheem, Hippolito, and Polo were a pack of wolves. Speaking of Polo, Seven and Chad haven't seen him in a great while. He was locked up for getting in an altercation with another motorist. The posse frowned upon Seven. Yes, they witnessed Seven and Boo fight. Polo missed that big event. He told DeShaun that he knew Seven and Chad. But he agreed with the rest of the posse. Polo wasn't too crazy about having Seven mingling with them. But whatever DeShaun says goes. His entourage had to respect his wishes.

When Seven got home, he saw Ingrid sleeping in the recliner. He kissed his mother as she slept. The Christian Bible fellowship played on the television. Seven saw his mother was at peace. The only peace she had was when she slept. Seven placed one hundred dollars on the coffee table. He turned out the light and went to bed.

Chapter 18

July 27 was here again, the big one four for Seven. The enormous celebration took place at a club with DeShaun and his entourage. Loud rap music played. The place was decorated with black and silver balloons, plastic plates and utensils in black and silver, and everything in sight. Seven wore his black Dickies with his black construction boots. His guests wore black clothing but looked very nice. DeShaun threw this party for Seven and made sure it was big. Over two hundred guests attended Seven's celebration. Most of them, he didn't know. Without a doubt, Seven got to know them. DeShaun introduced Seven to them as his son, the son that he regained. DeShaun wanted Seven right by his side.

DeShaun, Seven, and Chad drank. Chad told Seven and DeShaun he wanted to go by the street name Magnum. Chad thought it was cool. Seven and DeShaun agreed. Then DeShaun escorted Seven into the VIP section of the club. DeShaun and some of his posse sat at a long table. Seven could tell that it was another meeting—business meeting—on his birthday. Business never stopped regardless of the circumstances. Seven sat down in a chair at the end of the table as DeShaun took his place at the head of it. There was a known drug dealer by the name of Corey, who was stealing DeShaun's customers, crackheads that is. DeShaun wanted to approach Corey so he could move his operation elsewhere. DeShaun wanted it to be peaceful so the authorities wouldn't stick their noses in it if any trouble emerged.

Seven was going to meet with another known drug kingpin. This was some shit. Deep shit. DeShaun learned all this while growing up on the rough streets of Brownsville, Brooklyn. DeShaun's mother was never around because she was busy trying to keep a roof over their heads and clothes on their backs. DeShaun didn't like his environment growing up. When he was eight years old, the NYPD had a summer program where they would take kids from rough areas of Queens, Brooklyn, and the Bronx out to Long Island or Westchester County to stay with a family for the summer so they could get a taste of the rural and suburban life. DeShaun never forgot the family he spent the summer with in King's Park, Long Island. They seemed rich. They had a big house, lots of green grass and trees, and an enormous backyard with an in-ground swimming pool. That inspired DeShaun to live on Long Island. But his choice of career wasn't a good one. Just listening to the details of the conversation that was gonna take place inspired Seven.

A couple of days later, a dim, smoke-filled bar with alcoholic beverage neon light advertisements gave it an urban feel. A few guys sat at the bar, smoking and chugging down their beers. There was cursing as usual and playing pool that was right in the back. Like in the game of chess, the henchmen must protect the king. When it came to DeShaun's entourage, it was exactly that. Polo, Tool, and Ronell swaggered in first, with Nugget, Chief, TaTu behind, then came Seven with DeShaun behind him. Napoleon was right behind DeShaun. Two henchmen were on DeShaun's sides. Then there were three extra rows of henchmen behind. They came in peace. But when they entered the bar, it caused tension. The bartender felt something was going to go down. DeShaun's posse made their way toward the rear of the bar. The guys at the pool table saw DeShaun's crew coming their way. They immediately stopped playing their game. DeShaun had that much power, and Seven saw more of it.

There was a booth adjacent to the pool table where thirty-something-year-old Corey Mitchell, a funny-looking, brown-skinned, African-American male with a lazy eye, resided with two Latina women by his side. The three of them giggled, drank, and enjoyed each other's company until DeShaun and his posse made their presence known.

"What's up, Corey?" DeShaun greeted. Polo, Tool, Ronell, and the other three henchmen parted ways as DeShaun approached Corey. He tried to greet Corey with a high five.

Corey made a sour expression and felt threatened due to DeShaun and his entourage. "What the fuck is this? Why all the motherfuckers!"

"Be cool, Corey! You know me!"

"No, I don't know you. I know of you!"

"And I know of you!" DeShaun responded. He pulled up a chair as his posse gathered behind him. Seven was by DeShaun's side, just like a son's loyalty to his father. Then Corey's henchmen came to his defense at the last minute. They drew their firearms at DeShaun and his posse. They backed off. Seven's heart was ready to jump out of his chest. It raced a mile a second. He hid behind Polo. Seven shook like a leaf. *God, this is dangerous! Forgive me! Please don't let any bullets fly! Please!* Seven prayed in his heart. Maybe this was his time to meet his grandmother and father in heaven.

Due to God's grace, no bullets flew, just some bad words exchanged between the two kingpins. "Call your goons off, Corey! I come in peace, mother fucker." DeShaun pleaded sarcastically. Corey guffawed. Seven's heart pounded in his chest. Then all of Corey's goons backed off and withdrew their firearms. Seven took a deep breath as his heart pumped at a normal pace.

"Damn, you fools were shook!" Corey joked.

DeShaun rolled his eyes and got down to business. Seven then scrambled back to DeShaun's side. DeShaun indirectly insulted Corey about his operation needing new management. Corey knew where DeShaun was coming from and didn't like what he was hearing. DeShaun wanted to buy him out. Seven easily understood the conversation. It wasn't difficult. It was simple economics. Seven never knew about economics. He was just a kid. He learned from the best.

As DeShaun kept on egging about Corey's business operations, Corey became more and more annoyed. So did Seven. Corey wouldn't give in to DeShaun. *Why doesn't Corey just take his advice and get the fuck out!* Seven thought to himself. Unfortunately, it didn't work. Corey cursed DeShaun out. DeShaun took his vicious words like a man. *If that were me. I would have shot him!* Seven thought to himself again.

DeShaun and his crew left Corey's establishment in peace. There was no violence, just profane words thrown at DeShaun. DeShaun wasn't going to give up until he's king of the streets. Later that night, the black Lexus pulled up at a car garage. Hippolito peered from behind the open hood of a Toyota Camry, fixing the wires. DeShaun and Seven hopped out of the black Lexus as they approached Hippolito. As soon as Seven and DeShaun stopped at the garage, he knew this was going to be something good. DeShaun gave Hippolito a high five, then Seven and Hippolito gave the same. DeShaun's gift to Seven was for Hippolito to teach Seven everything that he wanted to know about cars, anywhere from oil changes to adding pounds of boost for speed—that's if you had a sports car. This was right up Seven's alley. Seven was going to learn about vehicles hands-on, then hit the street corners and make those pickups.

Seven was automatically promoted. He had the authority to tell guys on the corners what to do. Seven sat in the front seat of a navy-blue Suburban while Polo drove it. Seven went to every corner and made the pickups. The drug runners were now under Seven's super-vision, and he was only fourteen. This was embarrassing to them that they had to answer to a child. All Seven wanted was the money handed over. As for Chad, a.k.a. Magnum, he hung on to the corner, slinging. Magnum wasn't so lucky. He didn't get to hang out with the boss. But Magnum got to rub elbows with the boss's so-called son, which was a good thing.

That night, Seven came home. Ingrid became more and more distant from him. Ingrid really didn't have much to say. But she dealt with the situation. The money she took from Seven, DeShaun was behind. Ingrid was more responsible than he was because she was Seven's mother. Seven tried talking to Ingrid, but it turned into an argument. Ingrid didn't approve of the situation. She didn't want her utilities shut off. Due to the good amount of cash that Seven brought home, Ingrid ceased seeking employment for the moment. She wasn't gonna stick with this thing Seven had going. Later, Seven headed to bed and gazed up at the ceiling. He heard a televangelist on television. Seven made his way to Ingrid's bedroom. She sat up in her bed as she read her Bible. Seven watched her as he could see the comfort in her face. Ingrid then saw Seven leaning in the doorway. She reached her hand out to him. Seven swaggered to Ingrid like a toddler reaching to his mother. Ingrid hugged him. Seven felt small, like a baby again. Then he saw the photos of him and Angelika with Rocco next to the Jaguar. Seven grimaced. Ingrid talked about how she missed Angelika. And the thirty-first of July was coming.

The next morning, Seven smelled waffles and coffee in the atmosphere. The birds chirped as the sun beamed through his window. Seven opened his eyes with a smile on his face. Moments later, he swaggered into the kitchen and saw Ingrid cooking. Seven kissed her on the cheek. He went to the refrigerator and poured himself a glass of orange juice. He gulped it down then released an enormous belch. Ingrid gave Seven a dirty look. Seven didn't apologize for his rudeness. He sat down at the table and gazed at his Todd MacKenzie bike. He hasn't ridden it for a while since he met met DeShaun. Seven wanted one last ride before his advanced in life. Seven knew where he could head off to. But, he needed his energy in order to do so. He shoved the waffles in his mouth and was ready to conquer the world.

Moments later, Seven pedaled fast on his bike. It was a bit awkward for him because he was getting older and set his mind on four wheels. A car that is. A muscle car. This bike shit was for kids. It was time to move on. Seven rode alongside of the road, where cars passed by him honking their horns. Then Seven halted at a railroad crossing where the gate was down. The mechanical bell rang. There was a long line of cars that were waiting to cross to the other side of the tracks, including a couple of bicyclists. Then a diesel locomotive chugged along the tracks with rapid speed. Its horn tooted throughout the air. This was where Seven made his entrance into another world, a world he once knew and liked, but freaked him out at times. At the railroad crossing, Seven knew there was a meaning behind that railroad crossing. He wasn't good enough to become a professional race driver, become an entrepreneur or dwell within high society as one of them. Seven felt that way just by that railroad gate being closed.

The train passed. The gate opened as the railroad crossing signaled green. The cars and the bicyclists made their way across the tracks. And so did Seven. He raced as fast as he could so he wouldn't miss what he was looking for. Seven made his way on to Old Westbury Road. Seven rode past the large well-trimmed hedges and grass. And then Seven slowed down his speed and came to the large black iron fence. The security guards where on the job. There was no way Seven could probably see Angelika. *How is Angelika doing? What is she doing? How pretty is she now?* Seven wondered to himself. One of the guards at the iron fence noticed Seven lingering on his bike near the property. The guard knew Seven looked familiar, but he didn't bother to alert any of his colleagues or police. Seven knew the guard was giving him the evil eye. Seven didn't want to cause problems for himself or his mother. He headed back home. He pedaled as fast as he could.

When Seven began freshman year in high school, he knew some of the juniors and seniors. Some knew what Seven did on the side. Some seniors wanted Seven to provide them with drugs for the parties that they threw, some rich kids. Seven denied selling drugs and brushed them off. If they really got on his nerves, he'd curse them out. Then they became afraid. Very afraid. They backed off and never bothered him again. One thing DeShaun taught Seven was to never deal with rich kids because they'll get you into some serious shit. Seven kept it street. He never took DeShaun's business elsewhere unless DeShaun wanted to. Seven just studied hard and checked out the pretty girls in school.

There was one girl named LaToya, who was a fast ass. She swore every guy wanted her. LaToya was wrong. Dead wrong. Seven didn't. But she wanted Seven. Every time Seven and Magnum swaggered down the hallway, she threw her breasts in his face. Seven wasn't taken by her at all, because LaToya was a hood rat. She wore synthetic multicolored weaves. It wasn't becoming at all. LaToya dressed in extremely tight jeans with her butt poking out for the world to see.

She wore low-cut tops that showed cleavage. Latoya wanted Seven badly. But Seven didn't respond to her even when she said "Hello." Latoya took it that Seven was playing hard to get. But Seven wasn't playing at all. She wasn't good enough for him. He was too proud for a fourteen-year-old. Most fourteen-year-old guys would go crazy if a girl like LaToya was up in their face.

Then LaToya turned to Magnum. She smiled and saw Magnum was a cutie. Then Magnum kissed her on the cheek. They both held hands. Seven observed LaToya's promiscuous behavior. Magnum gave Seven a high five. Seven watched as Magnum and LaToya headed to the second floor. Seven proceeded to class. The late bell rang.

In English, the class read *The Catcher in the Rye* novel. Seven was bored by it as he always did with school. Seven looked among the large class of students; Seven spotted her, another girl, similar to Dilbrina. She was a beautiful and dark-brown-complexioned girl, about fifteen years old, with a nice short haircut and sported nice clothes; her name Gwendolyn Norton. She was just as bored as Seven was. Gwendolyn's eye wandered around the classroom. They caught each other's eye. Gwendolyn gave Seven a smile from ear to ear. Seven then returned that smile.

After class, the students grabbed their books and exited the classroom off to their next class. Seven scrambled over to Gwendolyn, and he already knew her name but wanted to know more about her. Gwendolyn smiled as she gave Seven her phone number. As time went on, Seven and Gwendolyn were an item. They dated, met each other's families, were intimate, etc. In between Seven juggling school and working on cars with Hippolito, a relationship with Gwendolyn and slinging dope for DeShaun became challenging. But Seven had to deal with it the best way he could.

Then junior year came. Seven and Gwendolyn were together for two years and looking forward to starting a life together. Seven was in love with Gwendolyn. With the money Seven hustled on the streets, he had a surprise for Gwendolyn. Seven walked her to class and gave her a passionate kiss before parting their ways..

That night, Junbug, Raheem, Hakeem, and some other hood-lums lingered on the corner where a bodega conducted business.

Junbug was a tall, slender guy in his midtwenties; he wore black, which made him look even thinner. He puffed on a cigarette. The headlights shined off oncoming vehicle. It honked. Junbug ran to the vehicle to exchange drugs for money. Then the navy-blue Suburban truck pulled up to the curb. Seven hopped out. "Where's the cash!" Seven demanded. Skeeter sat in the driver's seat and kept an eye on Seven taking care of business. He peered through his rearview mirror. Skeeter cracked a smile as he saw the drug runners obeying Seven. The drug runners handed over their pay to Seven. They lined up one behind another. Seven counted some cash that was given to him by Junbug. Seven counted twelve hundred dollars. Seven then gave Junbug his cut. Junbug then went back to business. Hakeem gave his cash to Seven. Seven counted as Hakeem tapped his feet on the concrete. Then Seven halted his counting and noticed that Hakeem was nervous.

"What's the problem?" Seven asked. Hakeem shook his head. Seven then proceeded to count the cash and halted his counting again. "You're short, Hakeem! One hundred dollars!" Seven said. Seven became irate and glared at Hakeem. Seven's heart raced as the tone in his voice became more and more aggressive. Hakeem needed the money for his daughter's tuition. When it came down to doing the pickups, you had to pay in full. If you need some more time or a loan, just ask. Don't try to steal from your payout. But Hakeem did a stupid thing. Seven pimp-slapped Hakeem. Hakeem cried like a girl. Seven immediately stopped himself and showed him some sympathy. Seven couldn't bear to hear a man cry.

Skeeter peered through his rearview mirror and observed Seven's actions. Skeeter was disappointed in Seven because he wasn't hard enough on Hakeem. Skeeter continued watching Seven take care of the other payouts. Then Seven swaggered to the car. He hopped in and slammed the door. "What the fuck is wrong with you, Seven? Did you get soft over night!" Skeeter bitched.

"Soft? I wasn't soft back there! Are you fuckin' kidding me!" Seven replied.

"I'm gonna have to talk to DeShaun about this!"

"About what?" Then the Suburban jeep sped off into the night as the wheels screeched.

Back at the minimart, several robust adult Rottweilers roamed the basement as DeShaun and his posse counted earnings from the store to drug sales in his office. Chief was third in command when it came to DeShaun's business. He took care of counting up the cash and did it when Skeeter wasn't available. Chief would also do pickups on the corners and made some bigger transactions when it came to a drug supplier, someone bigger than LaLo.

Pop, Nugget, and Tool watched the drug room. They received the cocaine there, and then it was made into crack cocaine. The three of them guarded like watchdogs as they carried Uzis in their hands. Ronell, Napoleon, and Polo took care of business in the store. There were stock boys and some cashiers that rang up customers' food. It was a busy atmosphere. You would have thought that Christmas was coming. Out of nowhere, Skeeter stormed into the establishment first. He was pissed. Seven then stormed in behind him. You could see the sour expression on his face. "You're gonna have to explain yourself to DeShaun!" Skeeter shouted. He headed to the back as Seven followed. Ronell and Napoleon glared at each other, trying to figure out what happened.

In DeShaun's office, Seven explained what he had done. DeShaun listened to Seven's every words and didn't feel he did anything wrong. Seven held the situation right. Skeeter became irate. Skeeter continued to go at Seven with such hostility. Skeeter grabbed Seven by the collar as they wrestled to the floor. DeShaun and Chief intervened. It was chaos. DeShaun then stopped Skeeter as he pointed a nine-millimeter handgun in his face.

"That's enough! Seven did fine!" DeShaun said as he pressed the barrel of the pistol hard in Skeeter's forehead. "I know you don't want take a bullet over something as petty as this!" DeShaun stated. DeShaun raised an eyebrow for Skeeter to take his advice. Skeeter then threw his arms up to drop the whole thing. "You owe Seven an apology," DeShaun said.

"Are you for real?" Skeeter scoffed with an "I can't believe this shit" expression on his face.

"Yes, I'm for real!" DeShaun nodded.

Skeeter inhaled and then shook Seven's hand. Seven and Skeeter put their differences aside and went on to doing business as usual.

Chapter 19

I t was Saturday noon, where the sun beamed as the birds sung their usual melodies. Seven had a surprise for Gwendolyn. Seven drove to Gwendolyn's house in the latest Volkswagen Jetta. The ride was black and very sharp looking. He sped on the highway as he usually did. He weaved in and out of traffic. Motorists became pissed off with Seven. One motorist gave him the finger. Seven laughed it off. He loved upsetting drivers by showing off his ride. But Seven had no time for that right now. He had to get to his baby, his other baby. Gwendolyn.

Few minutes later, Seven stopped short at the curb as the wheels squealed on the Volkswagen Jetta. Seven ran up to the door and rang the bell. A dog barked in the distance. Gwendolyn's mother, Mrs. Norton, answered the door. She wasn't too crazy about Seven seeing her daughter. Gwendolyn made her way to the door as she gently brushed her mother aside. Seven and Gwendolyn kissed. Mrs. Norton backed away with a look of disgust on her face. She didn't know for a fact, but Mrs. Norton had a strong feeling Seven was up to no good. Seven felt the negative vibes from Mrs. Norton.

Later, Seven drove as he held Gwendolyn's hand as she resided in the passenger's seat. The engine of the Volkswagen Jetta was weak. Seven listened to its sound. "Do you hear that engine, Gwen?" Seven asked. Gwendolyn shrugged her shoulders and had a dumb look on her face. She couldn't comprehend what Seven was getting at. "What do you mean, Seven?" Gwendolyn asked. Seven knew she didn't understand where he was coming. He tried to explain the sound of the car engine that was music to his ears. Gwendolyn still didn't get it and turned the radio on. R&B music played. Seven glared at her as he saw it as disrespect. He just brushed it off. "Maybe, she'll understand later." Seven thought to himself.

Seven and Gwendolyn stopped at the auto shop. Seven beeped the horn of his Jetta. The garage door opened. Hippolito came out in his soiled garage suit as he wiped his dirty, oily hands in the towel. The Volkswagen Jetta pulled into the garage. Seven could tell that Gwendolyn didn't get what he was about, something that interested him, which was racing cars. Seven jumped out of the Jetta, and he gave Hippolito a high five.

"What's up, Seven?" Hippolito greeted him.

"My baby needs a bit of adjustments." Seven said. Gwendolyn hurried out of the Jetta. She looked around, somewhat annoyed. "This won't take long, baby," Seven said. Gwendolyn smiled and nodded. She wasn't feeling this whole car thing. She found a place to sit down as she had a glum expression on her face. Seven strapped down the Jetta to a dyno. He popped the hood up and added the nitrous oxide system, better known as NOS, to the engine. Hippolito and his colleagues assisted Seven in any way they could. The turbo engine rumbled as the wheels spun slowly and then gained speed. The computer read the car's performance due to speed and horsepower. The computer read 500 miles per hour (mph) and 710 rear wheel horsepower (rwhp). Seven shook his head as he was satisfied with his ride.

Moments later, the Volkswagen Jetta backed out of the garage. Hippolito and his colleagues cheered Seven on. Seven then did a burnout with his fixed baby. Seven placed his foot on the brake and gas at the same time. Massive smoke emerged from the rear tires of the Jetta. The new-improved engine roared. The Jetta zoomed down the street with enormous smoke in its rear. Seven swung the car back around and sped to the garage. Gwendolyn smiled and applauded along with Hippolito and the auto technicians. Seven noticed Gwendolyn started to lighten up.

Night made its presence known as the Volkswagen Jetta thundered along Sunrise Highway with its headlights gleaming. The engine roared throughout the whole car. It was music to Seven's ears. Now, Gwendolyn got it. She loved the ride as she wore her seatbelt, of course. Seven could see it in her face. The Jetta was lightweight. The ride was smooth. Seven weaved in between cars. They honked their horns. Seven hoped highway patrol wasn't around.

"Seven, do you think we'll miss the late movie?" Gwendolyn asked.

"We'll be there in time for the coming attractions!" Seven said. Seven and Gwendolyn smiled at each other. Then he focused his eyes on the road.

Seven's ride made it possible. Seven and Gwendolyn made it in time for the coming attractions at the movies. The couple maneuvered their way through the crowded theater. Seven and Gwendolyn grasped hands as they held a large bucket of popcorn, a large soda, and candy. They took a seat in the corner and cuddled up as the movie began. Gwendolyn fed Seven some popcorn. Then Seven started to caress Gwendolyn's breasts. She pushed Seven's hand away. Seven respected her wishes and got a passionate kiss instead. That was good enough.

The movie was an old kung fu flick from the sixties. Seven liked watching kung fu movies from the latest to the most recent like Rush Hour, Rumble in the Bronx, and Romeo Must Die. After the movie, Seven sped through a fast food drive-through with his new-boosted Volkswagen Jetta. The turbo engine bellowed as the wheels screeched. Then it made a short stop. Seven rolled the window down as the cashier took his order. Seven wanted to talk to Gwendolyn about their future together. He just let Gwendolyn talk about what college she wanted to go to and what she was going to major in. Gwendolyn was about something and having goals in life. It was all about her, but that was okay. Gwendolyn was about something and pretty too. The only thing she knew was Seven worked as a stock boy at a minimart on Sunrise Highway in Hempstead.

Later, the Volkswagen Jetta pulled into a driveway of a house. The engine rumbled and then shut down as its headlights dimmed. Seven and Gwen exited the car. Seven could see the wonder in Gwendolyn's eyes. The house was a nice middle-class home where any man could start a family. Speaking of this home, DeShaun hooked Seven up with this property for putting in work for him on the streets. DeShaun had several real estate properties under his belt. Seven opened the front door with his key. Seven and Gwendolyn stepped into the living room; it was small and cozy. It was furnished with a sofa, loveseat, and recliner. A flat screen television hung on the wall. There was a fireplace and some pictures on the walls. There were photos of Seven as a child to the present time and his mother and other family members.

Gwendolyn strutted to the center of the room and looked around. She nodded in agreement with its decor. "Your mom did a good job with the place," Gwendolyn said.

"Thanks," Seven said as he gave his mother credit for beautifying his home. But, he knew who was really responsible for that.

"When do I get to meet her?" Gwendolyn asked.

"Soon. This is for you, Gwen." Seven said as he smirked.

"What! Are you kidding, Seven?" Gwen said shockingly. She strutted over to Seven and just gazed into his eyes. Seven saw Gwendolyn's watery eyes as she became emotional. They embraced each other and wouldn't let go. To Seven, it felt as if they were becoming husband and wife. Seven didn't want the baby mama drama type of relationship. That was bullshit. Most guys saw marriage as a prison. It's not a prison unless you're with the right person. Marriage was a huge step. Seven and Gwendolyn were still kids. For now, they just played house.

Seven and Gwendolyn did their daily routine. They went to school and worked. Gwendolyn's job was part time, and she got home before Seven did. She made dinner for both of them. Then he arrived home. Seven and Gwendolyn ate and then made love. Then Seven headed to the corners, doing the pickups and reporting to DeShaun. Seven returned home late that night. Seven wanted to fuck some more, but Gwendolyn was already asleep.

This went on for a while until their schedules got in the way. They had no time for lovemaking anymore. Seven's mind was on making money, busting his ass, risking his life. He visited his mother about five times a week. Seven's uncle Darren was home from the military. Darren spent years in combat in the Middle East. Seven and his uncle Darren already got into heated arguments. Ingrid told what Seven was doing. Since Darren's home now, Ingrid didn't have to take any more of the dirty money.

Seven set his mind on his car. Hippolito helped Seven to reconstruct the engine of his Volkswagen Jetta, which took almost a day and a half. Seven did away with the NOS. He installed a larger air filter to the engine. This was what gave his ride just as much speed or more than the NOS.

A few months of Seven and Gwendolyn living together, she became suspicious. Gwendolyn believed Seven had another girlfriend. Plus Gwendolyn didn't get to meet Seven's mother. What happened to that? Seven wasn't ashamed of Gwendolyn; it was just that he was participating in illegal activities in the streets. She couldn't take it. This was a big mistake. Gwendolyn already packed her things and moved out of her mother's house. Now she had to talk her way back home. Seven agreed. He figured they were moving too fast. Seven and Gwendolyn gave their last kiss and went their separate ways.

Chapter 20

It's been a few months since Seven and Gwendolyn called it quits. The temperature was eleven degrees and dropping. Extreme cold and winds whistled during the month of mid-January. Seven slumbered in his warm bed as the heater fan ran all night. His bedroom was like a hot summer day. Seven wore only his boxers and had light blankets on his bed. He opened his eyes to the high-pitched winds whistling. He sprung from his bed to the window. Ice and frost overwhelmed the entire neighborhood. He wasn't surprised at the type of wintery weather New York got, especially Long Island and upstate. Seven eyed his ice-covered Volkswagen Jetta in the driveway.

Later, Seven made it his business to check on his mother. A sheet of ice blanketed Seven's pathway from his door to the driveway where his Jetta was parked. Seven took baby steps as he made his way towards his ride with caution. His black Timberland construction boots were still good as Seven wore his thermal garage jumpsuit. That's all Seven wore. It kept him warm. In Seven's hands, he carried a shovel and an ice pick to get his ride out of this wintery shit. Seven checked the tires of his Volkswagen and saw the ice engulfed the entire wheel. He used the ice pick to free his wheels. As Seven chopped at the ice, it flew off the tires in small and large, cold, sharp chunks. Seven closed his eyes and held his head away to protect himself. He then did the same for the other three tires. Then Seven removed the ice from the front and back windshield. Seven went to the driver's side of his car and opened the door. The interior felt like an icebox. Seven sat in the driver's seat. Due to Seven's thermal garage jumpsuit, he couldn't feel the cold on his ass. He put the key in the ignition. Seven tried to start the vehicle up, but it wouldn't start. He tried and tried again. No luck. Then he stepped out of the car and popped the hood. He saw that the engine had frost on it. Seven was determined to give his girl strength. He poured antifreeze in the engine. Then he tried to start his baby up again. Success. She roared like a lion. Seven revved her engine as she continued to roar.

Then the Jetta backed out of the driveway carefully. Seven knew that he couldn't speed up. The Volkswagen Jetta turned on to the icy road. Seven drove very slowly and with ease. As he drove down the road, every tree, bush, sidewalk, and house Father Winter didn't miss. Icicles hung from every house like Christmas ornaments. It reminded him of Christmas that just recently passed. Sanitation and emergency vehicles were helping residents with their homes.

Moments later, Seven made it on the highway. The traffic was slow, but it was moving, which was a good thing. Another good thing was, raindrops began to beat against the windshield. It helped to melt the ice faster. But there would be slush everywhere. Seven put on his windshield wipers. It made a loud squeaking sound. Seven looked to his right as he saw a gentleman having car trouble. Emergency lights flashed on a tow truck. It passed Seven with tremendous speed. Seven proceeded on.

Later, Seven made it to his mother's house. He usually parked in the driveway of his mother's home, the home where he grew up. Someone else was parked there. "Who the fuck is that?" Seven mumbled to himself. Seven stopped short in front of his childhood home. Seven swaggered out of the Jetta. He slammed the door as he swaggered through the driveway. He looked inside the mango-colored Saturn. He saw metal military tags that dangled from the rearview mirror. "Darren!" Seven murmured to himself. Seven was pissed his uncle Darrin had the balls to take his parking space. *Who the fuck does he think he is?* Seven thought.

Seven still had the keys to his mother's house. He opened the door with his keys. Ingrid lounged in the recliner, watching Creflo Dollar on television. The entire house was extremely warm. The aroma of a roast beef was in the air. Seven was thankful that someone else was helping out his mother. But Seven felt defeated. He stormed past his mother while behind her as Ingrid lounged in the recliner. Seven stood in the kitchen entrance for a second. His Uncle Darren was six two and over two-hundred pounds of military strength. Seven didn't allow that to intimidate him. Darren boasted the roast with a boaster. It sizzled.

Darren looked over his shoulder from the oven and saw Seven standing there. Darren didn't greet his nephew with a hug or tell of his experiences in the marines. Darren pushed the roast beef in the oven and closed the door. He threw the potholder down on the counter. The two men glared at each other like two lions fighting to be king.

"The weather doesn't even stop you, does it?" Darren asked in a stern tone.

Seven swaggered to the refrigerator and grabbed a soda. He cracked the can opened and took one big gulp and tossed it in the trash can. Seven exited as Darren followed him. He headed into his bedroom, his childhood room, that was where he began to pack some clothes. His uncle marched in. Seven glared at him. "May I help you, Darren?" Seven asked in a stern tone.

"Who do you work for?" Darren asked. Seven ignored his uncle's question and continued to pack his belongings. "Who is DeShaun?"

"That's none of your fuckin' business!" Seven cursed.

"It is my business when it concerns this family. You're putting my sister in jeopardy!"

"There's nothing to worry about. You're here now, superman," Seven said. Seven finished packing his things and swaggered toward the door. Darren blocked his path. "Get the fuck out of the way, Darren," Seven threatened.

"You should have been drafted!"

"I don't want to be like you, walking around here like someone stuck a broomstick up my ass!"

Darren grabbed Seven by the throat as the two wrestled to the floor. Seven pushed Darren off him. Darren's back slammed against the wall. *Thud.* Seven scrambled out of his bedroom before Darren could get to him. Darren wound up knocking down Ingrid as she came in to see what the commotion was all about. Ingrid hit the floor like a ton of bricks. Ingrid looked at Seven. "What's going on?" Ingrid cried.

Seven hopped in his Volkswagen Jetta. Seven inserted the key into the ignition and started his girl up. He didn't bother to rev her engine like he usually did. The Jetta blasted off as Ingrid and Darren stormed out of the residence. Seven viewed his uncle's dumb military ass attempting to chase his ride. *Uncle Darren thinks he's Rambo! That's what the military will do to a motherfucker! Fuck your mind up! Make you think you're someone else!* Seven thought to himself as it screamed in his mind. No luck in the world could ever catch Seven and his baby.

Due to the altercation Seven and Darren got into, Seven forgot about the icy roads ahead. Seven proceeded to speed on the slippery road. The Volkswagen Jetta held up just fine. Then it hit Seven—the roads were icy. Then he decreased the speed of his vehicle. Seven headed to the nearest grocery store. He parked in the parking lot.

Meanwhile, Seven held a basket in his hand with a few things for his mother. Ingrid always did her own shopping when she had money. Seven went through aisles. He picked up some orange juice, apples, crackers, potatoes, milk, and Ensure. He wanted to put down the basket and walk out of the store. But he couldn't do it. Ingrid was his mother. She always did things for him. He headed to the cashier. The scanner beeped on each of the items being rung up. The noise was like an insect buzzing in his ear. It annoyed Seven a bit. Seven gave her the money as he packed his own items and swaggered out of the supermarket. "Keep the change," Seven said.

Back at Ingrid's house, she and Darren ate the roast beef that he cooked. Keys jingled at the door, and Seven swaggered in the house. Seven saw his mother and uncle eating at the table. The two were silent as Seven swaggered toward the kitchen. Darren stormed away from the table. And again, Seven and his uncle were engaged in another scuffle even before Seven could put the groceries down. The plastic bags fell to the floor. Seven and Darren wrestled to the floor. Seven punched Darren in the face. Then Darren hurled a punch to Seven's chin. Ingrid grabbed the phone to call 911.

"This is the 911 operator. What's your emergency?" the operator asked.

"My son and my brother are at it!" Ingrid shouted. The commotion could be heard in the background.

"Are there any weapons?" the 911 operator asked.

"No," Ingrid answered.

Surprisingly, Seven pushed his uncle off him. Seven brandished his nine-millimeter at Darren. Darren automatically put his hands in the air. Seven knew he wasn't gonna shoot his uncle. That's unless Darren came at him again.

"I'll shoot your motherfuckin' ass!" Seven hollered.

The 911 operator heard Seven's voice in the background loud and clear. "Ma'am, I thought you said there were no weapons involved. Ma'am?" the 911 operator asked. Ingrid didn't respond to the operator. "Hello, ma'am?"

"Are you really gonna shoot me! Come on, big man!" Darren challenged.

"Ma'am, I'm sending a patrol car," the 911 operator said.

"Don't! Please!" Ingrid pleaded.

Seven snatched the phone from Ingrid and hung it up. Seven couldn't believe his mother called the authorities. The look in Seven's eye would land him in jail for the rest of his life. Seven knew he better get the fuck out of there before the cops arrived. Darren still had his hands sky high. Seven easily put his gun down. "Mom, I can't believe you!" Seven said. "I guess you won't be needing me anymore!" Seven said. Seven swaggered out of the kitchen and stormed out of the house. He hopped back in his Volkswagen Jetta as he revved the engine then sped off.

Again, due to the fight between Darren and himself, Seven didn't pay attention to the dangerous conditions on the road. He stepped on the gas hard. The car started to skid across the icy road. The vehicle automatically went out of control. He slammed on the brakes. The wheels screeched. Then the Volkswagen Jetta swerved off the road and tumbled a few times. Seven felt as if he were in a wet garment clothes dryer. He thought this was the end. In his mind, he thought of all the people he knew. His mother, Ingrid, would go crazy if she lost her only son. *My uncle Darren, would he even regret the fight that we had ? And would DeShaun care if I died or not? Is it time for me to meet my father, grandmother, and God, who art in heaven?*

Finally, the Jetta tumbled into an icy, watery ditch. Seven's ride was upside. He felt extreme cold blowing on him. Seven shivered and knew he had to get out of there. He wasn't bleeding. But he felt sharp pains in his temple due to the car flipping over and the extreme cold. Seven's body hung upside down in the front seat of the car with his seatbelt on. He unfastened it. Seven's body landed on the roof of the car. The rush of icy water drenched the Volkswagen Jetta rooftop interior. The freezing cold water splashed in Seven's head and face. He spit the water that ran into his mouth. He choked a bit. The water drenched his backside. *This is it!* Seven thought again. Thank God, the water was shallow. Seven realized it and knew God has given him a chance. Seven then kicked the glass of the door out. Success. Seven slid his body out as he cut his hand on the glass. Blood streamed down Seven's hand like a river flowing. He crawled on the snow and then climbed his way up out of the ditch. Not only did Seven leave his baby behind, he also left a bloody handprint behind.

Later, Seven swaggered along the roadside. A couple of vehicles passed him by. Seven shivered as extreme cold numbed his entire body. He sneezed. Then Seven sneezed again. Few minutes later, it began to snow again. Seven swaggered on the sidewalks of Sunrise Highway. He coughed and sneezed again. His head ached even more. The pain went away for a moment and then came back. The headache became more intense.

Seven made his way to DeShaun's minimart. It was open. He went inside. The bell chimed. Seven saw the cashier scanning a customer's items. *Beep. Beep.* The sound of the scanner aggravated Seven's headache more—sensitivity to sound. The cashier saw Seven and smiled. Seven didn't return the smile. Instead, he collapsed to the floor.

"DeShaun! Seven passed out!" the cashier shouted.

Luckily, Skeeter was supervising the stock boys. He heard the commotion and noticed the young man stretched out on the floor. Skeeter rushed from the aisle and noticed Seven lying stretched out. "Holy shit, Seven! What the fuck! Get DeShaun!" Skeeter hollered. One of the stock boys ran downstairs to get DeShaun.

DeShaun dashed upstairs. "Seven, what happened!" DeShaun asked. Seven couldn't really respond due to his body being so weak. Seven was losing his natural color. He was blue in the face. "We've got to get Seven to the hospital," DeShaun said.

A couple of days later, Seven laid in a hospital bed still very weak. He caught pneumonia. Seven was in very bad shape. He could possibly die. His complexion was still pale. Nurses and doctors checked on his condition. DeShaun, Skeeter, and the rest of the posse were right by his bedside.

Seven opened his eyes and saw DeShaun and the entourage. He smiled. *Someone cared about me enough to get my black ass to the hospital! Thank God!* Seven thought to himself, *Where's my mother and my kin?* Seven thought again. Seven just let the negative thought from his mind go for now and just thought about getting better. He was glad DeShaun and the crew were there for him.

"You're gonna be all right, Seven," DeShaun said.

Seven felt at ease with DeShaun's words. Seven then closed his eyes and got some rest.

A car's engine revved as the brakes squealed of the latest Dodge Dart vehicle in a matte-black finish, the type of car that gave an edgy persona. Seven was behind the wheel of another ride, again in one of his racing adventures. The Dart sped along Sunrise Highway. It wove in and out of traffic. Seven's ride darted past an eighteen-wheeler truck. Then he made his way across some railroad tracks. The Dodge Dart thundered down Old Westbury Road and halted at the large iron gates. There were no guards. The gates just automatically opened. Seven smiled as he bolted down the long stretch of road that led to the Westland mansion. The Dodge Dart stopped short in front of the villa.

Angelika, now a beautiful seventeen-year-old girl, stepped out of the front door. Seven exited from the driver's side of the Dodge Dart to meet his honey halfway. Angelika and Seven engaged in a long passionate kiss.

"Angelika, get away from him!" said an irate voice.

Angelika and Seven's romance was interrupted by Mr. Westland's disapproval. Mr. Westland's attitudes were still the same. *Stuck-up, nasty, and tries to fit into a world that really doesn't like him,* Seven thought.

"No!" Angelika hollered to her father.

"What the hell did you just say to me, young lady!" Mr. Westland asked.

"I said no!"

Mr. Westland shook his head as he lit a cigar. He blew smoke into the air. "That's all right with me, Angelika. It's your funeral," said Mr. Westland.

Seven opened the passenger's side door for Angelika. She then hopped in. Seven shut the door as he got in on the driver's side. Then the Dodge Dart thundered away. It zoomed through the iron gates and down Old Westbury Road, going eighty-five miles per hour. The wind blew through Angelika's long ebony hair with her sleeveless T-shirt and jeans. Seven eyed Angelika from head to toe. It turned him on how beautiful she grew. Seven drove his ride on to the Long Island Expressway. Seven could really show off his stunts to Angelika. She chuckled at Seven as he drove his ride even faster. The engine roared. The Dodge Dart wove in between vehicles. Angelika then let out a burst of laughter. Seven knew it turned her on. And he knew that Angelika understood him, not like Gwendolyn.

Police sirens screamed in the distance. "Shit!" Seven cursed. Angelika looked over her shoulder toward the back of the car. She saw a patrol car. Seven peered through his rearview mirror and saw the cops on his ass. Seven picked up the speed of his Dodge Dart even faster. Then another patrol car with its sirens blaring in the air made its entrance on the highway, in pursuit of Seven and Angelika. She proceeded to laugh. "Two patrol cars are on us! My father did this!"

"No doubt!" said Seven. Then there's a third highway patrol car in pursuit of the forbidden lovers. Then a fourth patrol car pulled alongside the Dodge Dart. It picked up speed and swung in front of the Dodge Dart. It was surrounded by five highway patrol cars. Then a helicopter hovered from above.

"Is this it, Seven? Is this is how we're going to end?" Angelika asked with fear in her voice.

"No. This is our beginning," Seven said. Seven took his eyes off the road as he and Angelika kissed passionately. Then a bright light blinded the windshield of the Dodge Dart. Wheels screeched as vehicles could be heard crashing.

"Holy shit!" Seven cursed as he woke up abruptly from his sleep. He coughed violently. His body rose up from the hospital bed halfway.

"Seven! Thank goodness!" Ingrid praised. Ingrid began to pat Seven on his back repeatedly.

Darren pressed the button to alert the nurses. "Seven, you're gonna be all right, man," Darren said.

Three nurses rushed to Seven's aid. "Mr. Miles, are you all right?" the first nurse asked. Seven's coughing subsided; the second nurse gave him a drink of water. Seven sat up in bed as the third nurse gave him some more antibiotics.

Ingrid fluffed his pillow as Seven laid back down. He exhaled sharply as he saw his mother and uncle right before his eyes. He smiled. No words were exchanged. Ingrid clutched Seven's hand and kissed it. DeShaun was present in the room. He sat in the corner as he watched Seven interact with his kin. DeShaun informed Ingrid that Seven was in the hospital with pneumonia. Ingrid was grateful to him for telling her about Seven's condition. But still there was some tension. She didn't want Seven involved with a guy like DeShaun. She feared that something might happen to her son. As for Darren, he and DeShaun gave each other the evil eye. Seven could feel the tension between them. Darren kept glaring at DeShaun's clothes and saw he was a walking fashion show. He didn't want whatever DeShaun was doing to affect his family, especially Seven being just a kid. No matter what, Seven was just pleased with everyone being there for him.

That night, DeShaun had Hippolito and his team of auto technicians lift Seven's Volkswagen Jetta out of the ditch. An enormous tow truck had a crane attached to it to do the heavy-duty work. DeShaun and Skeeter watched as the Volkswagen was finally out. Seven's ride was secured to the crane of the tow truck. DeShaun shivered as his teeth even chattered. "Bounce! Hippolito, get the fuck out here!" The sound of the diesel of the tow truck drove away with the Volkswagen attached. Hippolito and his team then fled the scene in another vehicle. Then DeShaun and Skeeter hopped in the black Lexus and sped away.

Chapter 21

A month and a half later, mid-march, the air remained frigid, but there was no more snow to worry about. Spring was about to make its way in. After being separated, Seven and his baby were reunited. Seven felt stronger than ever, but not his baby. She was deathly ill. She had multiple dents on her sides, trunk, and the hood. Her front and rear windshields were busted with a few glass pieces in the frames. Her wheels were just fine. But her engine had to be checked most importantly.

Seven had to operate. The doctor's in. Immediately Seven put on an auto technician's jumpsuit. The metal body frame of the Volkswagen Jetta had to be stripped, which included the trunk and the hood. The busted windshields from the rear and front were removed. Hippolito's auto technicians took care of the dents in the body of Seven's ride. Seven focused on his baby's engine. The turbo engine was frostbitten. It was white with frost on it. Just like before, he added antifreeze to her engine. Seven got behind the wheel and started her up. Success. Everyone applauded. Seven knew his girl was going to fine. All that mattered was her engine. The Volkswagen Jetta's wheels were tested on the dyno. The wheels spun perfectly on it. Seven did an oil change on her just to be on the safe side.

On the other side of the garage, the team of auto technicians recreated the metal body of the Jetta. Also, on the damaged metal body, the color was rubbing off. Hippolito offered a paint job after the Jetta was finished. Then two auto techs carried a brand-new hood toward the front of the car. They placed it down over the engine. Brand-new metal strips were placed on the body of the Jetta, filling it out, also including the doors. The trunk was placed on the rear of the car. All this was then followed up with a paint job—a black matte finish. On top of all this work, brand-new shiny rims were on the wheels.

Finally, Seven's girl was good as new. The garage door opened as Seven revved her monstrous turbo engine. The Volkswagen Jetta backed out and made its way on to the street. Seven took her out for a test drive. Hippolito and his team cheered. Seven sped down the block as if he stole it. And Seven did exactly that. Enormous smoke emerged from the rear wheels of the Jetta. Meanwhile, Seven proceeded to speed up with his baby again. There were no worries about snow or ice. He and his girl were gonna be fine. The monstrous engine bellowed as he thundered his way on to the expressway. As always, Seven weaved in and out of traffic. Motorists were displeased with Seven's aggressive driving. He enjoyed speeding. It was a rush for him. Minutes later, the Volkswagen Jetta stopped short at the curb in front of the minimart. The monstrous engine of his car shut down. Seven swaggered out of his Jetta, slamming the driver's side door without even thinking about damaging his baby. He made his way into the mini mart as an elderly woman exited with groceries. Seven held the door for eighty- something year old senior. She remained him of his grandmother as they made eye contact. He then felt as if this were her testing him to see if he was doing the right thing. The elderly blessed Seven and gave him a warm smile. Seven returned the gesture and headed inside.

"How are you feeling, Seven?" the cashier asked with excitement in her tone.

"I'm cool."

"I was so worried about you. Everyone was."

"Thanks," Seven said. The stock boys and other employees greeted Seven with hugs and high fives. Seven headed down to the basement. It's dim as always, with some lighting around. Chief, Tool, and some other thugs played a game of pool as they saw Seven approaching them.

"What's up, Chief?" Seven greeted.

Chief and the other players threw down their pool sticks and embraced him. "You're better, man!" said Chief.

"We thought we were gonna lose you, Seven," said Tool.

"I'm new and improved," said Seven with an arrogant attitude. Seven felt the love from everyone. They were like the brothers he never had. His family. A family that will be there for him through thick and thin.

DeShaun witnessed his henchmen greeting Seven with hugs and high fives. DeShaun stood in the background and watched the interaction between Seven and his entourage. It's like a father watching his son playing with his friends. "Welcome back!" DeShaun shouted. Seven turned around and saw him. DeShaun embraced Seven. DeShaun noticed Seven wearing the dingy garage jumpsuit and had to get him into some fresh clothing.

Later, Seven took a hot shower at his house. He allowed the steam to stimulate his entire nude body. He grabbed the bar of soap, lathered up, and washed. Minutes later, his wiped the steamed mirror with his hands. Seven's reflection appeared before him. He noticed his body looked thinner. He lost weight. Seven wasn't pleased with his physique. He knew what to do. This was the right time for Seven to take care of that issue that he had with his body. He believed that by a person being frail, people viewed you as either weak or sick. And they would fuck with you.

Then Seven and DeShaun sat at a booth in a restaurant. A waiter poured water into their empty glasses and gave them a basket of rolls. Seven grabbed a roll, shoving it in his mouth. After Seven came out of the hospital, he had to drink lots of liquids and take a lot of medications. It's been a month and a half, but still Seven was thin. As Seven devoured the bread, DeShaun raised an eyebrow, wondering what the problem was. "Damn, you're hungry like a motherfucker."

DeShaun cursed. Seven nodded his head as he chewed and gulped the glass of water. He wiped his mouth with his napkin. "I've got to gain weight, yo."

"I agree. You need weight on you," DeShaun agreed as he sipped his glass of water and cleared his throat. "Speaking of weight gain, you'll need to do that because you're gonna have to go back on the streets," DeShaun said as he glared right into Seven's eyes and sipping his water. Then a pretty waitress placed two large dishes of shrimp, chicken, French fries, and veggies before Seven and DeShaun. Seven dug into his food and ate like a crazy. He devoured the food like a famished child in a third world country. Seven didn't even bother to make eye contact with the waitress. Usually, Seven would check out a beautiful female, but this time he was concerned with his body image. DeShaun chuckled as he noticed Seven giving massive attention to his food.

That night, Seven brought home some leftovers from the restaurant in a doggie bag. He devoured the shrimp, French fries, and rolls as he stood in his kitchen. Then he crumbled up the doggie bag and tossed it in the trash. He then ate a couple of donuts from the refrigerator. Whether it was junk or healthy food, Seven had an appetite. Before Seven went to sleep, he did sit-ups and push-ups. Sweat poured down his face and body. He exhaled sharp. Hot water poured from a showerhead as Seven allowed it to flow down his nude body. Then Seven exited the bathroom with a towel wrapped around his waist. He lay down on his king-sized bed and glared at the ceiling. Seven's mind was blank for a moment. Seven thought of the dream he had while he was in the hospital. Angelika was in it. *Why was she in it? Was she my soul mate? She's just a little girl. Angelika's about eleven years old,* Seven thought. Seven erased Angelika from his mind and closed his eyes.

It was hot, humid, and sticky night in mid-June, making it very uncomfortable for everyone. The thugs on the corner played dice and argued over money. Then a fist fight erupted. The two hoodlums exchanged punches over the disagreement. The fight made its way into the middle of the street. Russell intervened and broke it up. "Fuckin' chill!" Russell hollered. "Stay the fuck away from each other. I'll keep the money.

"I need that for my kids!" the first thug whined.

"How many kids do you have?" Russell asked.

"Five," the first thug replied.

"You're dumb. Keep your dick in your pants. DeShaun doesn't care about your problems," said Russell.

A monstrous engine could be heard in the distance. Russell and his associates weren't fazed by the engine's sound. It got louder and louder. Then it drowned out Russell and the drug runner's argument. Russell turned and saw that it was Seven. Even though Seven was younger than the drug runners on the street, they were deathly afraid of him.

"Shut the fuck up, fools," Russell shouted to the other drug runners. They noticed Seven's presence and became submissive. Seven rolled the window of the Volkswagen Jetta with a not-so-happy expression on his face. Russell scrambled to the vehicle. He smiled and played up to Seven. Russell noticed Seven had more muscle on his body. Russell became intimidated by Seven because he wasn't a scrawny something anymore.

"Pay up!" Seven demanded. Russell's hands began to quiver as he handed Seven a bundle of cash. "Come you, motherfuckers! Pay the fuck up!" Seven demanded again. He counted the cash that was given to him by Russell. The other drug runners lined up one by one.

Then another monstrous Hemi engine of the latest Dodge Ram in black pulled up alongside the Seven's Jetta. Chad, a.k.a. Magnum, was behind the wheel of the muscle truck. His truck had nice, shiny rims and tinted windows with a blaring horn that sounded like a steamboat. Magnum worked hard and got to roll with DeShaun and the OGs of the crew. Magnum worked day and night on the corner. Just like Seven, Magnum was doing pickups from drug hustlers. The two cronies gave each other high fives and embraced. Due to the distraction, one of the drug runners named Jug took off running.

"Holy shit!" Seven cursed.

"Get that motherfucker, Seven!" Magnum encouraged.

The Volkswagen Jetta blasted off down the street after Jug. Magnum stayed and continued the pickups from the rest of the runners on the corner. "Don't even think of running the fuck off!" Magnum said. He gave them the "I dare you" look.

Jug was a skinny, braids- and baggy-clothes-wearing, somewhat drug addict thug—a crackhead at that. Seven stepped on the gas extremely hard as the monstrous engine roared. Jug scurried into the empty parking lot of a shopping center with its closed businesses. Headlights beamed right on Jug's ass. Jug stumbled to the concrete. His money flew out of his hand and scattered all over the ground. The wheels of the Jetta screeched, missing Jug by a few inches. It stopped. The headlights shined directly in Jug's face. Seven hopped out of his car with the engine still running. Seven kicked Jug in the stomach three times as he lay on the ground. Jug cried like a baby as he coughed up blood. Jug spat it to the ground. This time, no more excuses. Seven wasn't feeling sorry for anyone.

"I need the money, please!" Jug pleaded. Seven didn't say a word to Jug. Seven gathered up the cash from the ground. "Please, Seven."

Seven stared at Jug and still didn't say a word. Seven counted the cash and recognized a one-hundred-dollar bill looked counterfeit. Seven raised an eyebrow. "This is a fake hundred dollar bill! You were gonna pass this on to DeShaun! That's why you ran!" Seven hollered. Seven continued to kick Jug in the back and chest repeatedly. Jug cried like a baby. "What the fuck am I supposed to tell DeShaun! Huh!" Seven asked with an aggressive tone. "What am I supposed to tell him!" Seven demanded answers. Jug proceeded to sob but still didn't respond to Seven's question. Seven grabbed Jug by his jacket and hauled him to the backseat of his Volkswagen Jetta. Seven thrust open the back door. He then realized that Jug was bloody. "Shit! You're bleeding over all the fuckin' place!" Seven cursed. Seven knew he had to have Jug answer to DeShaun even though Seven didn't want blood all over the backseat of his ride. But Seven had to do it. He forced Jug inside and slammed the door.

As Seven drove at a medium pace, Jug cried and cried and cried. Seven eyed Jug through the rearview mirror to the backseat. The crying irritated Seven. Seven restrained himself from hitting Jug.

So Jug continued to cry. "I've got five kids to feed, man. Seven, you know how it is!" Jug cried.

"I don't know how it is!" Seven responded.

"Don't you have kids?"

"No, I don't! I don't go around sticking my dick in every female out there! Is this about child support payments?" Seven asked.

"Are you taking me to DeShaun?" Jug asked.

Seven didn't a say a word. He glared at Jug in the backseat through the rearview mirror. Jug proceeded to cry because Seven hit the nail right on the head. Seven drove fast due to the crying that got on his nerves. The turbo engine of the Volkswagen bellowed.

Moments later, Jug sat right before DeShaun as he presented the phony one-hundred bill in his face. Seven, Magnum, Skeeter, TaTu, and his other henchmen surrounded DeShaun. Jug cried and begged for clemency. When it came to DeShaun's money, there was no mercy. DeShaun leaped over his desk and pimp-slapped Jug. Jug plummeted to the floor. He cried like a girl. DeShaun went crazy of course. "Where the fuck is the rest of my dough!" DeShaun shouted as he held Jug by the shirt. Jug's face was bloody as hell. "You've got the motherfuckin' nerve to slip me a counterfeit! Are you stupid! Or do you think I'm stupid!" DeShaun really didn't believe in doing away with someone. He believed in snitches. DeShaun glared at Seven and nodded. Seven knew what DeShaun wanted him to do. Seven thought about the counterfeit bill Jug tried to give to him. What if Seven didn't realize that phony bill? Then Seven would have gotten stitches. Seven hauled Jug out of DeShaun's office. Jug screamed and screamed. His screams made Seven angrier.

In the alleyway of DeShaun's establishment, Seven hurled multiple punches to every part of Jug's body—face, head, and abdominal area. The more and more Jug screamed, the angrier Seven became. Then the punches became more and more fierce. DeShaun and his henchmen watched the entire thing. Then DeShaun saw Seven was caught up in the red zone, like a Rottweiler ready to kill. DeShaun grabbed Seven and had to snap him out of it. "Seven, chill! Yo!" Seven then spat on Jug.

A couple of weeks later, Seven graduated high school. He didn't attend, but there was a girl he wanted to get with. Her name was Tamara. She was a medium-brown-skinned African-American girl about seventeen years of age. She was pretty with a figure shaped like an hourglass. A graduation party was being given by one of the students. Seven and Tamara didn't go because they had their own graduation party. At Seven's house, Seven and Tamara were fucking up a storm in his king-sized bed. Sweat trickled down their bodies as the air conditioner was on. The more and more Seven and Tamara got it on, the harder the air conditioner had to work.

After that episode, Seven and Tamara really weren't into each other romantically. They were more on the friendship level. They spoke very little in school, and now they were just getting to know each other. Tamara told how she was going to move to California to attend UCLA. She wanted to pursue acting or some area of the entertainment business. It was like history repeating itself, another Dilbrina, a bragger.

Seven listened and nodded. Seven couldn't wait to drive this girl home. Tamara was full of herself. Tamara swore she was going to be the next Halle Berry. *Hell no! In your dreams!* Seven thought to himself.

Later that night, Seven and Tamara ate dinner at a nearby diner. They clanked glasses to congratulate each other for their success. "Here's to us, the graduating class, and may the future be bright," Seven said.

"I'll drink to that," Tamara said. She gulped down her drink. Then Tamara continued to talk about her promising career in Hollywood, how famous she was going to be, and how much money she was going to make. This time Seven didn't hold his tongue. Seven didn't mean to rain on her parade, but how many people actually made it to Hollywood big time? That's a one in million chance. Tamara frowned because she didn't like to hear the realities of Tinseltown.

On the way home from the restaurant, the turbo engine bellowed as Seven thundered along Sunrise Highway. Seven and Tamara didn't glance at each other. Not even once. She was pissed that Seven sounded so discouraging. Tamara hated that. Seven felt bad and didn't mean to ruin her aspirations. "You could let me out here," Tamara said.

"Here?" Seven asked with an eyebrow raised.

"Yes, here," Tamara said. She rolled her eyes and had an attitude.

Seven halted his Jetta at the curb. "Tamara, I'm sorry. I didn't mean to say that."

"But, you did," Tamara said.

"I wish you all the luck in the world," Seven said with honesty in his voice. There was a bus stop a few feet ahead of the Volkswagen Jetta. Tamara grimaced and let herself out of the car. The bus pulled up to the bus stop. She raced for the bus. Seven watched as she got on. The bus zoomed down the street. Seven turned red in the face and pounded his fist on the steering wheel. He drove like a bat out of hell.

Chapter 22

Another enormous birthday bash was thrown by DeShaun for Seven at a lavish hall in Glen Cove. Seven turned eighteen and felt stronger, not just physically, but also mentally. Tiana wheeled out a huge five-layered chocolate cake with eighteen lit candles. Everyone sang "Happy Birthday" to Seven. Seven appreciated the celebration that DeShaun put so much work into. But Seven didn't want to do the whole "happy birthday" celebrations anymore. *This is for babies. I'm a man now,* Seven said to himself.

Later, as the celebration proceeded, rap music blasted from the speakers. Everyone danced. A sexy girl named Kim grabbed Seven by the hand to the dance floor. DeShaun and his henchmen cheered as they saw Seven with Kim. Kim was a fair-skinned African-American female with long braids, pretty, and sported a tight red jumpsuit with matching pumps. Kim rubbed her buttocks against Seven's pelvic area. Seven felt an erection coming on. *Happy birthday to me,* Seven said to himself as he felt himself getting harder and harder.

After the party, Kim bounced on Seven's lap in the driver's seat of his parked Volkswagen Jetta. They moaned like there was no tomorrow. Seven squeezed Kim's breasts. Then they reached a climax. Kim screamed as if she were being murdered, but no. It was the pleasure. "Holy fuck!" Seven cursed as he reached his peak during his sexual encounter. They both exhaled sharply. Sweaty, Seven and Kim gazed into each other's eyes and kissed.

Kim was different from Tamara. She didn't brag at all. She got to know Seven. Seven told about his grandmother and his father, who taught him about fighting with fists instead of a gun. Kim loved that. Then it was Kim's life story. Kim told how she was on her own since fifteen years old. She had to resort to the street life in order to survive. She didn't get into detail. But Seven imagined what she had to do. He felt sorry for her and didn't want anything bad to happen to her. Seven asked what she wanted in life.

Kim kind of shrugged her shoulders and cocked her head. "Maybe a writer?" Kim said.

"What medium?" Seven asked.

"A screenwriter," Kim answered.

"That's cool. Would you write about your life?" Seven asked.

"No! I'd rather use my imagination," Kim said. She had some ideas for a good science fiction thriller; something Steven Spielberg or George Lucas would do. Seven was impressed with her imagination. Seven knew this girl could really go far in the world if given the opportunity. Seven made a deal with Kim. He wanted Kim to give up the street life. No more selling any of her goods. Kim looked at Seven like he was crazy. Seven could tell that she didn't believe a word he said. She couldn't believe it because it was coming from a thug. Kim usually sold her goods to thugs and guys who wore three-piece suits. None of them ever talked nicely to her. They wanted Kim to fulfill their fantasies.

"Do we have a deal, Kim?" Seven asked her with a dead-serious expression on his face. He raised an eyebrow. Seven still saw Kim wasn't taking him seriously.

"All right. I'll do it," Kim said immediately.

Seven shook his head in disagreement. He knew Kim was pulling his leg, in this sense. "I don't believe you," Seven said.

"Why not?" Kim asked.

"I can sense it. You gonna head right back to the corner. Aren't you afraid of losing your life? Or getting sick?" Seven asked in curiosity.

Kim shrugged her shoulders and exhaled. She had no family and no one she could really trust. Kim had to do what she felt was best for her. Even though Kim had a brilliant mind for writing, the streets continued to call her in order to make a fast buck.

Finally, Seven gave up. It was like talking to the wall. He couldn't change her. *If this is what she wants to do, then that's on her.* Seven kissed Kim on the cheek, and they said their good-byes to each other.

Meanwhile, as Seven thundered down Sunrise Highway, he thought about Kim. What a waste, a genius mind lost to the streets. *Am I gonna to be a lost to the streets? Seven thought. Seven then lit a cigarette and took a couple of puffs. Then he exhaled smoke rings. If given the opportunity with NASCAR, he'll take it. He'd be the only African-American in that sport. Seven thought. I love speed, and that's my passion. I can't give up my passion. Check out me and baby on the road,* Seven thought again. He eyed other motorists on the highway and then began to speed it up. It was as if he were on the NASCAR track, racing professionally. Then sirens blared in the distance. Seven's heart raced. "What the fuck did I do? I've got to get the fuck out of here!" Seven said to himself. "I can't go to jail," Seven said, and then he slowed down his ride. Two patrol cars were right behind him and then exited off the highway. Seven was relieved as he took a deep breath. He saw that several patrol cars surrounded a dump truck. Then Seven's cell phone rang. It was Magnum. It was still Seven's birthday, and the night was young.

Later, headlights of the Volkswagen Jetta beamed as it pulled to the curb of Magnum's home in Commack. TaTu's navy-blue Toyota Camry, BiBi's black caravan, Bay's Mercedes-Benz, Boo's matte black Camaro were all parked one behind another in Magnum's driveway. Seven hopped out of his car. He greeted his cronies with high fives as they checked out Polo's turbo engine of his black Cadillac CTS coupe. The engine of Polo's ride was nice. The sound was very crisp and mean. Magnum got everyone together because he wanted to celebrate Seven's birthday more. Seven would love this.

"Seven, let's celebrate your birthday to the fullest," Magnum said. Polo's wristwatch read 2:39 a.m. Polo revved the engine of his Cadillac CTS Coupe, and the other mean engines of the Mercedes,

Toyota Camry, Camaro, and Audi roared like a pride of lions. It was the loudest sound a person ever heard. Seven knew the NASCAR races sounded just like this. Probably louder. Seven revved the turbo engine of his Jetta. He blasted down the road with the other racers right behind. Massive engines roared throughout the night.

Minutes later, on the Long Island Expressway, Seven and his cronies zoomed past each other along the dark, empty expressway. A devilish smile surfaced on Seven's face. He put his pedal to the metal and passed Bay's Mercedes. Seven waved good-bye to Bay.

"Holy shit!" Bay cursed. Bay stepped harder on the gas and caught up to Seven's Volkswagen Jetta. Then the Cadillac CTS Coupe took the cake. Polo laughed as he left all of them in the dust. As Seven and his friends continued to challenge each other, their engines echoed. "Happy birthday, Seven!" Polo shouted.

Three days later, the birds sang on the morning of July 31 as Seven slept on his king-sized bed. He opened his eyes as he focused on the ceiling fan above. Seven knew what day it was. It was Angelika's thirteenth birthday. Seven wondered what Angelika would get since her father was wealthy and shit. *Angelika would probably take a trip to Paris or California. Or Mr. Westland would take her on a shopping spree. Or Mr. and Mrs. Westland would probably throw her a lavish party,* Seven thought as he smiled to himself. All he could do was wish Angelika all the best. "Happy birthday, Angelika."

That night, Seven thundered down the LIE (Long Island Expressway) with his Volkswagen Jetta. The turbo engine bellowed as he weaved in between cars. Like always, motorists cursed Seven and gave him the finger. Right behind the Jetta was Boo in his Camaro, TaTu in his blue Toyota Camry, and BiBi in his black Dodge Caravan. As far as Polo, Magnum, and Bay, they were busy putting in extra work for DeShaun. DeShaun found out about the drag racing on the expressway. He didn't like it at all. It could put his operation in jeopardy. If Seven and his friends got caught, police authorities would find something on them and it would be traced back to DeShaun.

Several highway patrol cars were on pursuit. They were determined to get these street-racing thugs. Red and blue police lights flashed in his rearview mirror. Sirens wailed in the air. Seven had two patrol cars on both sides of him. But there was a station wagon with a family of four in front of him. Seven blared his horn continuously for the station wagon to get out of the way. But the station wagon was blocked by another vehicle right next to it. The patrol rammed the side of the Volkswagen Jetta. Seven tried to keep his Volkswagen under control.

Boom! Seven heard the sound and felt his Jetta steering out of control. Then the station wagon picked up speed as Seven increased his speed. The Volkswagen Jetta reared into some grass and halted. The engine was still running. Several highway patrols surrounded the Jetta. The officers brandished their firearms.

"Get your arms in the air! Right now!" an officer shouted with a rifle pointed at the driver's side of the Jetta. Seven easily made his way out of his ride with his hands sky-high. "On the ground!" the officer demanded. Seven did what the highway officer wanted. He lay down on the ground. Dozens of officers ran up on him. Seven was handcuffed and taken into custody.

Chapter 23

A caged-window prison bus drove along a stretched road on a hot day in mid-August. Correction officers carried rifles as they guarded both the front and the rear of the bus. The prisoners, mostly African-American men ranging from seventeen year of age and up wore beige-colored prison suits while shackled to one another. Thieves, murderers, rapists, and white supremacists convicted of the most horrendous crimes. Seven was charged with street racing and possession of an illegal firearm. He was only eighteen, and the judge sentenced him to two years in prison. Seven was sent to one of the toughest prisons in Upstate New York. He resided by a window and didn't give the other convicts any eye contact. Seven was a bit scared. What was gonna happen to him? Seven knew he had to be tough. If he was strong arms on the streets for DeShaun, he had to be strong arms in the pen. Someone had their eye on Seven from the other side of the bus. Seven glanced over and saw the nasty-looking convict. He gave the disgusting thing a dirty look and turned eyes in the other direction. From the corner of Seven's eye, he knew this fool still watched him.

Boo, BiBi, and TaTu were convicted of the same crimes as Seven; they served different times, some more or less charges. All Seven knew was he had to spend a couple of years behind bars, an eternity in hell. Ingrid passed out in the courtroom when Seven was sentenced. It was like death to her. DeShaun blew his top because he loved Seven like a son. And he was losing Seven. Of course, DeShaun couldn't be present in court. He heard from Magnum about Seven's sentencing. The same went for Boo, BiBi, and TaTu. DeShaun experienced a bit of a financial setback but was able to still compete with his drug rival Corey across town.

The prison bus then halted at a tall fence with barbed wiring on the top. A tower with guards kept watch of the premises as they bore rifles. The correction officers were accompanied with guard dogs barking their heads off. The gate opened as the prison bus pulled onto prison grounds. Then it halted as the diesel engine shut down. Then the prisoners were led out like African slaves arriving to America on the slave ships back in the eighteenth century. The guards watched their every move as they grasped their rifles.

Later, prisoners were ordered to strip naked as guards searched for any weapons they may have hidden on their bodies. Seven felt funny about taking his clothes off around a bunch of men. Seven glanced around as he saw the other convicts undress as ordered. Then a middle-aged, tattoo-ridden, muscular Mexican gang member glared at Seven. "Are you ashamed of your body?"

"Shut the fuck up!" Seven cursed. Seven then began to take off his shirt and then his pants. He only had on his boxers. Seven could sense that he was being stared at. He glanced over shoulder as the Mexican gang member blew Seven a kiss. "What the fuck! I'm not the one!" Seven said.

Then an African-American guy in his midtwenties witnessed the incident. "Don't let that bother, yo!"

"He's been fuckin' with me since we got here."

"Just stand your ground. Don't back down from anyone," said the African-American convict.

"Thanks, man," Seven said.

"I'm Jamal."

"I'm Seven."

"Seven? Is that your street name?" Jamal asked.

"No. That's my real name," Seven replied.

"That's cool, yo." Jamal laughed.

Then Seven took off his boxers, exposing his penis, balls, and buttocks. The head correction officer hollered at the top of his lungs. He ordered the convicts to line up against the wall. Seven, Jamal, and other prisoners were right behind one another and did as they were told. The Mexican OG (original gangster) wasn't far away. He was three men behind Seven in line.

"Lift your arms!" the correction officer commanded. Seven and the prisoners did it. "Lift up your balls!" the correction officer hollered. "What the fuck! He's got to be kidding!" Seven scoffed.

"Just do as you're told," said Jamal.

Seven shook his head and sucked his teeth. Seven reached his hands down on his testicles and lift it up. This was the most humiliating thing anyone could go through, your body being searched from head to toe. The Mexican OG peered at Seven's penis. Seven didn't notice. But Jamal did.

"Seven be careful. He's checking you out," Jamal advised.

Seven noticed the Mexican OG peering at his penis. Seven's heart raced, and he balled his hands into fists. "Are you fuckin' gay or some shit!" Seven shouted. The Chicano OG blew Seven another kiss. Seven then hurled a punch to the Chicano OG's face. It was a hardcore punch. He plummeted to the floor, unconscious. Several corrections officers began to beat Seven with billy clubs. "What the fuck!" Seven shouted in pain.

"Put him in the hole!" the head officer shouted. The guards hauled Seven butt-naked through the prison as the other convicts watched in shock. Then they approached solitary confinement. The guard unlocked it with a key and opened the door. Seven's prison clothes were thrown in. Seven was then thrown into the hole, nude. Seven bled from his nose, and he had pain in his side. Seven curled in a fetal position on the cold concrete floor. The pain intensified. Seven prayed to God to make the pain go away. Seven hoped his appendix didn't break. He coughed up blood then shut his eyes and slept.

Hours and hours went by as Seven groaned in pain on the floor. Seven was curled up like a fetus in his mother's womb. A tray of food was slipped through the slot of his cell. Seven could hear it. He was in a world of his own. Then the hours turned to days. Correction officers peered into Seven's cell to see if he was okay. Since Seven didn't budge. A medical team was brought in to check Seven out. The prison medical team checked his breathing, took his blood pressure and heart rate, and saw he lost body weight. Again, Seven was losing the body that he worked so hard for from losing it due to him catching pneumonia from his car accident to now being beaten in the penitentiary. The medical team carried Seven out on a gurney as he was rushed to the hospital.

That night, Seven squinted his eyes and saw he was in a hospital. He had blurry vision. Seven tried to move his arms but really couldn't. His hands and feet were cuffed to the bed. He pressed the button to alert the nurse. Correction officers were guarding Seven's every move. But where was he going? The officers came to Seven's aid, followed by the nurse.

"How's your side, Mr. Miles?" the nurse asked.

Seven tried to sit up but couldn't. The sharp pain was still in his side. "This shit still hurts!" Seven cursed as he endured the agonizing pain. The nurse gave him a pill and some water. Seven took it as he breathed sharply.

Ingrid and Darren entered into the room. Seven smiled as he was relieved to see his family.

"Hey, baby. How are you?" Ingrid asked as she pulled up a chair to Seven's bedside.

"Not good at all."

"Hey, Uncle Darren."

"How are you doing, man?"

"Again, not good," Seven said.

Ingrid preached the Bible to Seven as he lay in bed. Seven listened to his mother as she read the Word of God. Seven was all ears.

Weeks past as Seven got better. Correction escorted Seven back to the big house with the general prison population with other inmates. Again, Seven's feet were shackled together as the guards escorted him to his cell. The guard unlocked the door of the cell as Seven was unshackled. Seven then swaggered into the cell. There was a cot to sleep on, a toilet where there's no privacy, and all kinds of profanity written on the walls from previous inmates. This was Seven's new home. There was a window where Seven could only see a patch of sky. A loud squeaking sound of the prison door slamming shut was heard as the keys rattled, locking it securely. The clunking footsteps of the guards left Seven's cell—all this for street racing and carrying an illegal firearm. Seven didn't want to wind up here again. "I didn't murder or rape anyone. Damn! Any little crime the judge would throw the book at you or give you a slap on the wrist. That shit certainly wouldn't happen in my case." Seven thought as he looked around his cell. He then shook his head at the shit he got himself into.

It was time for dinner. All prisoners stepped out of their cells with guards at every angle. They marched right behind one another like toy soldiers to the cafeteria. Seven got his tray as a cook put some nasty slob on it. Seven sneered at it. Seven carried his tray of food in his hands. He tried to figure out where to sit. Then Jamal beckoned Seven. Seven took a deep breath as he found someone he kind of knew. Seven gave Jamal a high five as he took a seat next to him.

"What's going on, my man? I thought you died."

"I'm cool," Seven replied.

"That's good to hear," Jamal said as he chuckled.

As Seven and Jamal chatted across the cafeteria, there was the Mexican OG. He devoured down his dinner. Jamal nudged Seven. Seven noticed the tattooed, oily thug ate like a pig with his fat lips. Food fell from the Mexican thug's mouth and on to his tray. Seven and Jamal made sour expressions and then turned their heads.

"Fuckin' nasty," Jamal said.

"He better not step to me again. I'll knock his ass out. I don't give a fuck. These guards can kill me," said Seven.

After dinner, Seven returned to his cell. Seven wondered what he was gonna do now. There were a couple of magazines, but they didn't interest him. He laid on the cot and stared at the ceiling. Seven's mind was blank. He shut his eyes, and it was lights-out for the entire prison. The prisoners stopped their boisterous behavior for the evening and saved it for the next morning. A guard paced back and forth, peering in cells, and made sure convicts were present. Seven dozed off every few minutes due to the guard's shoes waking him up. Seven tried as hard as he could to really get some sleep. And he wanted to have a dream, because this place was a nightmare. He wanted to think about his ride, which gave him freedom without being pursued by authorities. What about his future? What's going to happen to him after he's released from prison? Only time will tell. Seven closed his eyes as he tried to get some shut-eye.

Dawn approached as the sunrays peered through the prison walls' crack. Then the bell rang. The cells automatically opened as prisoners stepped out of their cells, facing the correction officers. Correction officers kept a sharp watch on every prisoner's move. The inmates marched down to the dining area. Few minutes later, Seven grabbed a tray as he got himself some nasty breakfast to eat. Seven made a sour face because he saw the slop that the prison served to the inmates. It was old, extremely lumpy, and slightly warm oatmeal, and probably expired. Seven had to eat. He scooped up the oatmeal with the spoon and shoved the nasty cereal in his mouth. Seven frowned as he washed it down fast with milk. He swallowed it whole. Then he coughed a bit. Then he took another spoonful of food and forced himself to eat. It was nasty. As Seven continued to eat the foul food, he visualized his grandmother's cooking. The so-called Sundays which took place every single day. She made sure her family was well fed. The roast beef, roast chicken, mashed potatoes, veggies, etc. This helped Seven to devour the shitty food.

Later, the courtyard clamored with inmates either playing basketball, lifting weights, or just hanging out in their own clique. The African-American inmates stuck together; so did the Latinos and the whites. There were some African-American convicts playing a game of B-ball and another gathered around, freestyle rapping. Seven stood on the side as he watched the two groups do their thing. Seven couldn't rap and he rarely played basketball.

Jamal swaggered to Seven's side. "What's up, Seven?" Jamal asked with a smirk on his face. He lit a cigarette.

"Nothing much," Seven responded as he gazed at everyone around him.

"You look like you lost your best friend."

"I did."

"How did that shit happen?" Jamal chuckled.

"The pigs took her away from me."

"Her?" Jamal asked with a look of confusion on his face.

"My ride."

"Your car." Jamal took a couple of puffs of his cigarette and blew smoke rings into the air.

Seven continued to look at the guys rapping. They dissed each other in the freestyle battle. Everyone guffawed. Seven and Jamal smirked as they heard the disses that were being verbally hurled around. Seven enjoyed the show, but he wished he had his ride. He and his girl would stunt for everybody—burnouts, doughnuts, quarter-mile runs, etc.—if his ride were around. He had to participate in some type of activity. It was either play basketball or lift weights.

Seconds later, players danced around on the basketball court like real players in the NBA. Seven was a good player, but it wasn't his passion. Seven dribbled the basketball and passed it to Jamal. Jamal dribbled the basketball and threw it in the hoop. Seven applauded as he gave Jamal a high five. Seven participated in the two activities available in prison, weightlifting and basketball. Every day, Seven lifted weights to build muscle on his body. He ran up and down the basketball court when the players weren't on it. This is how he got his exercise. Seven worked out a good sweat every day. Luckily, none of the other prisoners bothered him. That was God watching over his child even when he's not really doing the right thing. Even when a person isn't good, God is still good.

During Seven's days of activities, Jamal worked in the kitchen. Not only did Jamal work in the kitchen for the inmates, he also worked in the one for the correction officers. In their kitchen, the food was fresh and tasty. Jamal was allowed to eat from this kitchen as a reward for his hard work in both kitchens. He also slipped Seven some fresh food. Jamal wrapped a roast beef sandwich, soda, and some fruit. Jamal pushed a tray of magazines and other items down the hallway of the cells. Also in that cart was some fresh food for Seven.

Jamal halted the cart in front of Seven's cell. He opened the tray slot and slipped Seven some good food. Seven heard the squeaking of the slot as he got up from his cot and saw the fancy napkin. Seven swaggered over and grabbed his food. He devoured the sandwich and was satisfied with it. Jamal did this every day for Seven without the guards finding out. But there was a dispute among correction officers over missing food from the refrigerator where some of their food was stored. Seven and Jamal laughed about the situation as they hung out in the courtyard every day. Jamal heard about guards looking at inmates who worked in the correction officers' kitchen. So Jamal had to stop taking the food or he'll get caught. That was the end of Seven's fresh foods.

At dinnertime in the cafeteria, Seven sneered at his tray of nasty food. It was some stale chicken, bread, hard rice, and cold veggies. Even though, Seven tried to think of his grandmother's cooking in order to help him to deal with the nasty prison. He couldn't. He felt himself getting nauseated. He pushed the tray away and just sat there until dinner was over. Later, right before lights went out, Seven stared at the ceiling as he laid on his cot. Again, his mind was blank. There was nothing to think about. No more good food from the officers' kitchen, no calls from anyone, or not even a visit. Then there was the squeaking sound of the wheels on a cart that was pushed toward Seven's cell. The slot of his cell door opened. Another white cloth with possibly food in it was forced into the cell. Seven sat up in bed and grabbed the cloth. In the white napkin was a steak sandwich, french fries, fruit, and a juice. Also, there was a letter. Seven glared at the return address as he took a bite of his sandwich. It was from DeShaun. Seven tore the letter open and began reading. DeShaun's letter said, "What's up, Seven? Damn. It's nothing around here without you, yo. I hope you're doing all right and no one's fucking with you. Everyone misses and praying you get home quick."

As Seven continued to read DeShaun's letter, it was wholesome, so the guards didn't detect any criminal references within it. Corrections read every letter that was delivered to its inmates, so people on the outside had to be careful what they wrote. Seven knew DeShaun wouldn't forget him. It was the first contact from someone on the outside. Usually, when an inmate is incarcerated, the first person to see them is their mother. But not in Seven's case. It was DeShaun.

Seven made one collect call to Ingrid. Ingrid accepted the call. Darren tried to talk her out of it. When Seven and Ingrid were talking on the phone, Darren could be heard bitching in the background. He wasn't the only one. There was a long line of other inmates that needed to use the phone, and Seven felt a humungous thug breathing on his neck. Seven glanced over his shoulder and gave the thug a nasty expression.

"You're gonna have to wait, motherfucker!" Seven cursed as he continued to chat with Ingrid on the phone. Then Seven didn't want Ingrid to hear any conflict over the phone, so it wouldn't freak her out. Seven decided to end his call and told her that he loved her. He then slammed the receiver on the phone and swaggered away.

A few weeks later, surprise, surprise. A visitor was sitting behind a glass with a phone on the side. Seven swaggered by the other prisoners as they were busy chatting with their relatives. He sat on the opposite side of the glass, and it was Ingrid. Seven's face lit up as any child would. He felt himself regressing back to a child again. Seven snatched the receiver as Ingrid did the same. They had a teary conversation. There were things Ingrid wanted to say to Seven but knew she couldn't because of security's eyes and ears. Ingrid just spoke about Seven getting his life on track. What was he going to do? Seven shrugged his shoulder and didn't know.

"You better figure it out, Seven," Ingrid suggested.

Seven became very defensive when Ingrid spoke to him in a stern tone. "What do you mean I better!" Seven responded as he took a deep breath. Seven wanted his mother's love and not her harsh criticism. But Seven was locked up and knew it came with the territory. Ingrid proceeded to lecture him. As Seven always did, he just sat there and listened to her. Uncle Darren was present. He glared at Seven the entire time and didn't say a word. Ingrid broke down in tears as she lectured Seven. Then Darren took the phone and began his military lecturing. Darren spoke about how the marines was a good place for Seven to be. "Be all you could be." Seven wasn't having it. Seven hung up the phone and swaggered away. Ingrid sobbed. Seven already had a daddy and didn't need another one, especially someone with a broomstick up his ass.

Minutes later, Seven returned to his cell and stared at the ceiling as he laid on his cot. This time his mind wasn't blank. Seven thought of home. He could sleep in his own comfortable bed, wake up any time he wanted, eat his delicious, healthy foods, go out, and nothing but freedom.

For the next two years of Seven's incarceration, he kept himself out of trouble most of the time. He lifted weights in the courtyard and ate a lot of good food that was stolen from the correction officers' cafeteria. He constantly played basketball on the court with the other inmates. He and another player got into an altercation because of the ball. Seven and the guy exchanged punches, and they both drew blood from each other. The guard saw the fight from the tower high above and signaled the alarm. Everyone had to stop and lie on the ground. Guards rushed to the scene and took Seven and the inmate were taken into custody. This time, Seven had to go solitary confinement again. This time, it wasn't pitch-black. There was some light. Seven put his hand up in front of face to see if he could see it. He smiled.

Seven looked around at his surroundings. He saw a brown wall with more profanity on it. This was how the inmates felt when they were locked down. They talked to the wall. There was a white supremacist's writing on the wall. He expressed how the white race was topnotch and a racial holy war was coming. Seven saw it and shook his head. Then there was a guy who expressed his love for his girlfriend and missed her to death. And when he got out, they were gonna be together. Sounded like Romeo and Juliet bullshit. And there were other expressions on the wall by inmates who spoke from their hearts.

Seven didn't believe in writing his business on any wall. If he talked to someone, that someone was God. He's the only one who will be there 24-7, 365 days of the year and for the rest of your life. If you allowed him to be. Seven did just that. He shut his eyes, inhaled some air into his lungs, and then opened his eyes. A heavenly light shined upon him. Seven looked to the ceiling (God). He spoke from his heart. Aloud. "God, I'm sorry I've haven't been doing the right thing. I know you're not pleased with me right now. Please, get me out of this hell. This place is hell for sure. As Seven continued his loud talk with the creator. A correction Officer heard voices coming from Seven's cell. The guard eavesdropped on the conversation, but really couldn't understand because it was just gibberish. The female guard shrugged her shoulders and strolled away shaking her head. "I know you're here for me. I'm not going to talk to any wall, I'm gonna talk to you. I want to talk to you. I'm not to write my business on any wall. I give it to you. I know you're listening. Forgive me for not knowing the way, God. And please take care of my mother. Amen."

He laid down on the cold floor and fell asleep. There was a sound of the slot of the door opening with a tray of food. "Yo, Seven," a voice called him. Seven woke up from his sleep and ran to the opened slot of the door. A ray of light beamed into the confined cell. A tray of food was placed on the slot. Seven squinted his eyes because the light was blinding. "Jamal," Seven cried.

"Yeah, it's me. I heard you got put in here again. I brought you some food," Jamal whispered.

"Thanks."

"Keep your head up, fool," said Jamal. Seven took the food as the slot closed. The light was gone. While in solitary confinement, Seven ate well with the help of Jamal. There were of course no windows, so Seven didn't even know what time of the day it was. He could only guess. Seven focused his eyes on the direction of the door, where the food was placed and where there was a ray of heavenly light. But the slot didn't open for a week. Seven was really starving. He knew he lost his weight. He could just imagine how he looked. Then finally that ray of heavenly light opened as a tray of food was placed on it. Seven saw it.

"Jamal," Seven cried as he rushed to the door. Then the slot of the door closed as the heavenly ray left. "Jamal!" Seven cried again. There was no response. *Was that Jamal or not?* Seven wondered. Seven took the food and really couldn't see what he was about to eat. It wasn't pleasant. He took one taste, and it was the worst. Seven didn't know what it was, but it was shit, not actual, but some bad-smelling meat, stale bread, and cold veggies. Seven threw the food against the wall. "Jamal, where the fuck are you, yo!" Seven shouted. The correction officers heard Seven's scream from the cell. They simply ignored him as Seven went crazy. "Where's Jamal? I want some answers." Then the slot of the cell door opened as the heavenly ray of light came in. A voice spoke to Seven. "Jamal's expired," said the unfamiliar voice.

"Who is that?"

"Don't worry about it. I want you to stop hollering. Your friend is gone," advised the unfamiliar voice. The slot of the cell closed back unfamiliar voice. The slot of the cell closed as the heavenly light left in a flash. Seven could only think of the worst. "God, what happened to Jamal!" Seven cried aloud to the creator.

"Ah, shit. Fuck." Seven cursed in a low toned voice as he paced the floor.A week later, Seven hung out in the courtyard where the inmates played basketball. The inmate players glanced at Seven with his somewhat frail physique. Seven was thin again. And he felt tired. But he couldn't let anyone see his weakness. Seven heard that Jamal was stabbed to death by another inmate over the stealing of food from the officers' cafeteria. There would be no more good food. Seven was gonna have to get used to the shitty food they served.

As the days went on, Seven ate the shitty food, pumped iron, played basketball, and got into altercations with others crazy inmates. Seven received letters from DeShaun, Polo, and the rest of the entourage. All their letters were carefully written, without any references to crimes or BiBi's, Boo's, and TaTu's situations since they were jailed as well for street racing.

Holidays and birthdays sucked in the pen. Seven's birthday arrived. There were no happy birthdays and no lavish parties thrown by DeShaun. But Seven received birthday and holiday cards from his mother, DeShaun, and the posse with their signatures on it. During the last two years, Seven sucked it up and served his time. He became real stocky, a giant almost—a giant that no one dared to fuck with. Seven pumped iron on the bench. The clanking sound of the weights could be heard across the courtyard. The inmates were drawn to Seven's weightlifting skills. The African-American and Latino inmates cheered Seven on. But the white extremists sneered and made racist remarks under their breaths. Their attitudes didn't faze Seven one bit. Seven glared at the angry mob of whites as he swaggered away.

Seven received a letter from his little sister, Athena, with a couple of photos. She was nine years old and wanted to see her big brother, but this wasn't the right time. Seven wrote back to Athena and promised he was gonna make it his business to see her. Seven counted his blessings every day. He had people around him who cared.

As Seven's twentieth birthday approached, so did his freedom. It was the greatest birthday present in the world. Seven shoved his clothes in a duffel bag and exited the cell as guards waited for him. Seven stepped out from behind the prison walls. Seven felt the weight of enslavement being lifted off his back. His body felt strong and his spirit was alive. On the other side of those prison walls was the mango-colored Saturn car as Darren leaned against his vehicle, waiting for Seven. Seven recognized his Uncle's body language and the frown on his vehicle as he waited for Seven. Seven recognized his uncle by body language and the frown on his face. They stared at each other for a moment then turned away. The two didn't say a word to each other—strange for family members who hadn't seen each other for a while, regardless of the situation. Seven hopped in on the passenger's side as Darren entered on the driver's side. The engine of the Saturn started up and sped off.

During the long eight-hour drive from Upstate New York to Long Island, Darren and Seven still didn't utter a word. Dead silence. Seven remained quiet because he didn't want to argue with his uncle. Seven knew Darren was disappointed in him and was waiting for the right time to start preaching about the armed forces. That was inevitable, long preaching about making Uncle Sam proud. Seven expunged that thought from his mind and thought of his mother. He couldn't wait to see her.

When Seven got home, Ingrid waited at the door for him. She thrust the front door open. Ingrid clutched Seven and didn't want to let go. It was a long hug. Seven missed his mother too, but he started to feel a bit funny. Seven felt like a baby.

Ingrid then released Seven from her arms and took a look at him. "How are you, Seven?" Ingrid asked with a grimace on her face.

"I'm cool," Seven said nervously.

"You look good."

"Thanks."

"I fixed dinner for you."

Seven took a seat at the table as Ingrid fixed Seven a plate. Darren stood in the entranceway of the kitchen and stared at Seven. Seven ignored his uncle. Ingrid placed the plate of steak and rice with veggies in front of Seven. He devoured the food like there was no tomorrow. Darren grabbed a seat at the table as he took a piece of broccoli from Seven's plate.

"Why are you putting your hands in my food, Darren?"

"I apologize. I wanna talk to you."

"I don't want to hear it right now."

"You need to listen."

"I just got out the pen, all right. Get the fuck off my shit!"

"I'm on your shit. You've been putting your mother through some shit."

"Darren, please," Ingrid begged as she turned abruptly from the stove.

"This is what the fuck I have to come home to?"

"Yes, you do. You're just like your father. A thug."

"That's what I am."

"And you're proud of that."

"I'd rather be a thug than a tight-ass drill sergeant!"

"Get the hell out of here, Darren!" Ingrid shouted as she grabbed Darren by the shirt. Ingrid tried to escort Darren from the table and to the door. But she couldn't because Darren was solid muscle. "Go home, Darren. This is my son. Let me handle it!"

Darren respected his sister's wishes and exited through the rear glass door. He slid it opened as he pointed at Seven. "This ain't over! You hear me, Seven!" Darren said with a determined expression on his face.

"Shut the fuck up!" Seven murmured as he continued to eat his dinner.

Ingrid sprinted to the rear glass door and slid it shut. She leaned against it and inhaled. A smile slowly emerged on her face. "I'm happy you're home."

"Thanks. I am too," Seven said as he continued to chow down on his food. Ingrid then fixed herself a plate and sat it down at the table. She sat across from her son that she hasn't seen in years. They had a lot of catching up to do.

Chapter 24

Not too long after Seven and his mother had a long talk about him getting his life on the right track, Ingrid's words went through one ear and out of the other. Seven's head was like a rock. A fool. Pigheaded. Seven wanted to do what he wanted to do. Seven wanted to see if his experience in the pen would help him conquer the streets. He dared the streets to challenge him.

Seven swaggered into DeShaun's minimart where it was jam packed with customers. It felt as if Christmas was coming. Tiana rang up customers as fast as she could. Then she saw Seven and dropped what she was doing. She left a long line of people waiting to get checked out. The stock boys noticed Seven and welcomed him with open arms.

Boo stocked the shelves with canned good. He peered from the aisle as he gasped. "My man, Seven!" Boo said as he swaggered toward Seven.

"Boo, what's up? When did you get out?" Seven asked as he embraced him.

"Four months ago," Boo answered.

"Where's DeShaun?" Seven asked stupidly.

"You know where he is."

Seven and Boo swaggered down the dark stairwell. As they came to the bottom of the staircase, there was a loud growl coming from within the darkness. An adult male Rottweiler with a thick link chain around his neck guarded DeShaun's office with sure loyalty. The dog salivated from its mouth.

Polo swung the door open. "What's the problem, Sting!" Polo hollered as he grabbed the dog by the collar. Sting proceeded to bark. "Seven, holy shit!" said Polo with enthusiasm. Sting became uncontrollable, continuously barking. "Get in the office, Sting!" Polo commanded. The four-legged animal trotted inside. "DeShaun!"

DeShaun swaggered out of the office with a cigarette that hung from his mouth. He puffed smoke into the air as he saw Seven right in front of him. DeShaun welcomed Seven home with open arms along with his entourage. DeShaun's employees in the store and thugs on the streets welcomed Seven home. DeShaun gave them a good tongue-lashing about their drag racing. He told them about a drag strip over in Riverhead where street racers could show their stuff. Seven would quickly do the pickups for DeShaun and then head over to the auto track. It would prevent Seven, TaTu, BiBi, Boo, and whoever else from being under police radar.

They drove out to Riverhead a few days later to check the drag strip out. A white Camaro revved its engine as smoke emerged from the rear tires. The tires screeched. It moved up to the starting line. Seven and his friends watched as the white Camaro was ready to blast down the track. Seven noticed the red light in the middle of the two lanes on the track. Seven nudged Magnum. Magnum looked at the red drag strip light. Then it turned green. The white Camaro thundered down the track. Seven loved the atmosphere. It felt as if he were at a NASCAR race. Seven smiled at DeShaun and loved what he did for him. DeShaun shook his head and knew this was the right place for him to be instead of the corner, where anything could happen. On top of that, Seven had to work his way back up the ladder again. DeShaun offered Seven a temporary car for the time being. It was a Cobra Mustang in black. Seven loved it. He hooked it up as he pleased. Seven gave the turbo engine extra pounds of boost, put some shiny rims on the wheels, and made the dashboard larger. There was one problem: Seven's probation officer came to check on his status every now and then. In order to keep the officers off Seven's case, DeShaun paid them to go away. And they did. So DeShaun went back to busy as usual. Seven knew his duties—pickups and fuck-ups if the drug hustlers refuse to pay. Seven did plenty of that.

One night, Seven and a drug hustler in Rochdale, Queens, exchanged multiple punches. The drug hustler was putting up a good fight, but Seven got the best of it. The other drug hustlers on the corner watched the confrontation unfold before their eyes and knew not to butt in. Seven had the clout with DeShaun's posse. Seven threw one good punch to the hustler's chin. The hustler crashed to the concrete. Seven grabbed the cash from the hustler's pocket. He then brandished his other nine-millimeter handgun that was given to him by DeShaun. All the drug hustlers gave up by giving up their cash to Seven. As Seven held that nine millimeter in his hand, he remembered he was jailed for the other illegal nine-millimeter gun. Seven moved quickly as he gathered the money from the hustlers and sprung into his Cobra Mustang and sped off. The engine's blaring reverberated into the night.

Seven did the same task day in and day out for DeShaun. He got the cash from the hustlers and returned it to DeShaun. DeShaun saw Seven's loyalty and hard work. DeShaun rewarded Seven with a puppy Rottweiler. The puppy came from a Rottweiler kennel out in Riverhead. DeShaun placed the puppy in Seven's arms. Seven was happy with the dog. DeShaun didn't like pit bulls. He couldn't stand the look of them.

Keys jingled at the front door of Seven's home as he entered. This was the home that DeShaun provided for him. It still remained the same way that he left it. Seven made his way inside with the Rottweiler puppy in his arms. He looked around and saw that everything was in order. Seven placed the puppy on the floor and headed upstairs. Seven checked out his bedroom. His king-sized bed was still neatly made. On his dresser, his colognes and personal things still remained. Then he checked his closet. Seven's clothes and footwear were fine. Then he checked the bathroom. It was fine. Seven smiled at himself and headed back downstairs. As Seven came closer to the bottom of the stairs, he smelled something shitty. There was a pile of feces right in the middle of the floor. "Fuck, yo! You can't be shitting in my house!" Seven said to the dog as if the puppy understood what he was saying. Seven grabbed some cleanser and paper towels to clean the mess up.

It was dinnertime. Seven thrust open the refrigerator, and a foul smell emerged from it. Seven turned his nose up and slammed it back. He opened it again because he had to get rid of the spoiled food in it. Seven tossed it in the trash. He then opened the freezer and threw out some frost-burned ice cream and meat. Seven had to go shopping.

Later, Seven's Mustang Cobra peeled in a parking space of a supermarket. The puppy Rottweiler resided in the backseat. Seven looked at the dog as he sat comfortably in the backseat. "Don't give me no shit!" Seven said to the dog. Seven hopped out of his Mustang and headed into the store. Inside, Seven had a shopping cart of steaks, french fries, juice, and protein drinks for himself. Then he pulled the cart down the pet aisle. Seven looked around for the best dog food for his Rottweiler pup. He grabbed a large bag of puppy chow and sneered. It wasn't good enough. He looked at the Alpo dog food and turned up his nose. He didn't want to give his dog this shit.

At home, Seven cooked two rib-eye steaks in the oven. He placed one on his plate and then placed a rib-eye steak on a plate for his puppy. It was cooked right from the broiler. The Rottie pup chowed down on it. "You like that?" Seven said to the puppy as he smiled at the animal. "If I eat steak, then you eat steak," Seven said. Seven sat down at the table and ate his dinner. That's all Seven did— eat, lift weights, and do his street duties. He really became stocky. People feared him. When Seven walked down the street, they crossed to the other side. If he swaggered into a room, people's hearts raced. When Seven entered into a store, security followed him, and when he made his way through a parking lot, people popped the locks on the car doors. No one dared to fuck with Seven. Seven knew he was powerful and embraced it. DeShaun saw the change in Seven's physique. He had himself a real street solider. Fearless. Powerful. And bold.

Word on the street was that Corey ruled the street and expanded his business. Corey and his posse overthrew kingpins in the Bronx and Westchester Counties. DeShaun wanted to run Corey into oblivion. DeShaun wanted his money, hustlers, cars, women, and everything he possessed.

Three nights later, Polo drove with Seven, Magnum, TaTu, BiBi, and Bay in his black Cadillac CTS Coupe. He would have taken another vehicle, but he didn't think to. The Cadillac CTS Coupe drove down a dark alley that was the rear of Corey's establishment. Two robust security guards stood at the door. A few thugs exited and entered. Seven and the rest of the crew put ski masks on their faces and cocked their firearms. They were ready for war. The billiard room was a full house. Seven had to find the safe where Corey's money was stored. And whatever else was around. Whoever else was around.

Rap music played from Polo's phone. Polo answered it. "Yo!" Polo replied as he lit a Philly blunt. DeShaun resided in the back-seat of Magnum's black Dodge Ram with the cell phone to his ear. Magnum occupied the driver's seat of course. "Are those fools ready?"

"Yes," Polo answered. Polo hung up his cell. Seven and his cronies leaped in action. They stormed toward the security guards, full force. Seven's pistol whooped one guard. Magnum pumped several bullets into the other guard's legs. Blood spewed through his pants' legs as he plummeted to the floor. He laid in agony. Seven and his crew made their way inside. Some thugs stood around in a red-lit hallway, smoking blunts. Seven acted fast. The atmosphere reminded him of hell with its demons plotting their next lust of sin. Seven shot bullets from his guns into the legs and feet of the thugs. They collapsed to the floor, crippled. Magnum beat one of the thugs with his fist and stomped on him. Seven crept down a reddish stairwell. He had to look for the safe or something valuable. Corey and his cronies were seated at a large table with lots of money, a JetScan, and an opened safe. "Jackpot!" Seven mumbled to himself. Seven beckoned Magnum and pointed toward Corey's profits.

Bullets began to fly. Corey and his cronies duck for cover as they exchanged fire. Gun smoke and the sound of loud popping filled the air. Rap music blasted from upstairs, where customers relaxed.

The music drowned out the crimes being committed from below. Gunfire continued as Seven had to get Corey. Seven struck Corey in the abdominal area and legs. Seven began to sweat under the ski mask. He couldn't wait to take it off so bad, but he couldn't. He had a job to do. Corey was stretched on the floor, motionless. Seven looked down at Corey and hoped that he didn't kill him. Then the gunfire seized. Seven and his crew went for the cash. The safe was already opened. Seven shoved every last bundle of the money in a plastic bag. Seven browsed to see if there was anything else of value. Seven removed Corey's gold watch, chains, and rings. Corey and his crew were laid out. Seven and his cronies fled the scene as they leaped over the thugs stretched out on the floor.

DeShaun's cell phone rang as he lounged in the passenger's seat of the Dodge Ram. "What's up?" DeShaun asked as he grinded his teeth.

"DeShaun, we got almost everything. Cash, jewelry, and shit." Seven said.

"Cool. Bring your asses!" DeShaun responded. Seven quickly hung up his cell phone as he and his posse dashed out the rear door. Seven panted as he sprung over the corpses. He panted. Then they stormed into the Cadillac Coupe as it sped down the dark alleyway and on to the street. Its wheels squealed.

A week later, Seven sped in his Mustang Cobra as the engine bellowed. Seven loved his car and was very proud of it. It was like a father being proud of his son. Seven added additional touches to his ride. He tuned up the engine even more, and he installed professional race cars seatbelts and added another pair of shiny rims on the tires. Seven never stopped working on his car. He always thought of something new to add or subtract. The black Mustang Cobra zoomed down Sunrise Highway and then halted at a red light. It pulled behind a gray station wagon, where an eight-year-old boy peered through the rear windshield. His eyes widen as he saw the shiny black sports car. It was the kind that was on every little boy's wish list.

"Dad!" the little boy cried to his father. His father was in the front seat, on the cell phone, which he's not supposed to be doing. The black Mustang Cobra switched lanes as its engine revved. The little boy pressed his nose against the window of the station wagon. Seven noticed the little boy's nose pressed against the glass window. Seven snickered. It reminded him of a little pig. The kid then gave Seven the thumbs-up on his car. The traffic light turned green. Seven beeped his horn and thundered down the highway. The engine roared as it weaved in between other motorists. Seven continued to speed up. You would think Seven learned his lesson. But no. Seven stepped on the gas and had his freedom of speed.

Seven was on his way to see his baby sister, Athena. He held on to the letters Athena wrote to him while he was incarcerated. Athena lived with her mother, Maureen, and her grandparents in Mineola. Athena was a third grader who got B's and C's. Her beautiful coca brown-skinned, long thick ponytails that draped to her shoulders made her the apple of everyone's eyes. She loved riding her bike, playing with her dolls, and looking at magazines like *Homes and Gardens* and *Unique Homes*. For a nine-year-old girl, she loved houses, especially mansions. In Athena's neighborhood, mansions weren't too far away.

Seven's engine could be heard a mile away. Athena opened the door of the two-story colonial home with her mother Maureen right behind her. The bawling turbo engine got closer and closer. The fierce muscle car stopped short in front of the home. Athena's face lit up as Seven emerged out of the driver's seat of his black Mustang GT 500.

"Seven!" Athena shouted as she raced to her brother's arms. Seven and Athena clutched each other. The last time Seven saw Athena was when she was a year and a half old. Seven could have seen Athena during those years, but there was still tension between Ingrid and Maureen even after William died.

"How are you doing, kid?" Seven said as he kissed his baby sister.

"Fine," Athena said. Seven noticed Maureen in the doorway. Seven nodded to her. Maureen sashayed towards him and Athena. The expression on Maureen's face was bitter. Seven knew it wasn't his fault he and Athena were the aftermath of their so-called love triangle. Maureen still had ill feelings towards Ingrid and some towards him. Maureen gave a slight smile and hugged Seven. Seven could sense that Maureen was being phony about it. Maureen just wanted Athena to see her big brother.

"How are you?" Seven greeted Maureen as he gave a slight smile in return.

"I'm fine," Maureen answered, not so pleased. She folded her arms and began to interrogate Seven. "How do you make a living?"

"I'm assistant manager in a grocery store," Seven answered as he raised an eyebrow.

"A grocery store?" Maureen responded. She then raised an eyebrow and knew something was not right about Seven. It was obvious; Seven was thugged out and wild. His clothes were baggy and black, and he drove an aggressive car. She didn't want Athena getting any bad influences from her older brother. Maureen was thankful she didn't have a boy, because she'd really be in trouble. Seven didn't appreciate Maureen drilling him.

"What happened to 'Hello' or 'How you doing?' instead of you drilling me?" Seven suggested. Seven refused to argue in front of Athena. Maureen then toned it down. "I came to spend a little time with my baby sister. If that's okay with you?" Seven said as he scratched his forehead.

Maureen shook her head and kissed Athena. Maureen acted as if this was going to be the last time she was going to see her daughter. "Take care of my baby. I'm holding you responsible," Maureen said.

"Don't worry. Athena's in good hands." Seven opened the door on the passenger's side of the black Mustang GT500. He slammed the door. Seven then got in on the driver's side. "Fasten your seatbelt, Athena," Seven advised. Athena fastened her safety belt. Seven put his on as well. The black Mustang GT500 car's engine started up. It revved and sped away. Athena waved to Maureen. Maureen waved in return as she tried to give a smile.

During the drive in Seven's Mustang, Athena talked and talked and talked and talked. She was just a kid. Seven didn't mind at all. Athena spoke about how her grandfather brought home magazines of mansions. And then they would ride through the upscale neighborhoods of Garden City. Athena yapped so much she didn't even notice Seven speeding.

"How are you doing in school?" Seven asked as he kept his eyes on the road.

"Good," Athena answered and then went back to the subject that interested her. "Anyway, Garden City is gorgeous. Have you been there?" Athena asked as she glared at her big brother. Athena noticed Seven's persona. He was good looking, tough, and he drove a mean machine.

"No. I've been to Westbury. There are a lot of rich people there," Seven said.

"Do you know any rich people?"

"Yeah. I once knew someone rich."

"A boy or girl?" Athena asked.

"A girl."

"Do you still see her?"

"No."

"I like your car." Athena changed the subject.

"Thanks. You wanna get something to eat?" Seven asked Athena as he glanced at his baby sister, now all grown-up.

"Yes," Athena said. She continued on her conversation about mansions and rich people.

Seven listened to how she wanted to become rich. Maybe she would go into real estate and/or some sort of lucrative career. Athena opened the door to Seven's past, which was Angelika. She stuck to Seven's mind like glue. He wondered how Angelika was. She would pop in his mind every now and then.

At a restaurant, Seven and Athena resided at a booth and waited to have their orders taken. Athena flipped through Unique Homes a real estate magazine that Seven purchased for her from Barnes and Noble. She pointed out which mansion she loved the most. And then Seven pointed out which ones he loved the best. Just by flipping through this magazine, it sparked a lot of memories of him and his mother at the Westland mansion when he was a kid. A stunning, fair-skinned waitress switched her hips towards their table. She was twenty-something, pretty, with a body shaped like an hourglass, with brown shoulder-length hair.

"Good afternoon. My name is Candace. I'll be your waitress," said Candace.

"Hello, Candace," Seven said with seduction in his tone. Athena snickered at Seven coming on to the waitress. Seven couldn't take his eyes off her. She smiled as she attempted to take their order. Seven and Athena then quickly looked over the menu.

"Do you guys need a while to decide?" the waitress asked as she smiled at them.

Seven made direct eye contact with her. "Give me the Philly cheesesteak sandwich with fries and a Coke." Seven ordered as he kept his eyes on the waitress. Then he checked out Candace's buttocks and breasts. Athena ordered a simple burger, fries, and soda as well. The waitress grabbed the menus and strutted away. Athena snickered again. "What's so funny?" Seven asked as he glared directly into his baby sister's eyes.

"You like her?" Athena giggled as she covered her mouth.

"Why are you laughing at me?"

"Because you're funny, Seven," Athena said as she burst into laughter.

"Shh! Everyone's looking at us," Seven whispered. "She's pretty," Seven said as he thought about getting the waitress's number. He stared at Candace from a distance as she took orders from other customers. Seven had to wait for the right time.

A couple of hours later, Seven and Athena finished eating their food as Candace came and collect their plates. "Would you guys like any dessert?" Candace asked as she smiled.

Seven eyed her straight in her face and then grinned. "That's okay," Seven said as he continued the grin that he wouldn't let go of. "May I have the check and your number," Seven said. Candace snickered as she strutted away with the empty plates.

Athena really began to crack up. "Why are you cackling so much, huh? Seven asked Athena as he tossed a five dollar bill at her. "Thank you." Athena said as her cackling subsided. Then Candace came back with the check. Seven looked at the bill as he counted a fat bundle of cash from his pocket. Athena raised an eyebrow as she saw Seven counting his money. Seven placed down the payment for the meals and a fifty-dollar tip. "And your number, Candace." Candace blushed as her cheeks turned red. "What's the problem, Candace?" Seven asked.

"I'm flattered, but I have a boyfriend," Candace said as she collected the pay for the bill and her tip. "I can't take this," Candace said in a nervous tone.

"Don't worry, that's for you. Get yourself something pretty," Seven complimented as he and Athena left.

During the drive home, Seven rode through the affluent neighborhoods of Garden City. Athena's eyes bulged as she saw gorgeous homes just like in the magazines. There were many mansions, some old and some recently built. You could tell by the fresh stone, brick, and cement.

"Look at that one there. How much do you think that one cost, Seven?" Athena questioned.

"Probably over a million or two," Seven answered.

"Whoa! Look at that one!" Athena said with enthusiasm as she pointed at the property. Athena loved Garden City, with its luxurious homes and people with their affluent lifestyles. It was like Beverly Hills, but no hot weather and palm trees. Seven wanted to drive to Westbury, where Angelika resided, if she still lived there. He didn't want Athena to start bugging him about the rich girl he once knew. Maybe, Angelika's probably in California or Paris or some affluent place. Moments later, Seven dropped Athena off at home. She kissed her big brother on the cheek and said good-bye.

Seven drove slower than usual. This was a first. He knew why he was doing it. Seven drove down Westbury Road with its enormous well-trimmed hedges. The lamppost kept the surroundings beautifully well lit. The black Mustang drove past the gated entranceway where guards kept an open eye. *Maybe Angelika did move,* Seven thought to himself. *No. Maybe she's just at home chillin',* Seven thought again to himself. Seven smiled because he was comfortable with that thought since no one was around. He was going to make it his business to see her again. Just a glimpse of Angelika.

Chapter 25

A year later, it was just a few days after Seven's birthday. He was twenty-one. Seven's now driving a black Dodge Charger with the Hemi Super Bee engine. Seven's proud of his new ride. It was given to Seven as a gift from DeShaun, who rewarded him for successfully overthrowing Corey. Seven did the job well without being under police radar. DeShaun's operation ruled the streets and generated more than six hundred grand a day. DeShaun got customers from every walk of life—black, white, Latino, rich, poor, old, young, middle-aged. It didn't matter. All he wanted to do was please their high. Due to Seven's profitable earnings, he showered his mother with gifts beyond her belief. He purchased Ingrid extravagant fragrances, nice clothes, a new refrigerator—anything she wanted or needed Seven had it delivered to the house. There were times when Ingrid refused to accept her son's offerings. Darren knew Seven was giving his mother these gifts and just had to cope with it.

On this late afternoon, July 31, Seven drove his Charger through the affluent neighborhood of Westbury. Today was Angelika's sixteenth birthday. Seven drove down Westbury Road as an expensive sporty blue Ferrari raced past him., as well as a burgundy Maserati and a silver Cadillac Escalade with clamoring rich white kids. A bunch of aluminum balloons that read "Happy birthday" took up the entire backseat of a metallic blue BMW that made its grand entrance as it accelerated past the black Dodge Charger. The turbo engine bawled. Seven became irate with this blond-haired, blue-eyed rich kid behind the wheel. "What the fuck?" Seven cursed as he raised an eyebrow and wondered where these rich kids were headed to. Seven immediately thought about Timothy from years ago, Angelika's childhood friend. "Is that Timothy?" Seven asked himself. Seven put his foot on the gas and raced behind the sporty metallic blue BMW.

The line of luxurious cars halted at the gate that led to the Westland mansion. The black Dodge Charger halted at a red traffic light a couple of yards from the enormous gates. Seven saw the security guards check everyone in the vehicles. Then they were allowed through the enormous iron gates to the Westland mansion. Angelika was definitely having a soiree. House music could be heard from behind those gates. Seven pictured in his mind what was probably going on.

Balloons, streamers, and other party favors gave the atmosphere that birthday vibe. There were long tables of food, snacks, and drinks. A large ice swan sat in the middle of the table with a punch bowl. "Happy birthday, Angelika." Angelika's friends Cassandra, Timothy, and other cronies shouted. Her friends embraced Angelika with hugs, kisses, and gifts. Angelika developed into a lovely young lady. She grew a little taller, and her hair was longer and styled to give her the Farrah Fawcett look. The scent of Juicy Couture fragrances emerged from Angelika's petite body—original Juicy Couture, Viva La Juicy, Couture Noir, and other fabulous scents that made a person know she was present.

Angelika's outfit was a red jumper from Chanel that her mother bought for her. She also wore black pumps from Chanel with her Juicy Couture jewelry, and she wore makeup that consisted of foundation, eye shadow, eyeliner, mascara, a little blush, and red lipstick. She had a wardrobe from Juicy Couture, the Gap, American Eagle, Banana Republic, etc. Angelika wore nothing but the best. And she always shopped till she dropped.

Angelika danced with Timothy to the House music. The music became groovier. The party guests got on the dance floor and boogied. Angelika was getting older and just lived for the moment. She didn't really think about the future. But for Mr. and Mrs. Westland, Angelika's future was very important. Mr. Westland didn't worry about college or her having a lucrative career. He wanted Angelika to marry into wealth. And he knew the perfect candidate. Angelika's parents watched as Angelika interacted happily with Timothy. Timothy was close to the Westlands, and he seemed to like Angelika. Mr. Westland had an agenda.

Still waiting at the traffic light, Seven revved his Hemi engine. The traffic light signaled green. The black Dodge Charger thundered down the road. Seven knew he wasn't going to get past those gates. He'll figure that out later. Rap music blasted from his cell phone. The caller ID read "Mom." Seven answered, "What's up, Mom?"

"I'm at the market. Can you come and get me." said Ingrid as the clamor of the busy supermarket was loud in the background.

"Where are you, Mom?" Seven asked.

"I'm at Stop and Shop in Bay Shore.", said Ingrid as she continued to push her shopping cart full of food.

"Why did you go to the store by yourself?" Seven asked in a stern tone.

"I have to shop. And don't raise your voice at me," Ingrid yelled back at Seven.

Seven sucked his teeth. "I'll be there to pick you up," said Seven as he hung up.

An hour later, Ingrid browsed the cookie aisle. She checked the price of the Chips Ahoy! cookies. It was 1.99 on sale. Ingrid placed three of them in the cart. Then Seven swaggered down the aisle behind her. "What's up, Mom?" Seven greeted her with a kiss and hug.

"How are you, son?" Ingrid asked.

"I'm chillin'," Seven replied.

"The Chips Ahoy! are on sale for 1.99. So I bought three packs for you."

"You don't have to do that," Seven said. "Where's Darren?"

"He had a date. Darren's got to have a life too," Ingrid said.

Moments later, Ingrid and Seven loaded their groceries on the register, ready to be rung up by the cashier. The cashier's hair was nicely styled and wore attire that made her approachable. As Seven loaded the food on to the register, the cashier scanned the items quickly. Seven acknowledged how pretty she was as he kept glaring at her. He could sense a fuckin' attitude. Seven couldn't stand women with attitudes.

They were the worse type of females to deal with. Most guys would simply retreat when a female gave them an attitude. But, when it came to Seven he put them in check. "Who the fuck does she think she is?" Seven thought to himself as he sneered at her. He noticed her nametag read "Margo."

Cashier Margo scanned the last item and totaled the order. "One twenty-two eighty," said the cashier.

Ingrid searched for her money in her purse. Seven quickly grabbed the bundle of cash from his pocket and handed Margo two hundred dollars. Ingrid had her money in hand. "Don't worry, Mom. I got it," Seven insisted as he handed the cashier the cash. Then Ingrid handed her cash to Margo. Margo became confused on whom to accept the money from. "Take the fuckin' money!" Seven cursed at the top of his lungs. It sparked attention from other shoppers in the store. Margo then snatched the cash from Seven's hand. "I know you didn't just do that shit!" Seven bawled.

The supermarket bookkeeper rushed over to register. "What's the problem?"

"Your cashier has a real attitude." Seven carried on.

"I sincerely apologize," said the bookkeeper as she took the money and gave Seven back his change. Then the bookkeeper packed up the groceries.

Seven glared at Margo as she shied away. Seven snatched some of the groceries and swaggered out of the supermarket. The bookkeeper finished packing up the rest of Ingrid's food and placed it in the shopping cart. "Thank you. I apologize for my son's behavior," said Ingrid.

"That's okay. Have a nice day," said the bookkeeper.

Ingrid wheeled the shopping cart out of the store to Seven's car.

Meanwhile, during the drive home, Seven and Ingrid had it out. Seven knew it wasn't the cashier's fault. Seven was pissed. A bunch of snobby rich kids had to have their way on the road. Seven hated to be cut off. That's a slap in the face to any driver on the road.

"What was your problem embarrassing me like that!" Ingrid said.

"Embarrassing you? How? This wasn't about you! It was that cashier!"

"Something else is bothering you," said Ingrid as she eyed him right in the face.

Seven became quiet and focused his eyes on the road. He drove at a medium speed as he exhaled. Seven wasn't going to tell his mother he was cut off by some rich kids. He wasn't even going to tell her he was pursuing Angelika. He knew she'd disapprove because of his thug lifestyle. *Speaking of rich kids, maybe, I shouldn't pursue Angelika. She's probably a snob,* Seven thought to himself.

The black Dodge Charger peeled into the driveway of Ingrid's home. Ingrid and Seven hopped out of the car, at each other's throats. *This behavior of Seven's could land him in jail again,* Ingrid thought. Seven opened the trunk of his Charger as he grabbed the groceries and hustled into the house. Inside moments later, Ingrid lounged in chair at the kitchen table as Seven stored the food away. She shook her head in disappointment. Seven felt his mother's unhappiness, especially when he did something as extreme as that. Seven placed the canned goods in the cabinet then put the meat in the freezer.

"Leave the rib eye out. You know you want me to cook it," Ingrid said as she didn't take her eye off Seven. Seven smirked as he placed the rib-eye steak on the counter. Then he put the cereal and more canned goods in the cabinets.

After dinner, Seven and Ingrid ate the rib-eye steak and didn't really have much to say. Seven felt that a lecture was about to jump off from his mother on his boisterous ways. "You're still running the streets for DeShaun, aren't you?" Ingrid was right on point. There was displeasure in her face. Seven chugged down his drink and slammed the glass on the table. "Could we please change the subject, please." Seven pleaded in a subservient tone.

"No." Ingrid hollered as she slammed her hand on the table.

"Why are you questioning me now? You've been taking my money and gifts for, God only knows how long!" Seven said.

Then Ingrid was lost for words. Ingrid took her last bite of her food and then placed her dish in the sink. He didn't mean to make Ingrid feel bad. But he was doing something bad. Seven sold poison to the world. Even though he did this, it wasn't his responsibility for the drug users' habits. Ingrid differed on the issue. Seven stormed away from the kitchen table, leaving an almost-empty plate. He gave Ingrid a peck on the cheek and left. He slammed the door shut. Seven jumped in his black Dodge Charger and backed out of the driveway. The engine rumbled. The tire screeched. The muscle car thundered down the road as night approached.

With Seven and his Charger, he knew he had to be more aggressive on the road, cutting people off. *Fuck it! I own this motherfucker.* Already, he began bad road habits. A lime-green-colored Toyota Prius was a few feet ahead of him. In the next lane was a funny purple car, something that was for those stunt car shows. The black Dodge Charger accelerated past the funny purple car and then swerved in front of it. Seven then cut right in front of the Toyota Prius. He peered through his rearview mirror and snickered. The black Dodge Charger left the poor little Toyota Prius in the dust. Seven had a heart of stone. He picked up his speed so he wouldn't witness any accidents or someone being a witness to an accident that he caused.

The night was young, but Seven headed home. Most of his friends were busy hanging out. DeShaun left several messages on Seven's cell to hang out. No street duties. Seven wasn't in the mood. He wanted to hit the sack and just be left alone.

That night, Seven focused his eyes upward at the ceiling in his king-sized bed. His Rottweiler pup slept in a doggie bed large enough for this type of breed next to Seven's bed. Seven's eyes became heavier and heavier. But he couldn't sleep. Depression overwhelmed Seven. He felt an emptiness inside him. His spirit's dead and needed to be uplifted.

A King James Bible sat on his nightstand. He looked to it and grabbed it, flipping through the paper-thin pages all through the Old

Testament to the New. Seven didn't know where to start. He halted at the Gospel according to John, chapter 1, "In the beginning was the word, and the Word was with God, and the Word was God. He was in the beginning with God." Seven squinted his eyes and didn't get it. He tried to understand the Good Book on his own without his mother's interventions. He kept reading chapter 1 of John. As Seven kept reading the scripture, he got it. He placed the Bible back on his nightstand. Since the day Seven and his mother were at the Westland estate, he somewhat felt as if they were second-class citizens. Due to their big parties, glitz, and glamour, it washed all that away. He's not a kid anymore. Seven's a man and wanted to be treated with respect. But if someone is going to be disrespectful, you're sure in going to get a full serving of it in return. Seven cleared his mind and closed his eyes. All Seven had to do was focus on God and things would fall into place.

Chapter 26

The next morning, there was no sun. Gray skies dominated the heavens. Raindrops hit the earth like the sound of a crowd applauding at a Broadway play. Seven slept on his back as he heard the sound of the heavy rain. He then opened his eyes and looked toward the ceiling. Thoughts from the night before popped into his head, the reenactment of those rich kids bullying everyone out of their way. *When they eat at the restaurant, they probably left the waiter/waitress a small tip or nothing at all. Those rich fucks probably ran red lights and tried to run people down. The police probably saw everything and turn their heads. Chances are, they even belittled their help.* It's a good thing Seven had God, because he knew his temperament. If Seven didn't, he'd be in jail or dead for fuckin' up some rich kid.

Minutes later, Seven dragged his feet along the floor as chewed-up doggie toys were in his path. He kicked them to the side. Sting slept in the center of the floor. Stuffing from the toys were all over the floor. Seven trashed it. The Rottweiler woke up and glared at Seven. "Are you ready to eat?" Seven asked the dog as if Sting understood. Seven grabbed some old rotisserie chicken from the refrigerator and put it in his doggie pan. The four-legged hound understood when Seven headed to that ice box. Sting devoured the poultry in a

205

matter of seconds. Then he placed some cheese from the refrigerator and tossed it in the puppy's dish. Again, the Rottweiler devoured it. Seven had to walk this puppy because he didn't want any accidents in the house.

Later that morning, Seven walked his puppy Rottweiler at a local park. The sun came out, but with cool temperatures that made the day a comfortable one. Joggers jogged. Children clamored in the a.m. hours. Elderly people resided on benches, enjoying the ducks in the nearby pond. Sting sniffed around, trying to figure out where to do his business. Sting finally made number 2 in the bushes. Seven gazed at a young African-American female, fair skinned with a slender body, jog by. Seven eyed her as she jogged her way out of the park. Then there was another African-American female, fair skinned, pushing a baby stroller. Seven was still dazed. He couldn't snap out of it. The girls that he spotted reminded him of Angelika. He wasn't going to let any obstacles get in the way of him reuniting with his friend. Seven had no idea how Angelika may look now. But he knew she was beautiful.

Seven's eyes continued to wander around the area to see if there were any other females of similar type. No, that was it. Then he snapped out of it. Seven's eyes panned around and stood there dumbfounded with a dog leash in his hand. Seven searched the park grounds high and low for his dog. There was a German shepherd barking. Seven noticed the German shepherd and its owner kept the Rottweiler puppy company. The dog owner was a white male in his early fifties, strong built, and wore police attire. In the distance, Seven noticed a line of German shepherds with some police officers doing some training exercises. There were police vehicles that read "Suffolk County K-9 Unit." Seven's heart raced as if he saw a ghost. Seven then did see a ghost.

He swaggered across the enormous lawn at a fast pace. He constantly looked over his shoulder, hoping the officer wouldn't ask if the Rottweiler pup was his. *I'm not going back to jail for any drug charges. These cops will find out every bit of info on me and I'll be sent away from life,* the nervous thought ran across Seven's brain. Finally, he made it to his black Dodge Charger, hopped and sped away.

Meanwhile, during the drive home, Seven continuously peered into the rearview mirror. He was going to miss Sting. Maybe, he would be better as a K-9. K-9 police units mostly use German shepherds, but once in a while, they'll use Rottweilers. Sting would be of good use. *What the fuck am I going to tell DeShaun? I know he's going to ask me, "What happened to the dog I gave you?" What the fuck do I say? I can't tell DeShaun that the pup got hit by a car. I'm sure as fuck not going to tell him I came across some police K-9 officers and I had no other choice than to leave the puppy that played with the K-9 dog and officer. Now what?* All these questions ran through Seven's head.

He focused his eyes on the road. His cell phone vibrated. Seven checked on the caller ID. It read "DeShaun." Seven swallowed his fear and answered the call. As Seven greeted DeShaun with "What's up?" DeShaun asked and wondered why Seven didn't want to hang out. Seven claimed a severe headache overwhelmed him that night and he had to get rid of it. Anyway, DeShaun wanted him to do some pickups over in Roosevelt, Long Island, one of DeShaun's drug spots. Without hesitation, Seven was right on the job. There's nothing Seven couldn't do for DeShaun. After Seven hung up his cell, Seven navigated his black Dodge Charger over to Roosevelt, not too far from where he was. The Hemi engine bellowed as the muscle car thundered down the road.

Over in Roosevelt, in front of a grocery store, it looked like a semilit area. Two drug runners, Chip and Hobbit, were busy exchanging drugs for money. Chip was a tall, kind of pudgy twenty-four-old thug with his front chipped tooth. He liked the way it looked, and then everyone gave him the name. It was due to him getting into a physical altercation with a girl. This girl was three times his size. Chip and the girl hurled punches at each other, which led to his tooth being chipped. It humiliated Chip that he almost got his teeth knocked out by a female. Chip's partner, Hobbit, a dwarflike thug in his late-thirties, seemed like someone you would laugh at due to his size. But, if anyone dare to laugh at him, Hobbit would clamp down on them like a pit bull. Most of the time, he was like Mr. Frodro in the Lord of the Rings movie. Happy, adventurous, and everyone loved him

Then a loud echo of a car engine was heard in the distance. Chip and Hobbit didn't really pay any attention to it. Then beaming headlights blinded them as they were still in the process of their transactions. Chip squinted his eyes and turned his head away.

"Who the fuck is that?" Hobbit shouted as he stepped in front of the unknown muscle car. The headlights dimmed as Hobbit gasped.

The black Dodge Charger became prominent before his eyes. The Hemi engine proceeded to rumble. Seven stepped out of his ride as he left the driver's side door open. Seven confronted Hobbit. Hobbit cringed as he didn't dare challenge Seven's authority.

"What the fuck are you in front of my ride?" Seven questioned as he eyed Hobbit from head to toe.

Hobbit automatically handed over his cash to Seven. Seven counted it and glanced at him. Chip then made his way over to Seven's side. The drug runners always became nervous when it was time for the pickups. Seven knew the runners like he knew the back of his hand. He handed Hobbit his cut of the money. Hobbit smiled and swaggered away. Chip handed Seven his bundle of cash. Seven and Chip got along better than any of the other runners. Chip put in his hours, overtime, paid on time, and was never short on a dollar. Seven noticed Chip's performance and was thinking about
putting in a good word for him. They gave each other hi-fives as Chip went on his way. Seven dashed into his muscle car and took off as the engine bellowed through atmosphere.

Meanwhile, back at the minimart, DeShaun, Skeeter, TaTu, and Polo counted up cash that was earned from other dealers on the streets. Some of them stood in line as if they were paying their utility bills. DeShaun paced behind Skeeter and Polo as they collected the cash and then placed it in the JetScan. TaTu stored the cash in the safe. DeShaun kept close watch on everyone and everything, especially since he rebuilt his business.

Like a father waiting for his son to come home, DeShaun constantly glanced at his watch. "Where's Seven, yo?"

Outside of DeShaun's office, his Rottweiler guarded the door. Seven approached as the dog rose to his feet and barked. But the bark wasn't a menacing one; it was more of a friendly one. The dog received a pat on the head as Seven rung the buzzer. Skeeter thrust the door open. Seven rushed in. Inside, Seven handed DeShaun bundles of cash. DeShaun wanted to go to the strip club and see some T&A.

Seven felt those females were too easy. He wanted a challenge. Most guys were lazy to be challenged when it came to females, especially the thugs who claimed to be hard and couldn't back their shit up. They wanted the females to pursue them. DeShaun needed to get his mind off things and relax with some ass in his face. Seven had places to go and people to meet, one at the supermarket and one at a mansion. Which one of these women would give Seven the time of day? Probably neither. Seven had plan C. He'll join DeShaun for some T&A.

Chapter 27

A week later, a stock boy collected shopping carts in the parking lot of a strip mall. He pushed them into one another and wheeled them back toward the enormous supermarket. The establishment sat in the middle of smaller businesses. There was a nail salon, a pizzeria, a coffee shop, a bookstore, etc. Lots of cars occupied the spaces, which left no opportunity for other customers. The roar of the Hemi engine echoed in the distance as the black Dodge Charger made its presence known. Seven drove his ride around the lot, looking for a space. No luck. Determination was the key with Seven. Make a way out of no way. But still he drove around the lot with his muscle car, angry as a motherfucker. The exit door of the supermarket swung open as Margo, the cashier, strutted to the coffee shop. Seven noticed her from his rearview mirror. He slammed on the brakes for a second and then proceeded driving so he could cut her off the other way. Instead, Seven peeled into space where another vehicle pulled out of. Seven shut down his Charger and swaggered into the shop.

Inside, there was a long line as Margo waited her turn. Seven stood in line with two people in front of him. He had to think fast. How was he going to apologize to Margo? Then Margo ordered a cream cheese bagel and small coffee. Seven jumped ahead of the line and placed a twenty-dollar bill on the counter. "I'll pay for that!" Seven cried.

Margo looked and saw Seven. Her heart raced, and her eyes almost popped out of her head. Immediately, she shoved her ten-dollar bill into the cashier's hand. "Please, ma'am, take the ten dollars."

"Relax, Margo. I got it!" Seven insisted as he gave her a smile. Margo rushed out of the coffee shop. Seven was in pursuit. "Sweetheart, I'm sorry. Honest."

Margo ignored his apologies and kept on walking. Seven grabbed Margo by the hand.

"Let go of me!" Margo demanded.

"I'm sorry for my bad attitude. My fault." Seven continued to apologize.

Margo backed away as Seven kept coming toward her. "I'm sorry. Honestly. Let's go in the coffee shop."

"I'm not going anywhere with you. I don't know you. We'll stand here in front of everyone and talk." Margo and Seven made eye contact.

Seven had a smile on his face and snickered. Margo wasn't amused. She wanted her food. Margo didn't want her break to be ruined. Thirty minutes of hell with this guy. She put on her sweet girlie act to get Seven going.

"Where's my food?" Margo sighed.

"Holy shit! I paid for your food and forgot it," Seven said as he felt like a complete ass in front of her. "Don't go anywhere. I'm gonna get it." Seven dashed into the coffee shop. Margo stood there as some of her coworkers witnessed the scene.

"Is everything all right, Margo?" asked a co-worker.

"Yeah," Margo said as she shrugged her shoulders.

Seven then swaggered back out with Margo's food. He gave Margo the nice white little bag with her coffee and bagel. Margo didn't say "Thank you" or even smile. She drank her coffee and ate her bagel while Seven yapped how pretty she was. He explained why he cursed at Margo because she seemed very stuck up. So the only way to get her attention was to curse at her. Margo begged to differ. There's no excuse.

"You shouldn't take things so seriously," Margo explained. She then apologized in return. It was that time of the month.

Seven guffawed. "All this over your menstruation." Seven continued to guffaw.

"Keep your voice down!" Margo shouted as she blushed. Margo glared at him because it wasn't funny at all, women suffering with pains in the sides, stomach, legs, etc.

Seven's amusement subsided as he realized he and Margo weren't starting off on the right foot. He wanted the opportunity to take Margo to a movie or dinner so they could get better acquainted. Margo was flattered, but she refused him. Seven was a complete stranger, and he insulted her. Seven understood and smiled. There were slight smiles, handshakes, and it broke the ice. It was peaceful. Seven dashed into his black Dodge Charger and started her up. The wheels screeched as it took off in a flash.

He was back on the Sunrise Highway again, speeding. The black Dodge Charger kept up its swift pace. Highway patrol officers were on the side of the highway, waiting for the next speed demon. Seven kept on speeding and picked up the pace even more. The black Dodge Charger weaved in and out of traffic. He raised an eyebrow and wondered what was going on with them. *Why aren't I being pursued like last time? Whatever the fuck!* Seven thought.

Seven's mind went right back to Margo. He really wanted to take her out, but she felt Seven was coming on too strong and just wanted one thing. Seven really didn't do that unless a female had a reputation for being real loose. And he could tell Margo wasn't the type. But you never knew what kind a woman is in the bedroom. Sweet at the movies, then a freak in bed. There's nothing wrong with it. Unless you're with one person, then it's fine. Seven didn't even bother to allow Angelika to cross his mind. He focused his eyes on the road and thought of his baby with her four wheels, 720 horsepower, and Hemi engine that he boosted. She could get Seven from point A to Z in no time at all. She was his first love, and he and she were one. The drag strip was a place where Seven could get back into the swing of things. But the street was where it was at.

Seven arrived at the minimart when the sun was about to set. A few customers entered and exited the establishment with product in hand. Tiana rung up customers as usual. She's usually quiet. She maintained a classy appearance. Tiana wore her hair long and black, with a nice T-shirt with blue jeans and sneakers. It was totally different from what she usually sported.

Why is Tiana looking so classy now? She probably figured that the ghetto fabulous look doesn't work, Seven thought to himself. Seven waved at her. Tiana's face lit up like the lights on a Christmas tree. Tiana wanted to chat with Seven, but she had to take care of customers. Seven proceeded downstairs and headed into DeShaun's zealous Rottweiler. The Rottie guarded the door as it usually did. Seven confronted the 120-pound creature and dared it to challenge him. Then the four-legged beast rose on its paws and barked in a friendly manner. Some of DeShaun's henchmen goofed around the pool table without a care in the hood. The thugs didn't pay attention to the dog's barks.

Seven rung the buzzer as he hugged the dog. Seven felt bad because he lost his puppy to a cop, the loss of a best friend, even though it was a short time with a puppy. Seven didn't know if he wanted a dog. If he did, there would be no walks in the park. Seven noticed that no one responded to the door. There's clamoring from inside of DeShaun's office. Seven sprung to his feet and rung the buzzer again. Skeeter swung the door open." Who the fuck is it!"

"It's me, fool," Seven hollered in return. Skeeter hauled Seven into the office by the collar and slammed the door.

Static emerged from the holsters of police officers' radios. Among the sound of the officers' radios was DeShaun's radio that played Earth, Wind, and Fire in the background. Cigarette smoke filled the air, making it hard to breathe, especially if a person had asthma. The boys in blue stood before DeShaun's desk, counting bundles of cash. Seven and Skeeter bickered as the sound of the static continued throughout the office. Seven took notice as his heart pumped hard.

What are the cops doing here? What the fuck is going on? Seven asked himself but wouldn't dare ask Skeeter. Instead, Seven gave

Skeeter a look of "What's going on?" He then whispered in Seven's ear and told him. DeShaun made a deal with the boys in blue. They wanted to make extra money. These officers were to sell narcotics to more customers outside of the community. Then DeShaun would cut them a share of the profit. In Seven's eyes, this was a bad a move on DeShaun's part. He wasn't gonna tell DeShaun how to run his business. But the law was being involved in their business. Pigs are dirty and crooked. This deal was gonna go wrong. Dead wrong. Seven just kept his mouth shut and went along with the program. He stepped farther into the office and saw the transaction between DeShaun and the officers.

DeShaun noticed Seven's presence. DeShaun then introduced Seven to the officers. Seven wasn't crazy about the introduction but played along with it. The reason was DeShaun knew Seven loved to drag race on the street. The officers were not to patrol Sunrise Highway from 1:00 a.m. to 4:00 a.m. so Seven and other racers could occupy the road to do their stunts with their babies.

Chapter 28

A couple of months later, the autumn season was in full bloom. The trees' leaves changed colors of red, yellow, and brown as they fell to the earth one by one. Walking on autumn grounds where the leaves fell was like struggling through a knee-high snow in the winter. Sixty-five-degree temperature with a light wind blew through the air. With this type of season or with all four seasons, the Westland estate was becoming, even at the entrance where the enormous iron fence stood tall where it caught everyone's eye.

Along the tall well-trimmed hedges, manicured lawns, and its now-autumn trees on Westbury Road, two young girls strolled on this Sunday afternoon. Angelika and Cassandra, now sixteen years of age, have grown into beautiful young ladies. Both Angelika and Cassandra were similar in appearance even when they were kids. The two girls dressed alike and were like sisters even though they were of different races. Cassandra and Angelika didn't see that. They were best friends. Both girls sported designer clothing, either from the Gap or Banana Republic, which were blue jeans, girlie tops, and high-top sneakers. Angelika and Cassandra were on their way to Angelika's house. They snacked on some chips and soda.

"Don't hog up all the chips, Cassandra. Leave some for me," Angelika said.

"I'm not," Cassandra replied.

As the two girls were bickering over the goodies, the sound of a loud engine could be heard in the background. The girls didn't react to the sound until it got closer and closer and closer. Then Angelika wondered where that noise was coming from. Cassandra paid no attention. She continued to devour all the chips and gulp down the soda. Then the black Dodge Charger zoomed down Westbury Road as it slowed its pace. Angelika saw the noir muscle car approaching.

Seven had his window rolled down as he and Angelika caught each other's eyes. Seven knew that had to be Angelika. But Angelika didn't know the stranger was once her childhood friend. Angelika didn't return the smile. Seven understood Angelika's position on not trusting strangers even though he was sure it was her.

Cassandra then noticed the guy in the black Dodge Charger and wondered who the stranger was. "Wow. He's cute," Cassandra said with her mouth full of chips. Then the muscle car picked up speed.

"So what if he's cute," Angelika said as she grabbed the soda from Cassandra. Angelika took a sip and shook the empty can. "Cassandra! You drank it all. Why didn't you get another can?" Angelika sighed as she sucked her teeth. Then up ahead, a traffic light turned red. Seven halted at the traffic light. Alongside him, the latest Jaguar with a familiar face from Seven's childhood passed. Seven noticed the affluent-looking African-American gentleman much older now. He knew this had to be Mr. Westland.

"Dad, wait up! Dad!" Angelika screamed in the distance.

"Mr. Westland! Wait up!" Cassandra pleaded.

Mr. Westland peered through his rearview mirror and saw his daughter and her friend dashing towards the car. He unlocked to doors. "Girls! Get in!" Mr. Westland said as he kissed Angelika.

"What's up, Dad?" Angelika said.

Then it was definitely Mr. Westland and Angelika. Seven glared at her as she then caught his eye. Then the showdown between Mr. Westland and Seven began. They eyed each other from the driver's side of their vehicles. Seven didn't even admire the fabulous sporty Jaguar Mr. Westland was driving. Seven's eyes were fixed on Mr. Westland.

He knew the thoughts that were going through Mr. Westland's head. *Who the hell is this thug eyeing my daughter? This hood. This ruffian. This goon. This menace to society.* Mr. Westland would fight to the death for his daughter.

Then the traffic light turned from red to green. The black Dodge Charger then thundered down Westbury Road. "Bastard!" Mr. Westland murmured. Angelika and Cassandra witnessed the entire staring match between Mr. Westland and the thug in the menacing muscle car. The girls looked at each other in wonder, shrugging their shoulders. The Jaguar zoomed through the fancy iron gates that guarded the Westland estate.

As Seven proceeded down Westbury Road, he made his way on to the Sunrise Highway. Seven pictured Angelika's face just right as he thought she would be—beautiful and seemed to be good spirited. Just by Angelika making eye contact and smiling at him made a thug's day. *Does she remember me? Or maybe it's just a handsome thug she's laid eyes on for the first time,* Seven questioned in his mind. He had to tell his mother. Ingrid would be thrilled that Seven saw Angelika. Angelika was the daughter Ingrid never had. But she was like her child. He kept smiling to himself because he couldn't get Angelika's face out of his mind. Seven stepped on the gas of his Charger and headed to his mother's house.

Later at Ingrid's house, her eyes popped out of her head just by hearing Angelika was grown-up and gorgeous made Ingrid proud. Seven spoke of trying to reunite with Angelika. Ingrid wasn't crazy about the idea due to her being fired by the Westlands years ago. Ingrid knew this would cause trouble for Angelika, Seven, and even herself. There were other issues Seven had to face if he dealt with Angelika. He's not of the same economic status as she was. Plus there was an age difference that could land Seven behind bars. Ingrid voiced her opinion as Seven ate his dinner slowly, and it sunk in his head. Seven's been to prison before. He wasn't in any rush to go back there. He had to think of a way to get to Angelika and how to keep himself from getting into any trouble with the authorities. Seven wasn't going to give up that easy due to the threat of money, an age difference, an iron fence, and the police. A thug had to work it out.

At dusk, the sunset created an orange autumn sky. The air became cold and crisp. With this type of weather, a person could catch a cold if not properly dressed. As Seven drove his black Dodge Charger, he dressed according to the weather. Seven wore his black sweatshirt. The Hemi engine made the interior of his vehicle warm. He didn't even have to turn on the heat. He cleared his mind and was on his way to the auto track. He and his cronies had to discuss something that troubled them. DeShaun's business dealing with the police wasn't good at all. Seven had a negative feeling about that. Seven put a Philly blunt in his mouth, lit it up, and inhaled. He blew smoke rings into the air. The car became smoky. He didn't care at this point. The Philly blunt was cheery flavored, and the aroma scented the car.

Later, the auto track was packed with racers. A silver Audi blew smoked from the rear of its tires as it did doughnuts with lots of space on the other side of the parking lot. Polo, Magnum, BiBi, Bay, and the rest of the crew were busy having their private meeting. Their rides were lined alongside each other beautifully, like flowers in a garden. Magnum waxed the rims of his blue Dodge Challenger. The entourage gathered around Polo as if he were a preacher in church. The only one who wasn't present was DeShaun, and neither was Skeeter. Guess they were busy making business plans with the boys in blue. It was the topic of conversation. Polo had a rap sheet with his run-ins with the law. He loved to burn rubber on the block but didn't want to risk his freedom. The track was okay. Polo wanted to know what the rest of his partners wanted, especially Seven since he's been wanting to race since childhood. Professionally.

As Polo kept preaching his views on the situation, the rest of the crew were puzzled by DeShaun's decisions. They didn't want to step on his toes. The Hemi engine could be heard a mile away. Polo stood on the hood of his Cadillac CTS Coupe. That's a crazy move. He could see the black Dodge Charger in the distance as its headlights beamed and made its way into the parking lot. Polo smirked and got off the hood of his ride. He then ran his hand across the hood. Luckily, no dents. Polo would never do that again. The black Dodge Charger parked alongside the other cars, adding to the showcase. The Hemi engine shut down as Seven swaggered out of it. He slammed the door and headed toward his posse. Seven didn't utter a word. He just greeted everyone with high fives. Seven added his two cents as he knew exactly what the topic was. Polo agreed with Seven on not racing on the block. Seven hit the nail on the head. Anyway, Seven didn't want to go back to the pen for street racing. His sentence would probably be doubled from what it was the last time he was convicted.

Without DeShaun around, Seven was in control. So since Seven made his decision not to fuck with the streets, then the rest of the posse made the same choice. It was that Seven was scared. The boys in blue could set DeShaun up. They're tricky like that. Also, when Seven had a goal, he wanted to make sure that there were no obstacles in the way that could cause lots of difficulties. The goal. Angelika. Seven and his posse had their minds made up and did what they loved: stunting their rides. Smoke emerged from the rear tires of a race car. Wheels screeched on the auto tracks. The drag strip light turned green as the racers took off down the strip.

Chapter 29

The tires of Seven's muscle car squealed as smoke emerged from them. Seven drove his ride at a fast pace. He didn't stop or worry about any police. The Hemi engine bellowed as he relaxed to the sound of it. Music. Music. Music.

Thanksgiving was right around the corner, and the weather was getting frigid. He kept the heat on high in his ride. Seven didn't need to wear his jacket as he drove. He only sported his light long-sleeved T-shirt, black jeans, and construction boots and always puffed on a cherry-flavored Philly blunt. The black Dodge Charger thundered down Westbury Road. Seven waited to see if he could catch Angelika. There was no chance in hell he would see Angelika outside those iron gates again. Or maybe he would. *Stalker!* stalked Seven's mind, reminding him, maybe he might be coming on too strong. *Fuck it!* Seven thought to himself. *Whatever I want in life, I'm going to get it! That's what thugs do. That's one of the purposes of being a thug.* Those thoughts flooded Seven's brain like a river.

A traffic light on the corner of the intersection on Westbury Road turned red. The black muscle car halted at the red traffic signal. Seven remembered stopping his ride at this same traffic light where Mr. Westland pulled up beside him. He never forgot the stares and Angelika's beautiful gawking at the visual confrontation. Seven looked to the empty lane next to him. No sign of Mr. Westland pulling up beside Seven again. Instead, a Subaru pulled up and stopped. Seven's eyes bulged. A heavy-set gentleman, hunched over, with salt-and-pepper hair, occupied the driver's seat. Seven rolled his window down as he stuttered a bit.

"Rocco!" Seven cried. Rocco turned to see who called him from his driver's side window. He squinted his eyes due to him not recalling the face. The window of his Subaru rolled down. "It's me, Seven!" Seven cried again.

"Holy mackerel!" Rocco shouted.

Moments later, the black muscle car and Subaru were lined behind each other. Seven and Rocco embraced due to them not seeing each other for years. Rocco got older and was planning retirement soon. He lost some weight. He got some gray hair not only on his head but on his face as well.

Rocco saw that Seven had grown into a man now, of course, but a different type of man, a menacing one. He noticed Seven's attire—lots of black. The car Seven drove was a black menacing speed demon. Rocco wouldn't allow any negative thoughts to cross his mind. But a person's appearance was their advertisement. Rocco told about how he and the staff felt when Ingrid was fired two days before Christmas. Everyone missed them so much, including Angelika. She still always talked about Ingrid and Seven.

And then heading right down the road was Angelika and Cassandra goofing off, giggling, and cracking the corniest jokes. Seven and Rocco continued to talk. Seven saw Angelika approaching. Angelika immediately rose an eyebrow at this stranger smiling at her. Seven finally caught Angelika outside of those mansion gates that guarded the palace where she resided. Rocco did the honor of reintroducing Seven and Angelika.

As soon as Angelika heard this was her childhood friend before her, instead of a handshake, Angelika and Seven rushed into each other's arms like long-lost lovers. She was dumbfounded and didn't know what to say. Angelika hoped and prayed she'd see Ingrid and Seven again. And here Seven was, this tall, well-built, good-looking ruffian that people feared. Angelika didn't see it that way. Immediately she asked about Ingrid. Seven told her that everything was cool, and they got along fine even after Ingrid was terminated. Angelika felt guilty about that.

As Angelika and Seven talked, Cassandra purposely cleared her throat to grab Angelika's attention. Angelika then realized her rudeness. She then introduced Cassandra to Seven. *Who is this guy? He's so ghetto? But he's cute. What does Angelika see in him?* Cassandra's judgmental questions ran through her mind. The two childhood friends only chatted for a bit and were going to catch up with each other later. Angelika and Seven exchanged phone numbers. Angelika smiled from ear to ear. The same went for Seven. He made his move; now Angelika had to make hers.

Seven shook Rocco's hand and was off. Angelika couldn't believe how handsome Seven turned out to be. He had swag. Angelika saw that Seven had a powerful persona. Seven hopped in his black Dodge Charger and bolted away. The look of love was in Angelika's eyes. Cassandra could see it and felt it was wrong. Seven wasn't the guy for her.

The black Dodge Charger took jabs at other motorists on the highway as the sun set early in the distance. Seven didn't worry about any patrol officers because DeShaun had that much under control. Rap music blasted from Seven's cell phone. It was a text message; from DeShaun. Seven checked it out. DeShaun bitched about being shortchanged on the streets again. He always took care of the knuckleheads on the block. Seven had work to do as the Hemi engine bawled of the Dodge Charger.

Later, a brick flew through the passenger's side window of a cheap-looking Toyota. Glass shattered inward, cutting twenty-two-year-old Russell. Blood streamed from his mouth. He spat it to the floor. Seven then reached into the car and snatched Russell out through the busted passenger's side window. Everyone looked on in horror but minded their own business. The black Dodge Charger sat in the middle of the street with its engine still running as the driver's side door was left open. Thugs knew not to fuck with Seven's muscle car, a street racer's ride, even though it was an opportunity to steal.

Russell pleaded for Seven to have clemency on him. Seven ignored his cries and couldn't stand the bitch screaming, like a girl that is. Russell was slammed to the pavement, and punches were hurled by Seven. No clemency was in Seven's heart. His aim was to get the money from Russell and whoever else owed DeShaun. Russell cried like a child. Seven looked around at the other thugs on the corner. They automatically gave Seven respect. The hoodlums lined up one behind another and gave Seven their money. They didn't want their asses whooped. Seven gave the most vicious ass-whoopings and beat-downs. The fierce ruffian jumped in his Dodge Charger and blasted away. The wheels screeched, leaving an enormous cloud of gas-fumed mist.

At the minimart, cash was counted in the JetScan. DeShaun handed the boys in blue some cash for keeping his enemies as far away as possible. The buzzer buzzed. Skeeter peeked through the peephole as he puffed on a cigarette. He thrust the door open as Seven swaggered in with a pissed-off attitude. Seven halted in his tracks as he saw DeShaun in the middle of a financial transaction with the cops. Seven gave them the dirtiest look ever. He knew he had to back the fuck off because this wasn't his business. It was DeShaun's. And DeShaun did what he felt was right for his business and for his crew.

The boys in blue went on their way. Seven threw down a bundle of cash on DeShaun's desk without making eye contact. DeShaun eyed Seven directly in his face and knew something wasn't right. "Seven, what's wrong, man?" DeShaun asked as he snickered. He handed Skeeter the money. Seven shrugged his shoulders and played it off. He told DeShaun he lost his dog. DeShaun frowned and wondered, "How the fuck did you lose your dog?"

"I was walking him in the park, and he wound up running to a K-9 officer and his German Shepherd," Seven said. DeShaun couldn't believe his ears. It sounded credible. Seven told DeShaun he had no other choice than to hop into his ride and get the fuck out of Dodge. DeShaun smiled and nodded due to Seven doing the right thing. Whenever there were police around, *bounce*. That was one rule DeShaun imposed. No one is to speak with officers unless they're doing business. At this point, Seven was acting like a bitch, snap the fuck out of it, and thug up.

Seven cradled another Rottweiler puppy in his arms. This time is was a female. Seven wanted another male, but there were only females left. He had no other choice. She was a beauty. This time Seven was gonna keep a closer watch on her to make sure she didn't run off. DeShaun had no problem replacing something that Seven lost. He told the truth, and there were positive results. But when it came to lies, DeShaun's results were negative. Back to square one, Seven carried the puppy Rottweiler in a cardboard box. She whimpered and bounced around in the box. Seven loved every minute of his new puppy. Car keys jingled as Seven opened up the driver's side door of his Dodge Charger. He sat the box in the passenger's seat. Then the Hemi engine revved, and the muscle car sped away. During the drive home, Seven glanced at the puppy constantly just like he did the first one. "No walks in the park for you," Seven said to himself.

At home, Seven didn't have to worry about getting any dog food. The female pup sat before an empty doggie pan. Seven poured some dry dog food into the bowl. Seven laughed as the pup took tiny bites out of the bowl. Seven had to think of a good name for this dog, a female name. His mind was blank and couldn't think of anything unique. He really wasn't attempting to name her now. Seven needed to catch up on some Zs. In his bedroom, Seven stretched as he took off his boots, his T-shirt, his undershirt, and then his pants with only his boxers on. He hopped in his king-sized bed as his eyes became heavier and heavier. Seven's eyes finally shut.

Chapter 30

On Thanksgiving Day, most people were going to relatives and friends for the holiday feast. Seven laid in bed, staring at the ceiling (God). He felt the cold crisp air seeping through the cracks of his bedroom door. The strong wind whistled outside of his window. Almost every tree was bare. Old man winter had arrived. Seven turned his head toward the window. The weather had taken shape. What was on his agenda today? Of course, he had to spend time with his mother. And then he would have to drop by DeShaun's as well. Then Seven's cell phone vibrated. He turned and glared at it for a moment. The caller ID read: Mom. Seven flipped his phone open. "What's up, Mom?"

"Happy Thanksgiving, baby?" Ingrid greeted her son with a holiday cheer.

"Happy Thanksgiving to you too," Seven replied as he sat on the side of his king-sized bed.

"What time should I be expecting you?" Ingrid asked.

"I don't know." Seven yawned.

"Dinner is at three. So be there."

"I will. I love you, Ma. Later.," Seven said to his mother as he disconnected his call on his cell. Seven laid back down in his bed and looked towards the other side. The huge king bed was too big for just him. He needed a female to fill that empty space, a beautiful girl who would wake up beside him every morning. Whoever that girl may be. This king-sized bed made a man want to grab any old female. But not Seven, he was careful what female he laid down with. Thank goodness Seven's bed wasn't a California king; that would be even worse.

That afternoon, Seven and his baby thundered down Sunset Highway. Smoke from a cigarette hung on the side of Seven's mouth as he drove with one hand. Seven always had the most serious expression when he drove. He loved speeding. He took it very seriously. He didn't allow anyone or anything to get in their way. The American muscle car weaved in and out of traffic as its horn honked. First stop was DeShaun's. Even on this holiday, Seven had to put in work. It was only a half day.

DeShaun's minimart was open for business. The black Dodge Charger peeled into a parking space in front of the store. Seven swaggered out of his car and headed inside. The scanner beeped on the register as Tiana rang up groceries as always. She had to take care of an extremely long line of customers doing their last-minute holiday shopping. TaTu bagged customer's groceries in order to help Tiana's line move faster. "What's up, TaTu? Happy Thanksgiving."

"Happy Thanksgiving, Seven," TaTu said as he shook Seven's hand and then continued to pack customers' food.

"DeShaun's downstairs?" Seven asked.

"Of course! Where else would he be?" TaTu said.

Seven then left TaTu's side and made his way down the cereal aisle. As he swaggered through, he gave the stock boys high fives.

"What's up, Seven? Happy turkey day!" a skinny pants-sagging stock boy greeted.

"Happy Thanksgiving, motherfuckers!"

"You too, motherfucker!" another stock boy shouted.

Seven made his way down the basement steps as he pounded on the door with force. He heard loud music and clamoring of voices on the other side. The foul odor of marijuana seeped through the cracks of the door, which stunk up the air. Seven then rapped at the door again. Magnum swung it opened and gave Seven a high five.

"Happy Thanksgiving," Magnum greeted as he snatched Seven inside. The office door slammed.

Inside, DeShaun and Polo counted the cash before closing early. DeShaun was having Thanksgiving dinner at his house. Polo prepared a beautiful feast for everyone. He was in his second year of culinary school and wanted to become the next Wolfgang Puck. Polo loved to show off his skills and had everyone enjoy his meals.

Seven told DeShaun that his mother was having dinner at three. DeShaun snickered and told he could swing both dinners but to tell his mother he might be a little late. DeShaun asked about the puppy that he gave Seven. "Is the dog okay? No more run-ins with the laws?"

Seven laughed. No more of the puppy befriending a police officer. Seven kept a sharp eye on his four-legged friend.

At the Miles' residence, Ingrid, Darren, and other family members sat around the beautifully set table, waiting for Seven's arrival. It was going on three-thirty. Ingrid's family was anxious to enjoy their holiday dinner.

"Where the hell is Seven?" Darren hollered as he pounded his fist on the table. The silverware rattled.

Ingrid sat at the head of the table with a glum expression. Then keys rattled at the door, and Seven swaggered in. His family members cheered. "It's about time, Seven, my brother!" One of Seven's male cousins, Rasheed, shouted.

Rasheed was a five-percenter. The five-percenters were affiliated with the Nation of Islam. They had the same beliefs as they did—how the black man should be independent, strong, and take care of his responsibilities and his life. Seven agreed with some of the things they preached concerning African-Americans.

Seven resided in a chair at the end of the table as Ingrid was head of the table. He kissed his mother on the cheek and grabbed her hand. The rest of the family did and bowed their heads as Ingrid said the blessing. "Lord, thank you for allowing me and my family to see another holiday. Please bless us and protect us from all the evils in the world. And thank you for my son, Seven. He's alive, and keep watch on him from the temptations of the streets. Amen," Ingrid said as she finalized her prayer.

Everyone at the table gawked at Seven and could tell something was going on him and it wasn't good. Seven noticed the stares from his family. Darren gave the biggest stare of them all. "Why do you have to put me on blast like that?" Seven whispered to Ingrid.

"Praying for you is putting you on blast?" Ingrid responded as she whispered in return. Seven cringed in his chair as he didn't make eye contact with anyone. Then the different dishes of the feast got passed around.

Later, Seven laid on his bed in his childhood bedroom. His family members could be heard laughing, cheering at the Thanksgiving football game on television, and enjoying themselves. Seven thought about why his mother humiliated him like that. "She should have kept my business on the low. I don't spew out her business. Shit." Seven thought to himself. Then there was a knock on his halfway opened door. "Come in!" Seven shouted as he sat up in his twin sized bed.

Rasheed pushed the bedroom door wider as he observed Seven lying in his bed. Seven and Rasheed greeted each other with high fives. Rasheed heard Seven was hustling, street racing, and going wild in the streets. Rasheed knew he couldn't do anything to change Seven. He wasn't gonna preach to Seven. The only thing he could do was pray for him. Seven appreciated Rasheed not lecturing him like Darren. Speaking of Uncle Darren, he stood right in the doorway of Seven's childhood bedroom. The strong marine waited his turn to lecture the knucklehead. Rasheed gave Seven a high five and exited the bedroom. Seven's jaw dropped as he was shocked by Rasheed allowing this marine to scare him off. Darren grabbed a chair and sat before his nephew. Seven knew what was gonna come out of his uncle's mouth—the same ole shit. *Straighten up! Get your life together, boy. Stop running the streets. You're gonna wind up six feet under!* Seven said to himself as he foresaw his uncle's words.

"I'm praying for you, Seven. The whole family is. We just want what's best for you." Darren's voice cracked as he expressed himself.

Seven's eyes bulged as his uncle shed tears. Seven couldn't stand the sight of a man crying. Seven comforted his uncle. "I'll be fine, Uncle Darren. There's nothing to worry about," Seven whispered in Darren's ear.

Then Seven was off to DeShaun's house. The black Dodge Charger raced down the road. Seven thought about what his mother and uncle said. *It's in God's hands. He'll handle it,* Seven thought to himself. God's almighty and powerful. Now Seven was off to the devil's playground. The black Dodge Charger parked in DeShaun's driveway, which was occupied by other vehicles. Clamoring could be heard from the home's interior. Seven hopped out of this muscle car and rang the doorbell. Tiana opened the door and gave Seven a big holiday hug and kiss. "Happy Thanksgiving, baby."

"Same to you, Tiana," Seven greeted in return. He stepped inside as he saw that DeShaun's home was overcrowded. Everyone greeted Seven with holiday wishes, hugs, and high fives as he maneuvered his way from the living room to the dining room. The music and television were on simultaneously. DeShaun resided at the head of the dining room table as a king would normally sit. The food on the dining room table was almost gone. Polo cooked a fabulous feast. Seven could tell by the leftovers it was good. Alcoholic beverages were on the table. There was the smell of liquor in the air.

DeShaun then recognized Seven and scrambled from his throne to embrace him. "How are you, Seven?" DeShaun asked with the smell of liquor on his breath.

"I'm cool," Seven answered as he raised an eyebrow.

DeShaun wanted Seven to join them for a drink and celebrate.

Later, Seven did just that. Seven had a glass full of liquor and cracked dirty jokes all night. Everyone guffawed at his every joke and gesture. "Happy Thanksgiving, motherfuckers!" Seven hollered. DeShaun and his crew proceeded to laugh. Magnum saw how intoxicated Seven got. He had to get Seven home.

Later, the black Dodge Charger pulled into the driveway, driven by Magnum at 3:30 a.m. on Black Friday. TaTu parked his Toyota Camry right behind. The headlights of the Charger shut down.

Magnum exited the driver's side of the muscle car and got Seven from the passenger's side of the vehicle. He escorted him to his house. Magnum grabbed Seven's keys from his pockets and unlocked the door. He pushed it open. Seven staggered in with Magnum behind.

"Seven, come on, man." Magnum encouraged him as he tried to get Seven upstairs. Magnum pushed the door open of Seven's master bedroom. "Seven, lie down, man," Magnum insisted.

Seven plopped on the bed. "Holy shit!" Seven murmured.

"What's up, yo!" Magnum asked.

"The room is fuckin' spinning," Seven said.

Magnum's eyes widen; he knew what that meant. He panicked. TaTu swaggered upstairs. "Yo, TaTu! Get a pot from the kitchen! He's about to explode!" Magnum screamed. TaTu ran downstairs, raced into the kitchen, and grabbed the largest pot. He ran back upstairs with it. "Hurry!" Magnum rushed TaTu. He snatched the pot and held it to Seven's mouth. Seven knew he had to regurgitate. But not yet. He felt hot. Seven sat up and took off his boots.

"Seven, lie down, man," Magnum insisted.

"It's hot, yo!" Seven hollered as he took sharp breaths.

"Do you still have to throw up, man?" Magnum asked with fear in his eyes. Magnum didn't want Seven throwing up on him. TaTu stood in the doorway to avoid seeing or smelling vomit. Seven continued to take off his shirt and then his pants. Then the saliva in Seven's mouth got thick, and he became hotter and hotter. And then *pow!* Seven sat up immediately as Magnum right on the spot held the pot to Seven's mouth. Seven threw up. The smell of liquor, turkey, and sweet potatoes stunk. Magnum turned up his nose to the foul regurgitated Thanksgiving dinner. TaTu stood outside of the bedroom and could hear Seven spewing his guts out. "Damn!" TaTu sweared and cringed. Seven continued to spew as he took a deep breath and knew it was over.

"Are you all right, Seven?" Magnum asked with the look of disgust on his face. Seven nodded his head and lay in his bed. Magnum carried the pot to bathroom and dumped it in the toilet. You could hear him spraying air freshener. "Yo, could someone get me some ginger ale and feed my dog!" Seven shouted as he groaned in bed.

"All right," TaTu said; he was right on it. TaTu headed downstairs and grabbed a can of ginger ale. He then grabbed a glass and aced back upstairs. TaTu stood over Seven's bed as he cracked the can of ginger ale open and poured it in the glass. "Here you go, man."

Seven sat up and grabbed the glass. He gulped down the ginger ale as if it were a beer. Then he let out an enormous burp. The aroma of vomit filled the air once again.

"Holy shit!" TaTu cursed. Seven slept in his bed. He didn't move, not once. Magnum and TaTu left him with the can of ginger ale on his nightstand.

Hours and hours went by as Seven continued to sleep. It was a way of him fighting off the nausea and alcohol. That's what most people do when they were intoxicated. Seven changed his position in bed. He glanced at the clock. It read 7:30 a.m. Outside, peeking through Seven's bedroom window, the cloudy white dismal day lit his room up a bit. The headache that Seven was experiencing became more intense due to the light. He couldn't get up and close the blinds. He just dealt with the migraine. Seven pulled the covers over his head and went to sleep.

Several more hours passed as Seven's cell phone vibrated. The buzzing could be heard from the other side of the bedroom. It was late afternoon. Again, he didn't move or change his sleeping position. Seven squinted his eyes as his vision was blurred. Seven had a feeling it had to be Angelika "That's got to be, Angelika? I didn't *give* my number to anyone else but her. As soon as I get my shit together,. I'll get to her,." Seven thought to himself. More and more hours went by as he slept. Night came. Then the early morning hours arrived, and Seven heard buzzing from his cell phone again. He turned to where his pants lay on the floor. His cell phone proceeded to buzz. Seven turned his back on it and went back to sleep. He closed his eyes. There were no dreams, no semidreams, just a peaceful slumber.

Saturday afternoon was another dreary and cold day. Seven laid on his back and opened his eyes. His stomach was back to normal again. The migraine subsided as he was ready to conquer the world again. More buzzing came from where Seven's pants were. Seven reached into his pocket and answered his cell. "What up?" Seven answered as he lay back down.

"Seven, hi. It's me, Angelika," Angelika replied.

Seven sat up erect in his king-sized bed with his jaw dropped open. Angelika tried reaching him for the last past couple of days. Seven caught Angelika's call this time and wasn't gonna let her get away. "Jingle Bell Rock" by Brenda Lee played in Seven's ear from over the phone. Angelika's mother, Mrs. Westland, interrupted Angelika while she was on the phone.

"How about this shirt for your father?" Mrs. Westland asked Angelika's opinion.

"It's all right," Angelika responded.

"Tell Timothy I said hello," Mrs. Westland insisted.

Seven heard Mrs. Westland's every word from over the phone. He raised an eyebrow and sucked his teeth. Angelika told Seven not to pay any attention to her mother. Timothy was present in Angelika's life. As far as Seven recalled, Timothy was his age, white, rich, and had his nose stuck up in the fuckin' air. Seven sure as fuck wasn't threatened by Richie Rich (Timothy). He was still pissed about Timothy cutting off on Westbury Road. Anyway, Seven and Angelika planned to meet each other on Sunday. That's the perfect day where it's quiet and people got to focus on each other. But Seven couldn't figure out where. He didn't want to meet Angelika out in the street and then drop her off on the street. Seven wanted to pick Angelika up at her door and drop her off at her door. Seven remembered when his mother was terminated by Mr. Westland. Seven feared no man. He'll face Mr. Westland, man to man.

Sunday arrived on this Thanksgiving weekend. The hustle and bustle of Christmas shopping continued. The sun kept peeking in and out of the clouds in the sky. Seven woke up from his slumber and stretched. He looked forward to seeing Angelika again. Seven didn't get too involved with Christmas. It was about Jesus Christ. The way it's supposed to be. Not about Santa Claus, Frosty the Snowman, and Rudolph. Ingrid loved Christmas trees, decorating, and going to church, praising God. Seven looked at the clock. It read ten thirty.

Minutes later, water from a showerhead poured down Seven's nude body. Then he lathered with a bar of soap. Next, he wrapped the towel halfway around his body, and he wiped the fogged-up cabinet mirror. He brushed his teeth, trimmed the facial hairs on his face, and shaved a little. In Seven's bedroom, he put on his thermal garage jumpsuit and then his construction boots. It was freezing outside, so he didn't need anything else.

Seven stormed into the kitchen, where his puppy Rottweiler resided. The dog was growing. Seven grabbed some chicken from the refrigerator and fed it to the dog. He still didn't name his dog yet. It didn't cross Seven's mind. Then Seven left his home. Outside, Seven headed to his Charger. The neighbors were putting up Christmas decorations. The Hemi engine of the Charger started up and revved. Then Seven backed out of the driveway. He blasted off as the wheels squealed.

Thoughts ran across Seven's mind. He wondered what his friends did last night. *Did they go street racing? They probably did,* Seven asked himself. Seven checked the messages on his cell phones. He put it on speaker phone. Angelika left three messages. Seven saved them. Then he got one from his mother. Ingrid had lots of leftovers from Thanksgiving. He loved leftovers, especially from the holidays. Magnum's message was loud and clear. Magnum, TaTu, and the rest of the crew drag-raced along Sunrise Highway from Rosedale to Islip. The distance between the two towns were over fifty miles. It was a racer's paradise. No police presence. No looking over your shoulder. Freedom. Also, Magnum said that DeShaun fell ill too due to the excessive drinking, which caused nausea and then lots of vomiting. Like father, like son. DeShaun and Seven drank together and caught ill.

Later, DeShaun laid in bed, half asleep in his home. A liter of ginger ale sat on his nightstand. The doorbell rang. He couldn't move. He counted to three and then got the strength to get out of bed. DeShaun held on tight to the banister to avoid falling as he headed downstairs. He looked out the living room window. DeShaun swung the front door open.

"What's up, Seven?" They embraced each other. Seven could see DeShaun's tired, worn-out expression. DeShaun plopped in the lounge chair as Seven sat on the sofa. DeShaun closed his eyes. "I heard you got sick too, Seven. How are you feeling now?" DeShaun asked.

"I'm cool. How about yourself? I got the news from Magnum."

"Really? He was just here. I'm getting there," DeShaun slurred with his eyes still closed. He then tried opening his eyes. But he still had a bit of a sharp pain in his head. "Ouch!" DeShaun screamed as he held his hand to his head. He raced from the couch and headed straight for the bathroom which was also on the first floor. He lifted the toilet seat and disgorged. Seven swaggered to the doorway as he watched his mentor, his boss, his father figure sick as a dog.

"Get me that bottle of ginger ale in my room." DeShaun coughed.

Seven hurried to the kitchen, then the doorbell rang. He did a three hundred sixty degree turn towards the front door. He swung it opened as Skeeter and Tiana had their hands full with bags of groceries. Without any words, all three of them sprinted to DeShaun's bathroom, where he had his head over the porcelain bowl.

"Where that ginger ale? DeShaun hollered. Luckily, Skeeter brought bottles of them. Skeeter snatched it from the bag and opened it immediately. DeShaun gulped down the soft drink beverage that's a home remedy for nausea. The he released an enormous belch that left an odor of food from his stomach.

Moments later, DeShaun ate a bowl of chicken soup on a bed tray. That did the trick. He seemed to be feeling better after that last gruesome episode. It pleased Seven that his boss was bound for recovery.

The minimart resumed business as DeShaun took another day off to gain his strength back. Skeeter gave orders for now. He made sure of the payouts were taken care of and that no one was trying to pull a fast one or dodge DeShaun. Seven did his duties and reported to Skeeter with the earned cash from the corners. Seven earned his cut from the illegal earnings and hopped in his Charger and sped away. The Hemi engine bellowed with its screeching good year tires.

Off to the Westland's, the black Dodge Charger made its way on to the Sunrise highway.

As Seven drove, he felt as if he were going back in time, when he first arrived at the Westland mansion as a child. He loved the thought of seeing that beautiful estate again, but not the pleasure of seeing Mr. Westland. He focused on Angelika. How beautifully she had grown and still seemed to be kindhearted. It was only a twenty-minute drive to Westbury. As fast as Seven drove, it only took ten minutes. He hoped he wouldn't drive it into disaster. With Mr. Westland, that is. Seven's an adult. He's not some little kid that won't speak his mind. He dialed Angelika's number on his cell phone. It rang.

"Hello?" Angelika answered her cell shyly.

"Angelika, baby. It's me, Seven."

"Hey, babe. Are you coming over?" Angelika asked.

"I'm on my way now," Seven said as he placed a cigarette in his mouth as he drove with one hand. As the couple tried to figure out what they were going to do, Seven wondered how he was going to see Angelika beyond those enormous iron gates. *Let's see what happens,* Seven thought to himself. Finally, he halted at the corner where those enormous iron gates stood. He alerted Angelika that he had arrived. Angelika phoned the security guards at the gates that she was expecting company. She described the car Seven drove and his name.

One of the guards saw the black Dodge Charger pull up to the booth. The guards needed Seven's ID. He handed the guard his photo ID. It was an authentic New York State driver's ID. DeShaun knew some people at the DMV who hooked him and his posse up with IDs. The guard gave Seven his ID back, and those majestic gates opened as if heaven's gates were welcoming him home. The black Dodge Charger zoomed down that stretch of pavement that led to Angelika's home. As Seven drove, he glanced over both shoulders and saw that the sumptuous mansion hasn't changed.

Angelika could hear that Hemi engine approaching. The front door of the Westland mansion opened as Angelika stepped out. She had a big smile on her face, and her heart raced. It was as if Seven were coming home from a war and the two lovers were reunited. The black Dodge Charger halted as the engine shut down. He stepped out of his ride. Angelika and Seven raced into each other's arms. They embraced for a while. Olga stood in the doorway with a broom in her hands. She smiled and knew it was Seven. She became teary eyed.

"I missed you," Angelika said.

"I missed you too," Seven replied with a smile on his face. His eyes wandered around the place. Just by Seven getting a closer look at the grand mansion, still nothing has changed. Except for Angelika, she has grown into a woman. Seven noticed Angelika had nice T&A. It turned him on. "Is that Olga?" Seven asked Angelika.

"Yes, it is," Angelika answered.

Seven headed over and gave Olga a hug. She jumped for joy because the once handsome little boy was now a handsome grown man. She constantly kissed Seven on the face. "You are so handsome, Seven," Olga praised him. She asked about Ingrid. Seven told her that Ingrid was fine and she had no worries. But she did have worries. Ingrid worried about Seven's well-being. *Was he going to wind up in prison for a long time or was he going to be buried six feet under?*

Anyway, Mr. and Mrs. Westland weren't home. They were doing what everyone else was doing: Christmas shopping. Angelika's parents loved shopping in Manhattan. Fifth Avenue was their spot. Angelika didn't go because she wasn't too much of a help for her mother when it came to picking out gifts for her father. Mr. Westland had all the gifts in the world. Every day was Christmas for the rich. So Angelika didn't care to help her mother pick a gift.

Angelika and Seven took a tour of the mansion. They headed inside. Of course, the foyer was first. The huge chandeliers glistened as Ben sprayed a bottle of Windex as he stood on a ladder. Ben's gained a little weight and still looked the same. Seven and Angelika maneuvered themselves around the eight-foot ladder, Seven observed the rest of the staff vacuuming, polishing, and dusting. Ben was busy with his task. He didn't recognize Seven, especially if someone's on an eight-foot ladder. Angelika did the honors and reintroduced Seven and Ben.

"Ben, you remember Seven. Don't you?" Angelika asked.

Ben stopped polishing the chandeliers with the dust cloth. He gasped as he headed down the ladder and embraced Seven. Seven couldn't believe how the staff still remembered him. The Westland staff still had love for Seven, just like Angelika. As Angelika and Seven made their way throughout the mansion, from the foyer, living room, kitchen, family room, and beyond, Angelika introduced Seven to the new staff members. Seven smiled. One of the maids offered Seven a soda. He accepted.

Angelika and Seven toured the living room. It was about the same. Except for that eight foot statue that stood in the corner. Mr. Westland put the sculpture on the option block at Christie's for four hundred thousand. That's the same statue that freaked Seven out on Halloween. He's never been that freaked out since his grandmother died. Now, the living room was statue freak- out free. Angelika and Seven marched upstairs to the third level. He wanted to see the guest bedroom that he occupied. Angelika opened the bedroom door. The guest bedroom was pretty much the same but a bit different. Angelika and Seven reminisced about the time they saw their first snowfall and the preparations for the Fourth of July celebration from the window. And then they played in the enormous yard in the rear of the mansion.

Then the two headed to the next room, which was Angelika's bedroom. It wasn't pink anymore. Exotic red blanketed the walls with cheerful wall decor of ballerinas, angels, and a mural of Angelika as a ballerina. Angelika took actual ballet for a while but gave it up two years earlier due to bleeding toes. The pain was the worst thing in the world. Her parents became upset with her because she didn't stick to it. Angelika wasn't gonna ruin her feet to become twinkle toes at Lincoln Center. Angelika's stuffed animals and dolls from her childhood were still in her room. Figurines were an additional touch to her bedroom setting. Seven noticed the color of the bedroom had sex appeal. Seven took this shade of red as a turn-on. He wondered if Angelika was still a virgin. Seven wasn't going to ask her, but would allow Angelika to tell him on her own time. Timothy couldn't have hit that. But, you never knew what these rich kids did.

Angelika gave Seven looks of seduction. Angelika seemed like she was ready to go all the way. She had a bit of a rebellious side. This had nothing to do with Seven being there. It was in Angelika all along. So Seven didn't want any shit falling on him. He knew how Mr. and Mrs. Westland were. He took the last sip of his soda and handed the can to Angelika. "All done?" Angelika asked with a smirk on her face. She held the can in her hand as she and Seven took a walk down memory lane.

Angelika and Seven headed into the dining room. Thanksgiving at the Westlands as a kid immediately popped into his head. The turkey was dry as shit. Ingrid cooked a turkey much better. Seven never forgot the ballroom with that enormous flocked Christmas tree which stood ten foot high with black, silver, and white ornaments. Seven pictured Mr. Westland chatting with silver-spooned mouth Timothy. He turned and saw the corner he sat in as a child. He watched the entire Christmas party before him. Then Seven looked at Angelika as she leaned her slender body against the wall. Angelika smiled at him and wondered what the matter could be. Seven recalled Angelika as a little girl who never looked her nose down on anyone.

Then she pushed open the glass door of the mansion, which led to the porch overlooking its enormous lawn and beautiful gardens. The dismal day proceeded as Angelika and Seven stepped out onto the concrete porch. Seven looked around and experienced this heaven man created. The couple strolled through the rose garden, which slept for long winter's nap. Then they strolled past the garden of closed tulips and hardly any greenery. Angelika and Seven walked across the bridge over a lake. There were no signs of swans or ducks or any type of wildlife. The stone altar could be seen in the distance. It's quiet. Peaceful. The altar was adjacent to the lake as the two made their way to it. They sat there quietly still. It was cold.

Seven went into deep thought of his grandmother. And thought of heaven where she dwelled. It seemed as if Angelika and Seven knew what they were feeling, their childhood. They glanced at each other with smiles. They headed out to the larger lawn area. Here's where Mr. and Mrs. Westland threw their parties. Whether it be birthdays, Fourth of July, a barbecue, or Halloween maybe, depending on the weather. *Now this is God's creation.* Angelika and Seven looked down at the swimming pool area with a cover over it.

"I remember when you swan from one end of the pool to the other," Angelika said a she smiled.

"You still remembered?" Seven asked as he raised an eyebrow.

"How could I forget?" Angelika replied.

This pool will be ready to go in a several months, Seven thought to himself. He pretty much remembered everything from the past. But he wanted to look forward to the future. Angelika felt pretty much the same. Angelika wanted to hang out. Seven agreed.

The Hemi engine roared as the black Dodge Charger blasted down the highway. The fast car excited Angelika. Her hair blew in the wind even though it was freezing cold. She didn't mind. And of course, Seven didn't mind at all. As he drove his car, he glanced at Angelika's hair blowing in the wind.

"Where are we going?" Angelika asked with enthusiasm in her voice.

"Where do you want to go? Your choice, Angelika," Seven suggested.

"I don't know," Angelika said as she bit her nails.

Seven wanted to see a movie, but didn't want it to seem as if he were moving too fast. Maybe, go get something to eat and catch up on things. The movies would be next time. If there was going to be a next time. Seven just wanted to focus on now and see where things go.

In a beautifully set diner, waitresses served some customers with turkey dinners. Angelika and Seven resided at a booth, where they ate steak and potatoes. The two soon-to-be lovers constantly made eye contact as they devoured their food. Seven tried to figure out what he wanted to say to Angelika. The same was on her part. Seven wasn't gonna tell her about his street activities. He didn't want to turn her off or scare her.

"What do you do for a living?" Angelika asked.

"I'm assistant manager in a minimart," Seven responded nonchalantly. Seven gulped down his soda then asked Angelika the same thing, but backed off. He remembered, Angelika didn't work. She was rich. Seven became quiet. He didn't know what to ask. Then it hit him. "Do you have a boyfriend?" Seven asked as he shoved a piece of steak in his mouth.

"Not really," Angelika answered as she shrugged her shoulders and gazed into his eyes. "Why?"

"Because you're beautiful," Seven said with guts.

"Thanks," Angelika said.

"Have you been thinking about me over the years?" Seven questioned. He glared Angelika directly in her eyes.

"Yes."

"Don't lie," Seven said.

"I'm not. I really have," Angelika said.

"How do you feel being here with me?"

"It's nice."

"What's nice?"

"Being here with you. Catching up on old times. I miss your mom," Angelika said.

Seven smiled and put another piece of steak in his mouth. "She misses you too," Seven said with his mouth full. Seven told Angelika the things that have been going on with him and his mother. They struggled financially and then Ingrid found another job in order to support the household. Seven fabricated this story to Angelika. Tears trickled down her cheeks, and then Angelika sobbed. Seven felt guilty because Angelika was feeling it. Seven grabbed her hand and comforted her. He assured her that she had nothing to do with Ingrid being fired. And neither did he. It was Mr. Westland's boozie ass.

Angelika was shocked to hear Seven curse about her father. But then she realized it was true. Mr. Westland wanted Angelika to associate with affluent people and build friendships with them. Cassandra and Angelika have been friends since they were kids. She didn't feel her father was forcing a friendship between them. Cassandra was her classmate. But Timothy was a forced friendship, and now he's becoming a forced boyfriend. Angelika wanted to choose her own boyfriend or husband. Money talks, and bullshit walks. She wondered why Seven came back to her. Despite all that has happened, why would you step foot back on a property where your mother was fired? The memories bothered Seven, but he had to be strong about the situation when it came to Angelika. He would have to face it like a thug.

Later, Seven pumped gas into his black Dodge Charger at a not-so-crowd gas station. Seven kept his eye on Angelika from the side mirror where she sat in the passenger's seat. Seven smirked. He placed the gas hook back on the tank and paid the gas attendant. A convenience store sat in the background. Seven dashed in and purchased a dozen roses. He swaggered back into his Charger.

"How are you, Angelika?" Seven asked as she smiled. Angelika smiled in return as Seven offered the dozen roses to her. "For you," Seven said with a look of sincerity on his face.

"Thank you, Seven," said Angelika. She loved the beautiful bouquet of roses and saw him as a gentleman. Seven sped off as the Hemi engine was blaring.

During the drive home, Angelika kissed Seven on the cheek. Seven didn't dare ask what that was for. Seven smiled. He didn't want to make the moves on her yet. Just take it slow. But when it came to Seven getting sex, he went elsewhere. Seven wanted to ask how her relationship was with Timothy. Were they just friends, or was it more? Mr. Westland would have arranged any type of relationship that he approved of. Angelika cradled the bouquet as if she were holding a newborn. She wanted Seven to become her new boyfriend. She didn't care about the age difference. It was only four years. So what?

The black Dodge Charger arrived at the large iron fence with its monstrous engine. The guard in the booth saw the menacing car with its rightful owner. Seven rolled the window as the guard approached, and Seven was behind the wheel and Angelika in the passenger's seat. Samuel, a slightly overweight gentleman dressed in his police uniform, had his hand held on his holster as if he wanted to shoot Seven. Seven glanced down to where the guard had his hand held. Seven kept his cool.

Angelika noticed it as well. Her sweet, innocent persona melted Sam's heart. She was an angelic-looking, beautiful girl who wanted nothing more than to have fun. Then the majestic gates of this castle widened. The Dodge Charger zoomed into the estate. Angelika waved to Sam. Seven shook his head. He remembered Samuel as a kid. He even had an attitude toward Seven as a kid. So any poor African-American boy was a threat to anyone or anything. That was some shit.

Now, shit was about to fan as the black Dodge Charger pulled up to the Westland mansion. Older now, dressed in slacks, dress shirt, a sweater vest, and shoes from some fancy designer, Mr. Westland stood at the top of the steps. The affluent realtor wasn't pleased. Word got back to him that Angelika was sneaking around with some thug that had been lurking around the estate. Mr. Westland made it his business to take care of business.

Mrs. Westland stood by her husband's side. Seven saw Mr. Westland was ready for war. Seven didn't give a fuck. So was he. Seven exited the driver's side of his muscle car as Mr. Westland opened the passenger's side door where Angelika sat.

"Get out of there!" Mr. Westland demanded. Angelika hopped out. He then slammed the door of the Charger back.

"Don't motherfuckin' slam the door of my ride!" Seven cursed. Mr. Westland and Seven hurled words at each other from a distance.

"Stop it, both of you!"

The verbal war continued between Seven and Mr. Westland. He knew Seven was the one who lurked around with his menacing ride. But the pompous realtor didn't know Seven was the kid from years ago who participated in staring matches with him. Then Mr. Westland squinted his eyes and tilted his head. He gawked at Seven because he looked familiar. Then it came to Mr. Westland. "I know you." Mr. Westland said.

"Remember, you fired my mother years ago." Seven made it clear to Mr. Westland's recollection. Mr. Westland calmed down but was still angry because the devil came back into their lives. As far as he was concerned, Seven was stalking Angelika. Mr. Westland was about to ask Seven why he was there and what he wanted with Angelika.

"I wanted to see an old friend. Is that a crime?" Seven shouted. Mr. Westland didn't buy the heartfelt story. He just wanted Seven as far away from Angelika as possible. "I'll call you, Angelika," Seven said as he hopped in his muscle car. The engine rumbled.

"I don't think so!" Mr. Westland yelled as he gave Seven a look of disgust. Seven smirked and thundered away in his Dodge Charger. Mr. Westland gave Angelika the evil eye as they marched into the mansion. The front door slammed as a verbal war erupts between Angelika and her father.

Meanwhile, Seven drove his Charger to the fullest capacity. He stuck a Philly blunt in his mouth and lit it up. Seven patted himself on the back for standing up to Mr. Westland. Most thugs would've run like bitches. He didn't care how Mr. Westland felt about coming back into their lives. It's not about Mr. and Mrs. Westland. It's about Angelika. He just wanted to see her. Now, since he saw how beautiful she was, Seven may possibly want more than friends. Seven stepped on the gas and blasted down the road. The Hemi engine bellowed through the night.

Chapter 31

December 21, "The Spirit of Christmas Past" by Enya bellowed from the Bose radio in the family room of the Westland mansion. A cozy fireplace crackled as Mrs. Westland wrapped gifts for her husband and her daughter, Angelika. Gift wrapping paper and ribbons were scattered on the table. Surprisingly, Mrs. Westland loved doing this herself. She loved Christmas. Angelika loved the holiday as well. The young teen strutted into the family room and began to help her mother.

"I don't need your help, Angelika. Go watch television or something," Mrs. Westland yelled.

"All right." Angelika threw the Christmas wrapping paper down and stormed away.

Mrs. Westland continued wrapping a gift and then stopped. She realized that she can't lose Angelika. She didn't want history to repeat itself. Mrs. Westland lost the love of her father due to her marrying Mr. Westland because he's African-American. She sobbed as always when the holidays came around. Mrs. Westland wiped her tears and ran upstairs to Angelika's bedroom. She inched toward the door and knocked easily. "Angelika?" Mrs. Westland said softly. She opened the door and stepped into Angelika's princess-like bedroom. Silence. There was no television on. No radio on. No Angelika. "Angelika!"

Mrs. Westland cried. Her fears overcame her. Angelika probably ran off with Seven somewhere. That's every parent's nightmare to have your daughter involved with a guy from the other side of the tracks. Mrs. Westland wanted to give Seven a chance, maybe try to get to know him. She felt guilty about firing Ingrid years ago. When Mrs. Westland thought about it, it was just a misunderstanding. Seven just wanted to feel rich. Who could blame him, especially around Christmas. All Mrs. Westland could do was hope that Seven and Ingrid were doing okay. Well, she guessed they seemed to be all right by Seven's sharp-looking appearance and handsome muscle car. Mrs. Westland didn't want Angelika getting involved in any type of trouble that Seven may be involved in. She scrambled downstairs, calling her daughter. "Angelika!"

Angelika headed out of the rear door of the mansion with her cloak. She resembled a wintery princess. The trees were bare. The air was extremely cold and crisp. A cloud of her breath could be seen throughout the air as she spoke. Angelika waltzed her way from the rear of the mansion to the front, where the monstrous engine of Seven's Charger awaited her. She raced into the muscle car. Seven then laid a kiss upon her lips. Then it turned passionate. Their friendship elevated from friends to lovers—more intimate, that is. Angelika's parents didn't like it at all. Seven and Angelika fell for each other pretty fast. They went on their dates, the movies, dinners, and she watched Seven street-race. Seven brought Angelika home all hours of the night, which caused tension between Angelika, Seven, and her father. Another thing, Mr. Westland was concerned about Angelika and Seven becoming sexually active. He worried about her getting pregnant and getting sexually transmitted diseases. Angelika and Seven didn't make love yet. But they came across that path several times. Angelika wasn't sure if she was ready. Seven backed off and gave Angelika time. He respected her wishes and didn't want to fuck things up.

"Angelika!" Mrs. Westland cried in the background. Angelika's mother raced out of the front door.

"Seven, go!" Angelika screamed to him. Seven revved his Charger and sped off.

"Angelika!" Mrs. Westland sobbed as she watched Angelika take off with public enemy number 1. This wasn't about Mrs. Westland's life, but Angelika's. Mrs. Westland didn't know what to do. A rusty old reddish-brown railroad track sat abandoned for years where anyone could stroll along the tracks. This was the place for old memories of childhood friends. Lovers would spend their moments together, or kids would adventure out. Angelika and Seven did just that. Angelika balanced herself along the rail of the track as Seven held her hand. Surprisingly, Angelika didn't lose her balance off the rusty rail.

"Ballet sure did you justice." Seven cackled.

"I know. I can do the balance beam too."

"Really?"

"Yes, really," Angelika answered confidently. Angelika stepped off the rail as the young couple continued to stroll along the tracks. Silence always seemed to draw Angelika and Seven closer together. Strangely, Seven could tell by Angelika's body language and facial expressions what was on her mind. The same went for Angelika when it came to him.

Christmas was only a few days away. Angelika wanted to be with him. Plus, she wanted to see Ingrid. Angelika hadn't seen Seven's mother in years. Angelika wanted to buy Ingrid a gift from the mall. Seven remembered crossing the railroad tracks every time he and his mother were off to the Westlands as a kid, like the Mason-Dixon line, which separated the North and the South due to the Civil War. Wars occurred in countries, families, or individuals, always dividing them—different beliefs, cultures, races, religions, economics, etc. Angelika didn't see any difference even though there was. But Mr. Westland saw everything. The silence continued between them. Angelika and Seven's kiss made music for old man winter.

At the shopping mall, a gentleman dressed up as Santa Claus rang bells in order to get people to donate as much as a penny to help the needy. Angelika and Seven threw some change into the Salvation Army red bucket. The young lovers held hands as they marched inside. Angelika and Seven maneuvered their way through shoppers as they rushed into Macy's.

"Happy holidays. Would you like to try Angel?" asked the perfume vendor as she sprayed the fragrance on Angelika's wrist.

"Perfect." Angelika said an idea came to her. Mrs. Westland's signature fragrance was Angel. The Angel fragrance by Thierry Mugler was introduced to the world in the early 1990s. Angelika remembered the scent of the star-shaped blue perfume on her mother from the time she was born. Ingrid loved the expensive fragrance but couldn't afford it. So Angelika was going to make her happy this holiday. Later, a cashier at the Angel perfume counter wrapped the three-point four-ounce fragrance in gold wrapping paper. Seven counted a bundle of cash from his pocket. Angelika then quickly pulled out her American Express Gold card from her pocket and immediately shoved it in the sales clerk's face. Seven stopped counting his cash. He felt embarrassed as he saw Angelika's gold card. He let it go. Angelika smiled at Seven as if to say, "Not to worry." She took care of Ingrid's gift. But what was the purpose if Angelika could buy those things herself?

Seven felt threatened by that gold card. That gold card represented her father, his wealth—four hundred million, that is. *Was this another one of Mr. Westland's way of making me feel inadequate? Angelika didn't have that card on her before on our other dates. Why the American Express all of a sudden?* Seven asked himself. "Angelika, what do you want for Christmas?" Seven asked as he gazed into Angelika's eyes.

A smile from ear to ear surfaced on Angelika's face as it lit up like Christmas lights. "I want you, baby."

"Are you sure, Angelika?"

"Of course, I do. Why?" Angelika asked as she could hear the dubious tone in Seven's voice.

"It's nothing."

"I know your mom will love her gift."

"You think?"

"I know so."

Seven laid a kiss on Angelika's cheek. They exited the department store as it became more crowded.

Back at the Westland estate, night arrived. A festival of Christmas lights was everywhere. They led from the iron gates throughout the property. The Hemi engine of the black Dodge Charger could be heard a mile away. Samuel resided in the security booth as he ate cake and drank coffee. The "Twelve Days of Christmas" by Frank Sinatra bellowed from the radio. The monstrous engine drowned out the holiday song. It was extremely loud. Samuel jumped out of his skin as he turned. The menacing Charger halted at the booth. The tires released a loud screech. Seven rolled the window down on the driver's side of his ride.

"Merry Christmas, Sam!" Angelika shouted.

"Merry Christmas, Angelika," Samuel greeted her in return.

Seven didn't give a fuck if Samuel spoke to him. He was just there for Angelika. "Merry Christmas, Seven." Samuel gave him a holiday greeting. Seven nodded and smirked.

The enormous iron gates widened as the muscle car raced in. As Seven drove toward Angelika's home, he noticed the abundance of holiday lights. Beauty everywhere—holiday-lit reindeer, snowman, and other holiday characters on the lawn.

The Dodge Charger stopped right at the front door of the mansion. Surprisingly, Angelika's father wasn't waiting at the door. Seven noticed the so-called silence at the estate. Seven raised an eyebrow and knew Mr. Westland was up to some shit. Angelika and Seven exited the car. Seven knew he wasn't staying. He never stayed so Seven wouldn't get caught up in any shit with Mr. Westland. Instead, Mrs. Westland opened the front door and stepped out. She slightly smiled at Seven. He gave a quick smile and focused his attention on Angelika. Angelika and Seven embraced as they kissed.

"What time will you being picking me up on Christmas?" Angelika asked in her sweet voice.

"What time do you want me to come and get you?" Seven asked.

"As early as possible."

Mrs. Westland observed Angelika and Seven's loving moment. She felt their Romeo and Juliet romance played before her eyes. Mrs. Westland also saw how Angelika smiled and laughed. That's what love is all about. Not abuse. She hoped it wouldn't come to that.

Seven projected himself as a Prince Charming. Mrs. Westland had to go along with her husband's beliefs. Seven's a thug. And Angelika was just gonna have to learn the hard way. But Mrs. Westland hoped Angelika's lesson wouldn't wind up with deadly consequences.

Seven laid his last good night kiss on Angelika. Seven watched as Angelika marched towards the mansion. Angelika and Mrs. Westland's greeting was a war of words. Seven hopped in his Charger and honked the horn as a final good-bye to Angelika. She turned and waved. The overwhelming, clear holiday lights on the Westland estate flashed across Seven's windshield like lightning on a stormy night. Then it hit him. Every year, Jones Beach had the Christmas festival of lights. He'll take Angelika there on Christmas Day. Seven smirked to himself as he reached the enormous iron gates. Samuel could hear that Hemi engine coming in the distance. The gates widened as the black Dodge Charger made its way out.

Back at the Westland mansion, Angelika opened the double doors to her bedroom suite. In the corner of the room, stood a six-foot white Christmas tree with clear lights, red, fuchsia, and pink ornaments. Some of the decorations were butterflies, ballerinas, and bulbs. The Christmas ballerina decorations stemmed from Angelika's childhood. She loved decorating trees all over the estate. But, as she got older someone else did the decorating. She sure wasn't responsible for this holiday decor. She sashayed in with her Macy's bag and threw it on the chair. Mr. Westland waltzed in behind her daughter. Angelika took off her cloak and hung it up in her walk-in closet. She then took off her boots.

"Angelika!" Mrs. Westland called.

Angelika jerked as she placed her hand on her chest. "Mom, what's wrong with you?"

"I'm sorry."

"Why don't you make yourself known!" Angelika spoke to her mother in a stern tone.

Mrs. Westland didn't like the way Angelika was behaving, and she knew who was to blame. She just kept her mouth shut. But Mrs. Westland wanted to know where Angelika went with Seven, but as soon as Mrs. Westland yelled at Angelika, she was oblivious. Angelika told her the truth. Yes, she was with Seven. Mrs. Westland wanted to ask more questions about her relationship with this thug. *What drew Angelika to him? Does she believe he really care for her?* These questions played in Mrs. Westland's mind.

On the other hand, Angelika had questions of her own. "Why are you so against Seven? What did he do?" Angelika boldly asked her mother. Mrs. Westland expressed concern for her daughter. Mrs. Westland didn't find it amusing at all. It was serious. Mrs. Westland kept her cool as she browsed around Angelika's bedroom. She saw the Macy's bag.

"Is that my gift, Angelika?" Mrs. Westland shouted to her daughter with enthusiasm.

"No!" Angelika shouted in return.

"Of course, it can't be for yourself. It's wrapped."

"It's for Ingrid."

"Seven's mother?" Mrs. Westland asked as her voice kind of dropped. She raised an eyebrow as if to say, "Why her?" "You didn't go shopping for me, Angelika?"

"I'm gonna go for yours tomorrow," Angelika answered as she removed her sweater and jeans.

"What do you mean tomorrow?" Mrs. Westland asked in a stern tone.

"The store was extremely crowded, Mom," Angelika responded. She put on her pajama pants and top. She saw her mother opening the gift.

Angelika snatched it away from Mrs. Westland's hand. "What are you doing?" Angelika hollered.

"Remember who brought you in this world," Mrs. Westland reminded Angelika. Mrs. Westland then strutted out of her bedroom. Angelika held the torn gift in her hand. The woman at the department store did a beautiful job of gift wrapping. She barged out of her bedroom with the ripped gift in her hand. Angelika stormed into her parents' master bedroom. "Mom, wrap it please!" Angelika commanded as she shoved the half-ripped gift in her mother's face.

Mrs. Westland knew she was wrong for opening the gift that wasn't for her. It's Christmas, a time for giving. Mrs. Westland got all year, 365 days of the year, all Mrs. Westland's life, everything handed to her on a silver platter, waited on hand and foot. The good life. Mrs. Westland grabbed the Christmas wrapping paper and rewrapped Ingrid's gift. Angelika glared at her mother as she did the right thing. She hoped her mother felt bad about being selfish. Mrs. Westland's got everything going for her.

Minutes later, Mrs. Westland handed Angelika a beautifully rewrapped gift for Ingrid. "There you go," said Mrs. Westland as she felt better about doing the right thing.

"Thank you, Mom."

"So, how long are you gonna be at Ingrid's?"

"I don't know."

"What time is Seven picking you up?" Mrs. Westland asked.

"Early."

"This will be our first Christmas apart," Mrs. Westland said as her voice began to crack. She sobbed as if she were at Angelika's funeral. A guilt trip overwhelmed Angelika as she promised her mother she wouldn't stay all day with Seven's family. The telephone rang as Mrs. Westland answered it. Mr. Westland was stuck at the office and wouldn't get in until late. Angelika then marched out of her parents' master bedroom.

Angelika headed toward her bedroom as she held Ingrid's rewrapped present in her hand. She checked out the wrapping paper and tape to make sure it was perfect. Angelika placed the gift back in the Macy's bag. She brushed her long hair. The way her parents have been acting was cruel and heartless, Angelika thought to herself. She didn't want to be around them. They've got their snobbish friends and associates who engaged in gossip about their private clubs, expensive vacations, luxurious toys such as their yachts, fast cars, an abundance of fashion designer apparel, and their blameworthy gossip on how the poor were the cause of America's down fall in the world-wide economy. Angelika wanted to be with Seven and Ingrid. They were real people. That's how Angelika's gonna spend her holiday. She laid down in her queen-sized bed and closed her eyes.

Chapter 32

Christmas Eve morning, Angelika laid in her queen sized bed. Her bedroom suite was brightened due to the snow that arrived at night. Angelika opened her eyes and sprung from her slumber to the window. She saw that the Westland grounds were blanketed with the white stuff. Angelika snatched her cell phone to call Seven. But there was a text message. She read it. "I'm on my way." Angelika smiled to herself that Seven was right on target. She raced to her walk-in closet and grabbed what she was going to wear. Then she threw a bath towel over her shoulder and rushed into the bathroom.

While in the shower, Angelika thought of being with the person that you care about. Seven was her Christmas present. Then sex hit her. This was gonna be Angelika's first time spending the night with Seven. And she knew sex was going to be the gift. Angelika lathered up the soap with her wash cloth. She began washing her body and then stopped. Angelika glared at the marble shower wall and thought, *I have to be sure that I'm ready for this big step. I'm a woman now. I hope my parents are wrong about him. I hope Seven cares about me. Because I do care about him. I've always cared for Seven.* She exhaled and erased the negativity from her brain. She proceeded to wash up.

In the opulent master bedroom, where Angelika's parents resided, Mrs. Westland was sound asleep. But not Mr. Westland.

He stared at the ceiling with his hands behind his head. Angelika's movements were coming from her bedroom on the third floor of the mansion. He had a feeling that Angelika was gonna run off with some hood for the holidays. The Westlands always spent Christmas together like most do, of course. Mr. Westland sat on the edge of his bed. He slipped on his robe so he can have a word with Angelika. As he slipped on his slippers, a Hemi engine could be heard in the distance. Mr. Westland raced out of the master bedroom. He had to stop Angelika from leaving. But it was too late. Angelika already beat him to the front door as she swung it open.

She wore her dark-gray cloak and winter boots and held Ingrid's gift in her hands. The black Dodge Charger halted at the front door with its fierce engine. Seven hopped out of the car. Angelika and Seven rushed into each other's arms and kissed.

"Angelika! Angelika!" Mr. Westland cried to his daughter as he tied his robe. Angelika and Seven focused their eyes on her father as he marched toward them. "It's Christmas, Angelika! Where do you think you're going?"

"Merry Christmas, Mr. Westland," Seven greeted Angelika's father.

"Where are you going?" Mr. Westland asked Angelika.

"I'm going to spend Christmas with Seven and his family," Angelika said.

"We're your family. What about your mother? This will kill her!" Mr. Westland said.

"She'll be fine."

"We're having guests tonight," Mr. Westland continued to lecture Angelika. Seven opened the passenger's side door of the Charger as Angelika got in. "You son of a bitch!" Mr. Westland cursed as he waved his fists in the air.

Seven closed the door on the passenger's side. He didn't like the disrespect that came out of Angelika's father's mouth. Seven stepped to Mr. Westland. "Don't call my mother a bitch. You got that shit?" Seven said.

Mr. Westland balled his fists. He wanted to punch Seven right in the face but knew he couldn't because he knew he was no match for him. And he didn't want to lose his daughter. Mr. Westland took a couple of steps back from Seven.

Seven saw Mr. Westland balled his hands into fists. Seven glared at him and then gave Mr. Westland the eye to let him know, "Don't even try that shit."

"Again, Merry Christmas," Seven greeted Mr. Westland aloud. Seven got into the driver's seat of his ride. The Hemi engine bawled as Seven blasted away.

"Angelika!" Mrs. Westland cried as she ran out in her bathrobe and PJs. She sobbed like a baby. "Where is she going?" Mrs. Westland asked frantically. She proceeded to shed tears. Her husband held his wife in his arms.

Meanwhile, in the Charger, Angelika and Seven were free from the pressures of the world about their love being dangerous. Seven stepped on the gas as she sped through those large iron gates. Luckily, Samuel had it opened, or else Seven would have caused some serious damage. Anyway, the black Dodge Charger made its way on to the road. The muscle car halted at a red light. The Hemi engine rumbled as the slight smell of gas emerged to the front seat. Seven of course smelled it. But that was a normal smell when he sped the way he did. Seven and Angelika gazed at each other for a second. Then they kissed. "Merry Christmas, Angelika."

"Merry Christmas, Seven." Then the traffic light turned green. The black Dodge Charger sped off. Seven had a lot of things in mind for him and Angelika. But, of course, there were going to be family get-togethers. And Seven's family and friends were going to meet his love. Seven didn't mind showing Angelika off to the world. She was like an expensive jewel that he brought—an emerald, sapphire, ruby, pearl, or diamond.

Later that morning, the black Dodge Charger pulled into the driveway of Ingrid's home. As Angelika sat in the passenger's seat, she stared at the small tidy modest home. She remembered the last time she was here. Angelika reminisced about her short childhood times with Seven. They tossed rocks in the lake on the rear of their home. Seven kept cutting his eyes at Angelika. He got the sense she remembered everything. Angelika stepped out from the passenger's seat as she held Ingrid's gift in her hand. Seven exited from the driver's side as he slammed the door.

Then the front door opened as Ingrid stood in it. Her heart raced as if she were being reunited with her long-lost daughter. Ingrid held the widened screen door as Angelika rushed over. They embraced. It was a tear-jerking moment. Seven observed the scene, something out of a Hallmark film. Seven smiled. His stomach began to growl and felt some pain. "Mom, is dinner ready?"

"Yes, dinner's ready," Ingrid shouted in response. Moments later, after all the years that Angelika, Seven, and Ingrid have been apart, on this holiday, Angelika did the honors of blessing their meal amongst Seven's enormous family. Seven's kin consisted of Uncles, aunts, and cousins who drove up from Virginia and down from Canada. Ingrid celebrated Jesus every day of her life and even started early on Christmas Eve with large dinners for the entire family. Seven's family spent the holidays together in a small overcrowded house. Ingrid had a strong divine influence on Angelika. Seven was happy about that, but as far as he was concerned, he was a knucklehead fool. Angelika's blessing was still the same "God is great" blessing. *Angelika didn't mature in her prayers because my mother wasn't around. I don't blame Angelika.*

She's doing good by knowing how to bless a table, Seven thought. Seven's family opened their eyes, peering at Angelika and each other wondering how immature this young lady is and having no knowledge of God really. And yes, Seven had his eyes on his family if anyone dared approached Angelika about her juvenile prayer he was going to let their asses have it.

"Amen." Everyone said simultaneously.

Seven and everyone else at the table dug into the holiday feast. The homemade dishes like stuffing, string beans, mac and cheese and rolls got passed around. Darren did the honors of carving the turkey and that was passed around on a serving platter as well.

Angelika devoured the turkey, stuffing, macaroni and cheese, cabbage, and everything else in sight. Ingrid was delighted Angelika spent the holidays with her. It was the best gift ever. Seven always looked forward to his mother's dinners. Of course, Ingrid got that from her mother. The kitchen was extremely warm due to the oven cooking the turkey and stuffing. Dinner smelled really good. Christmas was in the air. Ingrid had the kitchen a bit decorated with a couple of Christmas figurines around, also snowmen, a Mrs. Claus, and the most important man of all—Jesus. The Jesus figurine sat in the middle of Ingrid's table all year round and was never removed. Jesus always kept Ingrid and Seven safe from harm. Seven made sure that his mother had a beautiful Christmas even though what was behind it was illegal.

In the living room, a six-foot green Christmas tree stood in the corner by the window. Red and gold ornaments gave it a classy look as the clear lights glistened. There were several gifts under the tree. They were all for Ingrid. Angelika's gift was there as well. Also, some Christmas figurines gave the place that holiday spirit. As Seven continued to eat his holiday food, which consisted of turkey, macaroni and cheese, stuffing, and collard greens, he couldn't help but listen to Angelika's past life story from years ago. Angelika became a really little bitch once Ingrid was fired.

The new nanny who was hired after the New Year looked like the malevolent nanny in the movie *The Omen*. She was a woman in her fifties, had a mole on her face, wore her hair in a bun, and had a British accent. It was the scariest thing Angelika's parents could ever do to her. They took Ingrid away from her and stuck her with an eerie-looking woman who looked like she was right out of a horror flick. Angelika prayed to God every night to make this new nanny go away. "God, please make Mildred go away and please bring Ingrid back. Amen." That was the new nanny's name, Mildred. No such thing happened. Angelika had to deal with losing Ingrid, but the new nanny was nice. After Angelika prayed, she cried like crazy because she missed Ingrid. Angelika gave Mildred the hardest time. Angelika wouldn't listen to anything Mildred told her. She threw toys around the room. Basically, Angelika messed up so Mildred would clean up, whatever that was. Angelika got a kick out of seeing Mildred work so hard. Angelika didn't care. She lost Ingrid. Yes, it was as if she lost her mother.

As time went on, Angelika began to lighten up. She and Mildred had regular conversations about school, what she wanted to be when she got older, and of course, friends. And yes, Angelika discussed Ingrid and Seven, how much they meant to her. Angelika threw it up in Mildred's face how Ingrid was better. She cooked better, prettier, kind, and didn't look frightening. Angelika insulted Mildred even though they were getting along. Angelika had a heart and apologized to Mildred. The insults made Angelika realize how much it could hurt someone. Just like Ingrid, Angelika began to love Mildred too. But it was a bit too late. One day, Mildred picked up and left. Angelika cried her eyes and blamed herself for being so mean. She should have given Mildred a chance.

A second nanny came to the Westland mansion to bond with Angelika. Rebecca—young, bubbly type, brunette woman, pretty, a former kindergarten teacher—immediately got Angelika's attention. At first, Angelika wasn't ready to bond with anyone else. All she knew was she needed a mommy. Rebecca asked Angelika about school. It was okay. Angelika focused on her schoolwork and read lots of books to Rebecca. Once in a while, Rebecca read to Angelika. When Angelika turned thirteen years old, there were no nannies for her. Angelika hated to see Rebecca go. During the years, Angelika and Cassandra hung out at the mall, movies, and other activities, especially the ones at school. When it came to Timothy, he didn't even exist. Angelika didn't discuss him in front of Seven because she wasn't into him.

Angelika expressed how happy she was to see Ingrid and Seven again. She loved Ingrid's cooking and wanted to learn how to cook just like her. And she was interested in other things Ingrid did around the house. Maybe one day, she'll be cooking for Seven. Seven couldn't believe his ears. *Angelika wants to play house with me. Is she for real? Does she know what it takes to cater to someone?* Seven thought. He was always thinking. Thoughts were running through Seven's mind when trying to put together a puzzle. Angelika smiled from ear to ear at Seven. Seven gave Angelika a quick smile due to him devouring his dinner.

Jones Beach celebrated their annual Christmas festival of lights show. Spectators drove their vehicles throughout the area where the holiday lights of Santa Claus, Rudolph, Frosty the Snowman, and other Christmas characters were on display. Angelika was the female whom he really had feelings for. As the black Dodge Charger drove around the area, Seven and Angelika gave each other the eye. Mariah Carey's "All I Want for Christmas Is You" blasted from another driver's radio. Seven couldn't stand that song. They played it too much. Angelika wasn't bothered by it. She kissed Seven on the cheek. Seven eased the brakes of his Charger as it halted right in front of the "Merry Christmas" light display. Then Seven and Angelika's kiss turned passionate. A car's honk honked right behind the Charger. Seven and Angelika snapped out of their moment of passion. "All right! Chill the fuck out, yo!" Seven yelled. Then the black Dodge Charger proceeded throughout the festival of lights show. Seven grasped Angelika's hand and kissed it.

Angelika and Seven strolled around the small Christmas village with its shops. Some had decorated windows kind of similar to Lord and Taylor's in Manhattan. But they didn't come close. A choir sang "Hark the Herald Angels Sing." Then a gentleman dressed in a Santa suit rang a bell, collecting for the Salvation Army. The cold breeze blew through Angelika's hair. The aroma of shampoo tickled Seven's nose. He sneezed.

"God bless you, Seven," Angelika said.

"Thanks," Seven replied. Seven sneezed again. He knew he wasn't getting a cold. It was Angelika's shampoo.

"God bless you, baby," Angelika said again.

"Thanks.", said Seven as he heard God's name come out of Angelika's mouth. He was proud that his mother was responsible for this blessing. Angelika resembled an angel on this supposedly religious holiday. It seemed as if she were on a mission from heaven to be Seven and Ingrid's guardian. Most rich people really didn't believe in God. Money was their god. It was obvious that Angelika was one privileged girl that did.

The two young lovers made their way into one of the gift shops. There were toys, games, house ware, candies, etc. Seven and Angelika browsed around as they clutched hands. Angelika's eyes were right ready to pop out of her head due to the beautifully decorated shops. Johnny Mathis Christmas music played from the speaker in the ceiling. Seven noticed the nice holiday items. He wanted to buy Angelika something but didn't want to feel like an ass. She probably had her American Express Gold card. *Why bother? Fuck it! Stop being motherfuckin' intimidated by a piece of plastic,* Seven thought. His eyes wandered around the shop. Seven looked back at Angelika and saw she continued to browse at the other items. Seven wanted to get something much more expensive than what he saw in the shop. Angelika was mesmerized by the animated snow village train set in the center of the floor.

Seven wrapped her arms around Angelika's waist. "Are you ready to go?" Seven asked as he kissed her on the cheek.

"Yes," Angelika said as she smiled.

Seven grabbed Angelika by the hand and exited the shop.

Zales jewelry shop in the mall had a reputation for selling the finest jewels in the world. Seven hauled Angelika inside. Seven knew Angelika had seen diamonds, pearls, rubies, sapphires, and other fine jewels all her life. Angelika didn't seem impressed.

"What's this all about?" Angelika asked Seven as she squinted her eyes.

"See what you like."

Angelika looked through the glass cases at the fine earrings, necklaces, rings, etc. Then right before her eyes, Angelika saw a diamond-cut swan necklace. Angelika gazed at it. She knew she could have anything in the world, especially with her father's money, but it was a different feeling when your boyfriend bought you a gift.

Seven stood directly behind her. "Do you like that?"

"Yes. It's beautiful," Angelika answered.

Seven noticed the look on Angelika's face. It's as if she never saw diamonds before. The jeweler came over and assisted them. Minutes later, Seven placed the diamond swan necklace around Angelika's neck as she gazed at her reflection in the mirror. Seven slightly smirked. Angelika looked like she was a movie star on the red carpet at the Oscars in Hollywood.

"I love it," Angelika said as she turned around and kissed Seven. The expensive necklace made Angelika felt as if she were on top of the world. She would treasure this necklace for as long as she lived. She continued to wear the necklace that Ingrid gave to her years ago and now the necklace Seven gave her.

Seven and Angelika exited the double doors of the mall. The Salvation Army Santa Claus rang a bell for donations for the needy. Seven and Angelika dropped some change from their pockets into the pail. "Thank you. Merry Christmas," greeted the Santa Claus. There was a man selling live Christmas trees. Angelika and Seven headed toward the trees. The smell of fresh pine filled the cold air.

"Let's get a tree, Angelika," Seven said.

"Sounds good," Angelika responded.

Seven grabbed a six-foot tree as Angelika grabbed some clear Christmas lights and a bunch of ornaments.

Later, the black Dodge Charger parked in the driveway of Seven's home. The engine shut down as well as the headlights. The sky was clear with a full moon on this Christmas Eve night. Keys jingled at the front door as Seven and Angelika stepped into his dark house.

"Seven, I can't see anything," Angelika said. Then a growl came from within the darkness. "Seven, what is that?" Angelika was startled.

"It's just my dog," Seven replied. Then the lights came on. Then Seven's Rottweiler trotted toward Angelika. Seven's Rottwciler was still a puppy but a bit bigger. Angelika halted in her tracks as she saw the animal. "Don't worry, she's still a puppy. You'll be fine." Seven laughed.

The Rottweiler came over and sniffed Angelika and the bags. "What's her name?" Angelika asked.

"I didn't name her."

"What do you mean you didn't name her?"

"Okay, you do the honors, Angelika," Seven said.

"Anastasia," Angelika said.

"Are you serious, Angelika? That's some Walt Disney bullshit."

"It's not bullshit, Seven."

"All right. Anastasia it is. Where do you want to set the tree?" Seven asked as both of them gazed into each other's eyes. Seven laid a passionate kiss on Angelika. Seven wrapped one arm around Angelika as the other was holding the heavy tree. As Seven and Angelika proceeded to lip-lock, Seven leaned the tree against the wall. Seven wanted some pussy right now. They'll decorate the tree later. As the passion moved along, Seven took off Angelika's cloak. He tossed it on the couch. The kissing, hugging, and moaning emerged from them. Seven reached his hand up Angelika's sweater. He fondled her nipples. Things were getting hot and heavy. Seven could tell Angelika's first sexual experience would be right, with the right guy like himself. Seven removed Angelika's sweater, exposing a sexy Victoria Secrets bra in red. Seven loved the way the alluring lingerie fit on Angelika, but he then took that off.

Angelika's feelings were as mutual as Seven's. She was ready to lose her virginity. Angelika unbuttoned Seven's black Dickies shirt, leaving him with an undershirt. She put her hands up Seven's undershirt and caressed his nipples. The kissing and moaning was right in the middle of it. They made their way up to Seven's bedroom. He lifted Angelika up as she wrapped her legs around his waist. He placed Angelika down on his king-sized bed. Seven pulled Angelika's pants off and then fingered her vagina. Seven felt Angelika's heavily discharged vagina. Angelika lay her head against the pillow as Seven continued to finger her. Her moans and groans turned Seven on. Sexy. Seven was doing what a motherfucker was supposed to do. He then took her panties off. And he then took off his pants and boxers.

Angelika saw a penis for the very first time, Seven's that is. It was enormous. *OMG! Is that gonna hurt?* Angelika thought to herself. Seven spread Angelika's legs apart as he pushed his penis into her vagina. Angelika felt the huge push of Seven's body organ. The feeling was a bit painful, then Seven made it his goal to please her. And he did. Then they changed positions. Angelika was on top of Seven as she moved her hips like a belly dancer. Their moans were like the hymns of a choir. Angelika's first climax came through. She screamed. Then the second one made its way right after. Seven knew he was the shit. He flipped Angelika on her back and made sure the third climax was gonna be fire. Seven thrust in and out of Angelika really hard and fast. Sweat poured down his body as he glared Angelika directly in the eye. She released the biggest scream. A devilish smile surfaced on Seven's face—a job well done. He then pecked Angelika on the lips.

A couple of hours later, Angelika strung Christmas lights on the live tree as she wore one of Seven old long t-shirts. Seven resided in the recliner and allowed her to do the work. A Charlie Brown Christmas played on television. This reminded Seven of when he and Angelika were kids. They'd watch the Christmas specials on TV and eat holiday goodies. By Seven being with someone he cared about he got into the Christmas spirit. He got his holiday treat: pussy and a blueberry Philly blunt. He lit it up with a cigarette lighter and inhaled. Then he blew smoke into the air. Angelika sniffed the air as she smelled the sweet fruity scent. She turned and saw Seven with the thin-looking cigar in his hand. She frowned at Seven chillin' in the recliner.

"Okay. How do you like the tree?" Angelika asked as she stepped back to get a better look at her work.

The six-foot tree was decorated with red and gold ornaments with clear lights. Seven could see the beautifully decorated tree from his seat. "That's good." Seven complimented. He inhaled his Philly blunt again. "Do you want some hot chocolate?"

"Yes. Thank you."

The aroma of a steamy, hot cup of chocolate rose into the air. Seven offered it to Angelika. She took the cup and sipped the hot beverage. Seven continued to smoke his blunt. This was Seven's way of celebrating the holiday. Seven and Angelika sat in front of the Christmas tree. Christmas is the most wonderful time of the year. But it's especially wonderful when you're with the one person you cared about. Angelika thought of her parents and wondered how every-thing was going. She knew they were pissed at her. Seven advised Angelika to give her parents a call. And so Angelika did.

Mr. Westland's voice could be heard bellowing through the receiver of Angelika's cell phone. Angelika voiced her views on her leaving home on Christmas Eve. It wasn't as if she ran away or she and Seven were going to tie the knot. They just wanted to celebrate the holiday together without any interference from them. Mr. Westland argued that he wasn't going to do that. It was her life. And whatever she does was her business. Angelika didn't believe that. She was his only daughter, and he wouldn't throw his daughter to the wolves. *Would he?* Angelika asked herself.

Then Mrs. Westland's voice bellowed from the cell phone. Seven heard the entire argument about him between Angelika and her parents. Seven sat in the recliner and shook his head. Angelika then hung up on her mother. Seven gawked at Angelika as he saw her eyes become watery. Her tears trickled down her cheeks. Seven took the last puff of his Philly blunt and put it out in the ashtray. Seven then wrapped his arms around Angelika. She sobbed in his arms. She then stopped. Angelika didn't want Seven to think that she wasn't happy on this holiday. Seven and Angelika engaged in a passionate kiss. She then wrapped her legs around Seven's waist. Seven pulled her panties down from under an old T-shirt that she wore of Seven's. Seven laid Angelika's nude body in the recliner. He took the T-shirt off Angelika as he removed his boxer. Now, they were ready for round two.

Chapter 33

Christmas morning, Ingrid opened up Angelika's gift. She could smell the Angel perfume within its tight plastic seal. Seven and Angelika watched her as she proceeded to open the gift. Ingrid sniffed the fragrance. She sprayed a couple of spritz on her wrist. Angel was a strong perfume. Seven sneezed. Angelika raised an eyebrow. "He's sneezing again. God bless you," Angelika said.

Seven loved the smell of good foods and fragrances, but for some reason, his nose wasn't pleased. Seven rushed out of the living room as he continued to sneeze. Angelika and Ingrid glanced at each other. The bathroom door slammed. Ingrid knocked on the bathroom door. Angelika was right by her side. "Seven, do you have allergies?"

"No."

"You didn't have this as a child."

"And so?"

"So? Maybe you just have a sensitive nose."

Seven blew his nose. It sounded like a fog horn. Ingrid noticed the diamond-cut swan necklace on Angelika's neck. Ingrid smiled and could tell it was a pretty penny. She knew how Seven was able to afford something like that. Look at the beautiful holidays Seven was able to give his mother. Ingrid didn't want to mess things up between her son and Angelika. But Angelika has always been like a daughter to her. God forbid if something were to happen to Angelika due to one of Seven's drug deals gone wrong. Then the toilet flushed. Seven swung the door open. He took sharp breaths as he rushed to his childhood bedroom. "Are you all right, Seven?"

"I'm cool," Seven yelled from the rear of the home. Seven laid on his twin-sized bed. Obviously, he was too big for it. He didn't care. Seven needed to lie down. He could sense Angelika making her way to his bedroom. She learned more and more about the years that they've missed out on each other. And there she was as Angelika, standing in the doorway of his boyish-looking bedroom. Posters of fast cars and NASCAR Champ Todd MacKenzie were on the wall. Angelika remembered Seven always talking about racing as a kid. "Will he pursue this NASCAR sport or not? By him *working in a grocery store isn't gonna cut it,* Angelika thought. She recalled visiting this home years ago. She touched everything Seven had in his room. Seven just lay on the bed as he glared at her.

Angelika sashayed into Seven's room. She browsed. There were model cars, books, and magazines about cars on Seven's childhood desk. Angelika flipped through them. She abruptly turned. "Aren't you gonna stop me?"

"Why?" Seven asked in wonder.

"Because I don't know this stuff. Remember?" Angelika said with a salty tone.

"I remember." Seven chuckled.

"Do you spend the night here?"

"Once in a blue moon," Seven said as he stared at Angelika, waiting for her next question.

"Does it bring memories?"

"Of course. But I look forward to the future." Seven wanted Angelika to be a part of his future—she was a part of his past—but there were obstacles. He knew what they were but didn't want to think about them right now. He wanted to just enjoy the holiday.

Later, Seven's entire family clamored around the Christmas tree and exchanged gifts. Ingrid was showered with presents. She was worth every penny. Ingrid got two bathrobes, slippers, shoes, boots, and lots of perfume. Angelika mingled with Seven's family as they admired on how beautiful she was and how Seven was lucky to have her as his girlfriend. Plus, they even admired the expensive swan necklace that she wore around her neck. Angelika looked over and saw Seven hanging with his cousin Rasheed. Seven got some gifts but wasn't anxious to open them. He and his cousin Rasheed gossiped about the rich and poor in society, and racism. Angelika heard their entire conversation even amongst the clamoring of Seven's family. Rasheed condemned African-Americans who were privileged. Once they've achieved their success, what do they do? Move out of their communities and live among the whites.

That would be my father. How does Rasheed feel about Seven and I being together? Angelika thought. Rasheed gave Angelika a dry Merry Christmas and didn't acknowledge her presence. His concern was for Seven.

Then later everyone gathered around the dining room table as Ingrid blessed the holiday feast. "Dear Lord, thank you for another joyous holiday, where my family and friends are together." Seven opened his eyes and peered at everyone. Seven held Angelika's hand. He foreshadowed what his mother was about to say. "On this holiday is where you sent your beloved son, Jesus Christ into the world. Please keep my family safe from the evils of the world, especially my son. Amen." Ingrid concluded her prayer.

"Amen," Seven's family repeated. Seven gave Angelika the most pissed-off expression. He squeezed her hand real tight and wouldn't let go.

"Seven, you're hurting my hand," Angelika pleaded. Seven rose from his seat as he kept a tight grasp on Angelika's hand, which forced her up from her seat.

"You did it again, Mom, telling my business in front of everyone!" Seven argued.

Ingrid couldn't take Seven's ungratefulness anymore. "I'm praying for you."

"Baby, let's go," Seven said to Angelika. He hauled Angelika out of the house.

"What's the problem, Seven?" Angelika wondered.

"I'll explain later," Seven snapped at Angelika. Seven and Angelika headed to his Charger. Seven opened the passenger's side door. Angelika got in, continuing to argue. Seven didn't say a word. Ingrid sprinted to Seven's car. Darren and Rasheed were right behind her. The Hemi engine of the Charger started up, revved, and then thundered away. Ingrid tried as hard as she could to fight back tears. Her tears for were two people now: Seven and Angelika.

While in the Dodge Charger, Seven drove as if he were on the auto track or in a NASCAR race. Seven didn't spew a word to Angelika. He kept his eyes on the road then slowed down a bit. He wanted to cease the tension. But the tension wasn't between he and Angelika. It wasn't between him and his mother. Ingrid didn't want to bury her son or have him behind bars for the rest of his life. Angelika glanced at Seven and then focused her eyes in front of her. She became a bit afraid of him. This was the first time Angelika saw Seven heated. *Where are we off to? Is Seven taking me home?* Angelika questioned herself.

Then moments later, the black Dodge Charger parked in the driveway of a nice, well-lit home. The house was like a mini castle with nice trimmed hedges and lawns. Colorful Christmas lights were strung along the fence and the entrance into the home. Music bellowed from inside. The Charger's engine shut down as Seven and Angelika exited the car. Angelika wondered whose beautiful home this was. *Does Seven know rich people also?* she thought. Angelika didn't bother to ask who lived here. She'll soon find out.

Seven grabbed her hand as they headed to the front door. Seven rang the doorbell. Seven kissed Angelika on the cheek. The tension began to subside.

"Who lives here?" Angelika asked with caution.

"My boss. He's cool," Seven replied. There was no response to Seven ringing the bell. He rang the doorbell a second time.

Then Skeeter swung the door open. "Merry Christmas, Seven," Skeeter greeted Seven with a high five. Skeeter held a beer in his hand. Skeeter's eyes then popped out of his head as he saw Angelika. He smiled. "Who's this?" Skeeter asked with curiosity.

"This is my girl, Angelika."

"She's beautiful," Skeeter complimented.

"Thank you," Angelika said as she smiled shyly.

"Yo, Seven's here!" All of DeShaun's posse and party guests cheered as they saw Seven and Angelika maneuver their way through the crowd.

Magnum greeted Seven with a high five and embraced him. "Happy holidays, fool," Magnum said. Magnum embraced Seven and then noticed Angelika. "Who is this?" Magnum asked.

"My girl, Angelika."

"How are you doing, Angelika? Merry Christmas," Magnum greeted.

"Where's DeShaun?"

"He's in the kitchen."

Seven and Angelika proceeded to the kitchen. As they did, Angelika felt a bit nervous as she noticed the stares she received from the females at the gathering. The guys were giving her go-go eyes. Seven immediately grabbed Angelika's hand. They entered through the swinging doors of the kitchen. There was lots of foods and drinks. DeShaun and Tiana were busy mingling with some party guests.

"Merry Christmas, Seven!" DeShaun shouted. He embraced Seven. "Who's . . . this?" DeShaun paused in the middle of his sentence.

"My girl, Angelika. Angelika, this is my boss, DeShaun."

"Hello, Angelika. Merry Christmas," DeShaun gave her a holiday greeting with a smile.

"Same to you." Angelika replied.

Tiana cleared her throat while holding a drink in her hand. She rolled her eyes. DeShaun grasped Tiana's hand and kissed it. "And this is Tiana, my now fiancée. Check out the rock!" said DeShaun.

"Holy shit! You're tying the knot?"

"Yes, we are," Tiana said.

"Congrats, boss," Seven said.

"Thanks."

"Did you set a date?" Seven asked.

"Not yet." Tina answered.

"We're working on that. Hi, I'm Tiana," Tiana introduced herself to Angelika as she extended her hand. The two young ladies shook hands. During the course of DeShaun's holiday feast, Seven and Angelika ate a lot. Seven seemed to be okay now. Whatever was bothering Seven, he pretty much got over it. But he would still have to tell Angelika the truth about his hustling in the streets.

Meanwhile, on the drive home, Seven knew Angelika had to spend Christmas with her parents. Seven didn't want to interfere with her family. Let them work it out. The wheels of the black Dodge Charger screeched at the entrance of the enormous iron fence. Samuel was napping in the booth with his cap covering his face. The sound of the Hemi engine didn't even wake him. Seven rolled his window down.

"Samuel!" Angelika shouted from the passenger's side of the Dodge Charger.

Samuel's cap fell off his face as he was startled out of his sleep. "Merry Christmas, Angelika," Samuel greeted them with an exhausted smile. He picked up his hat from the floor and placed correctly on his head.

"Merry Christmas, Sam," Angelika greeted.

Samuel pressed the button for the opening of the fence. Samuel and Seven didn't say a word to each other. It didn't bother Seven any. The Dodge Charger sped in and straight down the pavement. Seven made plans for New Year's, if Angelika was available. On the other hand, Angelika wondered about New Year's as well. Will she spend time with him? She really didn't want to be around her parents. Angelika wanted to be around the man that she cared—supposedly.

The Dodge Charger ceased before the front door of the Westland mansion. Olga opened the door. Seven and Angelika got out of the car.

"Merry Christmas, Olga," Angelika greeted as she waved to her.

"Merry Christmas, Olga," Seven also greeted her.

"Merry Christmas," Olga said with the holiday spirit in her heavy accent. Then Mrs. Westland brushed past Olga, almost knocking her down. Mrs. Westland didn't even apologize to Olga. Seven and Angelika saw what she did.

Mrs. Westland noticed she was getting dirty stares from her daughter and Seven. She really didn't care. Like always, Mrs. Westland rushed in between Seven and Angelika and turned her back on him.

Seven felt the disrespect coming from this stuck-up bitch. *Where the fuck was her tight-ass husband?* Seven thought to himself.

Mrs. Westland grabbed Angelika by the arm. Angelika snatched away from her mother. They argued and argued. Mrs. Westland began crying. This was the first Christmas without her daughter around. Angelika and her mother argued, and it got so heated to point where Angelika forgot all about Seven. He slammed the door of the passenger's side of the Charger. Seven immediately sprinted into the driver's seat and blasted off. The Hemi engine roared throughout the atmosphere.

"Seven!" Angelika shouted. The Dodge Charger thundered into oblivion. How could Angelika allow herself to ignore Seven? She didn't mean for it to happen. What a messed-up holiday. Angelika was with the one she cared about, and interference got in the way. "Thanks a lot, Mom," Angelika yelled as she marched into the mansion. Mrs. Westland gave chase.

While inside, Angelika and her mother marched from the Christmas-decorated foyer to the living room, arguing. Mrs. Westland suggested Angelika go see her father in the study. Her father was disappointed with the choices she's been making. Jazz drummer Art Blakey music bellowed from the study. Angelika headed towards it as she opened the double doors. The music became louder. A ten-foot-high flocked Christmas tree decorated in black, white, and silver sat in the corner. Tons of Angelika's gifts were still under it and wrapped. Two lounge chairs faced a crackling fireplace. The aroma of whiskey and cigar smoke filled the air. Her father had company. That company was Timothy. Angelika heard their laughter amongst the music. Angelika took baby steps as she slowly approached her father. She was never afraid to face her father, but this time she was.

"Merry Christmas, Dad," Angelika greeted her father with a slight smile. Mr. Westland wasn't happy but played it off due to Timothy being there. Timothy sat in the opposite lounge chair. Timothy, now twenty-two years of age, dyed his hair black and wore tight pants and shirts. He looked gothic, and his fingernails were painted black. He looked peculiar. Timothy used to be this cute blonde that the girls admired and loved. Angelika thought Timothy was weird. But her parents differed. They felt Timothy was perfect for Angelika. She knew arranged marriages were for people in foreign countries, not the United States, where there is freedom to choose whom you wish to love.

Timothy attended New York University and drove home from the city back to Long Island on the weekends and holidays. He loved it and majored in business administration. Timothy wanted to invest in some type of business. He believed in being his own boss. He and Mr. Westland had a lot in common, which was business. Those two could talk all night about the economy, stock market, big and small businesses, partnerships, mergers, and business moguls, such as Bill Gates, Steven Jobs, and Jay-Z.

Angelika excused herself and headed to her bedroom. She waltzed past Olga as she did some dusting. "Good night, Olga," Angelika said.

"Good night, Angelika. God bless," Olga said.

Angelika took a couple of steps up the stairs as Timothy ran behind her. "Angelika, wait!" Timothy cried as he shoved the beautiful black and gold wrapped holiday gifts stacked on top of each other from small to large in her face. Angelika made a sour face due to Timothy being so aggressive. She smelled the liquor on his breath and another type of disgusting smell within the alcohol, a fecal odor. Angelika thought maybe it was just the liquor coming through his pores mixed with the cigarettes, creating that odor. Timothy then went to kiss Angelika. Angelika jumped back and made another sour expression due to the fecal smell being so strong on Timothy. Timothy didn't bother to ask what the problem was. He was too intoxicated to realize Angelika's bitchy attitude. "I'll open them later, Tim. Just placed them under the tree in the study." Angelika said as she dashed upstairs. Timothy just smiled and with no problem did what she said.

Angelika sashayed through the double doors of her bedroom suite. Emily snoozed in doggie bed. The pooch didn't respond to

Angelika being gone for a few days. She was sound asleep. Clear lights glistened on her six foot white Christmas tree with girly ornaments. She noticed more gifts under the tree. They were wrapped in beautiful red, fuchsia, and pink wrapping with gold ribbons. She checked out the labels on the packages. They read from: Mom and Dad. Angelika wasn't in the mood to open up any gifts at this time. Angelika cradled the pooch in her arms like a baby. "Emily, how are you? I missed you," Angelika said. She placed Emily back down in her doggie bed and strutted in her walk-in closet. Angelika took off her cloak, then her boots, sweater, and jeans. Then there was a knock at her door. "Come in!" Angelika shouted from her walk-in closet. She threw her pajamas on.

Mr. Westland approached her from behind. Angelika turned and saw her father standing in the doorway. The expression on his face wasn't pleased. Angelika knew he was about to bitch—bitch about Seven and them being together. Surprisingly, her dad discussed Timothy's future and how bright it looked. He was ready for a wife and family.

"Looking for a wife, a family, with who? Not me? Timothy isn't my type," Angelika said to her father. Mr. Westland wasn't happy with Angelika's opposition. He then went on to ask Angelika about what colleges she applied to. "I'm not even a junior yet!" Angelika bellowed.

The diamond-cut swan necklace still being worn around Angelika's neck shimmered with its jewels. Her father couldn't help but notice it. Mr. Westland complimented on it and asked if she bought it for herself. Angelika told him that Seven brought it. Mr. Westland knew Seven must being doing something illegal in order to afford something that he really couldn't afford. Mr. Westland made accusations about Seven possibly selling drugs or something of the sort. Angelika argued with him and didn't like the assumptions he made. Mr. Westland screamed his head off about how a lot of girls from these lower-income neighborhoods wind up living a life of hell. All those girls did was get romantically involved with thugs. It's not a black thing. It's a universal thing. There are girls in every walk of life who dealt with a guy that their parents disapproved of. Mr. Westland didn't want that for her.

I'm going to see Seven regardless. Angelika hollered as she brushed through her long hair. Her father's bitching continued. Mr. Westland could bitch until he's blue in the face. Angelika hoped her father would plummet to the floor right then and there. She swore she wouldn't even call paramedics to help him. Angelika's so ignoring him.

Mr. Westland noticed Angelika's body language that she wasn't paying attention. He halted in the middle of his lecturing. "Your mother and I are going to the ballet," Mr. Westland implied.

"And?" Angelika answered as she shrugged her shoulders.

"You usually come with us," Mr. Westland said as he's about to exit Angelika's bedroom.

"No." Angelika said. Angelika usually went to the ballet or the opera with her parents. But this time, she had other plans.

Mr. Westland then thought that if Seven really loved Angelika, why wouldn't he join them for dinner and the ballet, if he's really a gentleman or a ruffian? Angelika gawked at her father and knew that wasn't gonna happen. Seven would never go to the opera or the ballet. She wouldn't even ask him. "That's not realistic, Dad," said Angelika as she shook her head doubtfully.

"Then he's not really the one for you. Timothy would go."

"So? I don't care about Tim."

"That's how those ruffians are! Intimidated by everything that's different from themselves!" Mr. Westland testified. Mr. Westland was being judgmental. She threw her brush down on her vanity and turned the lights out. Angelika hopped in bed and pulled the covers over her head.

"Ask him," Mr. Westland demanded as he exited his daughter's bedroom.

Angelika gazed at the ceiling. She grabbed her cell phone and type in, "WHAT'S UP FOR NEW YEAR'S?" She sent the text message to Seven's phone. Angelika placed it on the nightstand. Then she smiled at Emily snoozing in her doggie bed. Angelika then turned on her back as her eyes were directed toward the ceiling. As she waited for Seven's response, she focused on God. *How does the almighty feel about situations like this. The Romeo and Juliet type of love, dangerous or forbidden loves. What was his take on Seven and Angelika's romance? He could see the future, knows it and controls it.* As Angelika wrestled with her relationship and God in the mix, she continued to wait for Seven's text message. She waited, thought, and questioned God. Questioning God is something you're not supposed to do. Angelika didn't know any better. She had a lot to learn. Her eyes became heavier and heavier. Then they shut.

Chapter 34

Red velvet curtains draped over a stage as the sound of an orchestra tuned their instruments. Then the curtains opened as applause erupted from an audience of spectators. A spotlight shined in the middle of the stage as a ballerina appeared. Her hair was fixed in a bun, and she wore a burgundy outfit. She looked similar to Angelika, probably biracial. The audience was captivated by her beauty and grace. Then the ballerina sprung to her toes and twirled to the orchestration. Mr. and Mrs. Westland held hands as they enjoyed the show. On this occasion, it was a double date, not just Angelika's parents, but Timothy and Angelika as well. She wore a black strapless floral embroidered Oscar Da La Renta gown, her swan necklace, black pumps. Angelika had her hair up in a bun. She looked as if she were going to the Oscars instead of the ballet. Timothy sported a tight-fitting Giorgio Armani tuxedo with black patent leather shoes. He overwhelmed his body with cologne. As Timothy sat next to Angelika, he inched his hand to hers. Just like Seven, Timothy was captivated by Angelika and knew he had a much better chance with Angelika then Seven did. Timothy attempted to clutch Angelika's hand. She turned her nose up and snatched her hand away from Timothy. The nasty odor annoyed her. Timothy noticed the swan necklace around Angelika's neck. It went lovely with her gown, but Timothy wasn't going to let some low life intimidate him with material items that were probably purchased illegally. Mr. and Mrs. Westland wore the proper apparel for the evening. Mrs. Westland longed in her satin black ballroom gown with an enormous bow in the back from Chanel. Her diamond earrings and necklace glistened on her like stars in the night sky. Her head was way up in the clouds. Angelika's father sported an off black and black tuxedo from Sean John.

Angelika really couldn't enjoy the show due to her not hearing from Seven for a couple of days. All sorts of negative thoughts ran through her mind. *Does Seven have another girlfriend?* Seven didn't call. Angelika sent text messages and called, and Seven still hasn't gotten back to her. While the show was in progress, Angelika checked her cell for messages. Nothing. Angelika exhaled and turned her cell off. She tried to focus her attention on the show, but a fecal odor came from Timothy. Angelika made a sour expression and held her nose. She then looked at her parents and saw how happy they were. Angelika wanted that happiness too. But not with someone they felt comfortable with. It was with someone she felt comfortable with.

Timothy then held Angelika's hand. Angelika snatched her hand away from him. Timothy gawked at Angelika and wondered what the problem was. She didn't even make eye contact with Timothy this time, or even the entire date. Angelika couldn't wait until this night was over.

On the other side of town, a spotlight shined on a small stage where a half-naked girl in a G-string and bare chested swung from a pole. R&B music bellowed from the speakers. A crowd of men gawked, cheered, and inserted one-dollar bills into the stripper's bikini. Among the crowd, DeShaun, Seven, Magnum, Skeeter, and the rest of his entourage enjoyed the show. Usually, men who had money made it rain with one-dollar bills in stripper club. DeShaun and his posse were cheap about it. They made it rain pennies. The posse threw the copper coins on the stage, where the strippers, after their performance, collected them. DeShaun wasn't doing this because he was broke. He felt a stripper were less than a dollar. Strippers were pennies. Some of the exotic dancers knew how DeShaun operated and felt about them. But they had to make a living, whether it was picking up pennies off stage after their performance.

Seven made cat calls to the strippers. He tossed some pennies on the stage and laughed. Seven really didn't want to be there. He had to stay away from Angelika until things cooled off between her and her parents. Seven didn't like the disrespect Mrs. Westland gave him. She did the same thing to him as a child, not acknowledging his presence, disrespecting his mother when she took care of her child that she was supposed to be raising. In the back of Seven's mind, he wondered where Angelika was. *Who was she with? Was she in the company of another guy? Who was Angelika with? Was she at home waiting for me?* The last question was selfish. Seven's thinking Angelika should just wait around for him, not have a life while he hung out with his friends and chilled. Wrong. Angelika did have a life. She may not be with the guy cared for, but life goes on.

Later, the black Jaguar pulled up in front of the Westland mansion. Olga greeted the Westland family at the door. Angelika stormed out of the backseat of the jaguar. She held up her glamorous gown in order to avoid tripping. She slammed the car door. Timothy gave chase. "Angelika, what's wrong?" Timothy asked her, out of breath. Mr. and Mrs. Westland witnessed Angelika and Timothy's friction. They stayed out of it and marched into the mansion. "Angelika, answer me. What did I do?" Timothy asked again.

"Why do you smell like shit?" Angelika asked with frustration in her voice. It's just not due to Timothy's foul odor. She missed Seven. He still hasn't responded to her calls.

"I don't know what you're talking about," said Timothy in denial. He sniffed himself and shook his head.

"Maybe it's you. Who have you been fooling around with?" Timothy implied.

Angelika turned red in the face and balled her hand into a fist. She wanted to punch him in the face. "What are you trying to say?" Angelika asked.

"You're the one lying with ghetto trash," insulted Timothy. A smirk surfaced on his face.

Angelika knew that what he said wasn't true. Timothy had skeletons in his closet and didn't want any of his bones to get out. Out of nowhere, Angelika hurled a punch to Timothy's face.

Mrs. Westland witnessed Angelika's actions from the second-story bedroom window. "Angelika!" Mrs. Westland screamed. She scrambled from the window and raced downstairs.

Timothy held his hand over his bloody nose. "My suit!" Timothy said.

"No one will notice," Angelika said as she folded her arms. She smirked. Angelika felt good about hitting Tim. Someone had to.

Mrs. Westland rushed to Timothy's side. Olga was right behind with a napkin. Olga gave it to Timothy to hold his nose. "What the hell has gotten into you, Angelika!"

Then Mr. Westland stepped out of the mansion. He glared at Angelika. He wasn't pleased. Angelika was acting very stupid. Mr. Westland stood right before her. "What the hell did you do?"

"He insulted me."

Mr. Westland exhaled. "Timothy, I'm sorry for Angelika's behavior. Apologize! Right now!"

"Fuck no!" Angelika shouted as she stormed into the mansion.

"Timothy! I'm so sorry. I hope your nose isn't broken."

"I doubt it. It's not your fault." Timothy said.

"Please go inside and clean yourself up," Mr. Westland begged. Timothy and Mr. Westland headed into the mansion.

While in the study, Angelika browsed around the enormous glistening Christmas tree glistened with the crackling fireplace in the background. She checked out the gifts that were given to her by Timothy. Angelika torn the gold wrapping paper and black ribbon off the first one and then tossed it in the trash can. Then she repeated the same thing with the second, third, fourth, and fifth gift.

Mr. Westland stomped into the study and noticed the gold wrapping paper and black ribbon in the trash. "That's garbage?" Mr. Westland asked as he raised an eyebrow.

"Yes, it's garbage."

Mr. Westland pulled out the gold wrapping paper, a beautiful black pearl necklace, a satin scarf, the latest Juicy Couture perfume, diamond earrings, and a red candy sweater from the trash can. Angelika's father glared at her with disgust. "What the hell has gotten into you? Your behavior is unacceptable. It's that ruffian? Isn't?

"Stop calling him a ruffian! Angelika argued. She marched out of the study as her heels clanked on the floor. Mr. Westland argued with Angelika from the study throughout the entire mansion.

"That's what he is! Face it!" Mr. Westland said as his voice rose. "You're so-called thing for this ruffian is going to mess things up for me."

"This is about you. I thought it was about me," Angelika said. "It's about you, your mother, and me! What the hell do you see in him? He has no future!"

"You don't know that."

"I do know! Most of them wind up six feet under or serve life in the big house!"

"What are you, a fortune-teller?"

"Anyone can be a fortune-teller when it comes to those people! I know he's doing something illegal."

"You're wrong!" Angelika hollered as she glanced over her shoulder with her father directly behind her. Angelika swung opened the double doors of her bedroom and marched inside. She kicked her high heels off.

"I bet you I'm right!" Mr. Westland answered as he entered into Angelika's bedroom suite.

"You're wrong!" Angelika screamed as she erupted into tears.

Mr. Westland ceased the argument because his darling daughter was hurting. He tried to console Angelika. She pushed her father away. "Leave me alone!" Angelika shouted.

"I'm not going forget this conversation," Mr. Westland said.

"Whatever!" Angelika hollered. Angelika's father exited his daughter's bedroom. She rushed to lock her bedroom double doors. Angelika wiped the tears from her eyes. Angelika looked around and saw her pooch wasn't anywhere around. Then there were scratches at the door. Angelika thrust it open as Emily trotted in. Angelika smiled at her little pompous pooch despite what she was going through. The company of a pet made all the pain go away.

Later that night, Angelika didn't bother to wait by the phone for Seven's call. She went right to sleep. Emily snoozed in her doggie bed on the floor. Angelika heard the buzzing coming from somewhere. Angelika raised her head from her pillow and looked about her room. The buzzing came from her purse that was on her dresser. She grabbed her cell. The caller ID read "Seven."

"Hello, Seven. How are you?" Angelika answered in a sweet voice.

"What up, baby. I'm sorry I didn't get back to you. I had to take care of some business with my boss," Seven explained.

As he continued, Angelika wondered if this business that Seven was talking about illegal or cheating. Angelika hoped that her father was wrong. What would she do if Seven was doing something criminal? She definitely knew what she would do if Seven was cheating: call it quits. Breaking up is hard to do. But you have to if you don't want to be taken advantage of. Seven didn't go into too much detail. Seven was hiding something from her. *God, please let my parents be wrong*, Angelika prayed to herself.

New Year's Eve was a day away, and Seven wanted to spend time with Angelika, go out to dinner and a movie, kiss when the clock struck twelve, and make love to bring in the New Year. That's what Seven wanted, and of course, Angelika did too. Now, Angelika got some sleep and couldn't wait to be with her love.

Chapter 35

New Year's Eve. What could be said about the last day of the year, which dragged in the New Year's within twenty-four hours? For this New Year's Eve, a blizzard was on its way to hit the New York Tri-State area, Long Island, Westchester counties, and even New Jersey. Seven puffed on a cigarette as he drove to the Westland mansion. The clock on his dashboard read: 8:09 a.m. The weatherman reported the major snowstorm was about to hit within less than twenty-four hours. Seven knew that if he and Angelika spent the day together, it would turn into her spending a couple of days with him, depending on the storm. That's what Seven wanted—he and Angelika together on a wintery night in his bed, fucking in the New Year.

This really pissed Angelika's parents off. The Westlands' daughter's rebellious ways made them nervous. Everything Angelika did was out of order, and it was Seven's fault. He couldn't be held responsible for Angelika's actions. The black Dodge Charger halted at the security booth at the enormous gates of the Westland mansion. Samuel drank his coffee and ate a doughnut as he heard the Hemi engine's approach.

"Happy New Year," Samuel greeted Seven.

"Happy New Year," Seven returned the greeting as he nodded his head.

The large iron gates widened open as the muscle car sped to the residence. The fierce Hemi engine echoed throughout the air. Seven hoped Angelika would be outside at the front door. She did that last time.

Not so. Mr. Westland waited at the front door, dressed in his pajamas and robe in thirteen-degree weather. The muscle car's wheels squealed. Seven saw Mr. Westland waiting where Angelika was supposed to be. These two were gonna go toe to toe. Seven and Mr. Westland glared at each other like they did back in the day. Seven glanced at the mansion, hoping Angelika would exit.

"Happy New Year," Seven greeted Mr. Westland.

"The New year is getting off to a bad start. I don't need your holiday greetings."

"Where's Angelika?"

Angelika rushed out of the mansion and breezed past her father. She and Seven engaged in a passionate kiss right before Mr. Westland's eyes. Angelika's father's blood boiled, and he waited so bad to call the police, but that would only make Angelika pursue this ruffian even more. Mr. Westland turned around and headed back into the mansion. He slammed the door. Angelika and Seven ceased their kissing due to the red door slamming. She looked back. Angelika felt as if she were being exiled from her home.

Seven opened the passenger's side door for Angelika. He slammed it shut. Angelika stared at her home. Her parents were allowing her to make her own decisions. She knew it wasn't because they didn't care. They wanted Angelika to come to her senses. The black Dodge Charger thundered away as the Hemi bellow could be heard miles away. Seven sped on the LIE as if they were being chased by cops. Seven kissed Angelika's hand. She blocked the thought out of her head of her father slamming the door on her. It hurt. Instead, Angelika focused on Seven's affection. She really needed someone in this time of need.

Seven and Angelika ate breakfast at the diner. The two of them devoured waffles with lots of syrup, butter, and whipped cream. The whipped cream gave Seven some ideas. Angelika began to blush, being aware of Seven's motives. What else could a man and a woman do all day in the house during a blizzard? Sex, sex, and lots of food. Then Angelika worried about Timothy turning against her father due to her actions. She didn't want her father to lose business associates and friends on her account. Angelika excused herself from the table. She dialed Tim's number on her cell. It was thirteen-degrees outside, Angelika stood in the frigid cold pleading for Timothy's forgiveness.

Timothy cursed Angelika out like never before. He almost suffered a broken nose. Timothy's mother saw his bloodied nose and asked what happened. He lied and said that he got into a physical altercation with a guy at a bar. Angelika was relieved that Timothy lied about the situation. Then he criticized Angelika for being with a loser. "What could Seven possibly do for you? What's his annual income?" Timothy questioned. "I'll be inheriting my father's millions in no time," Timothy bragged.

Angelika paced the cold concrete as Timothy proceeded to holler obscenities in her ear. "I've got to fuckin' go. Have a nice fuckin' life with your ghetto trash!" Timothy cursed as the cell clicked in Angelika's ear. Angelika stood frozen as the cold overwhelmed her body. Timothy had the last word on this one. She then turned her cell phone off and shivered. She dashed back into the diner. Angelika plopped down in her seat in front of Seven. He could tell that something was wrong. Angelika had to be honest with him. Angelika told Seven how her father wanted to arrange her dates, relationships, and hopefully arrange a marriage with a guy of their choice. Not hers. Her parents felt Timothy was the best for her. Angelika disagreed. Seven didn't doubt Angelika one bit. Mr. Westland seemed to be the type to do something so outrageous.

Then it was Seven's turn. He confessed going to the strip club and watching exotic dancers crawl on their hands and knees for some pennies. Angelika laughed it off. She didn't seem bothered by it. Seven wouldn't bring one of those women home to his mother. Seven's doesn't go very much. Because it's a bunch of pathetic people insecure about themselves. He wanted something more meaningful that's unusual for a ruffian. Most of them have multiple women and children. Seven wasn't gonna do that. Angelika loved Seven's honestly. She hoped it would continue throughout the relationship.

Next, it was off to see Seven's baby sister, Athena. He was supposed to drop by on Christmas Eve, but he got distracted by other things. Seven glared at Angelika and smiled. The black Dodge Charger stopped in front of the two-story colonial home. There were Christmas decorations on the property. Seven wanted Angelika to meet his baby sister, Athena. Seven rang the doorbell. Athena opened up the door as her jaw dropped. She was happy to see her big brother with a very pretty girl. Angelika smiled as she saw the thirteen-year-old girl with her hair in a bun embrace her brother and greet each other with holiday wishes.

Athena smiled from ear to ear when she and Angelika were introduced. Maureen then greeted Seven Happy holidays. Seven introduced Angelika to Maureen. Maureen shook her hand. Seven handed Maureen eight hundred dollars for Athena and herself. But he really wanted to give the cash to Athena. She was too young to handle that type of money. She's a kid. Maureen planned on depositing some of it in the bank account for Athena to go to college. Angelika witnessed Seven handling large sums of money again. She wondered why he didn't have a credit or debit card. Angelika kept her mouth shut.

On the drive to Seven and Angelika's destination, they listened to the weather report on the radio station 1010 WINS. After the intro of the radio station with it bells chiming, the weatherman updated the wintery storm that New York was anticipating. Supermarkets, Home Depots, and even Targets were crowded due to everyone's panic. Seven and Angelika hurried, grabbed a shopping cart, and wheeled in through the store. Seven and Angelika snatched almost everything they came across on the shelves. Angelika loaded three gallons of milk in the shopping cart, then eggs, lots of cheese, coffee creamers, orange, apple, and grape juices. And they didn't forget the whip cream, at least five cans of it. Then it was off to the meat department. Seven grab the rib eye steaks, two whole chickens, hamburger meat, bacon, and a roast beef. Angelika grabbed that even though she didn't know how to cook one. She'll ask Ingrid for a good recipe. Then Angelika knew to get some spices. She left Seven's side and headed into the cereal aisle. She grabbed a five-pound bag of sugar, salt, garlic salt, garlic powder, onion powder, paprika, oregano, basil, thyme, etc. Seven dropped three flashlights and lots of batteries into the cart. Angelika dropped the spices into the cart.

"Seven, what else do we need?" Seven asked. He recognized the coffee creamer. "How are you gonna have coffee creamer without coffee, Angelika?" Seven hinted Angelika.

"I'll be right back," Angelika gasped as she dashed back into the cereal aisle.

As Angelika returned to the cereal aisle, her cell phone went off in her coat pocket. She looked at it and saw the caller ID reading "Mom and Dad." Angelika accepted the call. "Hello, Dad."

"Angelika. Angelika, where are you?" Her father so desperately asked. He paced the floor in his study as the fireplace crackled.

"I'm in the supermarket," Angelika said.

"With who?"

"Who else!" Angelika responded as she grabbed an instant coffee, tea, and box of Fruity Pebbles.

"There's a storm coming, Angelika!" Mr. Westland hollered frantically. Mrs. Westland could be heard sobbing in the background. "Your mother's going crazy. Come home!"

"Let me speak to Angelika," Mrs. Westland cried as she got on the other end of the phone. "Angelika, what are you doing? Why are you spending so much time with him?" Mr. Westland shouted in the background. He then snatched the phone from his wife.

"The storm isn't going to be that bad." Angelika sighed.

"So why are you in a supermarket then, Angelika?" Mr. Westland hollered again.

"So Seven and I can have something for New Year's dinner! That's why," Angelika said as she stomped her foot on the floor. At the same time, Angelika dropped the can of coffee on the floor. She then dropped her cell phone. Angelika grabbed the coffee and cell phone. Mr. Westland's voice bellowed through the cell. She turned it off. Again, Angelika dropped the items in the shopping cart.

Seven turned abruptly. "Is that all we need, Angelika?"

"Plenty of food and sex for a wintery storm," said Angelika as a devilish smile went from ear to ear on her face. Seven loved the sound of that. The best time to fuck. Before that, Seven stopped off at his mother's house. Seven bought half of those groceries for Ingrid. Ingrid's ice box was extra full because her brother Darren dropped off some food. And Seven's cousin Rasheed also brought her some groceries. Angelika loved the idea of Ingrid being nestled in her home with plenty to eat. Angelika wanted to know if Ingrid was going to be okay. Seven assured Angelika Ingrid was tough as nails. The lovers focused on themselves as they left Ingrid's home. They were able to set their minds on "getting busy."

Later, Seven's construction boots, garage jumper, socks, under-shirt, and boxers, along with Angelika's coat, jeans, sweater, bra, panties, boots created a trail that led to Seven thrusting himself in and out of Angelika in his king-sized bed. Her legs tightly wrapped around his waist. Seven loved the power he had over Angelika, domi-nating her with every fuck that he thrust upon her. Angelika couldn't wait for moments like this. She always saw these types of things in the movies, whether it be a mainstream movie or erotic movie. Seven didn't even bother to turn the heat on in his freezing house. Just Seven and Angelika fucking a storm of their own brought their tem-peratures up, body heat that is.

During the moment of passion, their hearts could be felt beat-ing against each other. Balls of sweat poured from their bodies as they made contact with each other and merged into one, just like their bodies. The moment became intense; their hearts raced faster and faster. Angelika's cell vibrated from her coat. The cell ID read "Mom and Dad." It stopped. Angelika could hear the annoying buzzing sound but, of course, ignored it. She was busy with the guy that she cared about. The New Year was on its way in a few hours, and she didn't want anything to interfere. Seven and Angelika gazed into each other after achieving their climaxes. Seven laid a kiss upon her cheek.

As they both caught their breaths, the wind could be heard with its breath of fury. It whistled and blew strong, knocking garbage cans, leaves, and other things that were lightweight. Seven swaggered in behind her with a cup of hot chocolate.

"Thank you," Angelika said in her sweet voice.

Seven plopped in the lounge chair in his boxers and bare chest. He lit a cigarette and exhaled smoke into the air. He watched as Angelika sipped her hot beverage and kept eyeing him. *I guess she likes what she sees,* Seven thought to himself. He knew Angelika like he knew the back of his hand. Angelika noticed Seven's physique. He was built like one of those sexy Hollywood actors in the movies. She felt like the luckiest girl in the world to be with someone that's sexy and loved her. She hoped. These thoughts and feelings that Seven and Angelika had for each other were mutual. Seven took the last puff of his cigarette. Time for round two.

Seven approached Angelika as she sat on the seat. She wore one of his old T-shirt and no pants. Seven got up on her. They made eye contact. Angelika knew what that look meant. Seven lifted Angelika up and laid her on the bed. He lifted up the T-shirt and spread her legs open. Her pussy was ready for more. Seven saw the juices emerging from it. He stuck his finger in Angelika. She began to moan just like erotic stars in the adult films. Angelika was being pleased. He knew what to do. He gave her nothing but pleasure. Seven then caressed Angelika's breast and sucked on them.

"Happy New Year, Seven." Angelika moaned as her sex began more intense.

"Happy New Year." Seven moaned in return. There were still a few hours before midnight.

Live from Times Square in New York City, Ryan Seacrest hosted New Year's Rockin' Eve. The worldwide event blared from Seven's plasma screen television. A pop singer was right in the middle of her performance. The crowd of spectators clapped along to the song of a popular artist. Couples cuddled together due to the nine-degree temperature. Seven and Angelika lay in bed with a down comforter over them. Snowflakes trickled down on the crowd, who wore zany-looking New Year's Eve glasses, hats, and other party favors as they waited for the crystal ball to drop. No doubt they were freezing their asses off.

"I could never go to Times Square for any event." Angelika chuckled.

"I don't like the city. Too crowded. Too many buildings," Seven said.

"Skyscrapers," Angelika corrected him.

"Buildings. Skyscrapers. Same shit," Seven said. "It's not roomy like Long Island," Seven continued.

"Flat!" Angelika said again.

"Whatever, Angelika. Why are you correcting me?" Seven asked as he started feeling a bit embarrassed even though it was just he and Angelika. Seven noticed Angelika seemed to be changing on him. Or was it just at this moment, because he knew her parents had that self-centered, know-it-all attitude?

She apologized. Angelika didn't mean to belittle him. She was just like that. Seven wanted to tell Angelika to check her behavior. She really didn't think anything was wrong with what she was doing. Angelika gave Seven a peck on the cheek and watched the ball drop. Countdown. Ten. Nine. Eight. Seven. Six. Five. Four. Three. Two. One. Happy New Year! Confetti and streamers and balloons flew down over Times Square. "Auld Lang Syne" New Year's song played. Angelika and Seven engaged in a passionate kiss. "Happy New Year once again, baby," Angelika moaned.

After Seven and Angelika's moments of passion, what else could they do but eat. A microwave beeped as Seven took out two chicken broccoli hot pockets. He placed it on a plate and handed it to Angelika. She bit into the steamy hot patty. Seven did the same. Seven's refrigerator was full as their stomachs were. Angelika sat on the couch as she gazed out of the picture-framed window. She reminisced about the snowstorms, playing in the snow, and school closing, which was considered a snow day. She loved those days. Angelika remembered her and Seven playing in the snow on Thanksgiving. Seven smiled as it was very vivid in his mind. As Angelika went on, her arrogance was surfacing. Seven didn't know if Angelika realized it or didn't care. She talked about the places she and parents traveled to. Angelika bragged about France. She'd been there at least nine times. France was a beautiful country, rich in culture, the food, and locals were wonderful as well.

Seven raised an eyebrow as Angelika began telling him that she was French. Angelika didn't talk like this as a child. *I guess by Angelika vacationing in France so much, she felt right at home.* Angelika made two friends there and is still in touch with them on Facebook. Seven wondered why Angelika felt that she was French. She's biracial. Angelika didn't want to be looked upon as African-American or biracial. She sure couldn't say that she was white. So instead of a race, she just considered herself a part of an affluent nationality. Angelika had a hard time fitting in with anyone.

Angelika had some bad experiences, racism and all. While growing up in the neighborhood, some of the residents really didn't like Mr. Westland. Luckily, the majority did. But there were a few that despised the Westlands. At school, the boys were giving out Valentine's Day hearts and candies to the girls, except Angelika. Two little white boys said, "No boy loves a nigger." That statement was a stab in the chest at age eight. She cried all night when she got home. Angelika never told her parents because she didn't want her father to get into a confrontation with those crazy people. Just by talking about it, tears trickled down Angelika's cheeks.

Seven couldn't help but comfort her. He wanted to tell Angelika like it was. But he kept his mouth shut and allowed Angelika to speak what was on her mind. Angelika's got plenty of so-called friends in the neighborhoods and at school, but Cassandra and Timothy were the closest friends to Angelika. Throughout the Westlands' lives, Angelika's father was in denial when it came to racism. Mrs. Westland didn't discuss it because of her father's bias ways toward her African-American husband. Angelika's grandfather's name was Maximillian Covington. Angelika lied about her grandfather being in her life. He wasn't even in his daughter's life. Mr. Covington came from old money inherited from his father's real estate investments. Real estate was Mr. Westland's first goal. He sought employment at the Covington Realty back in the early eighties after graduating college and earning his real estate license. That's where Angelika's parents met. All the realtors were Caucasians, not a black or brown face in sight. Sparks flew between Mr. and Mrs. Westland. Raquel called

Mr. Westland and hired him on the spot. Mrs. Westland knew this man was going to be her husband. They kept the relationship on the low because of Mr. Covington. She knew he'd disapprove. Mrs. Westland worked closely with her father. She sold some real estate and taught Mr. Westland the ropes. Mr. Westland caught on quick and sold his first home. He made a pretty penny. From there, he kept on with selling and then appraising properties. On Mrs. Westland's (Raquel's) birthday, she received a gift of twenty-five million. Mr. Covington created a bank account of the money for her. But she closed the account and deposited the money in another bank. Her father was irate and then disowned Mrs. Westland (Raquel) when found out she was involved with Charles (Mr. Westland).

Over the years, Mrs. Westland has tried to win back her father's love. She felt if the money was a gift, she could do whatever she wanted. But when it came to Mr. Covington, he wanted to have the upper hand. On Mr. and Mrs. Westland's wedding day, Mr. Covington didn't want to hear it. When Angelika was born, he didn't want to hear it. With the family's success, Mr. Covington turned deaf ears to them. So this was the drama that's been going on in Angelika's life. Seven raised an eyebrow and tilted his head in shock to her painful life. Most poor people believe that most wealthy people have the happiest lives in the world. Not so. Angelika ended her story and looked at Seven. Seven knew he wasn't going to tell Angelika a fuckin' thing about the streets, even though nothing there was good either. Seven just got into Ingrid's life. Ingrid's been active in church for years and has been raising him. Until Seven made enough money, he left the nest. Seven didn't talk much about his life. He didn't even talk much about his Dodge Charger. He'll get into that later. For now, Seven's just taking it one day at a time. Seven clutched Angelika in his arms as they gazed outside of his snowy living room window. The snow was a sheet on the ground for now.

A few hours later, Seven and Angelika were at it again. The thermostat read ninety degrees. Seven's bedroom was like a summer day in July. Angelika's legs wrapped his waist as he kept thrusting in and out of her. Seven didn't think about how many times they had sex. Every guy doesn't care about how many times he fucks. This was the best holiday ever for Seven. Not just because he's getting lots of pussy, but also because he was with someone that he cared about. For Angelika, the feeling's mutual. *Does Seven really care about me? We're having sex a lot,* Angelika thought. But that immediately vanished from her mind as her orgasm kicked in.

Snow and wind continued through the hours of the night, through the night and into a brand-new day as sunlight beamed through the blinds of Seven's bedroom window. There was loud scraping along the pavement with a loud beeping sound with rumbles of engines. There were clamoring of voices coming from outside. Seven opened his eyes. As he glanced at his clock, it read 9:19 a.m. He sprung from his slumber in the nude. He slipped a pair of boxers on and headed into the living room. As Seven made his way through, the draft was extremely cold. He shivered as he rushed to the window. The snow blanketed most of the picture-framed living room window. It only left an eye's view to the outside winter wonderland. The emergency vehicles were busy clearing the roads, removing fallen trees and branches, and fixing power lines. Then some neighborhoods teens marched in the middle of the road because it was the best place for them to walk, one right behind the other with shovels over their shoulders, trying to help out residents and earn some cash. Seven always shoveled snow, especially for his mother. But before he could shovel for her, he had to shovel himself out of his own home.

Seven raced to the door and opened it. The snow blanketed the screen door from top to bottom. "Holy shit!" Seven murmured to himself. He then slammed the door and dashed into the living room window. Seven saw some teens marching in the middle of the street with the snow crunching under their boots as they carried shovels over their shoulders. It was if they were going to war. Seven knocked on his living room and tried to get the attention of one of the teens. Angelika grabbed Seven from behind. Seven jumped out of his skin. "Angelika, what's your problem," Seven cried. He didn't expect Angelika to creep up on him the way she did. He gave her the biggest attitude that morning.

"Why?" Angelika thought to herself as she gazed at him, shocked. Seven proceeded to call out to the teens. Then he caught the attention of one of them. "Yo! Come here!" Seven hollered.

A tall, skinny eighteen-year-old kid from down the street walked as close to Seven's house as he could. "What's up!" he greeted as he stuck his shovel in the deep snow. "You need some shoveling done?"

"Yes, I do. I need the front, rear, the side of the house dug out. And my Charger."

"Bet! Come on, fools. Let's shovel the house and his Charger!" he shouted to his friends. About eight teens headed over to Seven's property and began digging the heavy, cold snow. Seven then turned away from the living room window and noticed Angelika wasn't around. Seven marched into the bedroom. He saw Angelika lying in bed with a glum expression on her face. Seven didn't mean to yell at her, but she startled him. He got on top of Angelika and began kissing her on the face, neck, and then the lips, which was a passionate one. At this moment, Angelika wasn't in the mood for lovemaking. Seven blew it. "What's the problem, Angelika?"

"Why did you yell at me like that?"

"Angelika! You snuck up behind me!"

"Sorry!"

"I'm sorry too," Seven apologized in return. He and Angelika gazed into each other's eyes. The two didn't know if they wanted to make love or forget it. Seven rolled off Angelika as he gazed at the ceiling. Was the love gone? Or was it just the hot, steamy sex they wanted to accomplish between them? Seven didn't have a thing on his mind. But Angelika rolled on top of Seven with her lightweight body and began kissing Seven. "I'm not in the mood, Angelika."

Angelika raised an eyebrow and was having doubts. "Do you care about me, Seven?"

Seven looked at Angelika as if to say, "What the fuck!" "Why are you in doubt?"

"Because."

"Because I won't allow you to sneak up behind me! What if I had a knife in my hand or something!" Seven explained.

"What a way to start off the New Year."

"You think the New Year got off to a bad start, Angelika?" Seven asked.

"We're arguing."

"We're we arguing last night?" Seven asked in a calm voice.

"No," Angelika answered. The tension between them ceased. Seven wrapped his arms around Angelika and cuddled next to her. Seven didn't want a war between Angelika and himself. He was already at war with her father. Then a buzzing sound came from Angelika's coat pocket. Seven and Angelika both knew it was her parents. Angelika wasn't going to answer. But Seven encouraged Angelika to respond to her father's call. Angelika refused to answer. Seven then volunteered to answer it. She didn't care. Seven rose from his king-sized plush bed and grabbed Angelika's cell phone from her pocket. The caller ID read "Mom and Dad."

Seven answered the call. "Yes, Mr. Westland," Seven answered.

Mr. Westland's irate tone could be heard from the receiver of Angelika's cell. "Where's Angelika!" Mr. Westland shouted.

"I would appreciate it if you stopped hollering in my mother-fuckin' ear!" Seven cursed. Angelika sat up in bed as she heard Seven using profane language toward her father. She didn't want to intervene. Angelika surely didn't want tension between her and Seven. Seven immediately turned off Angelika's cell phone. He then looked at Angelika as if to say sorry. Seven gave the cell phone to her and kissed her on the lips. "I didn't mean it," Seven said in a lower tone. Angelika just shook her head and took her cell from Seven's hand. He glared directly into Angelika's eyes. She exchanged glares with him. They then engaged in a passionate kiss.

Later, as Seven and Angelika made their way out of his home, the pavement was slippery. Angelika almost hit the ground. Seven caught her before that accident was about to happen. The teens dug his Charger out of the waist-deep snow. He smiled. Now he could get to his mother's house and do some shoveling. The teens gathered around Seven like hungry stray cats. They held their hands out for money. Seven paid the kids fairly. He gave each a hundred dollars for a job well done. Angelika's jaw dropped as she saw seven giving the kids such a large amount of money. Mr. Westland hardly paid anyone for shoveling the estate. At least Seven didn't take advantage of people. Each of the teens was gratified.

Seven glanced back at Angelika and reached out to grab her hand. "Don't slip again." Seven chuckled.

"I won't," Angelika sighed. The two carefully took steps in the deep snow towards Seven's Charger. Seven opened the passenger's door of his ride with his keys. Angelika hopped in as Seven slammed the door. He got in on the driver's side and slammed the door. The Charger was like a freezer. Seven and Angelika could see their breath right before their eyes.

"Shit!" Seven cursed as he put the keys in the ignition. The Hemi engine started with no problem. Seven revved it a few times. The teens could be heard cheering from outside. Seven beeped his horn.

"You're a local Jimmie Johnson." Angelika laughed.

"Please. I'm me."

"You know what I mean."

"What do you mean, Angelika?"

"You're like a Jimmie Johnson of the streets. Long Island. You know," Angelika said.

Seven smiled due to the sound of Angelika's compliment. It made him feel proud and happy that Angelika acknowledged him. The black Dodge Charger backed out of the driveway with its engine rumbling and tires squealing. It turned on to the road and took off like a bolt of lightning. Then teens waved and gave him the thumbs-up.

While on the road, he didn't think about the dangerous conditions that could be right ahead on them. He remembered what happened a couple of years ago. His Volkswagen slid off the road due to bad weather. The Charger then slowed down because Angelika was also with him. That was the last thing Seven needed, an accident with him and Angelika both. "My baby's still running. Strong as ever." Seven guffawed. He's proud of his baby, tough as nails, strong as an ox. Real American muscle, motherfuckers! as Seven would say.

Seven had to get to his mother's to see if she's okay. Even though Seven didn't live with Ingrid, he didn't just bring her food. He always came to do odd jobs around the house. It still felt as if he were living there. The black Dodge Charger drove towards Ingrid's house. Seven's eyes bulged as his Uncle Darren shoveled the deep and heavy snow. Seven halted his Charger in the middle of the road. He pounded his fist on the steering wheel. "What the fuck!" Seven bellowed. Seven beeped the horn as it alerted his uncle. Darren headed over to the Charger as the window rolled down. "What brings you here?" Seven asked sarcastically.

"What kind of question is that! Someone's got to do it!" said Darren.

Seven felt the tension between him and his uncle. "What's my mother doing?"

"She's relaxing," Darren said as he stood the shovel in the deep snow.

Moments later, Ingrid poured hot chocolate from a pot into Angelika's cup.

"Thank you," Angelika said politely. Angelika sipped the hot beverage with caution in order not to burn herself.

Ingrid also poured herself a cup of hot chocolate. The two women sat in the living room where a small heater had the entire area warm. Ingrid and Angelika didn't get the opportunity to really talk last time because of Seven's exploding episodes. Ingrid remembered the mansion, the parties, the holidays they spent together, and so on—a walk down memory lane to such a beautiful place where Angelika resided. But things weren't as beautiful as they seemed. Angelika may have told Seven about the crap that went on with her family. But she didn't have the heart to tell Ingrid. The only thing she could tell Ingrid was that she's really happy that he came back into her life. Ingrid knew Mr. Westland disapproved because Seven was a ruffian. In Ingrid's mind, she had to agree with Angelika's father. Seven was a ruffian. Ingrid wanted to tell Angelika all about Seven's street hustling, street racing, fighting, and God only knows what. Ingrid figured she better keep her mouth shut because it would only bring Angelika closer to Seven. Hopefully, Angelika would see that Seven wasn't right for her. Ingrid went on to chat about her family background.

Meanwhile, Uncle Darren gulped down his cup of hot chocolate as Seven shoveled in the background. Seven glared at his uncle chilling out while he did the rest of the work. Seven wasn't in the mood for a hot beverage. He despised how his uncle always showed up unannounced. *Why doesn't he go shovel for his girlfriend?* Seven asked himself. Darren stared at his nephew. Seven caught his uncle's stares. "You didn't complete the walkway for the front door," Seven said. Seven swaggered toward the front doorway and began shoveling.

"I left the rest of the work for you because I knew you would get upset over me being here," Darren explained. He took the last gulp of his hot chocolate. He crumbled up his foam cup in his hand. "Seven, you finish the rest. I'm out of here," Darren said as he marched along the walkway of front door. Seven sneered at him. Darren pushed the front door open and slammed it.

Seven's face turned red. The tension between Seven and his uncle was high. Seven hoped Darren didn't go in there and start drilling Angelika. It's none of his business. Angelika would tell Seven if his uncle questioned her. Anyway, Seven took his mind off that. He proceeded to shovel the walkway. Angelika and Ingrid peered out of the living room window and waved to him. Angelika smiled at Seven. It was a turn-on seeing him do hard work. That's a real man. Then later he dug out the driveway.

As Seven did the hard work, Darren peered out of the living room window. He drank another hot beverage in a cup. Darren seemed to be taunting his nephew.

"What the fuck are you looking at!" Seven shouted.

"Nothing much!" Darren shouted from behind the picture window.

"Not today!" Seven shouted. Seven continued shoveling and just ignored his uncle. Seven didn't want to have a confrontation in front of Angelika. It was bad enough he's got to deal with Mr. Westland. Seven pushed the shovel along the driveway and pushed the snow into the grass. The driveway was cleared as Seven parked his Dodge Charger in it.

Darren exited the house at the same time. "Good work, solider!" Darren shouted as he saluted Seven. Seven got out of his car and slammed the door. "Are you motherfuckin' for real! You're not in the marines, yo!"

The engine of Darren's Saturn started up. He sped off. Ingrid and Angelika peered out of the living room window due to the verbal confrontation. "Stop, Seven!"

"He's been fuckin' with me ever since I got here!" Seven shouted.

"Please!" Ingrid shouted as she knocked on the window. Seven had tension between his uncle and her father. Angelika knew that Seven will tell what's going on. Right now, she's still in the dark about it.

On the way to the Westland estate, there was dead silence between them. The black Dodge Charger sped along the highway. The engine bellowed. You could feel the anger from it due to Seven. Angelika wasn't gonna let that put a wedge between them. "Seven, what happened?" Angelika asked with a bit of an attitude.

"My uncle's getting on my motherfuckin' nerves," Seven answered Angelika right away. "Why?" Seven asked abruptly.

"Don't let him get to you." Angelika replied.

"He does get to me."

"But when you do that Seven, the person wins."

"I disagree."

"Why do you disagree?"

"I'm not going to allow someone to disrespect me and get the fuck under my skin," Seven yelled.

"Yes."

"So what you're saying is bow down."

"Not exactly," Angelika said with some hesitation as she fidgeted in the passenger's seat.

"Are you serious! Like your father?" Seven said. He gawked at Angelika as she couldn't look Seven in the eye. "What's the problem, Angelika! Look at me!"

Angelika looked Seven right in the eye. Seven could see that Angelika was serious about him changing his tough ways. That wasn't reality. No ruffian allowed himself to be talked down to. She must be crazy. She must've been smoking something that no one knows about.

"I love you," Angelika sighed.

"What did you just say?" Seven asked as he slowed down the speed of his muscle car.

"I love you, Seven. I've always loved you," Angelika repeated.

Seven loved Angelika too. But he wasn't going to say it just yet. When the time was right. He cracked a smiled and gave her a peck on the lips.

The black Dodge Charger sped along Westbury Road as sanitation plowed the snow on the streets. The muscle car was able to pick up speed and make its way through the enormous iron gates without a problem. There were volunteers shoveling snow on the outside of the gates of the estate. Samuel sipped on his coffee as he saw Seven and Angelika in the Charger. The iron gates widened as Seven sped in. There were more volunteers shoveling snow. They were mostly teens hoping to get some cash from Mr. Westland. That certainly wasn't going to happen. No one could squeeze a penny out of him. The Hemi engine could be heard in the distance as Olga opened the front door of the mansion. Mr. Westland was expected to come to the door. Angelika and Seven stepped out of the Charger as they looked around.

"So, I'll see you soon," Angelika said.

"Yes. Very soon. Sooner than you think," Seven said. They kissed passionately.

"Bye," Angelika said as she backed away and made her way into the mansion.

Seven jumped into Charger. He revved the engine and sped off.

Chapter 36

Mid-January, the holidays were over. Everything was back to normal. DeShaun resumed business as usual with his minimart. Customers' shopping carts were full of food due to the threat of another blizzard. Scanners beeped like crazy as the cashiers scanned items. Stock boys stocked the shelves with food. TaTu kept an eye on the front of the store.

"Register five is opened!" TaTu hollered as he escorted a customer to the register. On the lower level, DeShaun conducted business as well with the boys in blue. Everything so far was going good with them. No arguments. No confusion. Things went smoothly even though some people got hurt all the way. The JetScan counted large sums of money . DeShaun handed the police officers large sums of cash for a job well done. They shook hands and went on their way. The boys in blue marched up from the basement through the aisle of the market and out of the establishment.

Seven pulled up in his Charger. The brakes squealed as the engine shut down. Seven hopped out as he saw the officers take off in their patrol car. To Seven it was whatever. He swaggered into the mart and was greeted with a five from TaTu. Seven waved to the cashiers. He didn't want to distract them from taking care of customers. Seven immediately headed into the basement. When he got down to the basement in the billiard area, there was no one in sight. And where was the Rottie DeShaun had guarding the door? Seven rang the buzzer.

Magnum opened the door. "What's up, yo?' Magnum greeted Seven with a high five. Seven swaggered in as the door slammed. The sounds of the locks latching could be heard. All of DeShaun's henchmen were gathered around as he discussed the updates of his monopoly of the streets. Rumor has it that Russell, one of the drug runners, has been short-changing DeShaun. Plus he disappeared. He hasn't been seen for a couple of months. DeShaun wanted Seven to take care of that. And he knew that Seven could.

Moments later, Seven was off in his black Dodge Charger to do the task that was asked of him. Of course, Seven sped along the way to Russell's house. Angelika crossed Seven's mind, and Valentine's Day was in a few weeks. He didn't know what plans he had for Angelika. But he'll get to that later. Right now, he had his priorities. Seven pulled out a Philly blunt and lit it up. He took a couple of puffs. He has to set his mind to getting DeShaun's cash.

The muscle car stopped in front of a small house. No one was around on this early afternoon. A dog could be heard barking in the distance. Seven hopped out of his car. He swaggered toward the door of Russell's home. The house was small and nice. The grass was trimmed as well as the hedges. With the money Russell stole from DeShaun, he sure kept his mother's home looking nice. Seven shook his head due to the well-kept property. Seven's heart raced as his face turned red as he sneered. He wanted to get Russell for trying to be slick. He rang the doorbell as he tapped his foot on the ground. Seven then balled his hand into a fist, ready to check Russell's chin and get that paper.

Then Mrs. Kemp, Russell's mother, in her midfifties, opened the door with a coffee mug in her hand. Seven's eyes widened as the angelic woman similar to his mother stood before his eyes. She smiled as anyone could see nothing but God in her face. Seven didn't want to disrespect Russell's mother because he sure didn't want any-one disrespecting his. Mrs. Kemp was known by neighbors not just as Russell's mother but as a woman who took care of children at a nearby day care center. The sneer on Seven's face then turned to a slight smile as his heart slowed down.

"Hello, Mrs. Kemp. How are you? Is Russell home?" Seven asked in a submissive tone.

"No. He isn't. Is he in some kind of trouble?" Mrs. Kemp asked with concern in her tone. Her facial expression became heartfelt.

Seven's rage then softened as he couldn't help but tell the woman a story in order not to upset her. "No. Everything's fine, Mrs. Kemp?" Seven lied to Mrs. Kemp as he swaggered back to his Charger and sped off. The engine reverberated through the atmosphere.

As Seven put his foot to the gas, he glanced over both sides of his shoulders, eager to get what was rightfully DeShaun's. Seven's rage surfaced to a boiling point. His heart pumped even harder, face turned red, and he drove even faster. He zoomed down every block and still no sign of Russell. Like the saying goes, "A man is one with his car." When Seven's heated, so was his Charger. The muscle car proceeded to zoom down the road until it merged on Sunrise Highway.

Where the fuck am I going? Am I really going to find Russell? Seven thought. Seven glanced over his shoulders left and right as he saw parking lots of strip malls filled with cars. Seven knew he wasn't going to find Russell here. He had to head back to the block, where he would have a better chance of catching his ass. Suddenly, Seven's eyes bulged. "Shit!" The Hemi engine of the Dodge Charger bellowed fiercely with its screeching wheels.

Russell strolled along a half-empty parking lot of a supermarket without a care in the world. He wore a black sweat suit with his white sneakers and windbreaker jacket. He hauled a large duffel bag over his shoulder. Rap music blasted through Russell's Beats headphones. The black Dodge Charger rolled up on Russell with its engine rumbling low and the headlights off. As Seven resided behind the wheel of his Charger, he made a sour expression. Russell didn't feel the muscle car's presence. Russell was in a world of his own. The Charger's headlights then beamed directly on Russell. He realized the beam of the light from behind him. Russell turned around as he squinted his eyes. He removed the headphones from his ears. Then the screeching sound of the Dodge Charger erupted. Russell's jaw dropped. He took off like a runner in a marathon. He dashed through every empty parking lot with Seven right behind him. Seven was desperate to get that cash. There were no people in sight to help Russell or witness the confrontation.

As Seven kept driving, he could see Russell's pace slowing down. Russell then stumbled to the concrete of an empty abandoned parking lot. He plummeted face-first, hitting his mouth to the ground. He spat blood out. The headlight of the back Dodge Charger was right up on Russell. The muscle car's wheels screeched directly in Russell's ear. The rumbling engine was over his shoulder. Then there was the sound of approaching footsteps coming right up on him. Russell then turned on his back. He saw Seven standing over him, looking powerful and menacing. Seven glared down at his victim and saw the duffel bag scattered on the side.

Russell continued to bleed and held his hands up. "Seven, it's all yours man!" said Russell as he held his hands up. Seven wanted to put more of a hurting on him but saw Russell's busted mouth and bruised face. Russell was hurt enough. Seven swaggered over to the duffel bag and unzipped it. Lots and lots of green dollar bills of twenties, fifties, and hundreds was mesmerizing to Seven. He closed the bag back up. He ignored Russell as he lay on the ground and began sobbing like a child. Seven couldn't stand when a man cried. Seven hurried to his Dodge Charger and hopped in. He placed the duffel bag in the passenger's seat. Smoke emerged from the rear tires as the black Dodge Charger took off. The Charger made its entrance on to the highway as it weaved between lanes. As Seven drove to DeShaun's, he constantly glanced at the duffel bag. The money was tempting. Seven really couldn't blame Russell or anyone who saw lots of cash right before them. *What would I do if had the opportunity to steal this cash?* Seven asked himself. *I would have to do something drastic like overthrow my own boss. Wow, the shit people will do for money.* Seven brushed these negative thoughts from his mind and focused how DeShaun was like a father to him and didn't want to be betrayed. *Hopefully, DeShaun doesn't do that to me. Shit happens.*

The *Queen Latifah Show* played on television while DeShaun resided in his executive's chair, enjoying the show. Skeeter and Magnum counted up money as they usually did. The buzzer buzzed. Skeeter took an enormous puff of his cigarette and dashed to the door. He didn't bother to ask who it was; he knew it was Seven on the other side of the door. He swung it open. Seven swaggered in with the duffel over his shoulder. Seven plopped it on DeShaun's desk right before him.

"You've got a surprise for me, Seven?" DeShaun asked with a smile. Just by the smile on DeShaun's face, Seven knew he was going to be pleased. Seven unzipped the bag and unloaded the cash. DeShaun relaxed in his chair without any type of astonishment. DeShaun had that faith in Seven. Magnum and Skeeter's jaws dropped as their eyes widened as the green blanketed DeShaun's desk. "Very good, Seven," DeShaun praised him with a calm reaction. He embraced Seven and patted him on the back. "Count this shit up, yo!" DeShaun commanded.

Skeeter grabbed the dough and placed in the JetScan. The machine began the count of the large sum of money. Magnum sneered at Seven due to him getting to Russell first. Seven didn't notice it, and if he had, Seven would confront the person on his beef. Seven wouldn't back down from anything. But this time, he didn't notice anything out of the ordinary.

Later, the black Dodge Charger parked in the driveway of Seven's home. He hopped out of the car and opened the front door with his keys. Anastasia greeted him at the door, wagging her tail and barking. He closed the door behind him. The foul odor of feces filled the air. "Fuck!" Seven hollered. He flicked on the lights and saw the pile of feces in the corner of the living room. "Fuck, Anastasia!" Seven grabbed a rag and cleaned up the dog poop. Then he sprinkled Carpet Fresh on the spot. Seven shook his head because he had to figure out how to train the dog from doing her business in the house. Then it hit Seven; he had to get a dog house and put it in the backyard. Anastasia could run free and do her business in the yard. But then Seven didn't like that idea. He would just have to take a chance and walk his dog despite of what happened to his other Rottie.

Seven stormed into his bedroom. He took off his construction boots and his auto mechanic jumpsuit. Nothing was on Seven's mind but getting to bed. He only had on his undershirt and boxers. Seven lay in his king-sized bed and gazed at the ceiling. Of course, someone did cross his mind: Angelika. He wanted to plan the most romantic Valentine's Day ever for her—lots of roses, candy, dinner, and lots of fucking. In Angelika's words, lots of lovemaking. To Seven, it was the same thing. Then his cell phone vibrated from his mechanic jumpsuit. Seven reached from his bed and grabbed his cell from his garment. The caller ID read "Angelika."

"Hello, baby," Seven greeted Angelika.

"How are you, Seven?" Angelika asked in her sweet, loving tone. She lounged on her small sofa in her bedroom suite with Emily resting in her arms. A late-night movie played on television. "Valentine's Day is coming."

"I know, babe. I'm getting ready for us."

"I want to see you before then."

"Yes. I'm gonna pick you up from school tomorrow. You attend Garden City Academy?"

"Yes. I do," Angelika said.

"We're going somewhere."

"That sounds good."

As Seven and Angelika continued to chat, he didn't want to let Angelika go even though he was dead tired. Seven dosed off and then woke up when Angelika shouted in his ear. He didn't mind her shouting at him. It woke him up. All in Seven's ear, Angelika spoke of the color red, how it's used for good and bad things. Red represented the devil, which Angelika avoided that conversation. Red was for Valentine's Day and Christmas. Christmas was long gone, and Angelika focused on the upcoming holiday. She loved the different shades of red—red violet mixed with purple, which made a fuchsia color, then the color of roses especially. Due to Seven being half asleep, he only heard portions of Angelika's chatting. Then Seven had to go before he really snoozed on her. The two love birds called it a night and anticipated the next day. Seven hung up his cell phone and placed it on the nightstand. Anastasia waltzed in the bedroom and leaped upon the bed.

"Get off the bed, Anastasia!" Seven shouted at the Rottweiler. The four-legged friend hopped off Seven's king-sized bed and lay on her doggie pillow on the floor. Seven exhaled and closed his eyes.

Morning arrived. Seven opened his eyes and felt the cold draft seeping through his down comforter on his bed. "How fuckin' cold is it?" Seven mumbled. Seven then threw the comforter off himself and really felt it. "Damn!" Seven shouted as he jumped up and shivered. He exhaled warm air from his breath. Anastasia shivered as she tried to find warmth. Seven couldn't believe his eyes.

"Anastasia! Come get in the bed!" Seven commanded the dog. The Rottweiler hopped in the bed as Seven threw the comforter on her. Seven headed to the hallway and looked at the thermostat showing the temperature was low. He forgot to put the heat on. "How could I forget?" Seven said to himself. He raised the heat high. Seven had the heat on when Angelika was here. But since it was just him, he didn't put the heat on. He thought more of Angelika than himself. He wanted to make Angelika feel comfortable and warm just like he planned to do when they spend their Valentine's together.

That afternoon, the black Dodge Charger halted in front of a beautifully well-kept school building with the work of old architecture. The American flag flew high from the flagpole that sat in the center of the school grounds. Then bell rang as a mob of students exited the building. Angelika and Cassandra strolled out of the building together without a care in the world. Angelika and Cassandra had plans that afternoon. They wanted to go to the mall. She told Cassandra she would go; she just remembered that she was supposed to be with Seven that afternoon. *What if my baby doesn't show up? Then I'll have to hang out with Cassandra,* Angelika thought. As the two girls kept walking, Angelika's pace became faster and faster. Her heart raced as she smiled from ear to ear. Seven leaned against his back Dodge Charger, so nonchalant. He wore all black as he usually did—black jeans, construction boots, a black turtle neck sweater, and a down jacket. He looked so handsome, strong, and fierce. Seven puffed on a cigarette as always. He knew he needed to stop before the cancer grabbed his ass.

Angelika rushed right to Seven and kissed him on the cheek. Seven threw his cigarette away and embraced Angelika.

"How are you?" Angelika asked in a loving tone. The look of love was in Angelika's eyes for sure. Cassandra took baby steps as she saw Angelika engaging in lovey-dovey with the strange hoodlum that all the neighbors have been talking about. "Oh, Cassandra. This is Seven. Seven, this is Cassandra," Angelika introduced them.

Cassandra extended her hand and then remembered Seven from years ago. His mother was Angelika's nanny and lived with the Westlands. The same went for Seven. He remembered Cassandra very vividly. He didn't extend his hand to shake Cassandra's. He knew Cassandra was a fuckin' phony. Seven focused his attention on Angelika. Angelika saw what Seven did but ignored it. Of course, Cassandra turned a blind eye to it as well. Angelika realized that she just couldn't leave Cassandra flat like that. Seven agreed, and they all headed to the mall.

While in the Dodge Charger, Seven glared through his rearview mirror at Cassandra in the backseat. She kept looking over her shoulder and not really talking that much. Seven and Angelika bragged about their love.

"No other couple in the world is like us! Right, babe!" Angelika said excitedly as she kissed Seven on the cheek.

Seven loved to see Angelika happy about them. There's no other guy like Seven. Most thugs are scared to say they love a girl because it's considered weak. As Angelika went on about her and Seven, Cassandra felt that they were being fake. No one falls in love with those types of guys—hoodlums, thugs, ruffians, a menace to society. They can't love anyone. They came from broken homes, only being raised by their mothers, no fathers, welfare and violence. Seven knew how the world viewed him just like every other African-American male. And he knew Cassandra really didn't like him. Like Seven really gave a shit. Cassandra definitely was a stuck-up one. Seven's concern was Angelika. They cared for each other, and that's all that mattered.

Through the slightly crowded shopping mall, Angelika and Seven held hands as they goofed around in a loving way. Cassandra lagged behind with a sour expression on her face. She couldn't believe this so-called romance. *What the hell is Angelika thinking? Does she expect a relationship like this to last?* Cassandra thought.

Angelika and Seven continued kissing each other and goofing off. Angelika turned around and saw Cassandra taking her time. "Cassandra, what's wrong?" Angelika asked. Angelika squinted her eyes due to the look in Cassandra's eyes. Seven gave Cassandra a dirty look and knew what the problem was.

"Can I have a word with my friend alone, please?" Cassandra asked Seven in a snobbish tone.

"Who the fuck are you getting an attitude!" Seven asked abruptly as he was ready for a war of words.

"I'm talking to you, homeboy," Cassandra replied.

"Bitch!"

"You called me a bitch!"

"That's right! Bitch! Bitch! Bitch!" Seven swaggered away in order not to get himself into any type of trouble, especially with Cassandra's caliber.

"Cassandra, what the hell is your problem?" Angelika asked in shocked tone. "Stop it!"

Cassandra ceased her insults as she watched the thug leave. Angelika gave Cassandra the most evil look ever. "What, Angelika?" Cassandra asked.

"How could you disrespect him like that!"

"Disrespect! He called me a bitch!"

"You called him a homeboy!"

"That's what the hell he is."

"And you're a bitch!" Angelika insulted Cassandra.

"You're next! He'll be disrespecting you!"

"Everyone knows my future!"

"If everyone is saying that he's an asshole, he is."

"And what about you, Cassandra? The guys that you've dated have been a walk in the park," Angelika said.

"They weren't as bad as this one! What about Timothy?"

"What about Timothy?"

"He's got a promising future as a stock broker. Timothy's excellent with numbers." Cassandra said.

"Good for him." Angelika raised her voice as she applauded for Timothy's accomplishments.

"Have a nice life with the thug!" Cassandra said as she stormed away.

Angelika stood there as she lost her best friend. And she did. Seven kept his distance as he saw Cassandra leaving Angelika's side. Seven headed over to Angelika and embraced her. "You all right, baby?" Seven asked in a caring voice.

Angelika took a deep breath and kissed Seven back. "Everything's fine," Angelika said. The two lovers clutched hands as they continued to browse the shops in the malls.

That evening, the black Dodge Charger zoomed through the enormous iron gates that led to the front door of the Westland mansion. Mr. Westland could hear that Hemi engine in the distance. He shook his head as he looked as if he were ready for war. Olga and Ben also stood at the front door with Mr. Westland for Angelika and Seven's arrival. Mrs. Westland stared from the second-floor window. Mr. Westland looked up at the second window of the mansion. He waved to his wife to get out of the window. She sucked her teeth and left. This time, Angelika's father didn't stand in the way of the muscle car. He allowed Seven to park his ride and drop his daughter off like a gentleman should. Seven came to a brief stop. Mr. Westland didn't move a muscle. Seven and Angelika both jumped out of his car and knew something wasn't right. Her father was being patient about this forbidden romance.

"Hello, Dad," Angelika greeted her father with a kiss. Mr. Westland returned the affection to his daughter. Surprisingly, Mr. Westland extended his hand to Seven.

Seven's eyes widened. He knew something was up. *Why the fuck is this motherfucker shaking my hand? This nigga's got something up his sleeve,* Seven thought. He shook Mr. Westland's hand.

Was Angelika's eyes playing trick on her? Her father finally having a change of heart? Angelika thought. The occasion could be happier.

"Let's have a drink, Seven. Shall we? After you?" Mr. Westland allowed Angelika and Seven to go into the mansion first. Then Mr. Westland headed in as Olga and Ben entered last as the door slammed shut.

Angelika grabbed Seven's hand and kissed him on the cheek as she headed upstairs. Mr. Westland and Seven made their way into the study. Seven was ready for whatever Mr. Westland was about to do. Then later, jazz tunes of Miles Davis played from Mr. Westland's Bose radio as he poured whiskey in two glasses. Seven looked around in the beautiful library that he once remembered as a kid. This was where Mr. Westland fired his mother. Now, it seemed as if Seven were back to avenge his mother's termination. Seven sensed Mr. Westland was still an ass. But Seven was going to stick it out and face this motherfucker. Mr. Westland offered Seven the glass of whiskey. "No, I'm cool," Seven said as he shook his head.

Mr. Westland placed the glass in front of Seven anyway. "Just in case you get thirsty," Mr. Westland said with a devilish smile on his face. "I've been thinking, and I shouldn't have jumped to conclusion. A young man like yourself is probably doing the right thing. And I just want to help you out any way possible," Mr. Westland offered as he took a sip of his liquor.

Seven couldn't believe what he was hearing from this tight-ass fool. *Is this for real or has Angelika's father been smoking something?* Seven thought. "I don't need any handouts," Seven suggested. But Mr. Westland set forty grand right before Seven's eyes. His eyes widened due to the fact that this was to chase him away. Forty grand could go a long way. Seven would have legal cash on him. This money wouldn't hurt, but it would hurt Angelika if he took it. Mr. Westland glared at Seven with the most devilish expression on his face. The man was in fact the devil, Lucifer in the flesh. The evildoer to keep this Romeo and Juliet romance apart.

Angelika had no idea what was really going on in the study between her father and the love of her life. Angelika and her mother were upstairs. They could hear the music slightly, but not the arguing between Mr. Westland and Seven. The walls were eight layers thick. Mr. Westland laid it on Seven; he packed the money in a black cloth bag with a pull string and threw it at Seven. "Take it and go!" Mr. Westland suggested. He hoped that this would get rid of Seven for good.

"And after this, what's next?" Seven asked Mr. Westland to see what his answer would be.

"You go on with your life."

"Are you motherfuckin' for real!"

"Yes, I'm motherfuckin' for real! It's as real as it gets!" The drum solo rolled in from the music as Seven's argument with Mr. Westland intensified. Their voices rose as they cursed and debated over what was best for Angelika. Seven knew he had to win this war of words. Mr. Westland had the upper hand at this point, not just due to his words, but also due to the money.

Standing outside of the double doors in the hallway were Olga and Ben, who heard the entire thing. Olga cringed as their words were slicing each other like knives. Ben stood there with a cup of coffee in his hand and then returned to the kitchen. Olga continued to stand there. Then the double doors swung open. Olga ran as fast as she could. She made her way into the family room.

Seven swaggered out. He didn't recognize anyone around. Seven was heated and didn't look back. Mr. Westland followed behind Seven. Seven thrust the front door open as he got into his Dodge Charger. The Hemi engine started up.

Mr. Westland continued to mouth off at Seven. "Don't spend it all in one place! I know guys like you! Money over bitches! Right!" Mr. Westland insulted.

Seven was shocked at Mr. Westland. *How could this man of such caliber allow those words to spew from his mouth?* Seven thought to himself. Angelika and her mother heard the loud arguing coming from outside. "You really shock the shit out of me, Mr. Westland!" Seven shouted.

"Believe me, I'm full of things that will shock you!" Mr. Westland responded as he marched toward Seven's muscle car.

Seven gave him the finger. The inky Dodge Charger sped off. Angelika stormed out of the mansion in wonder.

"Seven! What happened! What did you say to him? I thought you were getting along!"

"We were until he didn't like what I had to say!" Mr. Westland said.

"What did you say?" Angelika said in a calm and suspicious tone.

Seven drove his black Dodge Charger as if he were street racing other racers. But no one was around, just him and his baby. He sped along the pitch-dark long stretch of road that seemed as if it wouldn't end. There was no police, no critters, nor other drivers out at this time of night. He had the road to himself, because he wasn't in the mood for any bullshit. Seven gazed right through his front windshield and didn't blink once. The thought of him taking the money made him feel guilty. *Who wouldn't take a payoff? Let's be real about it.* But Seven really cared for Angelika. He wasn't going to forget about their Valentine's. He was gonna make it special. Seven would have to confess about the payoff before her father does. Or should he just keep his mouth shut?

Moments later, in Seven's bedroom, the forty grand blanketed Seven's bed. He paced back and forth, trying to figure out why he took the cash. Did he really need it? Seven thought. *No. I got my hustle on the streets and reputation as being the muscle of the streets. There wasn't really any need for the cash. But you never know that dough could come in handy. What if something were to come up?* All these thoughts and questions played in Seven's head. Anastasia lay in her doggie bed as she watched her owner mumbling to himself and stomping his foot on the floor. Seven hurled punches through the air as if he were hitting Mr. Westland. "Motherfucker! Shit!"

The Rottweiler knew this type of behavior from her owner wasn't normal. She moved from her doggie bed to the corner and cringed. Seven then noticed that Anastasia wasn't there. She was curled up in the corner, frightened. Seven shook his head, disappointed in himself. Then the vibration in his jacket went off. Seven looked at it and saw that the caller ID read "Angelika." Seven wasn't ready to face the music. He would get to that later. The cell just vibrated. Vibrated. Vibrated. And continued to vibrate. Seven resided in his lounge chair, staring at the cash on his bed as the vibrations kept coming in.

Chapter 37

Valentine's Day chocolates, romantic dinners, and bottles of champagne would be consumed by lovers everywhere. Diamonds, rubies, emeralds, and sapphires, would be worn by girl in the world due to her lover's appreciation. By Seven taking that money from Mr. Westland got him no sleep. Seven tried to shut his eyes, but the reenactment of Mr. Westland's pompous attitude played out in his mind like a fiddle. He could see the vile look on Mr. Westland's face. Then Seven thought about Angelika's reaction once she found out.

All I have to do is tell Angelika the truth. And if she cares about me, she'll stay, Seven thought to himself. He glanced over at the clock on his nightstand; it read 10:32 a.m. He sat up straight in his bed and looked around. Anastasia slept in her doggie bed. Seven noticed that his four-legged friend was growing. He smiled at the Rottweiler as she could see Seven smiling at her with her squinting eyes. Anastasia rose his head from the doggie bed, stretched and yawned. Seven took his mind off the hound. He had to figure out what plans he was going to have in store for Angelika. Like before, all he had to do was tell Angelika the truth about the money. *Does she already know?* Seven thought again. Seven grabbed his cell phone and checked if Angelika tried to call in the morning. Nothing. But, there were calls from Angelika from the night before.

Seven turned off his cell phone and held it tightly in the palm of his hand. He didn't know whether to call Angelika or not. If he did, she would turn his ass down. *I feel like a bitch right now! What the fuck!* Seven almost murmured to himself. Every time Seven felt like he's about to bitch out, he always checked himself. Seven sprung from his slumber and staggered into the bathroom. Warm water poured down Seven's nude body in the shower. He lathered with a bar of Dial soap.

Moments later, Seven wiped the medicine cabinet mirror with his hand. His reflection appeared before him. Seven noticed hair growing on his head, with some facial hair. He shook a can of shaving cream and applied to the top of his head then shaved it carefully with a large razor. It gave him the Mr. Clean look. Then Seven didn't shave much of his facial hair. He just trimmed it up. He looked very handsome; any woman would want to get with him, especially on this Valentine's Day.

The wintery February air swept through his bedroom from his windows. Seven plugged in his heater into the socket. The small heater began its magic. Seven's clothes laid on his bed neatly—a black and pewter checked sweater, a different style of black jeans, and his construction boots. This was what he was going to wear. No bright colors for him. Yes, it's Valentine's Day, but red wasn't Seven's color. Seven stood very handsomely in front of a full-length mirror with his Noir gear. Satisfied with his appearance, he had to make some adjustments. Adjustments to his bedroom that is. He changed the black bedsheets on his king-sized bed to a pair of black satin sheets. Then he fluffed the pillows and threw his black comforter over his bed. He looked around and had nothing else to make the setting more romantic. Then Seven's cell phone vibrated. Seven snatched his cell from the nightstand. "What's up, DeShaun?" Seven answered.

"We've got a fuckin' problem here!" DeShaun bitched.

"I'll be right there," Seven said as he turned off his cell. He looked at Anastasia wide awake in her doggie bed. Seven could read this dog's face.

In the kitchen, Seven poured her dry doggie food in her pan. The Rottweiler chowed down on the food. As Seven left his home, he allowed Anastasia to roamed the backyard for a moment to do her business. The Rottie did her business in the snow. Seven always kind of cleaned up behind her. He took a shovel and covered it with dirt and snow. Seven reopened the door and allowed Anastasia back into the house. Seven closed the door and locked it. He rushed to his black Dodge Charger and hopped in. He sped off as the Hemi engine echoed through the air. The roads were clear of ice and snow. There were medium to small piles of snows on the sides. But the temperature was extremely cold—fifteen degrees. Old man winter stuck around for the holidays from Thanksgiving until Valentine's Day.

Seven picked up his cell and dialed Angelika's number. He hoped that she didn't find out about the payoff from her father. There was a connection made to Angelika's number, but it kept ringing and ringing. But Angelika didn't respond. Seven exhaled. "Shit!" Seven cursed. He turned off his cell phone and threw it in the passenger's seat. He was definitely pissed at this moment, but he had to set his mind on other things right now. Seven drove his Charger even faster down the road. The Charger stopped short at the curb in front of the minimart. It's was quiet. No one was really around. Seven made his way into the establishment. The bell chimed as he pushed the door open.

"Seven! What's up, my nigga!" TaTu greeted Seven with a high five as he held a broom in his hand. Tiana was busy taking care of a customer at the register.

"Happy Valentine's Day, Seven!" Tiana shouted. She hurried by packing the customer's things so she could give Seven a hug. "So what are you doing today?" Tiana asked as she wrapped her arms around him. Seven felt awkward having his boss's woman hanging on him like that. Seven gently pushed Tiana's arms off him and stood a couple of steps away.

"DeShaun's here?" Seven asked as his eyes wandered around the place, hoping to spot his boss.

"Of course he is!" Tiana replied with a grin on her face.

It seemed as if she were drinking. Seven didn't smell any liquor, but still she's his boss's woman. Seven wanted to avoided conflict between him and DeShaun. Seven abruptly swaggered away from Tiana's sight. He headed down the dairy aisle, where he was greeted by the stock boys packing out dairy products.

"What's up, Seven?" one of the stock boys said as he packed out some milk. He gave Seven a high five.

"Chillin!" Seven responded. There were more high fives that came to Seven's way.

"You've got anything planned for Valentine's with your girl?" asked one of the stock boys.

"Yes," Seven answered. He rushed down the stairs toward the basement. Seven entered the dim basement, where he heard the growling of DeShaun's Rottweiler. The dog guarded his master's door like a pro. Also, there was clamoring coming from the other side of the basement. Some thugs argued over a game of pool. One of thug threw some money at the other one. "Fuck you!" cried the thug. Seven shook his head as he headed toward DeShaun's office door. The Rottweiler rose to his feet to greet Seven. Seven patted the dog on the head. "I've got a little girlfriend for you." Seven rang the buzzer.

Someone on the other side of the door peeked through the peephole. Then the door opened. Skeeter stood there with a cigarette hanging from his mouth. He blew smoke into the air. "Hurry up and get in here!" Skeeter demanded. Seven hurried in as the door slammed. DeShaun rocked back and forth in his executive's chair. The expression on his face wasn't a happy one. Someone pissed him off. Seven knew he didn't do shit. *Who did?* Seven asked himself. As the discussion between DeShaun and his entourage proceeded, Magnum was the topic of their conversation. *What the fuck did he do? He's one of DeShaun's best solider.*

Magnum's been stealing from DeShaun, just like the hustlers on the corners. While Magnum was watching the hustlers, someone should have been watching Magnum. He stole just as much as Russell did—fifty grand. Magnum and Seven were best friends. Where does this leave their friendship? Seven knew he couldn't continue his associations with Magnum.

DeShaun glared at Seven and, of course, knew of their friend-ship from childhood. It was time to end that friendship. DeShaun wanted Seven to see Magnum as a foe. That's a pretty hard thing to do when you've known the person all your life. Seven had to search for his best friend and possibly get into a serious dispute. Without DeShaun even asking, Seven drove around in his muscle car, ques-tioning drug hustlers on the block about Magnum.

One of them told that Magnum stole every penny of their cash and even shot anyone who refused to give it up. That made Seven raise an eyebrow. He took off as the brakes screeched and the Hemi engine of his Charger roared. Seven dialed Magnum's number on his cell. Seven was even more determined to get this job done for DeShaun. He would make sure that it didn't interfere with his plans.

"Yo!" Magnum answered on his cell phone.

"Where the fuck are you, fool?" Seven said, goofing off. He had to trap Magnum in order to get DeShaun's funds. Magnum told Seven everything. He was even stupid enough to tell Seven where he was and what he did. Seven played along with Magnum.

At a busy gas station, Magnum pumped his Dodge Challenger with gas as a cigarette hung from his mouth. How stupid he was. The gas attendant saw Magnum as he filled his muscle car up with gas.

"Sir, that's dangerous, what you're doing!" the gas attendant advised while he counted money in his hands.

"I'm cool!" Magnum mumbled with the cigarette in his mouth then took it out of his mouth and blew smoke into the air.

"You'll be hot!" the gas attendant said. He shook his head in disgust and marched off. Then a Hemi engine was heard about a half mile away. Magnum grinned. The sound of the engine got closer and closer toward the gas station. Then the black Dodge Charger entered the gas station. The Charger pulled alongside Magnum's Challenger. Magnum turned, smiling at his best friend.

Seven was ready for business with a straight face. He got out of his Charger and swaggered to Magnum with a mission. But Seven knew to play it cool. "What's up, yo!" Seven greeted Magnum with a high five.

Magnum threw his cigarette to the concrete and mashed the light out with his Timberland boot. "Chillin'!" Magnum coughed.

"Damn! You sound like you're coming down with something!" Seven said.

"Nah, man. I inhaled wrong, that's all!" Magnum replied. He pulled the nozzle from the gas tank of his Challenger and placed it back on the hook of the gas tank. The gas attendant came around to collect the money. "Here you go. Keep the change!" Magnum said to the gas attendant.

Seven sensed Magnum was hiding something. Seven admired the Challenger and wanted to challenge Magnum to a race. Magnum chickened out because he had to go to the Bronx to see his sick grandmother. *I thought Magnum's grandmother was in Atlanta. He's lying for sure! That money is somewhere in this Challenger,* Seven thought. "Did you tell DeShaun?" Seven asked.

"Why the fuck should I tell DeShaun!" Magnum said abruptly as he frowned. Then Magnum's frown turned upside down to a smile—a smile from ear to ear. Magnum was nervous, and there was a sudden personality change.

Seven looked around and saw the surveillance cameras. Seven had to get that cash from Magnum without being on video. "Come on. Let's race, Magnum! Are you chicken shit!" Seven teased him. Hopefully, this would get Magnum in a good place. "You're Challenger is shit!" Seven provoked Magnum.

Moments later, the two muscle cars drove under an overpass. No one was around, just Seven, Magnum, and their girls. Seven wanted to race his friend for old times' sake. Then it hit Seven. *If Magnum's grandmother was sick, why would he be sticking around to race? Magnum's got that cash.* Magnum didn't realize Seven was on to him. Seven got out of his Charger to give the details about their challenge. Magnum remained in his car and looked around nervously. Seven could see the suspicion in Magnum's eyes.

Out of nowhere, Seven hurled a punch to Magnum in the face. There was a loud crack when that punch was thrown. Seven kept his blows coming. Fierce. Bloody. Magnum tried to defend himself but was overpowered. Seven had to think quick as he was beating the shit out of his former best friend. Magnum attempted to inch his hand for his gun from his jacket. But Seven reached in Magnum' s jacket and felt the heavy firearm. By the feel of it, Seven could tell it was a Smith & Wesson. Then a bullet shot through the dashboard of his Dodge Challenger. Luckily, it missed Seven. As the struggle over the gun proceeded, a bullet shot through the windshield of the Dodge Challenger. Magnum tried to fire again. No luck. No more bullets. Magnum wasn't very smart. He only had two bullets in the gun. Seven had the best of the fight. He grabbed the gun and beat Magnum with the handle. Blood spewed from Magnum's mouth, nose, and there were cuts on the eyebrows.

"Where the fuck is the money!" Seven shouted. He looked over and saw a black garbage bag in the backseat. Seven gave Magnum one good last hit with the Smith & Wesson gun. He broke the backseat window with the butt of the gun. He reached inside and grabbed the bag. Seven opened it. Seven's heart sunk into his stomach. It was a bag of dirty laundry. Seven dumped the stinky, funky clothes to the ground. The clothes were spread out with Seven's foot. He wasn't going to touch anyone's dirty garments. No money. "Where the fuck is the cash!" Seven said frantically. Seven threw a couple of punches to his face.

Magnum inhaled sharp breaths as he took a beating from Seven. Seven tried to snatch Magnum out of the seat, but couldn't. The seatbelt had Magnum strapped in. Then Seven proceeded hurling punches to Magnum. Blood splattered on the dashboard and windshield. "Where the fuck is DeShaun's shit!" Seven demanded. He kept the punches coming and didn't get tired, not one bit.

"In the backseat," Magnum gurgled with a bloody mouth.

"What!" Seven hollered. Seven opened the rear door and saw there was nothing. He put all his might into ripping out the backseat of the Dodge Challenger. Then success. The fifty grand was buried in the car. Seven grabbed the garbage bag and stuffed the money in it. The black Dodge Charger then zoomed from under the overpass and on the highway. Jackpot once again. A job well done.

Seven unloaded the cash on DeShaun's desk. DeShaun, Skeeter, and the rest of the entourage applauded. He did it once again. Seven retrieved stolen monies from another fool trying to be slick. Unfortunately, that fool was his best friend. Former. DeShaun counted fourteen hundred dollars cash in Seven's hand. DeShaun couldn't be prouder, like a father being proud of his son graduating from college. Seven would be moved up in the rank of DeShaun's entourage. He became third man right behind Skeeter. Just like in the workplace, you got to work your way up the ladder. Polo's heart raced, and he balled his hands into fists because he was just bumped down by Seven.

Seven then became very arrogant about his new position. He had to now lead and watch everyone closely. By Seven doing a job well done, he had the rest of the day off. DeShaun asked Seven what he had in mind for Angelika. It was the typical Valentine's Day shit— roses, candy, and smashing. DeShaun and his entourage guffawed at Seven's views of the most romantic holiday of the year. Seven gave DeShaun and Skeeter a high five. Then he attempted to give Polo a high five, but he turned away. "Fuck you, nigga!" Seven roared. Polo didn't say a word. He took it like a man losing his position and being humiliated. He was the one who introduced Seven to DeShaun. Once, Seven took orders from Polo, and now it was the reverse.

Moments later, Seven sped in his Charger along the highway and bypassed other motorists. Next stop was the shopping mall. Seven wanted to get some things for Angelika and wanted to make his bedroom more becoming. Seven couldn't wait to see Angelika because he was horny as shit.

In the Godiva Chocolatier, the beautiful decor of gold-colored wrapped candies, lots of red hearts, teddy bears, and the cocoa aroma lit up the entire floor of the mall. Seven browsed around the shop, looking for the perfect gift. He noticed the cashier dipping the straw-berries in the melted chocolate. *Strawberries! That's a romance thing. And a one-hundred-piece box of chocolates and some other shit whatever comes to mind,* Seven thought. He grabbed the box of chocolates and a teddy bear, and the cashier prepared a box of chocolate strawber-ries. Seven paid the cashier and grabbed his bag, swaggering out of the store. Seven wandered around the mall, looking for other things that would tickle Angelika's fancy.

At the Westland mansion, everything was quiet. There were no sights of any type of Valentine's Day celebration. No party. Mr. Westland really didn't throw any parties for Valentine's Day. It was a personal thing to him. In Angelika's bedroom, an expensive maroon gown lay on a chair, just thrown there carelessly. Angelika wasn't interested in wearing it. She lay in her queen-sized bed, watching television. Emily slept at the foot of the bed. Light snoring could be heard coming from the pooch. Angelika raised an eyebrow as she heard her dog snoozing. She then turned her attention toward the box. *Can't Buy Me Love* movie from the late eighties played. Angelika took a deep breath and seemed bored with the film. She flipped through the channels with the remote control. Then *America's Funniest Home Videos* was on. Angelika left it there. She needed a good laugh.

Mrs. Westland sashayed into Angelika's bedroom unannounced. Mrs. Westland wore a burgundy gown with a train and black pumps. She looked like she stepped out of *Vogue* magazine. "Angelika!" Mrs. Westland called as she put her earrings on. Mrs. Westland halted in front of Angelika's bed and saw the gown negligently strewn on the chair. "Angelika, you're gonna ruin your gown! I spent a lot of money for this! Come on, Timothy will be here soon!" Mrs. Westland said as she held the gown on her hand.

"I'm not going, Mom," Angelika mumbled.

"Excuse me. What did you say, Angelika? You're speaking gibberish.

"I'm not going!" Angelika shouted in a more clear, stern tone.

"Get up and get dressed, Angelika! Right now!"

"I'm not going! Forget it!" Angelika shouted.

"Your father will hear about this! Charles! Charles!"

Mr. Westland strutted into his daughter's bedroom as he fixed the tie of his tuxedo. Angelika knew her father was going to start on her now. She proceeded to lie in her slumber. Mr. Westland saw his wife holding Angelika's gown in her hand. "Angelika, why aren't you dressed?" Mr. Westland asked.

"I'm not going," said Angelika.

Mr. Westland shook his head in disappointment. He knew what his daughter was doing. Who was she waiting for? "You're waiting for him? Aren't you?" Angelika looked at her father without saying a word. "He's not coming, Angelika," Mr. Westland said. "Whatever." Mr. Westland stormed out of Angelika's bedroom.

Angelika lounged in her bed with a disgusted expression on her face.

"What is it going to take for you to give up on this ruffian?" Mrs. Westland wondered.

"Nothing."

"Timothy will be a wall Street tycoon."

"Good for him!" Angelika shouted sarcastically.

"What's that ruffian's future? Jail? Death?" interrogated Mrs. Westland. She placed Angelika's gown on a hanger and marched into her walk-in closet. Mrs. Westland then marched out. "You really disappoint me, Angelika." Mrs. Westland stormed out of her daughter's bedroom. Angelika's cell phone rang. Angelika sat up in her bed and saw the caller ID. It read "Seven."

"Seven!" Angelika answered without a hello.

"Yes, it's me, babe. I'm coming to get you."

"All right! Perfect!" Angelika shouted.

Outside, Angelika's bedroom door, Mrs. Westland eavesdropped on Angelika's conversation. She leaned her body against the wall and shook her head.

"I missed you too," Angelika said. Angelika sprung from her bed and paced the floor while on the cell. "I'm so excited about this day."

"It's going to be cool," Seven said.

"Cool," Angelika replied. She turned off her cell phone. Angelika headed into her walk-in closet and had to pick out something red. She found her red blouse and a pair of jeans with some boots. Angelika made her way into the bathroom. She slammed the door.

Mr. and Mrs. Westland made reservations at a fancy restaurant for the evening. Mrs. Westland sat at her luxurious vanity. It was blanketed with bottles of the most expensive fragrances from the top fashion designers. She then sprayed a bottle of Alien perfume by Thierry Mugler on. The ingredients filled the master bedroom with notes of vanilla, cashmere, caramel, and white amber.

Her husband crept behind her and kissed her on the cheek. The affluent couple stared at each other through their reflections in the vanity. "Happy Valentine's day, honey," Mr. Westland greeted his wife with a dozen roses.

"Thank you, darling."

"Have Olga put this in some water."

"Olga!"

Olga rushed into the master bedroom with her head down in a very subservient manner. "Please put these in some water!"

"Yes, Mrs. Westland," Olga said as she took the dozen red roses. Mrs. Westland noticed Mr. Westland admiring himself in the full-length mirror.

"Does this tuxedo make me look different?" Mr. Westland asked his wife.

"What do you mean different?"

"It seems like every time I wear a tux, it feels like the same thing. Maybe I should have worn my Armani suit."

"You look very handsome. There's no need to start pulling yourself apart," Mrs. Westland encouraged.

"I'm going to see if Angelika's ready," Mr. Westland said. He stepped away from the mirror and exited the master bedroom.

Angelika got dressed in her walk-in closet. Mr. Westland just marched in without notice. He knocked to the wall to get her attention. Angelika abruptly turned around as she took a deep breath. She covered up all important parts of her body. "Dad! Knock!"

"I did!" Mr. Westland apologized. He noticed Angelika was half dressed. He hid on the outside of the walk-in closet. He leaned against the wall and knew his daughter was a fool for this ruffian. "Angelika! Seven isn't coming!"

"Why do you keep saying that!" Angelika shouted as she marched out of the walk-in closet fully dressed. Angelika put on her red boots that hung in her shoe rack. Mr. Westland saw that Angelika was dressed in jeans and a red blouse, not even thinking about her Valentine's Day date with Timothy.

"Damn, Angelika!" Mr. Westland shouted at the top of his lungs.

"What!" Angelika shouted in return.

The doorbells chimed. Mr. Westland glared at Angelika. "Put the gown on! Timothy's going to be disappointed!"

"That's the way the cookie crumbles!" Angelika said with sarcasm. She had a smirked on her face because she saw that her father was pissed.

"No! I'm not going anywhere with you!" Angelika screamed.

"You need to leave well enough alone!"

"Why!" Angelika asked as she threw her hands in the air. She wanted her father to explain himself.

"Angelika! Timothy is here!"

"Damn!" Mr. Westland stormed out of Angelika's bedroom.

Angelika peered out of the window and saw Timothy's metallic BMW. Angelika wasn't impressed by him. *He's nasty. He's not the person I used to know as a kid. Who is he really now?* Angelika thought.

"Angelika! Get down here!" Mr. Westland hollered like a man gone insane.

Angelika thrust her bedroom door open and stormed downstairs. "Yes!"

"Timothy's waiting. We're all waiting!"

Timothy stood in the foyer dressed in his tuxedo with a smile on his face. But he raised an eyebrow in wonder. He marched over to give Angelika a kiss on the cheek. Angelika pushed him away.

"Don't! You still smell like shit!" Angelika shouted as she turned up her nose.

Timothy held his head down in shame. Embarrassed by Angelika's remarks, Timothy turned red in the face.

"Angelika! What the hell has gotten into you! Get the hell out of my sight!"

"I will!" Angelika bellowed at the top of her lungs as she stomped back upstairs.

"We'll have a serious talk when I get back! You hear me!" Mrs. Westland shouted from the bottom of the staircase. Angelika did a double job of embarrassing both Timothy and her father. "Tim! I'm sorry." Mrs. Westland hugged Timothy. She kind of turned her nose up when she embraced him. Mrs. Westland smelled something fecal coming from Timothy. But she chose to ignore it. "Angelika has gone too far!"

"Don't worry. It'll be just the three of us. Maybe we'll talk business. Or I'll find some hot chic at the restaurant," Timothy said as he kept himself in good spirits.

All three of them hopped in the Jaguar, which was being driven by Rocco. Angelika didn't bother to look out of any window or care to hear the Jaguar leaving the property. Angelika lounged on the small sofa in her bedroom suite. "The Other Side of the World" by the late Luther Vandross played on her computer. Surprisingly, Angelika learned about Luther Vandross from Mr. Westland's music collection. He was the best R&B artist when it came to lovers. Every couple in the world probably had Luther Vandross on right now. People would say that Luther Vandross's music was baby-making music. But that's not the goal. Angelika just wanted Seven to make love to her.

Angelika lay on the pillow of the sofa, waiting for her love to make his entrance. That would be by the sound of that Hemi engine. Waiting didn't seem like a problem for Angelika. She closed her eyes and listened to Luther Vandross's music and envisioned her and Seven.

A few miles away, the ebony Dodge Charger sped along the curvy road. No other cars were in sight as he had the entire road to himself. Seven puffed on a cigarette as he focused on getting to Angelika. A box of Godiva chocolates, Marc Jacobs perfume, and some roses laid on the passenger's seat. Then up ahead was a railroad crossing. The gate was opened, and the light was on green. Seven noticed it and tried to see if he could make it to the other side of the tracks. But the railroad gate closed as the traffic light turned red. His Charger wasn't fast enough. This time his baby failed him. She needed more tuning. He pounded his fist on the steering wheel and halted at the railroad crossing. As Seven waited, he noticed everything around him was too quiet. There wasn't another car to the left of him. No motorists behind him or any vehicle around. The black Dodge Charger sat there all alone.

A blaring horn could be heard in the distance with a beaming light. A train chugged along the tracks at a medium pace. The clamor of the locomotive blocked all the other sounds that could be heard around Seven. Then a navy blue Dodge Caravan pulled alongside Seven quickly, on the driver's side. Suddenly, a round of bullets rang out, piercing the driver's side door of the Charger. Seven felt those bullets ripping into his body, repeatedly. The warmth of blood drained from his body. The locomotive chugged away down the tracks. Seven's eyes became heavier and heavier. His head fell on the steering wheel. The Charger's horn blared.

Two unknown men exited the rear of the noir Caravan. "Is he dead?" shouted the thug in the driver's seat. One of the unknown men opened up Seven's driver's side door of the Dodge Charger. The hoodlum searched Seven's pockets. Success. He pulled out a fat roll of cash from Seven's pockets. "Yo, this fool is loaded. Let's see what else we have here." The thug said. "Hurry up!" shouted another unknown thug in the passenger's side of the black Caravan. The hoodlum proceeded with his search and found a nine millimeter handgun from Seven's waistband. "He's packing too!"

"Come on, fool!, screamed the thug from the driver's seat of the Caravan. He pounded his fist on the steering wheel. Then Seven's cell vibrated. The second unknown thug noticed his cell and took. He saw that the caller ID read: Angelika. He wanted to play games with this girl Angelika, but couldn't. "Let's get the fuck out of here!" the driver of the Dodge Caravan shouted again. Instead, the second thug threw the cell to the ground and crushed it with his foot. Then the two mysterious thugs hustled back to the van. The wheels screeched of the murky van. The ruffians took off into the night. Seven kept his eyes and knew there could be some chance of survival. He hoped anyone would help. Seven's heart raced fast. Then it began to slow down. Seven fought to stay alive by taking sharp breaths. And the only thing Seven could do was pray. "God, is this it! I hope it's not my time, but if so, please take my soul. Forgive me for all the sins that I've done. I know I wasn't the best person that I should have been, but I tried. I know I did one thing that I'm proud of myself for. I care for Angelika. As a matter of fact, I love Angelika. I really do. I haven't told her yet. But if you get me through this Lord, I will tell her. Please spare my life. Amen." Then Seven's eyes shut.

The End

About the Author

Alexis Soleil is originally a screenwriter from Flushing, New York. She decided to adapt "From the Other Side of the Tracks" into a novel series. She loved the process of writing her story because Alexis was able to dig deeper into her characters thoughts, feelings, and beliefs. The descriptions of settings, a car, and situations. Novel writing is far more creative and lengthy than screenwriting. Screenwriting is short and to the point. Alexis loves fiction novels regardless of the genre. She read The Color Purple by Alice Walker, Toni Morrison's The Bluest Eyes, and Steven King's work such as Carrie, The Shining, and others. Alexis attended New York Film Academy where she studied film and earned her certificate.

CPSIA information can be obtained
at www.ICGtesting.com
Printed in the USA
BVOW08s1656090917

494451BV00001B/89/P